PENGUIN BOOKS

MALORIE BLACKMAN
Chasing the Stars

D0242375

MALORIE
BLACKMAN
Chasing
the Stars

PENGUIN BOOKS

PENGUIN BOOKS

UK | USA | Canada | Ireland | Australia
India | New Zealand | South Africa

Penguin Books is part of the Penguin Random House group of companies
whose addresses can be found at global.penguinrandomhouse.com.

www.penguin.co.uk
www.puffin.co.uk
www.ladybird.co.uk

First published by Doubleday 2016
Published by Penguin Books 2017

001

Set in Sabon 10.98/16.31pt and Franklin Gothic 9.9/16.31pt
Printed in Great Britain by Clays Ltd, St Ives plc

A CIP catalogue record for this book is available from the British Library

ISBN: 978-0-141-37701-8

All correspondence to:
Penguin Books
Penguin Random House Children's
80 Strand, London WC2R 0RL

For Neil and Lizzy, with love
as always

Perdition catch my soul
But I do love thee! and when I love thee not,
Chaos is come again.

Othello, Act III, Scene 3

Intelligence is the ability to adapt to change.

Stephen Hawking

AD 2164

1

'My turn!'

Dad jumped to his feet, straightening out his right arm in front of him. He moved his hand from right to left, nodding his head as he did so. Pumping his arm out to the side, then up, then out, then up, he then switched to his other arm to move it slowly but steadily before him, his head still nodding.

'*Grease*!' I shouted.

'Ah, but which bit?'

'Please!' I said, insulted. 'The song *Greased Lightning*.'

Dad straightened up, disgruntled. He was just winding up to mime the moves to the entire song and I'd spoiled his fun by guessing so quickly. He tapped his nose, pointed at me and smiled. 'I should've given you a harder one.'

'My turn.' I sprang to my feet as Dad sat down.

I loved playing film charades with Dad. We were the only two people on board who loved old twentieth- and twenty-first-century films. Pressing a make-believe switch to activate my imaginary lightsaber, I leaped high into the air while performing the side splits, all the while fighting off the imaginary foe who was trying to slice me in two.

'*Star Wars*!' Dad bounced in his chair.

'Ah, but which one?' I challenged.

'Which one of the whole series?' he exclaimed.

I nodded.

'Really?' Dad raised an eyebrow. 'I'm supposed to guess which one of the *Star Wars* films you're re-enacting?'

'Yep! And here's a clue: it's not one of the animated ones.' I continued to jump around, swirling my arm to deflect imaginary blows.

'Number eight!' said Dad.

My mouth fell open as I stared at him, stunned. 'How in the world did you get that?'

'Now if I told you that, you'd know as much as I do,' laughed Dad. 'My turn again. You'll never get this one.' He was already on his feet, his smile wide. I loved his smile. It was wide and infectious and made everyone else around him smile too, guaranteed.

'Why are you watching that? Again.'

At the sound of Aidan's voice I stopped the recording, swiping my hand downwards to dismiss the image playing in front of me. Dad's laughing face vanished. I turned my face away, quickly brushing my fingertips across my cheeks to smooth my expression.

'Vee, are you all right?' Aidan walked over to me.

I shrugged. 'Of course. I just like to watch recordings of Mum and Dad.'

A reminder of better times.

There were recordings of the whole family together but far fewer than I would've liked, and very little footage of just Mum and me. Her job had meant that she'd had very little free time.

Aidan frowned, his gaze intense. 'I don't understand. Watching them hurts you. So why do it?'

'They make me smile,' I replied. 'I don't do much of that any more.'

Puzzled, Aidan tilted his head as he regarded me.

'I laugh a lot. I don't smile much,' I explained.

'What's the difference?' he asked seriously.

'Not enough to worry about,' I replied at last.

Aidan reached out, one of his fingers brushing against my cheek just beneath my right eye. When he drew back his hand, a single tear lay on his index finger. He studied it for a moment.

'I don't like to see you sad.'

'Watching the recordings makes me happy too,' I said. 'That's the point.'

Aidan scrutinized me, those dark brown eyes of his not missing much, as per usual.

'Aidan, I'm OK.'

'True?'

'True.'

He stepped forward and gave me a hug. As he stepped back, I dredged up a smile which Aidan accepted at face value.

'No more recordings?' said Aidan.

'No more recordings.'

For today.

Aidan smiled and nodded, relieved. 'Now how about a nice game of chess?'

NATHAN

Son of a bitch! Agony detonated inside me, raw and devouring. I'd never felt anything like it. I wasn't so much crying out as screaming out in pain. My left foot and lower leg were completely crushed beneath the weight of fallen rocks and boulders. Gasping, panting, I had to make a superhuman effort to get myself together. If I gave in to the pain and panic slicing through me, I'd stand no chance at all. Grabbing hold of my left leg at the knee, I tried to pull myself free. I used my right foot to push and kick against the fallen boulders.

Nothing doing. The rocks weren't budging.

I was going nowhere.

Trapped.

The left leg of my environment suit was in shreds. Ironically the self-same boulder that had pinned my leg and ripped my suit in the first place was also the object now sealing the breach. But I'd lost a lot of oxygen from my suit in the process. When I came down into the mine thirty minutes ago, I'd had over ten hours of oxygen left in my suit. The heads-up display of my helmet now showed I had less than fifty minutes of air left. Which would see me off first? The intense cold, the carbon-dioxide atmosphere down here in the mine, or the blood loss from my crushed foot?

Having fun yet, Nate?

The sickly yellow lights which marked our route through the mine flickered and dimmed. In a few hours they would be switched off completely – not that I'd be alive to see that if I didn't get the hell out of here.

The trouble was, Anjuli was the only one who knew I'd come back down here to retrieve my tablet. That fact did me no good at all as she'd gone back to the barracks to get some rest. Knowing Anjuli she was already fast asleep.

And the filling in my life's-a-vindictive-bitch sandwich?

The moment I heard the ominous creaking and cracking which signalled a cave-in I'd started to run, but had dropped my damned tablet as I stumbled and fell. The tablet was about one metre behind me, buried under the same tonne or more of rubble as my leg, and undoubtedly sharing the same fate – smashed to pieces.

'HELP!'

Stupid to call for help when I knew there was no one around to hear me. But it made me feel like I was doing something. A pathetic something, a useless something, but something nonetheless.

I needed to do more.

The next shift was due to start mining at least seven kilometres away from my current location. The seams in the vast mines which crisscrossed this area were only excavated for a few months at a time before we moved on to a new section. The known seams were worked in a strict rotation. That's the reason I'd come down here to retrieve my tablet. I knew if I didn't get it now, I'd have to wait too many months before they opened up this section again. No way could I go that long with no lifeline to the world outside this mining colony.

But now I was trapped and alone.

If I didn't find a way to get out of here and fast, my buff and perfectly preserved but incredibly dead body would not be found for several months. I needed to figure something out. *Now.*

Forty-one minutes of air left.

'HELP! HELP ME!'

Nate, don't panic. You'll just use up your oxygen faster.

The agony in my leg made it difficult but I tried to compart-mentalize the pain, fold it up and put it to one side, so that I could come up with a way out of this.

My DE torch.

I dug into the side pocket of my suit over my thigh.

Please let it still be in there.

It was, thank God! I changed the setting from light to heat. The faint, high-pitched whistle told me it had activated properly. It gave out a concentrated beam that we used in the mine for precision cutting when necessary. Where would be the best place to cut into the boulders and rocks pinning my leg? If I got this wrong, the whole tunnel would come tumbling down on top of the rest of me. It dawned on me that cutting into the rocks that held me captive wouldn't work. Displacing any of them would just bring down more. The only way I was going to get out of here was to slice through my leg, just above where it was pinned, through skin and my shin, and muscle, blood and bone. The torch would cauterize as it cut but the pain would be excruciating.

Son of a bitch!

I was going to have to cut off my own foot.

I couldn't do it.

How could I?

But it was that or die for sure.

I switched off the DE torch, shaking my head. I simply couldn't do it.

I tried kicking against the rocks with my right foot again, heaving to pull my left leg free. All I got from that was a renewed blast of searing pain. In my panic, I was breathing too fast. I was going to use up all my remaining oxygen in double-quick time at this rate.

Thirty-seven minutes of oxygen left.

Face facts. Whatever happened, rescued by others or rescue myself, I was going to lose my foot. Damn! And I was so attached to it too.

Come on, Nathan.

Do it.

Get on with it.

You're not getting any younger.

My head was beginning to swim. Black spots were darting before my eyes.

I was going into shock. About to pass out. Wow, the good times just kept on coming. If I fainted now, these black spots would be the last things I ever saw.

Gritting my teeth, I switched on the DE torch again, adjusting the setting back to a focused beam of heat rather than light. Before I could change my mind, I directed it at my leg . . .

I woke up screaming.

'What the hell, Nathan?' said Mike, switching on his lamp.

I wiped my forehead, which was pouring with sweat. Pain, remembered but no less real for it, lanced through me. Damn it! I sighed as I sat up.

'The same dream?' Mike asked.

'Yeah,' I admitted.

'Why won't you let Doctor Liana give you something for that? Practically every other night you go through this. And when you go through it, so do the rest of us.'

'Some of us are trying to sleep over here!' an irate Pearl shouted from across the barracks. That was all I needed. She was a misery at the best of times. Deprived of sleep, she'd be yet another nightmare to contend with.

'Sorry,' I called out.

'Nathan, shut the hell up!' Corbyn shouted from further along the room.

I was feeling the love.

A ripple effect was happening throughout the barracks as more and more people began to stir. Time to escape before my arse got kicked. I threw back my bedcover and bent my left leg to rub halfway between my ankle and my knee. My real lower leg was back in the mine, probably still buried under a ton of rock. This bionic replacement, covered in synthetic skin, looked and behaved the same as my real leg and was certainly better than nothing; I could still feel the indented scar right around my calf and shin where the prosthesis had been attached to my body.

Knowing that sleep and I would be strangers for a while, I sighed and got out of bed. Slipping on my boots, I made my way out of the dorm. Mike waited until I was at the door before switching off his lamp. He was a good mate that way. After a brief smile in his direction, I made my way out into the compound, taking a deep breath of the still night air. The air here smelled and tasted different to what I was used to. More . . . citrusy. Maybe something to do with the plants and trees that grew around here. God, I sounded like Mike now. Mike would much rather hang out with the trees on this planet than any of us people.

I glanced up at the sky, full of stars I didn't recognize. That didn't make them any less awesome. Good word that. Awesome. And definitely under-used. I liked old, nearly obsolete words. That was one of the things I'd missed on the mining colony – access to words, new and old, especially the written kind. God knows this place was better than life back on the mining colony but there was still something empty inside me, a void that ached to be filled. This life, this place, it wasn't enough.

But for a while at least, it would have to do.

I looked around, trying to decide where to go. A light shone from the meeting house at the centre of the compound. Frowning, I made my way towards it. Wasn't it a bit late to be holding a meeting?

As I got closer, my steps grew quieter. Whatever was going

on, it was obviously not meant for common knowledge. I crept over to an open window, ducking down beneath it to stay out of sight. I heard Darren's voice, but then that wouldn't've been hard. The guy, who was Mum's second in command, had never been shy about speaking his mind.

'Cathy, this is madness. We need to activate the distress beacon,' Darren insisted. 'It's our only chance.'

'We've been here for over three Sol months. This is our home now. Are you really in that much of a hurry to be at the mercy of the Authority again?' Mum argued.

'No, but better the devil you know at this point. Quite frankly, I'd rather take my chances with the Authority than with the Mazon.'

My heart leaped. The Mazon? What was Darren talking about? Were we in danger from the Mazon? They were an enemy very few had seen but everyone knew about. I didn't know that much about them, but the stories of what they did to their victims had travelled fast, far and wide. Their hatred for all us humans was well-known.

'If the Authority gets its hands on us, we won't be sent back to the mines; we'll be publicly executed,' Mum snapped. 'You do know that, right?'

'Catherine, I know it's a hard choice between the lesser of two evils but we can't stay here,' said another voice. Sam this time, if I wasn't mistaken. 'The Mazon have made that perfectly clear.'

A moment's silence.

I risked raising my head to peer through the open window.

Mum, Darren, Sam, Hedda, Akemi, Doctor Liana and Beck sat at the round assembly table where most, if not all, of the decisions on behalf of us settlers were made. Almost directly opposite me, Mum began to turn her head my way. I ducked out of sight again, my heart thumping.

'I know it won't be easy but there has to be a way to reason with the Mazon,' Mum insisted. 'I'll keep sending out the transmissions. We've got to convince them that we're not the enemy. Quite frankly, they're our last hope.'

'Then we're in deep shit,' said Darren. 'Cathy, activate the beacon.'

'No. Not yet.' Mum dug her heels in. 'Not until we have exhausted every other option.'

Oh my God! We were in Mazon territory? Mum and the others had kept that quiet. And she was going to try and reason with them? Seriously? Well, good luck with that.

'The Mazon have only given us until the first sunrise to clear out,' said Sam.

'Cathy, we should activate the emergency distress beacon,' Darren urged.

'Not yet.'

'At least put it to a vote.'

'Darren, I didn't ask to be leader. You voted me into the role. You all did. So let me lead,' said Mum. 'I'm not going to activate the distress beacon until we have no other option.'

'By then it may be too late,' Darren said, exasperated.

'I refuse to believe that a race with the obvious intelligence of the Mazon can't be reasoned with,' said Mum.

'And if you're wrong?' asked Hedda quietly.

'We have to try,' replied Mum. 'I'm willing to take that chance.'

I raised my head again, just in time to catch the shared looks exchanged around the table.

Darren shook his head. 'Just as long as you remember you're taking a chance with all our lives, not just your own.'

3

'Aidan, is there any chance that you might make your next move before the last syllable of recorded time?'

'I'm thinking.' Aidan frowned, never raising his gaze from the chessboard.

I sighed. 'You've been thinking for over twenty minutes.'

Aidan's hand hovered over his bishop, who was pursing his lips with impatience, then moved slowly to hover over his rook, which had a darkening cloud over it, then back to his tetchy bishop.

Arghhh! This was the eighth time he'd contemplated the exact same move.

'Stop rolling your eyes,' my brother said, without looking up at me.

'Move then!'

'My bishop . . .' Aidan began ponderously, 'takes your knight.'

He snatched my knight as it reared up, and put his bishop in its place, then raised his head to grin at me triumphantly. I immediately moved my queen to E5. She glanced around the chessboard imperiously, then smiled with slow satisfaction.

Aidan stared at the board, then raised his head to blink at me like a stunned owl.

I winked. 'How d'you like me now?' Ha!

His frown deepened. 'There's a distress signal coming through.'

I glanced down at the screen that made up the right arm of my chair.

'Screen up,' I ordered.

Instantly a map of our immediate vicinity was displayed directly before me. Rotating my wrists slightly to adjust the command bracelets I wore, I scrolled across the map. There was nothing out of the ordinary. No blips, no beeps, no burbs. Nothing. I dragged my hand down vertically to remove the screen, then turned to frown at my brother. 'I can't see anything on the monitor.'

Aidan had a faux enquiring look on his face. 'No? I must've been mistaken.'

Yeah, right! Eyes narrowed, I glanced down at the chessboard. My queen now wore a thunderous expression. She wasn't the only one who was annoyed. 'Aidan, stop cheating!'

'I did not.'

'I swear if you don't stop cheating, I'm not going to play chess with you any more.'

'How did I cheat?' Aidan asked with indignation.

'My queen was on E5 and in three moves you would've been in check and begging for mercy – and we both know it. So why is my queen now on E6?'

The hologram of the chess set disappeared. Proof positive that Aidan had been cheating and was now going to sulk because he'd been caught.

'I'll take that as your resignation,' I said. 'That's three hundred and twenty-eight games to me and one hundred and ninety-one games to you, with thirty-four stalemates.'

I jumped up and did an impromptu victory dance. 'Go, Vee! Go, Vee! I win again. Yeah, me! Go, Vee!'

'Very mature! And I can't believe you're keeping the exact score,' sniffed Aidan.

'Getting the better of you is always an unforgettable experience.' I grinned, sitting back down. Plus, to be honest, it was getting harder and harder to win against him. In a few more months or even less I'd be lucky to win any at all.

'You need to get a life,' my brother said. 'And chess is a stupid game anyway.'

'Go wash your mouth out! Chess is a game of strategy, tactics and deeper thinking. It is a game of the soul.' I placed a hand dramatically over my heart. 'As well as the mind. And how come it's only a stupid game when you're losing?'

Aidan didn't deign to answer.

'Should I break out the cards? We can play Pairs if that's more your speed,' I teased.

'You don't hear me going on and on about it when I win,' said Aidan.

I snorted with derision. Actually snorted. 'You are joking, right?'

If my brother won at anything, he went on about it for hours, sometimes days, sharing every thought which had accompanied each decisive or winning move.

'Want another game of chess then?'

'No. You only win because you're better at cheating than I am.' Aidan swung round in his seat to face his navigation panel, effectively turning his back on me. He was such a sore loser. I mean, really? Getting bent out of shape over a game? But that was Aidan all over. He hated to lose.

I sighed. Now what should I do?

This was how I spent my days, playing games with my brother, where the outcome tended to be a given, or looking after the plants in the hydroponics bay or learning about as many different alien cultures and their languages as I could.

But that was it.

It should've been a lot, but it wasn't.

It should've been enough, but it came nowhere close.

It served to pass the time.

And God only knew I had more than enough of that, if nothing else. I swivelled right round in my chair, gazing out of the transparent dome that made up most of the roof of the bridge. A few distant stars and a lot of nothingness. It matched all the activities I pursued to occupy my mind and my time. Lots of nothingness to fill the empty hours. This was my life now. Each day I tried to find something – but it tended to be the same old something – to fill the moments, the minutes, the months. Life wasn't meant to be so predictable. The bridge I currently occupied was small – it could only hold eight comfortably – but I knew every piece of machinery, every byte of software, every panel, real and virtual. Apart from my sleeping quarters, this was the place in the universe I knew best.

It wasn't much. But it was all I had.

For want of something better to do I cast a cursory glance over the command panel and saw it immediately – a pulsing cursor at the very edge of my screen which disappeared almost at once.

'Aidan, what was that?'

'What was what?'

'Aidan, don't muck about. That looked like the signal from a distress beacon. You were serious about that?'

'I thought I saw an emergency signal but it was cancelled,' Aidan replied.

'Cancelled or extinguished?'

'I don't understand the question.'

'Never mind. The signal is back,' I said.

I bent closer to the panel in the arm of my chair for a better look. The signal was incredibly faint and getting weaker.

'Where does this signal originate?'

'Barros 5, the fifth uninhabited planet in the Barros binary star system,' said Aidan.

What on earth . . . ? That planet was inside Mazon space.

'Take us there,' I said.

'Vee, I don't think that's a good idea—'

'Aidan, take us there,' I ordered. 'Maximum speed.'

Twenty minutes later we were in high orbit around the so-called uninhabited planet. The trouble was, it was far from uninhabited. I had originally thought that maybe the signal came from an unmanned probe or an exploratory robot ship in trouble on the planet's surface. Now I was closer I was getting a jumble of life readings. The added problem was that my ship wasn't the only one in orbit. Two Mazon battlecruisers were several kilometres below me and firing at one particular area on the largest land mass in the southern hemisphere.

'What exactly are the Mazon firing at?' I asked.

'The scanners indicate eighty-five Terrans on the planet surface,' Aidan replied.

Stunned, I needed a moment or two to digest that information.

People.

People from Earth were down on that planet. People like me. But not for much longer if I didn't do something – and fast. But what? There was no way my ship was a match for the fire power of the two Mazon battlecruisers. If I tried to take them on in a knockdown, drag-out firefight, I'd be blasted to smithereens.

Think.

'Aidan, I need you to solo-transfer me directly into the engine core of both those Mazon ships,' I said.

Aidan swung round in his chair so quickly I'm surprised he didn't give himself whiplash. 'The core? Are you unhinged? You'll suffocate, then fry. Literally.'

'Not if I wear a protection suit and you shield me in each one.' I deliberately made my tone bright and breezy.

'Even with a protection suit, I can only shield you for fifteen seconds max, and if my calculations are out by even 0.001 per cent, you'll die,' said Aidan like he was telling me something I didn't already know.

'Don't miscalculate then.' I smiled with a bravado I was far from feeling. 'Transfer me into the core of the one closest to the planet surface, then back here. Recalibrate, then rinse and repeat. And I need you to get me into the second ship before the first ship realizes their engine has been sabotaged. OK?'

Transfer to the Mazon ship? *Piece of cake.*

Into the engine core? *Doddle.*

And not get caught? I could do that in my sleep and twice on Sunday. *Sorted.*

Ha!

Aidan stared at me as if I'd just lost my mind – which, quite frankly, was a distinct possibility. I admit, it was a pretty arseholic idea.

'No, it's not OK. You're really going to risk your life for some anonymous people down on the planet surface? That's just plain stupid,' said my brother. 'And even if you do manage to disable the Mazon ships, then what? We can't take that many people on board. Our maximum carrying capacity is seventy.'

'We'll figure that part out afterwards.'

'Vee, I know you believe in trusting your gut instincts but this is reckless – even for you,' said Aidan. 'We don't know who they are, or anything about them. I can't allow it.'

I stood up and went over to him. 'Aidan, there are *people* down there. People in trouble. I'm not going to insist on checking their credentials before deciding whether or not to help them.' I took my brother's hand in mine and looked into his dark brown eyes. 'They need help. That's all we know or need to know. I wouldn't be able to live with myself if we turned tail and ran, if we didn't at least try. So I'm ordering you to help me rescue them.'

'You'll die.'

'No I won't, because you won't let that happen.' I smiled. 'Think of this as the last scene of *Butch Cassidy and the Sundance Kid.*'

Aidan's eyebrows shot up. I winced. OK, maybe that wasn't the best example I could've given. 'Scratch that. Think of this as . . . as . . .' Nope, not *The Godfather.* Al Pacino had had one of his brothers shot. I was mentally scrambling for a film I'd watched that showed great family loyalty and a triumph over adversity. Come on! I'd watched thousands of twentieth- and twenty-first-century films over the years and had memorized every word of a number of them. So why was I having such trouble picking just one to mention now? 'Think of this as *Jeepers Creepers*!'

'The film where the brother dies at the end and the weird-ass creature ends up wearing his eyeballs?' asked Aidan drily.

Damn it! He was deliberately missing the point.

'But the sister was there for the brother and tried to save him,' I said. 'So this is like that situation but in reverse, 'cept you won't let me die 'cause you're my little brother and you love me.'

'I'm only your little brother by nine minutes and twenty-two seconds,' said Aidan, replaying an argument we'd had many, many times before.

'Whatever. Give me a couple of minutes to put on a protection suit, and then let's do this,' I said, already heading for my quarters, which were on the upper deck and within a stone's throw of the bridge. 'We don't have much time.'

I ran to my quarters. It took me longer than it should've to put on my protection suit because my room was a mess, and after I found it my hands wouldn't stop shaking. Now that I was no longer arguing with Aidan, the full import of what I was about to attempt hit me – and it hit hard.

My brother was going to transfer me into the engine core, the beating heart of each Mazon ship. Cells that gave out the same amount of energy as a small sun would surround me. I'd have around ten seconds to disable the appropriate cells in each Mazon ship's core before the energy permeated the force field I was relying on Aidan to wrap around me. After that, I'd have less than one second before my protection suit failed and I'd be vaporized. Aidan was going to have to divert all our ship's power, except for essential systems, to keep me alive within the force field.

If my plan failed but by some miracle Aidan managed to get me back to the ship in one whole living piece, we would be sitting ducks, with no weapons, no shields. No hope. The Mazon would know of our presence, and after one inevitable blast we'd be history. Aidan was right. This was stupid. Possibly the stupidest plan I'd ever come up with.

But there were people down on the planet.

People.

I hadn't shared a joke, a laugh, a conversation with anyone other than Aidan in over three years. That alone made it worth the risk.

A charge like electricity shot through my body. My mind was buzzing, my thoughts tripping over each other as they raced. This was the closest to instant death I'd ever been, or ever wanted to be; but for the first time in a long, long time I felt *alive*.

4

NATHAN

There was nowhere to run. Nowhere safe. The ground was erupting. The relentless din of screams, shouts, bomb blasts and collapsing masonry filled my ears. Debris and machinery flew through the air in all directions. Mum kept pulling me, but to where? There was nowhere to hide. Nowhere we could be safe from the bombs exploding all around us and the weapon blasts cutting straight through anything they touched. Some people were running back into nearby buildings or making for the barracks; others were trying to run out of the compound.

I saw Bertrand on his knees, crying and clutching Simone, his six-year-old daughter, to him as she screamed in wide-eyed terror. Snatching my arm from Mum's grip, I literally bent over backwards, one hand down, the back of my head almost on the ground – and only just in time, as a huge metal disc, intent on cutting me in half, sliced through the air just above me. A high, piercing whistle sounded. My heart sank. That whistling sound meant DE, or directed energy-weapons. The enemy had stepped up their attack. I knew only too well just how deadly directed energy could be. Two years ago that setting on my torch had detached a third of my leg from the rest of me. The ear-piercing whistling sound was getting closer.

Game over.

I sprang to my feet and hit the ground running. Mum grasped my hand as we raced for elusive safety. Ordinarily, I would've recoiled from holding my mum's hand. I mean, please.

But not today.

Not now.

'Get to the cavern in the mountain,' Mum shouted, though in the chaos of the destruction all around us her voice barely carried to me, never mind across the compound to the others running about trying to seek safe shelter. The bomb blasts going off around our compound effectively hemmed us in. The Mazon weren't stupid. And even if we did get to the cavern, what use would that be? The Mazon weren't going to stop until every last one of us was dead. Their merciless reputation hadn't been an exaggeration. They were the dogs of war and they'd bring down the whole mountain on our heads if they had to. As far as they were concerned, we were unwanted, unwelcome immigrants encroaching on their land.

We ran.

I tried not to focus on the bodies and severed limbs on the ground in every direction. The whole scene was of carnage. The random splashes of red soaking into the sandy soil of our com- pound were now so plentiful they were forming into rivulets.

And still we ran.

The undiluted screams of terror, panicked shouts and cries of others tore straight through me. And yet I didn't say a word. I couldn't. Besides, what was there to say? All I could do was run. And pray. A flash of resentment directed my focus back to Mum.

27

She'd been warned. The Mazon had told us not to try and settle here. They'd made it very clear that we weren't welcome. We'd been given just one day to be off their planet, but Mum had refused to deploy the emergency beacon until five Sol hours ago. The chances were slim to none that any vessel would be in the vicinity to even detect the signal, never mind come to our aid.

It didn't matter that this land was unoccupied. As far as the Mazon were concerned, it was their territory and theirs alone. We were intruders. Mum had tried to convince them that we weren't a part of the Authority and that all we wanted was to coexist in peace. I'd listened as she spoke at length about what we could bring to their table. Mum truly believed that reason could work with the Mazon. But we were the unknown, and as far as they were concerned, that meant we were to be feared and eliminated, not necessarily in that order. It would be laughable if it wasn't the exact opposite. We weren't a threat to anyone. Just a bunch of unwanted people seeking a better life.

This wasn't what any of us had had in mind.

Mum had been so sure we could win round the Mazon to her way of thinking. The bombs falling all around us were a testament to just how wrong she had been. Even though I was running for my life, a quiet sense of defeat tinged with sadness settled deep within me. I was only nineteen. There was so much I wanted to see, so much I still had to do.

No! I wasn't going to bow out like this. I needed to fight, not run. But how could I when the enemy were cowardly kilometres above us where our weapons couldn't touch them?

What we all needed now was a miracle.

5  VEE

'Ready, Aidan?'

'This is the worst idea in the history of bad ideas.'

'Aidan, I don't have time for this. Are you ready?' I said with impatience.

'I should be the one to go into the Mazon engine core, not you.'

'And we both know why you can't,' I replied.

He wasn't happy, but there was nothing either of us could do about that. If I went into the Mazon core, there was a minuscule chance I'd succeed. In there, Aidan stood no chance at all.

A moment's silence. My brother looked at me, a strange expression on his face. 'Don't die, Olivia.'

'Not part of my plan,' I tried to assure him. 'You don't get rid of me that easily. Think of this as—'

'Please. Not another film-reference failure,' Aidan begged.

He turned towards the console, but not before I deciphered his expression. He was scared. Actually scared. That shook me. I went over and hugged him from behind, around his neck, which he accepted for a couple of seconds before pulling away.

'Get off. Are you nuts? Oh wait, we've already established that you are!'

I smiled, though it didn't last long. 'Aidan, if something happens to me, do your best to rescue the people on the planet. OK?'

'You want me to rescue the ones who'll have brought about your death?' he said, aghast.

'Aidan, this is my choice. My decision. It's the right thing to do. So promise me you'll do what you can to save all those on the planet surface.'

'I promise I'll try. But that's all I promise.' Before I could reply, he added, 'Vee, on my mark.'

I crouched down, my protection suit in place, the visor of my helmet down. This was insane. The chances of this working were—

'Three. Two. One. *Mark*.'

A shrill whistle, an intense dragging sensation, and less than a second later I was on the Mazon ship. I had to close my eyes for a moment against the intense, blinding light. Even with my visor down, it felt like my retinas had been seared. I adjusted the light input of my visor to a more comfortable level. The urge to throw up was overpowering. That's why I hated this kind of transfer, but luckily I'd done it before so I knew what to expect. Even so, my mouth filled with saliva and I had to keep rapidly swallowing or I would've puked in my helmet. The heat in the core was almost unbearable, even wearing my protection suit, and there wasn't a thing I could do about that. Sweat was already dripping from my forehead and my skin felt like I was standing inside an erupting volcano.

With no time to waste, I looked around. The engine core of this massive Mazon ship was cylindrical in shape and about four metres in diameter, covering at least four levels, each roughly three metres or a storey high. Each level contained a narrow metal gantry in the shape of a cross to get from one side to the other, with what looked like fine metal cargo nets fixed vertically to the walls at regular intervals to allow access from one level to the next. From the look of the gantry I was standing on, it hadn't been used since the ship was first built. In this core, energy was a tangible thing, stinging my skin in spite of the suit I wore.

Ten.

I scanned the huge engine core. I had two more levels above me and one below. And beneath the lowest level was the reactor. Instant death. There wasn't a protection suit in the universe that could protect me from that if I fell into it.

Nine.

There they were. The core cells I was looking for. Two levels directly above. I had no time to climb. I'd have to jump, using my suit's limited propulsion system to move me up.

Crouch down.

Eight.

Jump! I leaped, reaching out with both hands above my head. Grabbing the underside of the metalwork, I swung myself round, crouched and jumped again, but this time I aimed not at the next horizontal gantry above me but the net next to the core cells I needed to sabotage.

Seven.

A frantic grab with both hands at the metal net. My left hand slipped, but my right hand managed to find purchase. My momentum swung me round and my back banged into the burning hot wall. I clung on for dear life – literally.

Six.

Dangling like a fish on a line, I tried to regain my equilibrium. I kicked out and swung back round to face the array of energy cells, by which time my right arm and shoulder were screaming in protest at having to take my full weight. Time was ticking by.

Five.

Looking straight up, I reached out with my left arm and grabbed hold of one of the energy cells directly above me. My visor readings told me I had one of the right kind.

Four.

Pull! Now that my feet were supported by the metal net, I could lean back slightly and lend my whole body weight to the task. I tried to pull the appropriate energy cell out of its housing. The thing wasn't budging. I wasn't going to make it.

Three.

It was moving! I held on tighter and yanked. Then grabbed hold of the one next to it and yanked that out too, allowing them to free fall around me.

Two.

I pulled the anti-energy unit off my belt and rammed it into the core, replacing the cells I'd just removed.

One.

A rush.

The dragging sensation was back.

An absence of light.

I couldn't see a thing.

'Vee, are you OK?' Aidan's voice came from directly in front of me.

Pushing up my visor, I blinked rapidly, my eyes re-adjusting to the normal light on the bridge of our ship, which was considerably more subdued than in the engine core of the Mazon ship. I took a deep breath, quickly followed by another. The cooler air on my face and in my lungs was most welcome. Now I just needed to stop feeling nauseous.

'Did it work?' asked my brother.

'We'll soon find out. Send me to the second ship. Same deal.'

'You should wait at least seven minutes to fully decontaminate,' Aidan said. 'If you go back now, you'll have even less time to sabotage the Mazon ship.'

'I can't wait. No time. I'll be fine. You'll keep me safe. Send me to the second ship.'

Aidan opened his mouth to keep arguing but the expression on my face obviously made him think better of it. I knew I was being terse with him, but if I didn't do this now, if I stopped to think about it for even a second, I'd bottle out. I pushed my visor back down, sealing it in place.

'Good luck, sis.'

A moment later and I was in the engine core of the second ship – except Aidan hadn't managed to get me into the middle of the relay core as before. Instead my feet were on the very edge of the gantry on the lowest level and I was tipping backwards. My arms spun like fan blades as I tried to regain my balance.

Ten.

I was slipping.

Oh my God! I was going to fall.

Nine.

I lurched forward and fell to my knees.

Eight.

I looked up. I needed to be on the topmost level, three storeys higher. It would take at least six seconds just to climb up that far, even using my suit's propulsion system, leaving me no time to sabotage the ship.

Seven.

What were my choices? No way could I make it to the right cells of the energy array in time to do any good.

Maybe if I . . .

Six.

Vee, don't second guess yourself. Do something. Fast.

A rapid recce: the cells that provided energy for the navigation and targeting systems and the cargo bays were the only ones within striking distance.

Five.

I raced along the gantry to the navigation-system relay cells.

Four.

Any sabotage here would be fixed in less than forty minutes. Thirty minutes, if I was unlucky.

Three.

Then I'd better make every moment count.

'Aidan, I need a few more seconds.' I spoke into the communications unit that was part of my helmet as I removed the closest cell and let it fall into the reactor.

Two . . .

'You don't have a few more seconds . . .'

'Hold on.' I reached for the adjacent cell to the one I'd just destroyed and dished out the same treatment. I pulled the anti-energy pack off my belt, but my hand – my whole body – was on fire and my focus slipped to the pain zigzagging inside me rather than the anti-energy pack. The display data inside my helmet was frantically flashing red. My suit was about to fail. The anti-energy pack fell from my fingers. I watched in dismay as it vanished into the energy reactor beneath me.

Searing light.

Unbearable heat.

I couldn't take much more. My protection suit wasn't going to last much longer, but I had to keep trying. I was just reaching for the next energy cell and had half pulled it free when the lights went out.

I was back on our ship, blinking as my eyes took longer than before to readjust. I fell to my knees, gasping against the intense pain ricocheting around my body. My stomach was heaving. I only just managed to unlock and pull off my helmet before vomiting with spectacular violence all over the floor. I vomited so hard and for so long that I'm sure there was a bit of cake from my first birthday party in among the smelly mess. The bridge's cleaning robot immediately emerged from its charging unit by the door to vacuum up the stuff and sanitize the area.

'Aidan! Why did you pull me out?' I asked when at last I managed to straighten up. 'I didn't have enough time—'

'One more second and you would've been vaporized,' he told me. 'You left it too long as it is. You have a number of second-degree burns and need to get to the medical bay.'

'No. The medi bay will have to wait until we've rescued the people on the planet surface,' I argued. 'You didn't put me down in the middle of the relay core like I asked. I had to improvise.'

'And I had to save your life. By the way, you're welcome,' Aidan said with attitude.

Justifiable attitude, I conceded.

I took a deep breath. 'Sorry, Aidan. I reckon we have maybe ten minutes max to evacuate all those people on the surface and it's going to take at least three minutes just to get down there.'

'You won't be able to save them all.' He was scrutinizing

the planet surface scanner. 'They're too scattered and the damage to the landscape is too great. Plus a number of them are already dead.'

'Put us down where we can rescue the greatest number,' I ordered. 'And let's do this quick, fast and in a hurry before the Mazon have the chance to fix their ships. Every moment counts.'

'For heaven's sake, Vee, why're you doing this?' Aidan asked.

I smiled, giving my brother an answer I knew would just aggravate him more. 'My gut is telling me it's the right thing to do.'

Aidan groaned. 'I swear one day your gut is going to be the death of me.'

I'd prayed for a miracle. What we got was the Earth vessel which had landed outside our compound. It wasn't quite what I'd expected or wanted, but hell, I'd take my miracles any way I could get them. The explorer-class ship was hovering about four metres off the ground to the east of our compound, blotting out the landscape.

And I've never seen anything so welcome.

Or so dreaded.

The bomb drops and DE bursts seemed to have ceased, which struck me as odd, but I barely had time to think about it. Pulling my arm out of Mum's grasp, I sprinted with her for the ramp which led from the ground to the belly of the Earth ship.

Mum and I weren't the only ones with the same idea. All around us, people were racing for the ramp. On the ground, the wounded were shouting for help and those in a worse way screamed in agony. The ones who really got to me were the severely wounded who didn't scream at all. A few stopped to help others to their feet before making their way to the ship. I slowed to help one of the silent wounded just to my left. Blood and more spilled from a wound in his gut as I tried to help him up. Mum looked at him, then at me, and shook her head. Gritting my teeth, I reluctantly released the guy as gently as I could. He lay on the ground, his eyes closed, his breathing laboured. And then, just like that, his breathing stopped. I stared.

'Come on, Nathan,' Mum urged.

With no time to even close the dead settler's eyes, we carried on running. There were so many around us who needed help, but when I slowed again, Mum turned to shout at me. 'Sort yourself out, Nathan. Then you can help the others. Keep moving!'

So for once, because it was convenient to do so, I did as I was told.

Darren, Mum's second in command, was on the ramp pressing people to hurry up. Now the bomb blasts had stopped I could hear him call out.

Then I saw her. Anjuli. About five or six metres to my right my best friend Anjuli was on her knees, blood trickling from a wound on her head. I sprinted over, pulled her to her feet and placed her arm round my shoulders and my arm round her waist as I urged her on towards the ramp.

'Ellie! ELLIE? Has anyone seen my wife? Where's my son?' Darren ran down the ramp, only to stop abruptly at the bottom. '*ELLIE?* Has anyone seen my son Martyn?'

No one replied as they ran past him into the belly of the ship. Mum, who was now ahead of me, slowed her pace so that Anjuli and I could catch up with her. When we didn't do that fast enough, she ran back to us and placed Anjuli's other arm round her shoulders. We practically dragged Anjuli up the ramp. When I knew she and Mum were safe and on the ship, I turned, ready to offer what help I could to those lagging behind.

'Mike, come on. Move!' I shouted to my friend, who was only just emerging from one of the few buildings in the compound that was still in one piece.

'I'm running as fast as I can,' he called back.

'Not fast enough if you still have breath to argue,' I yelled.

Firing a furious look at me, he picked up the pace. The compound was full of those who'd sought shelter wherever they could and were only just emerging now that the bomb blasts had stopped. Why they thought they'd be safer inside their dwellings than outside, where they at least stood a slim chance of seeing the bombs coming their way, was beyond me. Plus the fact that it was an Earth vessel which had come to our aid didn't exactly help. With the Mazon on one side of us and the Earth vessel on the other, we were between the proverbial rock and hard place. Now a wave of people were charging for the ramp.

'ELLIE?' Darren, who stood beside me, was still yelling for his wife.

BOOOOM!

The bomb blasts started again. Not in the compound this time but on the mountain a couple of kilometres to our west. In a panic, more people raced past me, but there were far more still in the compound, only just emerging from their hiding places.

The ramp I was standing on began to slowly rise.

'NO! WAIT!' Darren called out.

Before us, down on the ground, the panic was getting worse. It was now every person for themselves. Those who fell were not helped back up. The shouts and screams were getting louder.

And still the ramp kept rising.

Some flung themselves at the ramp and scrambled on. Now the ship itself was beginning to rise. Liana Sheen, our commune's doctor, jumped up to the ramp and only just managed to grab hold. The ship was rising faster now. Crouching down, I reached out to catch her as her hands began to slip.

'Darren, help me,' I called out.

Blinking, as if emerging from a daze, Darren grabbed my shirt and started pulling. Liana took hold of my wrists with both hands as I heaved her aboard. She fell forward onto her stomach, only to spring up again almost immediately. The ramp was now almost horizontal and still rising. Back on the ground I saw others frantically waving their hands and begging us to come back.

The ship kept ascending.

'Let's get out of here,' I shouted.

We raced along the ramp to the cargo hold, the renewed sound of exploding bombs pounding in our ears.

'Aidan, there are still people on the ground. We can't leave yet,' I protested.

'If we don't leave now, we won't leave at all,' my brother argued as his hands moved over the controls. 'One Mazon ship is still out of commission but the other one is on our tail. You only caused minor damage to their targeting and navigation systems. That's why it took them a few minutes to pinpoint our position, and why they hit the mountain instead of us, but I guarantee they're already correcting for that. The anti-energy cell you dropped into their reactor has bought us a few more minutes at most.'

'But what about all those people . . . ?'

'Vee.' Aidan swung round in his chair to face me. 'We can try and get the twenty-two we've rescued to safety or we can go back for the others and all die together. That's the choice.'

Oh my God. Only twenty-two . . .

'No other option?'

'No other option,' Aidan confirmed.

Silence.

'Get us out of here,' I said quietly.

The force of our acceleration upwards through the planet's atmosphere pushed me down hard into my seat.

Oh God! All those people . . .

Left behind.

Eighty-five people on the planet and only twenty-two rescued.

I should've tried something else.

Something more.

Tried harder.

'Seven seconds until we leave the planet's atmosphere,' said Aidan, his voice subdued.

'Once we've shaken off the Mazon ships, I want to swing back and pick up any survivors,' I told him.

'There are no survivors.' Aidan locked eyes with me. 'The Mazon have just detonated a proton bomb where we landed. There are no more life forms of any kind registering in that area on the planet surface.'

I stared at him. 'They're all dead?'

My brother nodded. 'And they won't be the only ones if we don't get out of here. We're not out of the woods yet, Vee.'

'Put the Mazon comms on audio,' I ordered.

Aidan tapped into their encrypted communications which he'd long ago managed to decipher. I could hear the Mazon chatter between their two ships. It was a series of clicks, whirrs and chirps, but I'd been studying them for long enough to have a reasonable understanding of their language. Aidan activated the UT, or universal translator, as a backup that I didn't need, but I guess he wanted to make sure I didn't miss anything.

And my brother was right. We were in big trouble.

'The detonation of the bomb on the planet surface will not be enough to deter the Terrans. We cannot allow them to escape our star system – or our justice. If we do, more Terrans will surely follow, and in far greater numbers. They are a threat which must be eradicated, as we have learned to our cost,' said the captain of the larger Mazon battlecruiser.

'But look how our assault has sent them scurrying like the vermin they are. Our proton bomb has annihilated all the cockroaches left behind. Their contamination has been eliminated. Those who have run away would be fools to return,' argued the other captain.

'Sister Sikess, we should press home our advantage. We should at least pursue their escape vessel and obliterate it. They started this war, not us.'

'I agree, Sister Sorres. Let us seek them out and destroy them. We have been wronged. Shall we not revenge? I thirst for vengeance against the humans. All humans.'

I couldn't bear to hear any more. 'Switch it off.'

'But Vee, we need to—'

'SWITCH IT OFF!'

Aidan killed the audio feed.

I clenched my fists, screaming inside. *Bastards!* 'Why didn't they just use their proton bomb to begin with and have done with it?'

'I suspect they were having too much fun making a game of picking off selected targets until you arrived,' said Aidan. 'Now they want to make sure neither you nor anyone else ever has any reason to return to the planet. That proton bomb will ensure nothing can grow or live on the planet surface for at least fifty Sol years.'

'Including the Mazon. They've ruined that planet for everyone, themselves too,' I said.

Aidan shrugged. 'They obviously believe that's a small price to pay.'

I couldn't take any more. The opposite end of the universe wouldn't be enough space between me and the Mazon at that moment. What had happened in the past had been an accident, tragic and terrible, but an accident nonetheless. The Mazon, however, refused to believe that.

'Get us out of here. Maximum speed.'

I sat back in my chair and closed my eyes. The Mazon didn't have to do that – slaughter innocent people. They were renowned for their xenophobia and considered all the planets in this system as theirs and theirs alone. But to massacre so many just to make a point . . .

Those people on the surface never stood a chance.

It barely registered that Aidan was walking towards me. Before I knew what he planned, I felt a sharp scratch against my neck.

'Ow! What the hell, Aidan?'

'It's medication to counter your radiation poisoning from the Mazon engines,' he said. 'It also contains something for your burns. You needed it now before your body goes into shock.'

'I repeat. Dahell! I could've done it,' I said, annoyed.

'Yes, but you didn't. And what is the point of swearing? I've often wondered.' Aidan returned to his seat at the navigation panel.

Glaring at him, I rubbed my neck where he'd just injected me. I appreciated his concern but I really could've done it myself. My neck was beginning to hurt where I was rubbing it. My skin would be ultra-sensitive for the next twelve hours at least, but I counted myself lucky to still be alive to feel it, unlike all those poor people left behind.

'Where are the survivors now?' I asked Aidan.

'In the cargo hold. Now that they've all been decontaminated, d'you want me to allow them to leave that area?'

'Of course. They're not our prisoners.' I frowned. 'Let them come up to the bridge.'

'We know nothing about them,' said Aidan. 'Are you sure about this?'

'I'm sure,' I replied. 'Direct them up here so they can be registered.'

Aidan's fingers tapped and slid over the command console before him. He operated that thing like a maestro. He was far faster than I could ever hope to be when operating the controls and I never tired of watching him work.

'So who are our new guests?' I asked after a while.

'Twelve males, ten females, including two children,' Aidan replied.

Children?

'Why on earth did they bring children to somewhere so dangerous?' I said, horrified.

'You'd have to ask them that, not me,' said Aidan.

Two children. How many more had been on Barros 5?

Vee, stop it! You did your best. What else could you have done?

'Vee, concentrate on the ones you *did* manage to help. They'd all be dead if it wasn't for you.'

I took a deep breath and forced a smile. My brother was right. I had to focus on the positive. After everything that had happened, to concentrate on anything else might send me over the edge.

8

NATHAN

A strange, strangled hush had descended on the cargo hold. Darren was kneeling on the floor, with his head in his hands, grief making his whole body quake. The ship we were on was still rising, juddering and jolting as we moved through the planet's atmosphere, leaving our friends and loved ones behind. I looked around, shaking my head. There were so few of us left. At first glance I'd say around twenty. Would we get the chance to rescue the others before the Mazon wiped them out? Without warning, the ship shook violently, knocking those few still standing off their feet. That last blast had been too close. If just one DE blast were to hit us, then we'd be toast.

Mum came and sat down next to me. She put her arm round my shoulder and kissed my forehead. I let it pass as it might be the last kiss I got from her. We were on an Earth vessel. That meant we weren't out of danger; far from it. A cocktail of emotions stirred within me. Back on the planet surface I really thought my last moments had come. Now here I was in the cargo hold of some anonymous Earth ship. Some of my friends were back down on the planet surface, no doubt still having to endure the continuing Mazon attack. I could only hope they'd make it to the cavern in the mountains. But was I any safer on this ship which could be blasted out of the sky at any moment?

Every second counted and was precious because it could be my last. I made a vow in that moment never to squander a single second of my life again. If by another miracle we got out of this alive, I would grab hold of life and squeeze every drop out of it.

A strange mist descended from the vents above us. I knew a moment's foreboding at the sight of it, but if someone wished us harm, they'd hardly go to the trouble of rescuing us first. However, this was an Authority Earth vessel. Had we really come this far only to be recaptured? The thought made me feel physically sick. I would fight and die before I let them take me back.

'Mum, d'you recognize this ship?' I whispered.

Mum shook her head.

I looked around again. What kind of captain was in charge of this vessel? Would he or she listen to the truth about us and at least give us a chance? Or had we jumped out of the frying pan and straight into the fire?

9

Focusing on the positive was so much easier said than done. All my thoughts were caught up with those poor people left behind on Barros 5. Just once I wanted to be able to properly help. All I seemed to do was dab and dabble at the edges, blotting up only a tiny amount of the damage from the mayhem around me. Just once, I wanted to be at the centre of doing some good for a change. I would make it my mission to get these people back home to Earth. I could do that, if nothing else.

As if on cue, the door to the bridge slid open with a hiss. These people hadn't wasted any time making their way up from the lower deck, where the cargo hold was situated, to the bridge on the upper deck. I jumped to my feet as a swarm of people flooded in. I took an eager step forward, then stopped.

People.

Lovely, beautiful people.

But so many of them. Too many to fit on the bridge. They were spilling out into the corridor.

A quick glance at Aidan for reassurance. He wasn't nervous like me, just curious. I straightened up and deliberately set my expression so that my anxieties were carefully masked. After years of just me and Aidan on this ship, the sudden influx of people was totally overwhelming. Someone was crying; there was a nervous cough, some fast panicked breathing. An assortment of smells hit me: sweat, blood, flowery scents, body odour and worse. So many people on board my ship, all of them staring at me and my brother. How many months and years had I spent longing for human companionship? Now it was here and this stream of people was shocking to my senses. And wondrous. And exhilarating. But mostly shocking.

These people, beautiful and welcome as they were, scared me. I caught sight of a five- or six-year-old girl with cropped brown hair, clinging to the leg of the willowy Indian woman beside her. I tentatively smiled at the girl. She didn't smile back but clung even tighter to the woman's leg. That was all right. The girl's expression was a reflection of how I felt inside. It was something we had in common and, strangely enough, made me feel slightly better. I could do this.

A woman with auburn-red hair and dark green eyes pushed herself through the crowd of mostly adults to stand before them. She was thin, with permanent grooves around her mouth that weren't laughter lines. This was a woman who hadn't had much to smile about in the past.

'Who's in charge here?' she demanded.

Aidan and I exchanged a glance.

'I am,' I replied. 'Nihao.'

'And you are?' asked the woman, completely ignoring my common language greeting.

'Vee Sindall. That is, Olivia Sindall, but everyone calls . . . called . . . calls me Vee. And that's my twin brother Aidan. He's younger. Who are you?'

God, I sounded like an inarticulate noob.

'I'm Catherine Linedecker. What d'you mean you're in charge? You're a child.'

'I'm eighteen,' I bristled.

'Where's the rest of the crew?' asked Catherine.

'My mum, Vida Sindall, was captain of this ship and my dad, Daniel Sindall, was the ship's doctor. They, along with all the other crew, died over three years ago,' I said.

'Died?' Catherine's tone was sharp. 'Died how? Of what?'

'A virus wiped everyone out except for me,' I told her. 'And my brother.'

'A virus? So now we've all been exposed to it?'

'No, the ship is clean. Whatever the virus was, it died along with the crew,' I said. 'I've carried out extensive biological tests all over the ship since then. There's no trace left of it.'

'What's the name of this ship?' asked Catherine.

'Earth Vessel *Aidan*. EV *Aidan*.'

'The same name as your brother?'

Obviously. The statement didn't warrant an answer.

'You departed from one of the main space docks orbiting Earth?' asked Catherine.

I nodded. 'Yes, we left seven years ago on a ten-year deep-space exploration mission.'

'You lived on Earth before that?'

'Yes, that's right.' I frowned.

'Anywhere else?'

'No, just Earth.'

It wasn't just that this woman asked far too many questions; it was also the way she asked them. Her tone was sharp and scratchy like shards of glass against my already sensitive skin.

A girl of about my age with short-cropped, spiky blonde hair and the bluest eyes I'd ever seen walked over to my brother, a determined look on her face.

'Nihao. I'm Erica.' The girl held her hand out towards Aidan.

Aidan looked from it to her and back again. Slowly he shook her hand. 'Hello, Erica.'

'Ooh! Very formal,' said Erica, one eyebrow raised. 'You're totally edible, aren't you?'

Whoa! My mouth dropped open.

'Erica, this is hardly the time or the place,' snapped Catherine.

'What?' said Erica. 'I'm introducing myself. There are rules about when I can and can't do that now?'

'Erica . . .' Catherine's voice held a barely disguised warning.

'I'm just letting him know I'm interested, that's all,' Erica argued, exasperated.

Me? I just stared. Erica was obviously a girl who gave zero damns about what anyone else thought. I liked that! Not only did Erica think my brother was fit but she wasn't shy about telling him so. I shook my head as I watched. Was she ever barking up the wrong tree though. Erica turned in time to see me shaking my head. Her gaze narrowed as she glared at me. What on Earth did I do?

Just then, two more men arrived on the bridge, pushing their way forward. The older guy with sandy brown hair and matching brown eyes looked around; then his fierce gaze attached itself to me with eagle's talons. He scowled like I was his worst enemy. I took a step back, my legs bumping against my chair.

The younger guy was about my age, I think, or maybe slightly older, with thick, raven-black, wavy hair that fell down to his shoulders. His dark eyebrows were straight, shaped lines above emerald-green eyes and he had lovely well-defined lips. OK, so I notice those kinds of things. But oh, those eyes! Not only were the lights on behind those eyes but there was a party happening. He and I regarded each other. Wow! He was definitely – what was Erica's word? – *edible*. He was a head and more taller than me, and his body looked like it knew the meaning of hard work. This guy was staring at me, his gaze intense, his expression unreadable. Self-conscious heat rose up from my neck to wash over my face. The younger guy's face didn't wear the same belligerence as his older friend, but maybe he was just better at schooling his features. Then, to my surprise, the younger guy smiled. It was the first sign of friendliness I'd seen from any of them. I tentatively smiled back. Whoa! He was gorgeous. Realizing that I was probably staring, I averted my gaze.

'You!' said the older guy as he pointed at me. His voice was gruff and deep, much deeper than my brother's. 'Did you give the order to abandon Barros 5?'

'Yes, I did.'

'Turn this ship round,' he demanded. 'There are still people on that planet. My family are back there.'

'I can't.'

'Damn it. Turn this ship round at once.' The man was a mad dog, howling at me – and just as terrifying. I stood up straighter.

'I'm afraid I can't do that,' I replied quietly.

'Darren, I'll handle this,' Catherine told him, but he stepped forward, completely ignoring her. His focus was solely on me as I was the one standing before the captain's chair.

'If you won't turn this ship round, I will,' said Darren.

Out of the corner of my eye, I watched as Aidan's hands moved swiftly over the controls, making sure that no one would be turning our ship or taking it anywhere without my explicit say-so. Saying nothing, I merely watched Darren warily. The man looked from my brother to me again.

'Please,' said Darren, trying a different tack. 'My wife and son are down there. We have to rescue them. *Please*.'

'We can't rescue anyone from the planet, because they're all dead,' said Aidan.

Oh. My. God! I glared at my brother. For heaven's sake! Couldn't he find a better way to let this guy know than just blurting it out like that?

Darren stared at Aidan. 'What're you talking about?'

'What my brother is trying to say is the Mazon detonated a proton bomb on the planet surface,' I replied before Aidan could. 'They didn't just kill all the people down there but every living thing is now dead – trees, flowers, animals, insects. Their bomb took out the lot. I'm so sorry.'

Darren's eyes misted over, but it didn't last long. He pressed his lips together until his mouth was just a gash across his face. Behind him, the cries and sobs of some grew louder.

For so long I'd yearned for the company of others. Selective memories told me that people brought happiness and laughter.

How strange I'd forgotten that with people also came grief.

'You should've waited to pick up more people,' Darren accused. 'You just left all those people back on that planet to die. My wife Ellie and my son Martyn are gone, thanks to you.' The daggers in his eyes shot straight through me and every single one of them exited my body taking a piece of me with it. I held my breath, drowning in the hatred of his cold stare, lashed by the venom in his voice.

'I tried to help,' I protested.

'You should've stayed longer, given them a chance to make it to the ship,' Darren insisted.

'I stayed as long as I could—'

But I didn't get any further before the guy standing next to him interrupted. 'Darren, if she'd stayed longer, none of us would be here now.'

'Stay out of this, Nathan. You didn't lose anyone. Your mum is right there.' Darren pointed to Catherine. 'None of your family got left behind to die.'

'I left it until the last possible second before taking off,' I said quietly.

'Vee did everything she could to save as many of you as possible,' said Aidan.

Mutters and whispers sounded at that. All those crowding onto the bridge were staring at me. The weight of their gaze almost made my knees buckle.

'Vee, you must forgive Darren,' said Catherine. 'He's still in shock. We all are.'

'Thanks to her, my wife and child are dead,' Darren accused.

I gasped, feeling his words like a stinging slap across my face.

'You need to thank the Mazon for that. *We* rescued you, you ungrateful turd,' said my brother furiously. He turned to me, his eyes sparkling with anger. 'Vee, I told you it'd be a mistake to get involved.'

'Aidan, that's not helping,' I said.

'Darren, I'm still in command here. Let me handle it.'

The red-headed woman, Catherine, grabbed at the older man's arm, trying once again to pull him back. He shrugged her off before taking a couple of steps in my direction. I could see his intent in his eyes. He was hurting and he didn't want to do it alone.

I was about to learn the hard way that no good deed went unpunished.

Darren was about to do something that we'd all regret. I couldn't let that happen. I spun round and put myself between Vee and him, my back to Vee.

'Darren, you need to calm down,' I said.

'Nathan, get the hell out of my way,' he hissed.

'No way. You need to back up,' I warned him. 'If it wasn't for Vee and her brother, we'd all be dead. Like Aidan said, if you want to blame someone, blame the Mazon.'

Vee moved to stand beside me. I risked a quick glance at her. She stood with her chin up, her head held high.

'Darren, is it? Well, I'm sorry for your loss, but believe me, Aidan and I did everything we could to help you. To help all of you,' Vee said.

'We couldn't stay any longer,' said Aidan. 'The odds weren't in our favour for rescuing any of you. If it wasn't for the time bought by my sister when she sabotaged each of the Mazon ships, none of you would be here now.'

What did Aidan mean by that? How could Vee have sabotaged the Mazon ships singlehandedly? A whole army would have had trouble doing that.

'I don't care what the odds said about getting us out of there in one piece. She shouldn't have left anyone behind.' Darren turned both barrels on Aidan before turning to Vee. 'My wife and boy are dead. I'll never forgive you for that.'

Next to me, Vee flinched. It was almost imperceptible but I saw it. I felt it.

'Why weren't your wife and child with you?' Aidan asked.

Darren's eyes narrowed. 'They were in our living quarters and I was working outside the compound when the Mazon opened fire.'

'Why didn't you go back for them?' said Aidan.

'I *tried*.' Darren was getting more angry with Vee's brother with each uttered word. 'Once the bombing started, I couldn't get to them.'

'Then you didn't try hard enough, did you?' Aidan challenged. 'I mean, you're here and they aren't. Every man for himself?'

Darren launched himself at Aidan. There was no other word for it. A second later, they were both rolling on the floor and Darren was punching the bloody hell out of Aidan's face. Some of us had to rush forward to pull him off. Darren was so full of rage, it took four of us to do it.

Aidan got to his feet, a satisfied half-smile on his face as he considered Darren. Aidan's bottom lip was split and a couple of drops of blood clung to the corner of his mouth. Slowly, his tongue snaked out to taste the blood. Wiping his lip with the back of his hand, Aidan's head tilted as he contemplated the blood smeared across it. As he raised his head to look at Darren, a strange expression rolled over his face. He was still smiling but there was an unnatural focused calm about him that made me want to take a step back.

'Aidan, stand down,' Vee urged her brother.

Aidan took a step forward.

'I said stand down. Damn it, Aidan, I mean it.' Vee moved in front of her brother. 'Don't you dare . . .'

Aidan turned to look at Vee as if her words were only just registering. The strange, focused expression faded. He stepped back.

'Vee, Aidan, I can only apologize for the behaviour of my second in command,' said Mum. 'I assure you, we are all . . . grateful for everything you did to rescue us.'

Wow! Mum's gratitude was a meagre dish, watery at best. I wasn't the only one who thought so. Aidan and Vee exchanged a pointed look before Aidan sat back down. Vee stepped further away from me to stand closer to her brother – and I couldn't say I blamed her. As first impressions went, we were all making a pretty piss-poor one. A tense hush reigned for a few moments as we all waited for someone else to break the silence.

'How long were you all on Barros 5?' Vee asked at last.

'Just over three Sol months,' Mum replied.

'Had the Mazon ever attacked you before?'

'No,' I answered before Mum could. 'They only became aware of our presence a day ago. That's when they warned us to leave their planet immediately and go back to where we came from or suffer the consequences.'

Vee looked at me. 'Which you took to mean . . . ?'

'You'd have to ask my mum that,' I replied. No way was I jumping in front of that question.

Looking deeply unimpressed, Vee turned to Mum and waited for an answer.

'I was hoping that with our actions we could persuade them that we were no threat to them,' said Mum, on the defensive. 'That we might even be a benefit to their community. And besides, we had no way of leaving the planet surface.'

'How did you get there then?' asked Aidan.

Mum and Darren exchanged a swift, calculated look, but not swift enough because Vee caught it. Her eyes narrowed slightly.

'A transport left us there,' Mum answered.

'Why would a transport ship deposit you on a planet in hostile Mazon space with no means of escape?' Vee looked to me for answers. Answers I couldn't give her. I met her gaze directly but didn't say a word.

Was that disappointment I saw in her eyes? I'd only just met her and yet I felt that in some way I'd let her down by not being honest with her.

'When you first arrived on Barros 5, why didn't you send out an emergency signal immediately so that you could be rescued sooner?' Vee asked. 'I know you could have done it because that's how my brother and I managed to track you down.'

Another look exchanged, between me and Mum this time. No one spoke.

'When the Mazon started firing on you, why didn't you fight back?' Vee asked.

Darren frowned. 'How d'you know we didn't?'

'I was monitoring the situation as we approached the planet,' Vee replied. 'All the weapons fire was coming from one direction.'

Mum's lips thinned. 'We were trying to establish a non-violent colony, to prove to the Mazon that they had nothing to fear from us. All we wanted was a safe haven and peaceful co-existence.'

'Are you serious? You do know that the Mazon hate us humans – right?' Vee said scathingly. 'They're the worst xenophobes in the quadrant. You can't preach peace to those who revel in hatred and hostility towards anyone who is different.'

'We had to try,' said Mum. 'Actions speak louder than words. We wanted to prove to them that they had nothing to fear from us. Besides, with no way off the planet, we had no choice.'

'You had a choice between living and dying,' Vee pointed out. 'And another thing: when this ship landed on the planet, some of you initially ran *away* from us, not towards us. What was that about?'

No one said a word.

'Well, Aidan, break out the dictionary. We have a ship full of scintillating conversationalists,' said Vee with enough sarcasm to make me wince.

11

Disillusionment was rapidly setting in. Is this what I'd risked my life for? Each and every one of them was hiding something. I didn't need to be Sherlock Holmes to figure that one out. Catherine asked a lot of questions but answered very few, Darren did his thinking with his fists and none of the others had much to say about anything. And the one with the dark hair – Nathan? – he was the biggest letdown.

When I first saw him and he'd smiled at me, I thought . . . I could've sworn . . .

Well, no matter. I'd been mistaken and that was all there was to it.

I glanced at my brother. The pointed look he gave me told me that he knew something wasn't quite right here too.

We might have been alone for the last few years, but I'd had direct dealings with the Mazon before, which was obviously more than this lot had. There was no reasoning with the unreasonable. No appeasing the unappeasable. Every word I'd read or heard about the Mazon said it was best to leave their planetary system alone and give them a very wide berth. They were a race who were terrified of change and as a consequence would do anything they could to make sure it never happened. The status quo was their religion. It was pure arrogance to expect the Mazon to change just because Catherine and her other colonists wanted them to. Where had they been that they didn't know that? Or maybe they were convinced that the Mazon would make an exception in their case? I had to admit, part of me grudgingly admired these people's optimism, misplaced and dangerously foolish as it was.

'I'm assuming you had weapons down on the planet?' I said.

'Enough to protect ourselves against the indigenous wildlife. Not enough to wage war,' said Catherine.

'Protecting yourself against the Mazon isn't the same as waging war.'

'We didn't have the fire power to protect ourselves against them effectively. Besides, how could we hope to convince the Mazon of our good intentions if we fired at them? Sometimes you have to show that peace is more than just a word.'

'By letting them kill you? That's showing them all right,' I said with scorn. 'And just now, Darren was ready to tear my head off.' I looked straight at him. 'If my brother hadn't deliberately provoked him to draw his fire, it'd probably be *my* mouth – or worse – bleeding by now, not Aidan's. So you're not all quite as peace-loving as you like to make out.'

Darren's lips disappeared altogether at that, not so much a gash as a paper-thin line. In that moment I knew I had made an enemy. Probably more than one. How many other survivors aboard my ship had loved ones who had been left behind on the planet surface? How many others now hated me because of it?

'What is wrong with you people?' A woman in her early forties with short, dark-brown hair and sad, pale blue eyes pushed past Darren. She cast a glance at Aidan, then took a step forward to address me directly. I braced myself, ready for another onslaught. 'Vee, I'm Doctor Sheen, but most people call me Doctor Liana. I don't blame you at all for what happened. I know you did your best and none of us would be here now if it wasn't for you. We don't all think – or act – like Darren.'

'Liana, I think I can—' Catherine began.

'I don't understand why you're all so ready to crucify this poor girl and her brother,' interrupted Liana, shaking her head. 'She risked her life to help us.'

'Thank you,' I said to the doctor, only slightly mollified.

'I've already apologized for Darren's actions . . .' Catherine began.

'Save it,' I dismissed. 'What it boils down to is you're all too principled to stand and fight but you have no qualms about condemning me for doing what you wouldn't.'

'We had no weapons that could affect the Mazon ships. They were way out of the range of our weapons,' Darren protested.

'Then isn't it lucky for all of you that I came along?' I made no attempt to disguise the contempt in my voice.

These people had been on my bridge for less than fifteen minutes and already I had a crashing headache and a pain in my chest like I hadn't felt since Mum and Dad died. It was going to take me another ten Sol months to get back to Earth's solar system. Ten months with these people.

Ten months of sheer and total hell.

 **NATHAN**

Well, I'm not sure how our initial meeting with Vee and her brother could've gone any worse. The tension on the bridge was a living, breathing thing. Darren was an arsehat at the best of times and this sure wasn't one of those. Yes, he'd just lost his wife and son, I understood that. We all got that. The Mazon were too powerful and too far away to blame. Vee and Aidan were right here. But he was being so damned unfair. I turned to face Vee. The beautiful dark brown eyes that had been soft and uncertain when we first came onto the bridge were now cold and hard as stone as they surveyed all of us – including me.

I didn't like that. At all.

'Aidan, get us away from the Mazon ships as fast as possible. Reconfigure our energy signature every few nanoseconds so they can't track us,' Vee said to her brother. 'Then could you scan and register these people. Provide any orientation they may need to help them find their way around the ship and settle in.' She turned to the rest of us. 'After that, I recommend you all meet up in the mess hall on this deck while my brother and your commander work out your various assignments. Aidan will also assign you sleeping quarters, most of which are below us on the middle or mid deck. In the meantime we shall resume our original heading back to Earth.'

Oh God!

There were gasps and groans at Vee's announcement. One person in the background exclaimed a very audible, 'No!' I think it was Jaxon, though I couldn't be sure. I looked at Vee. Her frown had deepened, bewilderment narrowing her eyes. Why didn't Mum just tell her the truth? Vee looked around the bridge, still puzzled.

'You're taking us to Earth?' said Mum, her tone sharp.

'That's the plan. We're ten Sol months, two weeks and five days away so I suggest you all make yourselves comfortable. It's going to be a long trip,' said Vee, adding under her breath, 'For everyone.'

'We can't go to Earth. We need to head for Mendela Prime in the Gamma Quadrant,' argued Mum.

Vee stared at Mum. 'Are you nuts? Mendela Prime is over twelve Sol months in the opposite direction. And to get to the nearest wormhole to make it to the Gamma Quadrant in that time, we'd have to travel for at least five weeks through Mazon space. In case you hadn't noticed, the Mazon are now actively hunting us. If we try to double back, we stand little to no chance of sneaking through their territory undetected. I'm not prepared to risk my ship like that. If you don't want to go back to Earth with me, then fine. I'll take you to the nearest neutral starbase from where you can send a sub-space message to Earth or Mendela Prime or wherever. No doubt you'll find a convoy that will pick you up and take you where you want to go.'

'That's not acceptable,' said Mum.

I winced. Could she sound any more arrogant? Not in this space–time continuum, I suspected.

Vee's eyebrows shot up. 'Well, excuse me all over the place but, acceptable or not, that's what's going to happen.'

'Are the Mazon really still after us?' asked Mum.

'Yes. As far as they're concerned, if they allow us to escape, other Terrans will surely follow. You've thrown down a gauntlet which they're not about to ignore,' Vee replied. 'I've been monitoring their comms. They're coming after us and they're not going to give up in a hurry. We can't match their fire power so our only hope is to outmanoeuvre or outsmart them, preferably both.'

'When was the last time you were at an Earth spaceport?' asked Mum.

'We set off nearly seven years ago on our deep-space exploration mission and the last time we docked at an Earth spaceport was when we reached the Alpha Quadrant's outer rim about three years after that. We haven't docked at one since then.' Vee frowned. 'Why?'

'So your ship's computer hasn't been linked to an Earth Authority hub in four years?' asked Mum.

'That's right. Why?'

'Then I'm sorry to have to do this but I don't have time to babysit you and your brother,' said Mum. 'Computer, this is Commander Catherine Linedecker CYL-Phi-Epsilon-803-1995. I am hereby invoking Earth Vessel Override Authorization Code 26-theta-upsilon and taking command of this vessel. Acknowledge.'

'Mum!' My heart sank down to my boots. Mortified, I closed my eyes momentarily, but that wasn't going to change this situation, much as I might wish otherwise. The faint whirr of the environmental control unit and the low hum of the ship's engine that reverberated throughout the entire ship were the only sounds on the bridge. It was as if we were all holding our breath, waiting to see what would happen next. Aidan observed my mum with a great deal of interest and very little concern. He wore the same strange smile he'd had on his face after Darren decked him. Vee, however, was somewhere north, south, east and west of severely pissed off.

'Seriously, Mum? Vee risked her life to rescue us and this is how you repay her?' I asked furiously. 'By taking her ship?'

'Don't argue with me, Nathan. This is far too important to leave in the hands of a child,' said Mum. 'We need to travel to Mendela Prime.'

'I've already told you, I'm eighteen, nearly nineteen, not a child.' Vee's tone was clipped and concise. 'Plus Aidan and I have survived just fine for the last three years without any of you.'

'Mum, this is so out of order.' I shook my head, my embarrassment growing in leaps and bounds. How could Mum do this? I know we were shaken up and still in shock over what had happened to us, but this was all kinds of wrong.

'Nathan, stay out of it,' Mum snapped.

She looked stressed and, worse than that, guilty. I doubted if anyone but me could recognize that in her expression but I was her son and I could read her like a picture book.

'Well, thank you for that demonstration,' said Vee quietly. Her contemptuous gaze slid from me to Mum. 'At least we now all know exactly where we stand.'

'Vee, the rest of these people are wandering all over our ship, *touching* things,' said Aidan, irritated. He was bent over his panel analysing something I was too far away to see, but he was obviously tracking everyone's movements and activities around the ship.

'Direct the ones who aren't already here to come to the bridge to be scanned and registered. Impress upon them that none of this ship's utilities or functions will work for them until they do,' Vee ordered.

'I tried to tell you this was a colossal mistake but you never listen to me,' Aidan muttered in a stage whisper.

Vee wasn't the only one to scowl at her brother. 'Aidan, enough.'

'They can't be trusted, Vee,' he said.

Vee's gaze swept around all of us on the bridge, her disdain obvious but mixed with something else. She regarded me, making no attempt to mask her expression, and her disappointment was a cord that stretched taut between the two of us, pulling at my insides. All the hurt she felt at that moment I wore as if it were my own. If this was a test, then we'd all spectacularly failed.

'Aidan, I'm going to my quarters and then I'll be in the hydroponics bay if you need me.' Vee didn't wait for a response, but walked towards the exit, her head high, her back straight. Those before her parted like the Red Sea to let her pass. We had all been effectively summed up and dismissed, even though Vee was the one who was leaving.

'I don't understand,' said Mum to no one in particular as Vee left. 'That override code should've worked.'

'After the rest of our crew died of the mystery virus, Vee modified this ship extensively, including the computer,' said Aidan. 'She put new protocols in place to make sure that no one but her and me could ever run this ship. It was a precaution to stop others – coming from any direction – from trying to take our ship or from turning it against us.'

'Aidan, you don't understand. We need to get to Mendela Prime, regroup and warn others about the Mazon threat,' said Mum.

'Then maybe you should've led with that, Mum,' I said, still furious with her, 'instead of trying to take Vee's ship away from her when you've only been aboard for a few minutes. Apart from anything else, that was plain rude. Why didn't you just tell her the truth? The whole truth?'

'As Commander of this colony, I have to do everything in my power, no matter how distasteful, to ensure our survival.' Mum tried to defend the indefensible. 'The Mazon threat—'

'As far as my sister is concerned, you and your friends pose the bigger threat at the moment,' Aidan interrupted. 'So accept the fact that you're going to be dropped off asap. Now if you'd all like to line up, I will scan you and assign you to your quarters on the mid deck.'

'And if we refuse to be scanned?' asked Mum.

'Then you won't be able to use any of the ship's facilities,' said Aidan. 'And that includes obtaining food and clothes from the utility dispensers. You won't be able to enter the medical bay or the hydroponics bay, which are both on the mid deck. You won't have access to the science or astrophysics labs on this deck. You won't get sleeping quarters assigned so you'll all end up sleeping in the corridors or the cargo hold. You will not be able to—'

'All right! We get it,' Mum said tersely.

'Ready?' Aidan asked evenly. And as far as he was concerned, that was the end of the discussion.

As for me, I wanted to run after Vee and apologize until my voice was hoarse. Mum should've just told her and her brother the truth. I headed over to Aidan to be first in the queue as no one else was showing any inclination to move.

'I know you have no reason to believe this, but we're not your enemy,' I told him.

'Didn't your commander state that actions speak louder than words?' said Aidan. 'Look at the panel over there face on.' He indicated the screen to his right. 'Then turn to give a left and right profile please.'

I did as directed, saying, 'Yes, Mum did say that, about proving to the Mazon that we weren't a threat. So?'

'Could you place both hands on this panel now?'

I placed my hands on the panel before him. A light shone beneath my hands followed by a sudden, almost painful warmth. My fingerprints, a palm print and a DNA sample had been taken.

I moved aside for Mum, who was next in the queue behind me. Slowly others got into line behind her.

'What about what Mum said?' I prompted.

'From where I'm sitting, you are all far more dangerous than the Mazon could ever be,' said Aidan.

'How so?' I frowned.

'The Mazon are an external threat. You people are on board,' said Aidan. He turned to my mum. 'What's your next move if Vee won't give up our ship? Are you going to bundle my sister and me out of an airlock, or do you intend to slit our throats while we're asleep?'

'We would never do anything like that.' Mum was outraged, but what the hell did she expect?

'No?' Aidan challenged her. 'Well, you'll forgive me if my sister and I don't turn our backs on any of you. And, Commander, you in particular don't strike me as someone who gives up in a hurry. You've already proved you can't be trusted.' He turned to me. 'Like mother like son?'

I glared at him, bitterly resenting his words. Aidan might think he knew Darren and my mum and the rest of the settlers. But he certainly didn't know me. Nor did his sister.

Right about now she was probably wishing she had ignored our distress beacon and continued on her way. Worse than that, she thought each of us was a real threat. As far as I was concerned, nothing could be further from the truth. I was going to make it my mission to convince Vee of that. I didn't want her to think badly of me . . . I mean, us. I wanted to get to know her, to see her smile at me again – and often. There and then I made a vow. If Darren or any of the others wanted to harm either Vee or her brother, they'd have to go through me first.

The thought startled me, not just because I'd thought it but because I meant it. Every word. And that worried me.

Why did I feel so protective of someone I'd only just met?

Not good.

13  VEE

Sigh. I sat cross-legged on the metal bench among the *tomtato* plants at the far end of the hydroponics bay. Another few days and I'd be able to harvest tomatoes from the top of the plant but it'd be at least another couple of Sol weeks before the potatoes at the bottom were ready to gather. Not that my tomtato plants were the highest priority at this moment. Shoulders slumped, I sat with a bowl of chilli con carne, my favourite meal, in my hands. Normally the smell alone was enough to cheer me up but for once it failed to weave its usual magic. I put a spoonful in my mouth and chewed slowly. The fiery taste wasn't doing much for me either.

Earlier, after I'd stripped off the protection suit in my quarters and put on my work clothes, I'd stopped by the medical bay to treat my burns, only to find the doctor, Liana Sheen, already making herself at home. She was attending to a number of people who'd been injured back on Barros 5, but the moment I entered the medi bay she was at my side.

'How can I help?' she asked, dredging up a tentative smile.

'You can't. I have some burns but I'll tend to them myself, thank you.'

'Let me do that for you,' insisted the doctor. 'It's the least I can do.'

'I can manage,' I said icily.

The doc sighed as I applied the skin regenerator for myself.

No doubt I came across as churlish but I was still smarting from all that had happened since she and her friends had come aboard. Injuries taken care of, I left without saying another word. Incredibly rude, I know, especially when she'd spoken up for me back on the bridge, but quite frankly by that point I'd had enough of all the refugees, colonists, settlers, whatever it was they called themselves. And though my body was almost back to normal, my mind wasn't. My thoughts were racing. The corridors of my ship were full of strangers who moved to one side as I passed and looked at me like I was a hydra with offensive body odour as well as nine heads. God knows I wasn't expecting to be lifted up onto any shoulders and hailed as a conquering heroine, but what had I done to deserve such angry suspicion?

And I still couldn't believe it. That . . . that woman, Commander Catherine Linedecker, had tried to take my ship away from me.

My ship.

She was lucky I hadn't locked up her and the rest of her friends in the detention cells on the lower deck for attempted piracy. From my quarters I'd DNA-locked all the weapons on board so that they wouldn't work for anyone but me and Aidan. Too little, but at least not too late. But now, for the rest of the journey back to Earth, I'd have to listen to my brother singing 'I told you so' at me in every available octave.

Oh joy!

The door to the hydroponics bay hissed open.

'Aidan, I'm not in the mood for company. And don't leave the bridge unattended,' I snapped, long before he came into view. 'I don't want that lot wreaking havoc on my ship.'

My visitors stepped out from behind the hybrid *plupple* trees close to the main entrance. Nathan I recognized. He stood before two girls, one of whom was Erica, and another guy, all around the same age as Nathan and me.

'Nihao, Vee,' said Nathan. A slight, hesitant smile was trying – and failing – to land on his lips.

'Hello,' I replied more formally. Friendly didn't work with these people. What were they all doing here? What did they want?

'D'you mind if we join you?'

'We?' I said pointedly.

Nathan frowned but then his expression cleared. 'Ah! OK. Let me introduce my friends.' He pointed at the tall, stocky guy who looked like he was of Chinese heritage. 'This is Mike. He's a plant freak. Anything that grows and he's there ready to give it a hug. He also works with Doctor

Liana when needed. He's a trained medic. The surly bastard to my left is Erica. There hasn't been a weapon invented that she can't handle. She also loves animals and is going to have her own farm one day.'

Erica scowled at him with a look that could halt an incoming missile at two metres. Nathan was introducing his friends like they were contestants in one of those matchmaker reality shows I'd sometimes watched as a child back on Earth. I pressed my lips firmly together to stop myself from smiling at Erica's expression. I'd hate to be on her bad side.

'Nathan, I'm sure Vee couldn't care less about my feelings towards animals,' said Erica.

I turned back to Nathan, wondering what was the point of all this.

'And this is Anjuli,' said Nathan, indicating the girl on his right. Her long, jet-black hair was streaked with burgundy and tied back in a ponytail. She had a tattoo of what looked like a moth inked on the brown skin of her neck. 'Anjuli is a genius with all things cybertronic – second only to me of course.'

'Is there anyone in the universe who adores you as much as you love yourself?' asked Anjuli seriously.

'You?' asked Nathan.

Anjuli snorted. 'You wish!'

I pressed my lips together even more firmly to suppress a laugh at the unimpressed look Anjuli gave Nathan. These were his friends?

'So now that you know who we all are, may we join you?' asked Nathan.

A moment's pause, then I shrugged. 'Help yourself.'

I uncrossed my legs and shuffled further along the bench to sit at one end of it, giving them plenty of room to sit where they liked. Nathan moved with impressive speed, and to my surprise sat down next to me. And I mean right next to me, with his thigh touching mine. I could feel the heat radiating from his body.

Anjuli sat next to him while Mike and Erica sat on the floor in front of us. I was suddenly inexplicably aware of my heart thumping in my chest. Now what? I had no clue what I was supposed to say or do next. I was out of practice when it came to being with people. Beads of nervous sweat were beginning to prickle my skin. I inhaled, trying to get it together. Hmm! I caught Nathan's scent, faint yet distinct as it was. He smelled of fresh perspiration and newly turned soil, a lovely earthy smell. Outdoorsy. I surreptitiously inhaled slightly deeper.

'Smells good.'

Busted!

Stricken, I stared at him. Had I made it that obvious that I liked the way he smelled?

'The chilli.' Nathan pointed to the bowl in my hand. 'That smells really good.'

'Oh! OK.' Phew! 'Would you like some?' I asked, my voice full of a reticence I barely recognized.

'Yes please. I'm starving,' said Nathan.

'There's a utility dispenser in the wall over there.' I pointed. 'Just press the food button and order chilli, hot or mild, or anything else you might like.'

'What kind are you having?' asked Nathan.

'It's in a category of its own. My own recipe. The dispenser knows it as "Vee's chilli".' I smiled. 'No one appreciates this one except me.'

'Why?' said Mike.

'It's not for beginners,' I replied.

'Fair enough.' He appeared not to require any further explanation.

'Not for beginners, eh? Is that right?' said Nathan.

What was that gleam in his green eyes? Had he taken my words as a challenge? I suspected Nathan was a guy who liked a challenge. The others stood up and headed over to the dispenser, all except for Nathan. He waited until they were out of earshot.

'Vee, I'm sorry about what happened earlier.' Nathan spoke softly. 'What my mum did was wrong.'

'You don't have to apologize—' I began.

'Yes I do,' said Nathan. 'I know it's not worth much, but it's all I've got.'

I studied him, trying my hardest to figure him out. Why would he feel the need to apologize for his mum? He met my gaze without flinching or looking away.

'Apology accepted,' I said at last.

He smiled, his eyes never leaving mine. God, he really was stunning when he smiled. Actually he was kinda striking, even when he didn't smile. And those eyes . . . Just looking at him was doing peculiar things to my insides. Or was that the chilli?

'Don't you want some food? I can show you how to use the dispenser to get anything you want.' I went to stand up but Nathan's hand on my arm made me sit back down again hastily. The touch of his hand had sent an electric shock racing over my skin. He withdrew his hand and I suppressed a shiver. It almost hurt to be touched after all this time. My skin was still ultra-sensitive.

'Can I try some of yours, just to see what it's like?' said Nathan.

What? Really? Why would he want some of mine when he could get a bowl of his own? My eyes narrowed. If he thought that being super-friendly would make me so dazzled and dazed that I'd hand over my ship to his mother, then he had another thought or five coming.

Come on, Vee, don't be so paranoid!

Why was I this jittery? I glanced down for a moment so he wouldn't see the confusion on my face. Schooling my features, I looked at him and said, 'Are you sure you want to share? I warn you, my chilli is a bit on the spicy side.'

'The spicier the better,' said Nathan.

We'll see about that.

'OK,' I replied.

On his own head be it!

The others made their way back to us and vied for free

space on the bench. Anjuli won. Mike and Erica ended up on the floor again. I'd need to put more chairs in here. Mike and Erica had chilli. Anjuli had chosen what looked like pea soup. Nathan took my bowl from me and, with a smile, shovelled my spoon into the chilli until it contained a serious heap.

'Nathan, don't you think you should get your own bowl of food?' said Erica after a quick glance at me. 'I mean, this ship did contain a mystery virus—'

It took a moment to catch Erica's drift. But only a moment.

Dahell! 'I'm not Mary Mallon, you know,' I fumed.

'Who?' Erica frowned.

'Typhoid Mary. She's supposed to have infected over fifty people with a disease called typhoid in twentieth-century America, back on Earth, but she didn't suffer from the disease herself,' I said. 'Don't think I missed the way you tried to imply that Nathan might catch something if he used my spoon.'

Erica's cheeks flamed red, though I'll say one thing for her, she didn't try to deny it. Nathan glared at her before lifting the full-to-overflowing spoon to his lips and shoving it into his mouth – and he kept it there for longer than necessary. It was all very well his making a point to Erica, but that was my spoon which I'd want back at some point. Erica lowered her gaze, suddenly fascinated by her own food. A slightly uncomfortable silence reigned.

'Vee, I don't know if anyone has said this yet, but thank

you for rescuing us,' said Mike. His smile was warm and genuine. The second person today to smile at me.

'You're welcome.'

'I bet that's not what you were thinking up on the bridge a short while ago,' he said drily.

I grinned. 'I wasn't wearing my poker face then?'

'D'you even have one?' asked Mike.

I shook my head. 'One of the things I forgot to bring on board with me.'

'Couldn't use a utility dispenser to manufacture one?' said Mike.

'Never had the need to before now. Should I revise that?'

'Not on my account.'

We exchanged a smile. I liked him. I sensed that Mike was a man of few words but that nothing much would get past him. He had an easy manner but shrewd, watchful eyes. I turned back to Nathan, ready to reclaim my food. For some reason Nathan was contemplating Mike, his emerald-green eyes stone cold, but the moment he realized I was watching him, his expression cleared and he began to chew the food in his mouth.

Surprised, I regarded him.

Why was he glaring at Mike? What was that about?

14

NATHAN

Damn it! Vee had caught me glaring at Mike, and Mike was smirking at me because he knew precisely why. I looked away from both of them and took another mouthful of Vee's chilli.

'Hey, this is good stuff!'

And I wasn't just saying that. It actually was really good. I don't know why I was surprised, but after experiencing the so-called food on the mining colony, the dried-out pack rations on the transport ship and the limited home-grown vegetables back on Barros 5, I suppose I'd been expecting more of the bland same.

'Like I said, it's my own recipe,' Vee said, watching me avidly for some reason. 'It doesn't really make its presence felt until after the second or third mouthful.' Huh? Hang on.

What the . . . ?

My smile slowly faded. Ow! My eyes began to mist up. My entire mouth was suddenly on fire. I chewed quickly and swallowed what was left with a gulp. Mistake. If I hadn't been trying to make a good impression, I would've spat it straight out. Vee's chilli had crept up on me and was now kicking my butt.

Son of a—

Panting like an overheated dog, I let my tongue hang out of

my mouth, desperately trying to cool it.

'Ow! Dafuq?' I gasped.

'I did warn you that it was spicy.' Vee stood up and headed for the utility dispenser. She ordered a glass of ice-cold cow's milk and brought it back to me, by which time my eyes were no longer merely misted over, but tearing up.

'Vee did say it wasn't for beginners,' Mike helpfully reminded me while I waited in agony for my tongue to spontaneously combust.

Erica and Anjuli just rocked with laughter as tears streamed down my face.

'Drink.' Vee handed me the milk.

I downed it so fast I don't think the liquid made contact with any part of my mouth, just the back of my throat.

'I'll get you another,' said Vee, 'but this time, let it flow over your tongue where it'll do some good.'

I couldn't speak. All I could do was nod vigorously, my tongue still hanging out of my mouth. Vee brought me another glass of milk, which I glugged down in one gulp as well, but this time I let it stream over my poor tongue as she had suggested. Instant relief. Thank God!

'Better?' Vee asked.

I wiped my eyes with the back of my hand. At least the tears had stopped streaming now. So much for making a good impression. Nothing excites a girl more than watching a guy make a damned fool of himself! If I could've found a way to slink out of the hydroponics bay, never to return, I would've taken it.

'That wasn't chilli, that was lava.' I coughed, handing the bowl back to Vee as she sat down. 'You seriously eat that stuff?'

Without saying a word, she put a full spoonful in her mouth and began to calmly chew. And I didn't miss the gleam of satisfaction in her eyes. My wide-eyed disbelief morphed into grudging respect.

With a grin, Vee took another mouthful, before licking the back of the spoon.

'How are you doing that?' I asked with genuine amazement.

'A soupçon of charm, a modicum of wit and more than a splash of badassery. Superior skills!' Vee told me. 'Want some more?'

'God, no! I mean, no thanks. It was . . . nice though.'

Oh God!

Vee raised an eyebrow. 'Great acting skills there. Worthy of Robert De Niro, that was.'

'Robert who?' asked Erica.

'Robert De Niro. He was a twentieth- and twenty-first-century actor. He was in *The Godfather Part II* and *Taxi Driver* and *Meet the Parents* among others and won all kinds of acting awards,' Vee replied.

'How d'you know so much about him?' said Erica.

Vee smiled. 'Films of the twentieth and twenty-first centuries are my predilection. We have a huge library of films on board and I've watched all of them at least twice. Most of them more often than that.'

'Why would you want to watch films from over a century ago?' asked Erica.

I admit, I was wondering the same thing too.

'For the same reason I read books or listen to music written throughout the centuries,' Vee replied. 'Good is good, regardless of when or where it originated.'

'You use a lot of fancy words, don't you?' said Erica, almost as an accusation.

Vee blinked at Erica in surprise. I winced slightly. Erica made it sound like having book learning was a crime. I frowned at her, not appreciating how she was implying that we were all as ignorant as a box of rocks and happy to be so.

'I don't have film and book learning like you do,' said Erica. 'The Authority didn't allow it. They didn't want us getting any ideas.'

'Erica . . .' Mike's voice held a warning.

Vee was puzzled. 'Why would the Authority care what you read or watch?'

Erica's lips clamped together. Quick accusatory glances passed between Mike and Erica which Vee caught. She looked to me for an explanation. I said nothing. Vee sighed.

'Well, the ship's computer has a huge library of books, music and films which can be accessed from your quarters at any time, so help yourself,' she said.

'What would you recommend?' I asked quickly.

Too quickly. Like, in-a-hurry-to-change-the-subject quickly.

'Another bowl of chilli for you that even a toddler could eat?' Vee replied.

Damn it! I was blushing. 'That sounds perfect,' I agreed. 'But I was talking about films.'

'I know.' Vee smiled. 'I was teasing.'

'Maybe you and I could watch some of your favourites together some time?' I suggested.

Vee's eyes widened as she beamed at me, obviously liking the idea. 'Yeah, OK. If you'd like.'

Wow! Her smile lit up the whole room. It'd be too easy to get lost in a smile like that, a smile that might even reach some of the darker places inside me.

Be careful, Nathan.

But I couldn't tell a lie. The idea of watching films or sharing music with Vee, well, it appealed.

'I'd like very much,' I said sincerely.

Ignoring the speculative looks of the others, I walked over to the dispenser and ordered a hamburger and another glass of cold milk. No more chilli.

'Did Aidan explain to you that there are utility dispensers in your sleeping quarters and you can use any dispenser on board to get whatever you want – food, clothes, whatever you need,' I said.

'Tell me more about your brother,' said Erica, a gleam in her eyes.

'He doesn't come out of a utility dispenser,' Vee replied.

That caused laughter.

'I wish he did.' Erica winked.

'We'd never get you out of your room!' said Anjuli.

'So go on, Vee. Aidan. Tell me more,' Erica urged.

'More like what?' Vee asked cautiously.

'What's he into? What does he do in his spare time? What kind of girls does he like? I'm hoping he's into girls rather than guys. Am I his type? What's his idea of an ideal date? Is he into films too? Music? Would he date a girl like me?'

'A girl like you?' Vee blinked at the verbal waterfall.

I wasn't surprised. When Erica started it was hard to get her to stop.

'Erica means a girl who can't shut up,' said Anjuli quickly before anyone else could reply.

'You'd need to ask him that yourself,' Vee replied.

I resumed my original seat, which wisely no one had tried to take in my brief absence. We all ate our food in a companionable silence now that the tense atmosphere had cleared. I stole a glance at Vee, only to find she was watching me. She immediately smiled, from a place that came from within rather than some polite effort she'd merely painted on her lips.

'Aidan said you modified this ship,' said Anjuli after a couple of sips of her soup. 'How?'

Vee shrugged. 'Made it faster. I improved the efficiency of the engine by almost thirty per cent.'

'Really? Just you and Aidan?' I asked.

'Well, it was more me than Aidan. I just used him to confirm my calculations and to see whether or not my changes would be feasible.'

'And . . . you've communicated your engine changes back to Earth?' said Anjuli.

Vee stiffened, immediately on her guard. 'There's no two-way communication with Earth, or any of Earth's outposts, this far out. Once I'm home and docked, they can download all my modifications when they uplink to this ship's computer.'

'What made you want to modify the engine in the first place?' I asked.

'I want to get home as fast as possible. My maternal grand-parents still live on Earth,' Vee replied. 'Plus, after the crew died, I didn't have much else to occupy my time, so it was either watch films or tinker with my ship.'

'Any chance you'd let me see the schematics of your changes?' I said as casually as I could.

If Vee was on her guard before, that was nothing to the expression on her face now. She was right, she had absolutely no poker face. 'Why?'

'Spacefleet design is my hobby.' I shrugged. 'There isn't a ship that I haven't studied in detail. None of the other settlers were much interested in the inner workings of ships, except Anjuli. And maybe Sam. And possibly Darren. Anyway, that's why I'm so fascinated to learn more about the modifications you've made.'

Vee took a last mouthful of her food, considering my request. 'What are your other hobbies?' she asked.

'Weapons design, military tactics throughout the ages, invent-ing stuff. I'm a hands-on kind of guy,' I said. 'So can I see your modified schematics?

'What does your mum think of your hands-on hobbies?'

It didn't escape me that Vee still hadn't answered my repeated question.

'She's still trying to figure out where she went wrong.' I smiled. 'Not that she knows half the stuff I'm into. What about Aidan? Is he into the same kind of things too?'

'Depends how you look at it.'

'What does that mean?'

'Aidan is interested in anything and everything to do with this ship.' Vee shrugged.

I waited for her to continue. Vee smiled but said nothing else. She watched me. Now it was my turn to force myself not to look away. Out the corner of my eye I saw Erica nudge Mike while all eyes were on Vee and me.

'I really am interested in your modifications, but for interest's sake – nothing more. I'm not spying for my mum or anyone else. You can trust me,' I said.

'I don't know you,' Vee pointed out.

'You will. And you'll trust me.'

Vee raised an eyebrow. 'You can guarantee that, can you?'

'Of course! Just look.' I waved my hand around in front of my face. 'Isn't it the most reliable, dependable, honourable face you ever saw?'

Vee raised an eyebrow. 'Er . . . compared to what?'

Ouch!

15

The look on Nathan's face made me laugh out loud. He was so cute when his ego got slightly and lightly stomped.

'Thanks!' he said drily. 'I think I'll let that slide.'

'As opposed to doing what?' I asked.

Nathan looked at me, a slight smile playing at the corner of his mouth, though he didn't answer.

'So how come this ship and your brother have the same name? Which came first?' asked Erica.

'My brother,' I said. 'This ship was commissioned and built eight years ago and named after Admiral Adam Aidan.'

'The one who died during the Barrington uprising?' said Nathan.

'That's the one. He and his crew died saving the lives of the rest of the fleet. It took the Authority a while to acknowledge their sacrifice though. I guess naming this ship after him once he was posthumously exonerated was a way of trying to make amends to his family for calling him a traitor and a coward in the first place. When Mum was given command of this ship, she said the fact that it had the same name as my brother and a hero was an omen. A good one.' My smile faded. 'Turns out the name wasn't such a good sign after all.'

Nathan placed a commiserating hand on my thigh, just above my knee. I smiled at him, grateful for his sympathy. He removed his hand but I could still feel the heat from it for seconds afterwards.

'But to look at it another way, you were lucky,' Erica said.

'Lucky?' I exclaimed. 'How?'

'How?' Erica spoke as if surprised I even had to ask. 'The whole galaxy has been yours to explore.'

Wow! Was she serious?

'Mine to explore *alone*. What's the point of going to amazing places and seeing incredible sights when I've had no one to share them with?' I asked.

'And no one to tell you what to do or where you can and can't go,' said Erica. 'Sounds great to me.'

Erica had a romanticized view of my last few years. Travelling alone and lonely had been soul-destroying. Only clinging to thoughts of home back on Earth had kept me from flying the *Aidan* into a star.

'It's not as good as going home,' I replied. 'Not as good as knowing you have somewhere to go and somewhere to belong and someone who cares waiting for you at the end of it.'

'Yeah, well, we don't all have that waiting for us,' Erica replied brusquely.

She was glaring at me. Again. What had I said wrong this time? All at once the atmosphere in the room started to get tense.

'As far as I'm concerned, it's not the destination, it's the journey and who you make it with that counts.' Nathan was looking at me as he spoke.

OK, Vee, you can look away now.

Vee, move your head! Look away now.

I couldn't get my neck to move. I just kept looking into Nathan's dark-green eyes, feeling like I was falling, drowning. It was only when Anjuli coughed meaningfully that I managed to tear my gaze away. All eyes were upon us. Heat flamed across my face.

'So did you get to explore any of the planets you must've travelled past?' asked Anjuli.

I could've kissed her! *Great change of subject. Thanks, Anjuli.*

'No, I didn't.'

'Not even one?'

'No.'

'But you could've? I mean, didn't you have the ship's robot to accompany you for safety?' asked Anjuli. 'Weren't you the least bit curious?'

I shrugged. 'The ship's robot was damaged beyond repair on one of the planets we explored over a year before the crew died. I wasn't prepared to risk landing on any planet without one, to be honest.'

'That's understandable,' said Mike. 'You and your

brother would've been far too vulnerable just by yourselves on some unknown planet.'

'Exactly. When the ship's robot was damaged, it couldn't be salvaged so the decision was made to scrap it.' Time to change the subject. 'I just want all of you to know how sorry I am about the friends and family you lost back on Barros 5. I know what it's like to lose loved ones.'

'We're used to it,' said Erica.

I frowned. How did you ever get used to something like that? Mike gave Erica another significant look which she didn't seem to notice.

'What happened to the original crew when they died?' asked Erica. 'I mean, what did you do?'

Strange question. What did she think I did? I wept. I hurt. I mourned. And I tried to move on.

'Standard funeral procedures. The bodies of those who'd died were jettisoned out into space,' I replied. 'Towards the end, only Aidan and I were well enough to do that. We'd stand beside the bodies, I'd say a few words and then they were gone.'

That had been the scariest, most unhappy time of my life. I still remembered my dad existing on a couple of hours' sleep a night as he and his two medical colleagues desperately sought a cure, until he too had become ill. I'd had to watch my mum and dad and the rest of the crew die by degrees. I never wanted to go through that again.

'It must've been lonely, just you and your brother,' said Nathan.

'It was, but at least I had Aidan. I don't know what I would've done without him, to be honest,' I admitted.

'You and your brother are very close, aren't you?' said Nathan.

'He's all I have. I'm all he has.' I shrugged. 'He kept me sane when our parents and the rest of the crew died.'

'And you haven't managed to figure out exactly what killed them?' asked Mike.

What should I say? The whole truth was out of the question. Best just to tell some of the honest edited highlights.

'At first Dad thought we might've picked up a virus from one of the unexplored planets we landed on,' I said, sadness folding its arms around me. 'Our decontamination procedures for unexplored, unregistered planets were very strict, though – so even Dad admitted that was highly unlikely. When the crew began to die, we wondered if maybe we'd been infected with a Mazon nano-virus. Some even thought that maybe the Mazon had deliberately infected us.'

The truth, however, was a lot more horrifying.

'Hang on – all of us were just down on the planet surface and now we're on your ship,' said Nathan.

I gave him a pitying look. 'You seriously think any of you would've made it past the cargo hold if you hadn't been decontaminated first?'

Nathan frowned, then his expression cleared. 'The mist coming out of the vents . . .' he realized. 'You've set up the cargo hold to automatically decontaminate anything in there.'

I tapped my nose and pointed to him. 'Safety and security are the top priority on this ship. Nothing and no one makes it out of the cargo bay without being decontaminated first.'

'And anything that doesn't pass the decontamination test?' asked Anjuli.

'Stays in the cargo bay or gets ejected from the ship – no ifs, ands, buts or exceptions,' I said.

'So how, with all that in place, did the virus find its way aboard?' said Nathan.

I looked down at my lap. I wasn't very good at lying so I didn't want to look any of them in the eye as I did so. 'I wish I knew.'

'How come you and your brother survived?' asked Mike.

'No idea. This universe is full to overflowing with the things I don't know.' I shrugged. 'What about all of you? Catherine said something about a transport abandoning you on Barros 5. I still don't understand why any Earth vessel would do that. Where did it pick you all up from? And where were you going?'

Nathan and the others exchanged looks which spoke volumes to those who understood the language. I didn't.

Nathan scrutinized me, then took a deep breath. 'Vee, we . . . all of us . . . we're *drones*. We used to live in the colony on Callisto, working the mines.'

I stared at him. 'You're a *drone*?'

I couldn't believe it. Anjuli and Mike stared at Nathan, just as stunned as I was. Erica's gaze moved from me to Nathan and back again, gauging my reaction. It was that more than anything that made me realize this was a joke. I laughed, more at my own gullibility than anything else.

'Good one, Nathan. You almost had me going there. Almost. Like you could be a drone! They're just sub-intellect labourers doing all the menial manual work that's too filthy or hazardous for normal people to do.'

Silence.

'Normal people . . .' said Nathan quietly.

Those two words and the look in his eyes wiped the smile right off my face. Oh my God. He was serious.

Nathan was a *drone*.

I stared at him, stricken. My last comment replayed in my head, destructive as an earthquake. The space between us opened up and grew wider with each passing second.

I winced. 'I'm sorry. I didn't mean that the way it sounded.'

'Didn't you?' Nathan asked.

We regarded each other, the only two people in our world at that moment, with a chasm as wide as the Earth between us.

There it was – that look I'd seen so often and knew only too well. Why shouldn't I recognize it? I'd worn it on my own face often enough before Mum and I were exiled to that shithole Callisto when I was fifteen. After we'd been exiled, all I had to do was look at the faces of the non-drone supervisors in the mining colony to know *exactly* what my place was in this galaxy. I was nothing in a place called nowhere. It didn't matter that we drones were human, we just weren't considered quite human enough. The supervisors had been physically and sexually abusive. Abusive? They'd been brutal. Every day was a fight for survival. I was one of the lucky ones. I quickly learned to fight back, plus I had my mum and Darren and a number of others surrounding me to try and keep me safe.

But not always.

I was born on Earth and lived there for the first ten years of my life. The next five years had been spent aboard the EV *Eachern*, the ship my mum had commanded. But then we'd been exiled to Callisto. That had been a baptism of fire. Just trying to survive there had given me a lot of time to view life from a different perspective. And from Callisto the view had been through shit-tinted glasses. Earth's history was scattered with artificial divisions – class, colour, culture, religion, gender, sexual orientation – all the things that made us truly human. Now, in 2164 AD, it was all about credits – those who had them and those who didn't: namely us drones. Not only did we have no credits but we had little to no chance of acquiring any. The Authority made sure of that. So effectively, once a drone always a drone, unless you had the one million credits required to buy yourself out of that life. And if you didn't have a spare one million credits with which to buy a life, then guts, determination, friends and a plan were a more uncertain, not to mention precarious, alternative. Failing that, the common choice was acceptance of life and death as a drone.

The latter wasn't an option as far as Mum or any of us who had escaped was concerned.

'I get it now. That's why none of you want to go back to Earth,' Vee mused. 'That's why your mum questioned me about the last time I'd docked at an Authority spaceport. If I had recently docked at one, this ship's computer would've been updated and would've immediately recognized all of you as fugitives.'

'Well done, Nathan.' Erica slow-clapped me, her expression thunderous.

'She didn't need to know that,' said Mike quietly.

'Yes, she did,' I argued. 'Whether we like it or not, we need her help. The best way to get it is to tell her the truth.'

'Don't talk about me as if I'm not here,' Vee protested.

'Stop looking at us like we're Mazon then,' snapped Erica.

Vee's expression set hard. 'I'm not looking at you like that because that is one hundred and eighty degrees away from what I'm thinking.'

'You're the one who said we ain't "normal people" – remember?' Erica reminded her.

'And I apologized for that,' said Vee. 'I've never met any drones before and the Authority drums it into us that drones are a certain type of person – that's why they're drones.'

Erica was still glaring but Vee met her gaze without flinching.

'Erica, calm down,' I said.

'Didn't you hear what she just called us?' Erica fumed.

'Yes, I did. And I also heard that she said sorry afterwards. So calm the hell down. You're being a pita.'

'How am I being a pain in the arse when all I'm doing is—?'

'Erica . . .' I warned.

Still irate, Erica clamped her lips shut. I knew from past experience that that wouldn't last long.

Vee turned back to me. 'Aidan scanned all of you, so how come we weren't alerted to your drone status?'

'What d'you mean?' I asked.

'Your drone microchips. The computer should've been able to detect those at least,' said Vee.

'The first thing we did when we escaped Callisto was to have the drone chips removed from the base of our skulls,' said Mike.

'I thought that couldn't be done,' Vee said.

'You thought wrong then,' Erica informed her.

Vee turned back to Erica to do some glaring of her own. 'Listen, I don't know what your problem is, but it sure as hell isn't me.'

103

'No? Well, I saw the way you looked at me when I shook your brother's hand,' said Erica. 'Even before you knew our status, you thought you and your brother were too good for us.'

Vee's eyes widened. 'Are you high?'

'What was that look you gave me earlier all about then?' asked Erica.

'Oh. My. God! You obviously liked the look of my brother and I was admiring the way you straight out let him know. Plus I was wondering how he'd respond to you and I was hoping he wouldn't hurt your feelings or make a fool of himself or show me up. Or all of the above. And that was it.'

'So you say . . .'

'Listen,' said Vee. 'You don't want to like me, that's fine. You want to put the worst light on everything I say and do, that's your prerogative. But I don't appreciate being called a liar.'

By which time they were both on their feet.

I stood up, as did Anjuli, and we both eyed Vee and Erica warily. Things were about to kick off, and when they did I wasn't looking forward to getting between the two of them. Mike stood and headed for the nearest plant that had caught his attention. He was making sure he was well out of it. *Thanks, mate!*

'You can't deny that our drone status has changed the way you think about us,' said Erica. 'I mean, Nathan shared your spoon to eat some of your chilli. Bet if he'd told you his status beforehand, you'd never have let him do that.'

'You don't know me,' Vee replied icily. 'You don't know anything about me, so don't you dare stand in judgement. Besides which, you were the one who didn't want him to share my spoon in case I was the one with lethal germs – remember?'

Erica blushed, then went on the offensive. 'I'm not wrong about sharing your food with Nathan though, am I?' she challenged. 'No doubt you'll be heading to your quarters to scrub your mouth out at the first opportunity. It's well known we drones carry a lower class of germs—'

Furious, Vee turned to me, locked her arms around my neck and kissed me – like her life depended on it. My mouth fell open in surprise, at which Vee's tongue darted between my lips. Only for a moment, but it was long enough. I wrapped my arms around her waist and returned her kiss with interest. I mean, it wasn't as if there was anything else I'd rather be doing. We kissed like we'd done it a million times before and were looking forward to the next trillion. My heart began to race, pumping blood at light speed all around my body. I would've been more than happy to keep going for another week or so, but Vee was the one to pull away first.

She and I looked at each other. I'm not sure what she was feeling but I knew I wanted more, a lot more. God, she really was beautiful. And the way she was looking at me . . . like she could see *me*, not the infamous Commander Linedecker's son, not a drone, not a victim. *Me*. I'd spent my whole life searching for someone to look at me that way. Anjuli coughed delicately behind us.

The strange expression on Vee's face cleared as she turned to Erica defiantly and said with a flourish, 'So screw you!'

Oh no! What have I just done? Kissed Nathan? Someone kill me now.

'Is this a *Manihot esculenta*?' asked Mike from somewhere behind us.

Huh? I turned to Mike. 'Pardon?'

'A *Manihot esculenta*? I'm right, aren't I? It's a cassava plant.' Mike smiled. 'I notice all your plants in here have to earn their keep. You're growing only plants that yield edible fruit. Right?'

What in the galaxy was he talking about?

'Computer, could you display a *Manihot esculenta* please?' Mike called out hopefully.

'If you want to activate the ship's computer, you need to start your sentence with "Aidan", not "computer",' I told him. 'And yes, it is a cassava plant.'

Oh God! How could I just launch myself at Nathan like that? What must he be thinking? But Erica spouting her nonsense had so annoyed me.

'Your ship's computer is called Aidan?' said Anjuli. 'That's different!'

'Not really,' I replied. 'Aidan is the name of this ship,

which is just metal and plastic without the computer to run it, so it made sense for the computer to have the same name as the ship.'

'Is that something you implemented when . . . you know, your parents and the crew died?' asked Anjuli.

I nodded. 'I also gave the computer Aidan's voice.'

Just keep looking at Anjuli. Don't look at Nathan. Oh God—

'Doesn't it get confusing, your brother and the computer having the same name and voice?' said Anjuli.

'Not really,' I said. 'If I'm not in the same room as my brother and I say his name, the ship's computer knows I'm addressing it, not my brother. Besides, the computer is sophisticated enough to figure out from the context of my comment or question whether or not I'm speaking to it.'

'Aidan, could you display a *Manihot esculenta* please?' said Mike, unnecessarily projecting his voice.

Immediately a number of 3D holograms of cassava plants appeared before him.

He turned to the rest of us, a grin almost splitting his face in half. And just like that the pissed-offness that had been burning through me at Erica and her comments faded away like vented plasma. I couldn't help smiling back at him. Yeah, I got why he'd asked the question in the first place, but he had managed to defuse the tension in the room.

Come on, Vee. Turn and face him. Get it over with.

A deep breath later, I forced myself to look at Nathan,

who to my surprise wore an amused look on his face.

'I'm so sorry, Nathan. I shouldn't have pounced and kissed you like that. That was out of order. I hope you'll accept my apology.'

'I didn't mind, so any time. And I really do mean that!' said Nathan with a wink that made me laugh.

He was a drone.

My smile faded, as did his.

Normal people.

The memory of the crass words that had fallen from my mouth made me wince. Normal people!

Dahell, Vee!

But how was I supposed to have guessed the truth? None of them had given me any clue as to their real status. Except . . .

'Wait a minute . . . when your mum tried to take over my ship she told the computer she was *Commander* Catherine Linedecker . . .' I said, still trying to make sense of it all.

'Years ago, Mum used to be the commander of her own Earth ship – EV *Eachern* – but she made the mistake of trying to operate above board,' said Nathan quietly. 'Mum couldn't be bribed and spoke out once too often about the corruption happening all around her, so over four Sol years ago, some of her enemies in the Authority framed her for some bogus crime she didn't commit and demoted her to drone status. She was sent to Callisto to work the mines and I was given the choice of an Authority military school or going with Mum to Callisto. I insisted on going with her.'

'You chose Callisto over military school?' I asked, astounded.

'She's my mum.' Nathan shrugged. 'My dad died when I was nine and Mum is the only family I have left. And even though she tried to persuade me to stay on Earth and go to military school, she needed me.'

I nodded slowly. I would've done the same in his shoes. At least, I like to think I would.

'Even after she was demoted, Mum still had some loyal friends so, after a lot of planning, she, Darren and some of the others were put in contact with the captain of an illegal transport,' Nathan continued. 'The captain took our credits and just about everything else we had of value in return for helping us to escape from Callisto. He was supposed to take us to Mendela Prime, but he forced us off his ship when we got to Barros 5 and left us just enough equipment to survive and to signal any Earth vessels in the area for help if needed. But that was all he left us. Most of us didn't even realize we were in Mazon territory, to be honest. Mum and some of the others decided that living on Barros 5 was our chance to make a better life for ourselves. Anywhere was better than Callisto.'

'Was it really that bad?'

'Vee, you don't have to die to be in hell,' Nathan replied.

I nodded slowly. If that was the case then Callisto was a place I never, ever wanted to see.

'I'm glad you escaped then.' I didn't know what else to say.

God, this was hard. I'd grown up 'knowing' certain things, like once a drone, always a drone. People who were born drones died the same way. Criminals and those who were traitors to the Authority had their citizenship stripped away from them and were relegated to drone status – and there they stayed. Once you slid down that slippery slope, there was no way back up. Born in that class or demoted to it, every drone was chipped to ensure they could never escape from their designated area. I'd never been in contact with a drone before, never mind a whole group of them.

And now they were swarming over my ship.

No! Not swarming. That was the wrong word. But I had a ship full of drones and what appeared to be eighteen years of miseducation and misinformation to re-evaluate. Even this short amount of time spent with Nathan and the others was enough to convince me of that, if nothing else.

'So now you know the truth about us and why we can't return to Earth,' said Nathan. 'What happens now?'

 **NATHAN**

This had been a roller coaster of a day and it wasn't finished yet. Vee now knew the truth about all of us, but what would she do with it? Her words 'normal people' still rang in my ears.

But then she'd kissed me.

Was that purely for Erica's benefit? I mean, it'd been me she kissed, not Mike. Was that because I'd been closer to her at the time? Or was there more to it than that, like her being the North Pole to my South? I admit, from the moment I saw her I felt strangely drawn to her and I had no idea why. I mean, I barely knew her.

'What happens now, Vee?' I asked again.

Vee shook her head. She sat back down. 'I need to think.'

'What's to think about?' asked Erica. 'Either you're gonna help us or you're gonna tell the Authority where to find us.'

'I need to think,' Vee repeated.

My heart sank. Had I made a colossal mistake, hitting Vee with the truth so soon? God, I hoped not. It was just that I didn't want any lies between us. The fact was, she was our one and only chance to get out from under once and for all. If she dumped us at a neutral space dock she might as well just dump us back on Callisto. We had no more credits to pay for the trip to Mendela

Prime, so it was guaranteed that sooner rather than later we would be betrayed for the bounty the Authority was bound to have put on our heads. The Authority would appear weak if it became known that some of us had escaped and made it to Mendela Prime. They'd never stand for that.

Unlike most, I wasn't born a drone so I'd experienced life from both sides. I knew which side I preferred. Those on the inside, who had a lot, had no clue what life was like for those of us who had nothing, and what's more, they didn't want one either. The Authority used us as cannon fodder in its conflicts, as test subjects to experiment on, as cheap, expendable labour. We were more plentiful and cheaper to produce than the robots who were prized by those on the inside as status symbols. Plus we drones served as a perfect way to keep those on the inside in line. We were a constant reminder of how far they could fall.

Vee's gaze was thoughtful as she studied me. Had she heard and understood anything I'd said after I'd admitted to being a drone? Drones, to those on the inside like her, were synonymous with the very worst criminals and scum-sucking lowlifes. Hell, I'd thought like her once. If I ruled the world I'd make it compulsory for those on the inside to swap places with a drone for a week. Just one week. Most of them wouldn't last one day if they had to survive the kind of existence we did. But there were some lines that didn't get crossed, or if they did it was via a one-way ticket. I'd met a number of people who'd been demoted to drones. I couldn't remember hearing of a single drone who'd managed to buy their way out of their drone status.

'What happened to the captain who dumped you on Barros 5?' asked Vee, as we all sat down again.

Not one of the questions I'd been expecting.

'No idea,' I replied. 'He's probably fleecing more credits off desperate people and dumping them God knows where in the galaxy the very first chance he gets.'

'What's his name?'

'Stefan Jersecky. He's captain of a rustbucket called the *Galileo*,' said Anjuli.

'Why d'you want to know?' Erica frowned. 'He's long gone by now.'

'He needs to be reported to the Authority. He needs to be stopped,' said Vee. 'He's profiting from the misery of others and not even giving them what they pay for. At least I can try to stop him. I can send a sub-space message back to Earth and report him.'

I grabbed her arm. 'No, you mustn't.'

Vee pulled away from me immediately. 'Why not?'

'Because Stefan knows the names of most of the ships that will help drones escape for a price. If he goes down, he'll make sure he's not alone.'

Vee frowned. 'It's not right.'

'Welcome to life as a drone,' I replied.

'If I do drop you off at the first neutral starbase, what will you do then?' asked Vee.

Erica opened her mouth to speak but I got in first.

'We'll just have to hope that we can hitch a ride on a transport heading for Mendela Prime before the Authority sends a ship to round us up and take us back to Callisto or, worse still, Earth.'

'But if you're not chipped, then how will the Authority find you?' asked Vee.

She really was clueless.

'You really think that you can put us all off at a starbase without anyone getting suspicious?' Erica said with scorn.

'We have no credentials and no credits,' said Mike.

'And the Authority will pay any amount to get us back and make an example of us, if for no other reason than to prove that no one can escape from one of their mining colonies,' I added.

'What if I were to speak to the Authority on your behalf?'

I took a deep breath before continuing. 'Vee, we can't go back to Earth. Don't you get it? I know my mum has done nothing to endear herself to you but she was the one who planned and fought to get us off that hellhole Callisto. There's nothing for us back there. We've been designated drones, and as far as the Authority is concerned, that's all we're good for. Back in Earth's solar system, we have nothing. No prospects, no future and, worst of all, no hope. That's not living, that's just being alive.'

How could I make her understand? How do you explain hell to someone who only knows it as a word and a concept?

'Commander Linedecker wanted something better for all us drones,' said Anjuli. 'Mendela Prime is big enough and well enough protected that the Authority can never find us, assuming they would expend the time and money to try and bring us back from that far away.'

'Isn't there anywhere closer and safer that you could go?'

Vee asked. 'I mean, this part of the quadrant really is the butt end of the galaxy. There are plenty of habitable planets between here and Earth's solar system.'

'None that want us,' I replied. 'Other worlds agree we have a problem but they want us to take our problem elsewhere. Most that we travelled to before we got dumped on Barros 5 refused us sanctuary and some worlds even threatened to shoot us down if we attempted to land. Believe me, after months of travelling on a filthy, cramped transport, we were almost glad to take our chances on Barros 5 if we couldn't make it to Mendela Prime. And for a short while it seemed ideal, until the Mazon became aware of our presence.'

'What's waiting for you on Mendela Prime?' asked Vee.

I looked her in the eye. 'A new life. A new beginning. Freedom. Somewhere where our lives matter.'

Hope.

'You've never been there before?'

I shook my head. 'But everyone on Callisto knows about Mendela Prime. It's the only place in the galaxy that's safe for us drones.'

Vee and I watched each other. I think she'd finally heard me. She didn't like what I had to say but she didn't dismiss it either.

Silence.

Vee stood up with a sigh. 'Time for me to get back to the bridge.'

I stood up too. I placed a hand on her arm. 'I'm sorry for inflicting our troubles on you when you've got more than enough of your own, but we really do need your help.'

Vee pulled away from my touch, the second time she'd done so. If she thought she was being subtle about it, she was wrong.

And it hurt.

Kissing me to prove a point to Erica was one thing. Having me touch her rather than the other way around was obviously something else entirely. Was she still angry with all of us because Mum had tried to commandeer her ship or just so disgusted by my status in particular that even my hand on her arm had her flinching away? If it was the latter, how did I deal with that? The *last* thing I wanted was for her to despise me.

But what else could I expect?

19

Please don't touch me.

Nathan's touch was doing funny things to me, burning into my skin and reminding me of everything I'd missed over the last three years. In the years I'd been alone, sometimes I'd close my eyes and touch myself, stroke myself, pinch myself or claw at my skin just so that I could *feel* and pretend the touch came from someone, *anyone* else.

'Sorry,' said Nathan, his hand dropping to his side.

'It's OK.' I forced a smile. 'Thank you for telling me the truth.' I headed for the door.

'Vee, I'd like to stay here and make the acquaintance of your plants, if that's OK?' asked Mike.

OK . . . that was kinda weird but I wasn't about to argue with him. 'Help yourself.'

'I'm going to my quarters. Nathan was a fool to tell you about us.' Erica stalked out of the room and marched on ahead. I watched her walk down the corridor, quite frankly glad to see the back of her. A little of her went a very long way.

Nathan and Anjuli fell into step beside me.

'I don't mean to be pushy, but what will you do now?' asked Anjuli.

'I'm not sure. My head is still buzzing,' I admitted. 'All I've dreamed about during the last three years is getting home to Earth but I see now that home for me is the opposite for you.'

'It must be overwhelming to suddenly have all of us on your ship after so many years of just you and your brother,' said Anjuli.

Gratefully, I smiled at her. At least someone understood. 'It is a bit of a shock to hear other voices apart from Aidan's – and my own.'

'I need to get something from my quarters,' said Anjuli. 'But I'll join you on the bridge afterwards if that's all right? I want to learn all about how this ship operates.'

'Is that where you've been assigned?'

Anjuli nodded, her face beaming.

'Then that's fine.'

She turned and headed in the opposite direction, leaving Nathan and me alone. I needed to say something before the silence between us grew too awkward.

'Nathan, thank you for telling me the truth. And I really am sorry for the way I reacted when you . . . when I . . .'

'Don't worry about it. I've never spoken of our life on Callisto to anyone outside our group before,' Nathan admitted. 'Non-drones tend to look down on us and assume the worst about us without a single question being asked or answered.'

'I'm not looking down on you,' I rushed to convince him.

Pause.

'I know,' said Nathan.

'You do?'

'Yeah, I do,' he replied softly.

I could quite easily grow to love that voice of his.

Vee, get a grip!

'You OK?' Nathan frowned, his hand back on my arm.

I stepped away from him. 'Yeah, I'm fine. I just have a lot to think about. If you'll excuse me, I really do need to head back,' I said. 'It's my shift and Aidan will give me grief if I'm late.'

I made for the turbo-lift, trying to make it look as nonchalant as possible. I didn't want Nathan to think that I was running away, though that was precisely what I was doing.

20

NATHAN

I had to jog to catch up with Vee. She was practically sprinting away from me now. Was my presence really that unwelcome? 'So what will you be doing on the bridge?'

'It's my watch, so I'll be . . . watching!' said Vee.

'Good answer! Want some company?' I asked in my best casual voice.

'Where were you assigned?'

'Mum hasn't assigned me anywhere yet because I was the first to be scanned and registered and then I went to find you,' I explained. 'So d'you mind if I join you?'

'Isn't there something else you'd rather be doing?' asked Vee.

'Nope.'

We regarded each other. I needed to persuade her that I wanted us to be friends – at the very least. I admit it, I found her intriguing. And not just because only she and her brother had survived when the rest of their crew had died. They'd been alone for three Sol years. Three whole years. I don't know how I would've coped under those circumstances. No matter how bad things had got in the past, I'd always had my friends, my mum and the rest of the drones in my corner. So no, she wasn't going to shake me off that easily. We resumed walking.

'How did you stop the Mazon from firing on this ship while you were rescuing us?' I asked.

Vee shrugged, then proceeded to tell me how she'd nobbled both the Mazon ships. More than once my jaw hit the floor but Vee spoke as if it were no big deal. With each sentence my respect for her rocketed. That she'd done all that to save us, people she didn't know, astounded me. It made my mum's attempt to take over her ship seem all the more shabby.

By the time we reached the bridge I was in awe. 'That has to be the gutsiest thing I've ever heard.'

Vee's cheeks grew darker, as did her earlobes. She was blushing. It made the brown of her skin even more appealing.

'It wasn't brave at all,' she denied. 'I was scared out of my mind.'

'If you hadn't been scared, it wouldn't have taken any courage to help us,' I pointed out. 'D'you know, if you had a sister who'd done all that and we weren't fleeing for our lives from the Mazon, I'd ask her out for a date on the spot.'

Vee blinked at me, stunned. 'You would?'

I nodded. 'In a heartbeat.'

Vee gave me one of her considering looks. 'What kind of date?'

'Dinner in the mess hall. Or better yet, dinner in the astro lab sitting in the middle of a 3D star chart,' I replied.

Damn! Could I make it any more obvious?

'Sounds lovely. Shame I don't have a sister,' Vee said at last.

'Yeah, a real shame,' I agreed.

We entered the bridge.

21

Well, I didn't expect that reaction! Nathan's admiration was making not just my face but my whole body burn. Not that I didn't like it. His admiration, that is. It was kinda flattering, in an embarrassing sort of way. He seemed so genuine and yet . . . why had he told me he and all the others were drones? I would never have guessed. To be honest, it wasn't just that I'd had nothing to do with drones in the past, but I'd never had any reason to think about them much either. It was just a given that they worked in service. Hell, back at school on Earth, we'd used 'drone' as an insult.

'*Drone brain . . .*'
'*You cry like a drone . . .*'
'*Your mother's a drone . . .*'
And much, much worse.

Now my ship was full of them.

Why had he told me? Surely his life – and mine – would've been so much simpler if he'd kept his mouth shut. But Nathan didn't strike me as someone who'd choose what was easy over what was right. I guess he wanted to explain why they couldn't return to Earth and needed to get to

Mendela Prime. But was that all there was to it? All Nathan's friends thought he was a fool to tell me the truth, yet he'd still done it. Why?

I hadn't quite figured Nathan out yet, but I would.

And what was all that about dating my sister if she'd done the things I'd done? He knew I didn't have a sister, so why say that? I had to admit, dinner while sitting in the middle of a hologram of stars and nebula sounded magical. Why had I never thought to do that before? Ideas like that were part of the beauty of conversing with other people; this was what I'd missed most over the last few years, but why didn't Nathan want to do that with me? Or was that his roundabout way of saying that he did? Or was that just wishful thinking on my part? I liked him. I mean, I *really* liked him, but I couldn't assume for a second he felt the same way. I mean, why should he?

My head was spinning like the outer hull of my ship. Hamlet had nothing on me.

Damn! I'd been away from people for far too long.

Back on the bridge, Aidan was sitting in my chair while Darren and Commander Linedecker sat at the navigation panel. Two other people – a black man in his forties and a white woman in her early thirties – were huddled around the weapons and tactical panels to the left of the captain's chair but I had no idea what they were doing. Nor had I any idea where the rest of the colonists were.

'Aidan? Update please,' I said as I headed towards him.

Aidan looked pointedly at Darren and Catherine before

turning back to me. 'The refugees have been assigned their quarters. A few have insisted on making themselves useful by going to their stations immediately.' Aidan nodded in the direction of the man and woman at tactical to illustrate his point. 'Dooli is in the science lab with the two female children, Simone and Khari. I hope she'll ensure they don't break anything. Most are in the mess hall. Darren and Commander Linedecker over there are examining our ship's log to find out as much as they can about us and our ship. They say it's so they can work out appropriate permanent assignments for our new crew as most of them aren't specialists, but we all know that's bull. Sam and Hedda, the two over there at tactical, are also raking through the computer logs. They insist it's to find out as much as they can about the ship. I did explain that they could do that from any control panel on board and that the science lab on this floor was at their disposal, but they're still here. I personally think none of them want to leave you or me alone on the bridge. I'm sitting in your chair because if I hadn't, one of them would've jumped into it and we wouldn't have got it back. I recommend we install some kind of ejector mechanism so that if the captain's chair doesn't recognize your buttocks or mine seated in it, it shoots the occupant out of the door. Would you like me to start working on such a device?'

By the time I'd reached the captain's chair, I was biting my lip to stop myself from laughing. Aidan stood up to let me sit down while the commander glared at him. That was my brother, subtle as ever.

'That won't be necessary, Aidan,' I told him.

'Well, if you're sure.' He sounded disappointed.

'Olivia, I believe we got off on the wrong foot,' said the commander. 'I'd like us to start again.'

'I'd like that too,' I agreed. 'But I'm still not going to hand my ship over to you.'

A slight pursing of her lips was the only indication of Catherine's annoyance at my words. 'Fair enough. But I hope you'll allow me and my colleagues to assist you in any way we can. You're not alone any more. You don't need to try and run every facet of this ship's operations by yourself.'

'Thank you. I'll bear that in mind,' I replied. I turned to my brother. 'Aidan, you can go and get some sleep if you like.'

He frowned at me. 'Sleep? No thanks.'

'Well, it's my watch now and it's been a long day. We all need to rest, so don't leave it too long – OK?' I smiled at him.

A moment's pause, then Aidan nodded. As I turned back to the commander, I caught the curious look Nathan directed at me, then at my brother. I'd have to be careful what I said with him around. Nathan was nobody's fool.

'Are the Mazon still on our tail?' I asked Aidan.

'We appear to have shaken them off for now, but I've left the ship on yellow alert,' said Aidan, adding, 'We both know they won't give up quite so easily.'

'You've had run-ins with the Mazon before?' asked the commander.

Uh-oh . . .

'Yes,' I replied.

'When?'

'Apart from when we rescued you, the last time was over a year ago.' I cringed at the memory. 'I ran into one of their exploration patrols travelling in deep space. I barely escaped with my ship and life intact. The time before that was three years ago, a few weeks before all the original crew of this ship died.'

'Your entire crew died in the space of a few weeks?' the commander gasped, aghast. 'I didn't realize it had happened so quickly.'

I nodded. She and the others didn't need to know any more than that. Those memories were not something I liked to dwell on. The external threats I'd encountered since the crew of the *Aidan* had died had been few and far between – an ion storm or two, running into the Mazon patrol, an asteroid belt and escaping the gravity well of a black hole. The rest of the time had been spent trying to get back home.

Meanwhile these people . . . they'd spent years or, in some cases, a lifetime on Callisto. I may not have known much about drones except what I'd been told, but everyone knew about Callisto. Of all the Authority's mining colonies on the different moons and planets it controlled, the one on Callisto was by far the most savage. It was the only place in Earth's solar system where the Aetonella bacteria, species *A. pentadensis*, could be found. The energy these bacteria produced when placed in special fuel cells kept not only my ship but every other Earth vessel made in the last eighty years up and running for decades and beyond. Mining those resources had led to the rise of the Authority's power and status, until it ruled not just one country but the planet Earth and all the other planets we had colonized since. The only trouble was, Aetonella bacteria lived in rocks deep beneath the surface of Callisto and excavating was icy-cold, back-breaking and hazardous work. Robots were too expensive to produce and too valuable to lose doing such work – at least, that was the Authority's party line. But drones? They were ideal for the job and would breed more drones for a fraction of the credits it took to produce a new robot.

I watched Nathan as he stood beside his mum and Darren to study the panel they were currently viewing. What must life have been like for him, to be thrown into that world with seemingly no way out? I could only imagine how terrifying it must've been. The screens relaying news and programmes from Earth to Callisto must've reinforced to the drones just how little they had and how little they were valued. In their shoes I would've done whatever I could to escape that moon too. If Callisto was half as terrible as the rumours and Nathan implied, it was more than bad enough. And then to be betrayed by the captain of the transport, followed by being attacked by the Mazon . . .

So far, if it hadn't been for bad luck, then these refugees would've had no luck at all.

I still remembered intense, whispered conversations my mum and dad had had with other grown-ups about the Authority when I was much younger. Conversations that had ended abruptly when I entered the room or when they realized I was close enough to overhear. I now knew enough to realize that the Authority wasn't totally benign, and that I was just lucky enough to be on the right side of it. The trouble was, the Authority was all I knew.

To me the Authority meant Earth, and home, and life as it once was and as I longed for it to be again. To me the Authority meant safety. I guess home was purely a matter of perspective. Earth was where I belonged. I wanted to see my grandparents and to breathe in air that wasn't constantly recycled.

Longing . . .

What were all the Callisto refugees on board longing for? And just what might they do if they didn't get it?

'Mum, how could you?'

The moment my shift was over I headed straight for Mum's room. I had a few things I needed to get off my chest, things I couldn't say on the bridge. And from the look on Mum's face when she opened her door, she had a fair-to-middling idea of what was coming.

'What choice did I have, Nathan?'

'You had the choice not to try and take Vee's ship away from her,' I replied at once. 'You had the choice to act like a decent human being.'

'Too much was at stake to leave to the whim of that girl,' Mum retorted.

'That girl?' I bristled. 'What does that mean exactly?'

'It means she's not one of us, Nathan. It means loyalty begins at home.'

Not one of us? What the hell . . . ?

'You were once an Elite too, Mum, or have you forgotten that? And *charity* begins at home, not loyalty,' I corrected, ice in my voice.

'Well, if loyalty doesn't, then it should,' said Mum. 'I heard about what you did. You had no right to tell her who we really are.'

'And what are we, Mum? Escaped drones who need help – or

space pirates with no morals and no conscience, ready to take her ship if she won't do as we say? You probably confirmed every negative thing Vee was ever taught about us.'

'Oh, stop being so melodramatic,' Mum dismissed.

Seriously?

I mean, *seriously*?

If she was trying to wind me up, then she was doing a first-rate job.

'You just don't get it, do you?' I said. 'The Authority took away everything we had and tried to take everything we are. It stripped you of your integrity and you don't even care.'

'Have you quite finished?' said Mum. 'I care about the ones who died back on Callisto following my escape plan, only to be shot to pieces by the security forces. I care about the ones who died on board the transport ship *Galileo*, and now I care about the ones who died on Barros 5 because I waited too long to activate the distress beacon. When I lie in bed tonight and every night unable to sleep because I'm going over and over in my mind all the things I could've and should've done differently, I care very much. I don't get it right all the time, Nathan. All I can do is try and work for the good of our friends. If I didn't care I'd have said "to hell with it" a long time ago and only bothered to get you and me off Callisto.'

'So what d'you want? A medal?'

'No, but some damned appreciation would be nice,' Mum snapped.

'What you tried to do to Vee was wrong, Mum.' I shook my head. 'I'm just sorry you can't see that.'

130

Mum and I glared at each other – in the same room together but light years apart.

'During the last few years, I've had to do a lot of things that were wrong just to live, Nathan,' Mum said quietly. 'We all do what we need to do to survive. Don't ever forget that.'

'Survival at any cost?' I asked scathingly. 'We've lived as drones for so long that we've become the Authority's dictionary definition of them? Is that it?'

'Grow up, Nathan, for God's sake! You still think of life as good or bad. You love or you hate, things are either right or they're wrong, people are either heroes or villains. When are you going to learn that life isn't that simple?'

I didn't need to hear any more of this. Casting one last disgusted look at her, I left Mum's room.

My door hissed open and Aidan walked straight in.

'Vee, are you OK?' He got straight to the point.

'No. But I will be,' I replied.

'True?'

'True.'

'Vee, you won't like this but I think we should limit access to the bridge,' said Aidan.

'Limit it to who?'

'Just us two. We managed to run this ship before all the refugees arrived, we can still do so.'

I frowned at him. 'We can't do that. And there were a lot of things on board that got neglected when it was just the two of us. And I like having others on the bridge. You're good at what you do, Aidan, but even you can't be everywhere at once and monitoring every system at once.'

'Then apart from us, I recommend we limit access to just those assigned to the bridge by Commander Linedecker,' said my brother. 'And even that is against my better judgement.'

'Why?'

'What happens if, no *when*, they decide to try and take the ship away from us again?' said Aidan.

I shook my head, thinking of Nathan. 'I don't think they will. Besides, if they try they won't succeed. The commander knows that now.'

'They could try and force you to give them the executive command code to run this ship themselves,' Aidan pointed out. 'Then they'd have no further use for either of us.'

I'd already thought of that. 'Which is why I won't be handing it over any time soon.'

Aidan shook his head. 'Vee, I don't trust them. They're drones.'

I frowned. 'So?'

'Don't give me that. They're drones. We both know what that means.'

But that was the trouble: I wasn't sure I did know, not any more.

'Aidan, I— Hang on. How d'you know that they're drones?'

He straightened up, looking at me defiantly. 'I overheard your conversation with them in the hydroponics bay.'

I frowned. 'Overheard? You mean you were listening?'

'You know I monitor your movements throughout this ship. That way I can make sure you're safe at all times,' said Aidan.

I knew he used the computer to track my whereabouts whenever I travelled around the ship and it had never bothered me before. It bothered me now.

'Aidan, if I'm alone, you can still track my whereabouts if you need to, but when I'm with others you're not to eavesdrop or record what I say or do. D'you understand?'

'Why not?'

I licked my lips, trying to put my feelings into words that Aidan would understand. 'Because like it or not, we're going to be stuck with this new crew for a while. I'd like to try and get to know them better, and knowing you're watching and listening to every word will be inhibiting.'

'You never used to mind my monitoring you when it was just the two of us,' said Aidan.

'That was then and this is now,' I replied. 'If I'm with any of them and I get into difficulties, I'll call for you. OK?'

I knew all I'd have to do was call his name out loud and the computer would immediately alert Aidan to my whereabouts.

'What if you can't call out?'

'It won't come to that. You worry too much.'

'I'm your brother. It's my job to keep you safe,' said Aidan.

'And you can still do that without listening to my every word. So please don't do it any more.'

'Very well.'

He didn't like it but he recognized a direct order when he heard one.

'Aidan, why don't you spend some time trying to get to know them?' I suggested. 'That's what I'm going to do.'

'Why?'

'Because whatever happens we're all going to be together for a long time,' I said. 'Besides, I think they have a lot to teach us. This is our chance to see the galaxy from another perspective.'

'Why would we want to do that?'

'For the sake of knowledge,' I replied, giving Aidan an answer he could understand. 'Isn't that why we're here? To learn?'

'These drones have shown they can't be trusted.'

'Nathan explained why his mum acted the way she did,' I reminded him. 'They're fugitives. Going back to Earth is the last thing they want.'

Aidan gave me an appraising look. 'Vee, they're not our friends. Don't let any of them fool you into thinking otherwise.'

'Aidan, I'm not going to spend the journey swimming in paranoia about our guests. I won't live that way.'

'You're a naive fool, Vee,' Aidan said disparagingly. 'The drones can't be trusted, and what's more, I'm going to prove it.'

Chicken eggs and chips! One of my favourite meals, and food I could only have dreamed of during my time on Callisto. Now I had four eggs and a mountain-high plate of chips in front of me and I wasn't enjoying it. It wasn't going down as well as it should have. It was my meal break and I only had twenty minutes before I was due back on the bridge.

A few days into our voyage and some of those in the mess hall were having a liquid dinner, having discovered the utility dispenser could dole out alcohol as well as food. That hadn't taken long. I shook my head as I glanced around the room. A few had glasses of Prop before them. It was like being back on Callisto at the end of a mining shift. There, too many had lost themselves at the bottom of bottles of cheap alcohol to numb their pain – physical and mental. Prop was the drink of choice on Callisto – a purple, oily, foul-tasting liquid. The stuff was muck but it did the job, bringing oblivion within a glassful. I'd tried it once and it had set my mouth, not to mention my insides, on fire. Once had been more than enough.

Aidan sat at the end of our table but he wasn't saying very much. In fact, he hadn't said a word since he'd sat down. His hands were cupped round the glass of dark brown liquid before him, his head bent as if he were deep in thought.

'So, Anjuli, when are you going to put Harrison out of his misery?' asked Corbyn, who sat opposite me and next to Anjuli.

'Harrison?' Anjuli scoffed. 'Oh please. I'll never be that desperate.'

'You two were inseparable once,' Corbyn reminded her.

Which was true. For a couple of months before we escaped from Callisto, Harrison and Anjuli had been all hot and heavily into each other. Then their relationship had turned sour because Harrison couldn't help being Harrison.

'Well, those days are over,' Anjuli dismissed.

'He still follows you around like a Garen puppy though,' laughed Erica. 'That man would lick your boots if you asked him to.'

Anjuli shuddered. 'I don't want that man's tongue near anything of mine, thank you very much. He makes my skin crawl.'

'Harsh!' said Corbyn.

'The lady doth protest too much!' said Mike, giving me a wink.

'What does that even mean?' Anjuli rounded on him.

Mike immediately held up his hands in a placating manner.

'Mike, don't be mean,' I said. 'You know Anjuli only has eyes and other body parts for you now.'

Anjuli's face turned an interesting shade of burgundy. Surprisingly, so did Mike's.

'She'd better sprout roots and leaves then,' Erica dismissed. ''Cause if it doesn't grow out of the ground, then Mike here isn't interested. And Harrison is ready, willing and able to comfort you at any time, Anjuli. Just sayin'.'

'Harrison was the biggest whore on Callisto and he's only interested in me because I was the one to dump him, not the other way around,' Anjuli said with ferocity. 'I do have standards, you know.'

'Harrison says you're different,' said Corbyn. 'He says he'd change for you.'

Anjuli dry-heaved a couple of times, then swallowed hard as she fanned her face with her hand. 'I just threw up in my mouth! Please, no more talk about him. Not while I'm eating.'

The back of my neck started to tingle.

'May I join you?'

I glanced up in surprise. Vee was standing beside me, a meal tray in her hand.

'Go ahead.' I indicated the empty seat beside mine, pulling it out for her. Of course she could join me – any time she wanted to!

Vee looked at me and smiled hesitantly. 'Someone's hungry!' She nodded towards my plate.

'Oh, that,' I said, blushing. 'God, I must look like a serious hog.'

'No. Just someone who likes their food,' said Vee, sitting down. 'Have you had the chance to explore the ship yet?'

'Not fully. I thought I might do that after my shift,' I replied.

'I . . . I can show you around if you'd like?' Vee offered. 'But if you'd rather explore alone or with your friends then—'

'No. I'd like that. I'll take you up on that offer,' I said quickly. 'If you're sure you don't mind.'

'I don't mind at all,' Vee assured me.

I glanced at her tray. The only thing on it was a bowl of watery soup with some kind of dumpling floating in it.

'That's all you're having?' I asked.

'I'm not terribly hungry,' said Vee, adding quietly after a pause, 'Nathan, may I ask you for a favour?'

'Of course. Name it.' I turned my chair so I was facing her, the others at the table all but forgotten.

'Could you tell me more about your life on Callisto?'

God! No. Not that. I'd just as soon put Callisto far behind me and try to forget about it.

'If you'd rather not, I understand,' said Vee softly, her hand on my arm, her touch gentle.

'No, I . . .' I sighed. 'What d'you want to know?'

'Tell me about when you first arrived there.'

Vee and I regarded each other. Not taking my eyes off her, I began to speak.

25

Since my initial conversation with Nathan about Callisto, I had thought of nothing but the refugees and what they'd had to endure on that moon. Every chance I got, I met up with Nathan to learn more. Every meal was spent in his company in the mess hall, usually sitting with him and some of his friends. My brother had joined us on a couple of occasions but barely said a word. Whenever Nathan spoke to me, however, I caught Aidan watching the two of us, his gaze intense. I know others at our table noticed it too. I intercepted more than one nudge or nod in my brother's direction.

Nathan and his mates had an easy camaraderie that I envied. Nathan tried to bring me into the conversation, but more often than not they spoke of their lives on Callisto.

I listened.

That much I could do. I may have been the outsider on my own ship but I was willing to learn. And I used every opportunity that came my way to ask Nathan questions about his life on Callisto and his life before that. He never snapped at me or was impatient but instead answered every single one of my questions with quiet conviction.

And the more I found out, the less I knew.

Another night, our shift over, Nathan and I sat opposite each other eating dinner. Though others were dining as well, we were left alone at the end of one of the long tables in the mess hall. We spoke of many things but inevitably our conversation made its way back to Nathan's life as a drone.

'Nathan, d'you have any good memories of Callisto?' I asked.

He thought for a moment. 'The friends I met and made, even if some of them are lost to me now.'

'That's the only good thing?'

Nathan nodded.

'Why has nothing been done about that place?'

'The only ones who speak out against it are the ones within in. No one else gives a damn,' Nathan replied.

I desperately wanted to deny his words, but how could I when he had first-hand experience of the indifference of non-drones? I picked at my meal of beef teriyaki, deep in thought. Nathan's hand beneath my chin made me jump. He raised my head to directly face him.

'You give a damn though, don't you?' he said.

The smile I tried for slid right off my face. I wished to God I didn't care, but he was right, I did. Very much. My mind was still spinning and I knew it would continue to do so until I made a decision. The way I saw it, I had a choice. I could abandon them to their fate, telling myself that whatever happened to them was not my problem, or I could put myself out and try to help, but the price of that would be high. Too high? My head told me to choose the former. Aidan would want me to choose the former. I was no saint and all I wanted was to go home.

'Vee, what d'you think of me . . . and all the other settlers?' asked Nathan.

I shrugged. 'I'm still getting to know all of you.'

'By now you probably know almost as much about my life as I do,' he said drily.

I doubted that very much.

'I didn't have to live through it,' I replied.

'No. Instead you had to watch your parents and everyone else on board the *Aidan* die before your eyes. Something else we have in common,' said Nathan.

'What?'

'We've both seen far more than our fair share of death.'

I couldn't argue with that. We shared a sombre look.

'Now it's your turn,' said Nathan.

'My turn to what?'

'Tell me about your life on board this ship before the crew died.'

I lowered my gaze. I really didn't want to dredge up old memories. The joy they brought was laced with sharp pain, but Nathan had opened up to me so how could I not do the same? With a sigh, I lifted my head and began to talk about Dad and our joint love of playing film charades.

That night I went to bed trying to come up with a plan

that would work for everyone. By morning, I'd made a decision – one of the hardest of my life – but my gut told me it was the right one. It was a decision that was going to hurt.

Once I was back on the bridge I activated the ship-wide announcement system.

'This is Olivia Sindall, acting captain of Earth Vessel *Aidan*,' I stated, my eyes on Nathan as I spoke. 'After much thought I have reached a decision. This ship will travel to Mendela Prime before resuming its course for Earth. Those who wish to disembark at Mendela Prime will be more than welcome to do so. Afterwards, if any of you wish to continue on to Earth with me, that will also be acceptable. That is all.'

Nathan inhaled sharply. Moments ticked by before he gave the briefest of nods in acknowledgement of what I'd just said. Neither of us uttered a word.

Stupid. *Stupid.*

I was probably making the biggest mistake of my life.

At this rate, would I ever make it home?

'Are you sure, Vee?' asked the commander. She had a light in her eyes I hadn't seen there before. It took a moment to recognize it for what it was – the light of hope.

'No,' I replied. 'But I'm going to do it anyway.'

'Vee, have you thought this through?' Aidan wasn't happy, to say the least. 'We need to get home.'

'And we will, Aidan,' I replied. 'It'll just take a while longer than we'd originally planned, that's all.'

'A while? By the most direct route and at maximum speed, it will take us twelve Sol months just to get to Mendela Prime, and then another eighteen months to make our way from there to Earth,' said Aidan. 'I can give you the exact amount of time to the second if you'd prefer.'

Like I hadn't already figured that out.

'Aidan, we're going to Mendela Prime,' I said. 'Could you plot a new course please?'

'Vee, you *need* to get home,' Aidan said urgently.

'And I will,' I replied, forcing a smile. 'In the meantime, could you follow my orders please?'

Aidan shook his head, but he turned back to his console to do as I'd asked and plot our new heading. I glanced around. Darren was giving me a strange stare. He looked like he had something to say, but then he turned abruptly and left the bridge. I sighed inwardly. Nothing I did would ever make that man forgive me for the loss of his family, but I wasn't seeking his forgiveness.

Maybe I was pursuing my own.

The hope of seeing Earth again within a Sol year had kept me going for so long. I would just have to pray I was strong enough to put my own hopes on hold for a while. Could I really do this? Delay my return home by so many months? Oh God! Was this yet another attempt on my part to make up for what had happened on board the *Aidan* three years ago? Probably. Plus deep down I still felt partially responsible for the lives lost on Barros 5. Logically, rationally, I told myself that there was nothing more I could've done. But logic was no match for my feelings on the subject. I had to do this, help the survivors. I just had to. No doubt they would all want to be put off on Mendela Prime. It would be a long lonely journey back to Earth without them. A journey I wasn't sure I'd be able to embark on again. Would I be strong enough to be alone with just Aidan for another eighteen months after we left Mendela Prime? I very much doubted it.

Loneliness was an insidious killer.

'Vee, I want you to know that we all appreciate this,' said Commander Linedecker. 'And believe me, we will do whatever it takes to fully assist you. I give you my word.'

'I appreciate that.' I smiled hesitantly.

The commander smiled back. A tentative truce had been established.

Time passed uneventfully, which was fine with me. A lot of the ship's work that had been part of my daily routine I now found lifted off my shoulders and I could sit up straighter because of it. The parts of the ship which hadn't been used in months, and in some cases years, like the science lab and the astrophysics lab, were once again fully operational. I was slowly getting used to a ship that had different smells, sounds and sights to what I'd grown accustomed to over the last three years. Having a crew again made me realize just how lonely I had been. It was truly wonderful to feel the ship beginning to live again.

*

Halfway through my shift and I admit I was already exhausted. Talking, listening, just being around people took far more physical and mental energy than I'd anticipated. I did my usual rounds of each deck of the ship as I always did once during each shift, and was pleasantly surprised by the cautious smiles and greetings from those I met along the way.

On my way back to the bridge, a woman's voice from behind me halted me in my tracks.

'Captain Sindall?'

I turned, half expecting to see my mum and someone calling her. I still wasn't used to hearing others call me 'Captain', I guess because I wasn't used to thinking of myself that way. A tall brunette woman with beautiful brown eyes walked up to me hand in hand with a slightly shorter blond man.

'Captain Sindall, I'm Mei and this is my partner, Saul.'

Saul's grasp of Mei's hand tightened almost imperceptibly.

Aw!

'Hi,' I said, searching for something to say next. 'Welcome aboard.'

'We just wanted to say thank you,' said Saul.

'For rescuing us,' added Mei.

'And for agreeing to take us to Mendela Prime,' said Saul. 'We know going there wasn't in your plans.'

'But we finally feel safe.'

'And free.'

'It feels like we're on our way home, even though we've never been there,' said Mei. 'Doesn't it, Saul?'

Saul and Mei exchanged a smile which whispered to all those watching that they didn't give a damn who knew how they felt about each other. I felt like a voyeur.

'Well, I hope you have a comfortable journey while on board,' I said.

'We've both been assigned to the astrophysics lab,' said Mei, her enthusiasm flowing over me. 'That's how we met, at AeriaTech Research.'

I'd heard of AeriaTech. That was one of the biggest and richest companies on Earth, with outlets on every continent. I wondered what had happened to exile both of them to Callisto, but much as I wanted to know, I wasn't about to ask. I'd learned from Nathan that you didn't ask that. People might volunteer the information but it wasn't done to ask.

Saul let go of Mei's hand to grasp one of mine in both of his. 'We owe you our lives and our happiness. Thank you.'

I slowly but surely drew back my hand. 'You're welcome.'

With one last genuinely happy smile, the two of them turned and headed back the way they had come, still hand in hand. I smiled as I watched their departure. Their happiness was infectious. I could only hope it'd spread around the ship. Now all that was required was for the Mazon to stay away while we travelled through their territory.

Back on the bridge, Nathan and Anjuli were at the navigation panel with Aidan. Anjuli and Nathan were deep in conversation but Aidan wasn't saying much. I'd have to have a word with my brother. He was coming across as aloof. He needed to fix that. Nathan looked up to smile at me before resuming his study of the screen before him. Sam and Hedda were at the tactical panels. Commander Linedecker sat in the captain's chair, but the moment I stepped onto the bridge she got up and, after a brief nod at me, headed over to the environmental panels to the right. I'd changed the access settings to allow the crew full access to all the equipment on board. We were going to be together for a long while, so a show of trust had to begin somewhere.

Once I'd read all the daily reports, I surreptitiously watched Nathan and Anjuli. I wanted to speak to Nathan in private later to learn more about his life, his hopes, his dreams. I valued every minute of the time spent with him. I sensed he could teach me a lot – if we ever got the chance to be alone. One of the dilemmas of having so many people on board. Conversation on the bridge was quietly animated. I was with people again.

Part of a team.

And I was quietly loving it.

26

I hesitated outside the medical bay doors. Something was wrong with me and I needed Doctor Liana's help but I hated doctors. Let's face it, I hated asking for help of any kind, but I wasn't getting any better. Once she told me what was wrong, then maybe I could fix it.

Pulling myself together, I entered the medi bay. I saw Doctor Liana at once. She was at her desk, reading something on her tablet. She only had one patient. Dooli lay on a bed, fast asleep, the monitor set in the wall above her bed displaying all kinds of information which meant nothing to me.

As I walked towards her, Doctor Liana looked over, then sat up. 'Nathan? What brings you to my neck of the woods?' she asked.

'Doctor Liana, I think I'm coming down with something,' I said reluctantly.

'Oh yes?' The doctor stood. 'Hop up onto one of the beds and let's take a look.'

I did as directed, a growing sense of trepidation washing over me. Being with Doctor Liana always brought back unpleasant memories. The doctor came over to me, put her hand on my forehead, then took my pulse the old-fashioned way – by holding two fingers against my inner wrist. I frowned at her as she removed her MMS, or mobile medical scanner, from her belt.

'So what makes you think you're coming down with something?'

I really didn't want to be here. The last time I'd had any dealings with Doctor Liana was when she operated on my leg to attach my prosthetic foot.

Not my favourite memory.

And she'd had to patch me up a couple of times before that too.

More harsh memories.

'Well?' the doctor prompted.

'Well, I keep breaking out in hot sweats, my body seems to flash hot and cold at odd moments and there's something wrong with my appetite,' I replied unwillingly. I couldn't do this. 'Look. You know what? Coming here was a mistake. I'm sure it's nothing. I'll sort it.'

I was already getting up off the bed, but the doctor pushed me back onto it. 'You can stay put until I've scanned you fully,' she said.

With a sigh, I did as I was told.

'Any other symptoms?'

'I'm having trouble sleeping and concentrating.'

'Anything else?'

Yes, but none I cared to mention out loud, even to the doctor. 'No, I don't think so.'

Doctor Liana gave me a studied look as she continued to scan slowly up and down my body. She shook her head. 'My scanner says there's nothing wrong with you. In fact, you're in rude health.'

'Which is exactly what I told you a minute ago,' I pointed out. 'I'm sorry to have wasted your time.'

I tried to get off the bed, but once again the doctor pushed me back down. 'Not so fast,' she said. 'Just because nothing is coming up on my scanner doesn't mean that there isn't something going on with you.'

'Like what? I thought scanners could pick up ninety-nine per cent of ailments and illnesses.'

'When do the majority of these symptoms of yours happen? Any particular time of the day or night?'

'Nope.'

'When you're doing a particular activity?'

I shook my head.

'After you've eaten any particular type of food? Could it be the onset of an allergy?'

I continued to shake my head.

'In the presence of any particular person?'

The head-shaking stopped. I stared at the doctor. 'Pardon?' I mumbled.

'Ah!' Doctor Liana said with satisfaction.

What the . . . ? 'I don't know what you're talking about.' A deep frown cut a trench between my eyebrows.

'Of course you don't.' Doctor Liana winked at me. 'Now in my expert opinion, if these symptoms have only recently started, you're either menopausal – which I'm inclined to rule out at this stage – or someone on board is causing your palpitations.'

'Seriously? That's the best explanation you've got? I thought you were a doctor, not a quack,' I told her frostily.

Ignoring my comment, she continued her speculations, a big-ass smile on her face. 'Now I'm assuming it's not one of us settlers who's turning you on. After all, you've been around us for years. There are only two new people in the equation – Aidan and Olivia. So which one of them is heating you up? Tell all. Enquiring minds want to know.' Doctor Liana grinned at me, delighted by her ridiculous deductions. She was way off base.

'Well, thanks for your time, Doctor Liana.' This time I jumped off the bed and there was nothing in the universe that could've got me back onto it.

'My advice?' she called after me as I made my way out of the medi bay. 'Figure out which of the two of them is doing it for you if you haven't already and then do something about it.'

I left the medi bay with the doctor's laughter ringing in my ears.

27  VEE

Each morning I awoke feeling more at peace with myself
and the galaxy than I'd felt in a long, long time. My days
now had a point and a purpose. I could do this. Getting to
know the new crew and helping them get to Mendela
Prime was the right thing to do, even though my brother
might believe otherwise. I'd worry about what would
happen after we reached Mendela Prime when we reached
that particular planet.

I could do this.

After a day spent fine-tuning the route to our new destination and using the ship's computer to run various tactical
simulations, I spent the final hour of my shift going through
the profiles of the new crew, memorizing faces, names and
assignments. The whole shift was pretty uneventful and I
was happy for it to stay that way, but ten minutes before
the shift ended, the ship's alert sounded, making me jump.
I hated that din. It was cacophonous and deafening and
never boded well.

'What?' I asked Aidan, my tone terse. 'The Mazon?'

'No, not the Mazon,' said Aidan, his expression puzzled.

153

'Three of the refugees – Mei DuLac, Jaxon Ramsey and Saul Turner – are in one of the cargo-hold airlocks and the evacuation protocol has been activated from in there.'

The full 3D images of the three he'd just named revolved slowly before us. I recognized all of them. Two of them I'd spoken to only the day before.

Dahell?

'One of them activated the evacuation sequence?' I asked, astounded.

Aidan studied his console. 'As far as I can tell.'

'Why would they do that? Does one or all of them have a death wish? Override it. Shut it down,' I said.

'I can't. It's been isolated and jammed. I can't shut it down from here.'

I stared at my brother. 'How long?'

'One minute, thirty-three seconds.'

Oh my God!

'What's going on?' said the commander.

Damn it!

I was already running for the door. 'Three of your friends are in the cargo-hold airlock and they've activated the evacuation sequence. If it's not shut down, they're going to be jettisoned out into space. Aidan, stay here and do what you can to override it.'

'I'll stay here too and help,' Hedda called after us.

I raced along the corridor towards the lift. Nathan was at my side. Sam, Anjuli and Catherine were running behind us. As we entered the lift, I said, 'Cargo hold. Emergency mode.'

Emergency mode ensured the lift went straight to the requested destination instead of stopping to pick up others who might have requested the lift. No one spoke during the seconds it took to get from the upper deck to the lower one. As soon as the lift door opened, I ran out into the cargo hold. I saw them immediately. My heart leaped into my mouth, then plunged down to my boots. On the other side of the cargo hold three of the colonists – Mei, Jaxon and Saul – were inside the airlock that separated the hold from the vast space beyond, and were banging frantically on the poly-glass panel of the door. The warning indicator above the door indicated they had twenty-five seconds left before the outer hull door opened, and counting. The airlock was in evacuation mode, something that was only supposed to happen when the ship was in imminent danger or on my explicit instructions. The warning siren screamed throughout the ship. Inside the echo-chamber of the cargo hold it was ear-splitting. I sprinted across the cargo bay, moving like the devil himself was chasing me. The absolute terror on the faces of the three colonists spurred me on to run even faster.

They were in trouble.

Mei, Saul and Jaxon began to float off the floor as the gravity unit inside the airlock ceased to function. I raced, my legs and arms pumping, but I was still several metres away from the airlock controls. The others were right behind me, sprinting across the hold. A warning alert from above the inner airlock door rang out, its continuous whine clashing dissonantly with the siren sounding throughout the ship. I was ten metres away when the outer hull door slowly began to open, revealing the vast inky blackness beyond.

'Aidan, abort the airlock outer door opening. Keep the nano-field in place. Aidan, do you hear me?' I cried out. 'And shut off the damned siren.'

The din sounding throughout the ship ceased. Only the constant warning wail from above the airlock itself could now be heard in the cargo hold.

'Why did you do it? Why did you activate the evacuation sequence?' I shouted.

'We didn't!' Mei cried out, grabbing for the guard rail which ran waist high around the perimeter of the airlock.

'We came in here to talk. Only to talk,' said Jaxon.

'The door came down.'

'The alarm started.'

'What's happening?'

They were all talking over each other in a panicked rush to be heard.

'Hit the abort button,' I urged, pointing to where it was situated next to the door on their side.

'I have,' said Jaxon, smashing his palm against it again and again. 'It's not working.'

'Help us!' Mei gasped.

'Do s-something.'

'Get us out . . .'

The three were free floating, only changing direction

when they bumped into each other. The outer hull door slid slowly but inexorably higher.

'Aidan, damn it. Don't let the nano-field drop. Close the hull door!' I shouted.

But still it kept rising.

The nano-field was a force field or wall made of pure energy that activated whenever a hull door opened or we had a hull breach, but here it would only last for a few seconds because as far as the computer was concerned this was a requested standard procedure. The nano-field was going to drop the moment the outer door was fully open, sucking out all the air in there and everything else that wasn't firmly secured. Mei's knuckles were white from gripping so tightly onto the guard rail. Jaxon's eyes pleaded with me to do something. Anything.

'Take off something,' I urged desperately. 'Tie it around yourselves and tie the other end to the guard rail.'

My fingers flew across the control panel outside the door as I input the command code to override the hull door opening. The code was ignored. I tried again. I had to stop it before—

Too late.

The nano-field dropped.

And just like that they all vanished, sucked out into the vacuum of space in a second or less. Shocked, I stared into the empty airlock.

They were all gone.

Next to me, Anjuli fell to her knees, burying her face in her hands. Someone was talking behind me, asking questions, but I couldn't hear a word. I just continued to stare into the empty airlock, totally stunned. My friends . . . gone. I wouldn't wish that kind of death on my worst enemy. The airlock warning alert stopped abruptly. The silence in the cargo hold was more deafening than the siren had been. Slowly the outer hull door slid down. The venting system gave a faint hiss as the airlock began to fill with air again from the vents above the door.

I was still trying to grasp what had just happened. I'd seen people die on Callisto – mining incidents and accidents happened all the time – but what I'd just seen was on a whole different level. During the Barros 5 assault, we'd all been terrified because none of us knew whether or not we'd survive. That uncertainty in itself had given us hope. But the terror on Mei, Jaxon and Saul's faces as the door opened . . . They knew they were going to die and there wasn't a damned thing they or anyone else could do about it. The look on Jaxon's face was something I'd never forget. I was helpless, totally useless. I was so sick and tired of feeling that way.

'Aidan, damn it, what just happened?' Vee called out. 'Aidan, answer me.'

A moment's silence, and then Aidan's voice rang out in the cargo hold. His voice surrounded us on all sides, strangely disturbing in the echoing silence.

'I don't know, Vee. I'm still trying to figure that out. Somehow, someone hacked into the ship's computer and gave the evacuation command when the three refugees were in the airlock, and whoever did it was skilled enough to make it look like the command came from *inside* the airlock.'

Vee was already marching back towards the lift. 'Aidan, where did the command actually originate?' she asked.

'I have tracked it down to a utility dispenser in the mess hall,' said Aidan.

What? A utility dispenser? That couldn't be right. Those things were given verbal commands and then they created whatever had been asked for. End of story. How on Callisto had someone managed to interfere with the ship's programming using one of those?

I ran to fall into step beside Vee. Mum and Sam were right behind us.

'Who's currently in there?' asked Vee.

A second or two passed before Aidan answered. 'Twelve of the refugees are in there at the moment, including the two children, Simone and Khari.'

'No one is supposed to be able to open the outer hull door except you and me,' said Vee.

'One of the colonists has found a way to bypass my security

protocols and access the system,' Aidan replied. 'The command to open the airlock outer door was definitely input from a dispenser.'

'How?'

The very question I'd been pondering.

'My guess?' said Aidan's voice. 'Programmable nanite technology. Someone introduced nanites into the ship's computer via the service module in one of the utility dispenser panels and the nanites did the rest.'

Son of a bitch . . . Nanites in the computer meant that the ship's computer was now infected and could be controlled at any time by the person who'd released them.

'Who? Who did it?' Vee was furious and totally focused on her conversation with her brother.

'I don't know,' Aidan's voice replied. 'But whoever it was, they obviously know of a back door into our computer system. We don't have full control here.'

'Are you broadcasting this conversation ship-wide?' asked Vee.

'No, just to your location in the cargo hold,' Aidan replied.

'Not another word until I'm back on the bridge,' Vee ordered.

I like to think I'm not stupid but I was still having trouble getting to grips with what I'd just heard. I grabbed Vee's arm and swung her round to face me. 'Hang on. Is Aidan saying someone deliberately sent my friends to their deaths?'

A moment's silence.

'Yes,' said Vee.

That one word sent a chill and worse down my spine.

'That's a lie,' Mum said furiously. 'I can personally vouch for each and every settler on this ship. None of them would ever do something like that.'

'Well, it wasn't me and it wasn't my brother,' said Vee pointedly as we all entered the lift.

'Don't be ridiculous.' Mum was irate. 'What possible reason could any of us have for killing Mei, Jaxon and Saul?'

'I don't know. You tell me,' said Vee. 'But I agree with Sherlock Holmes. When you've eliminated the impossible, whatever remains, however improbable, must be the truth.'

'Who? What?' said Mum, perplexed.

'Sherlock Holmes, the great detective, but that's not important right now,' Vee dismissed. 'The point is, someone on board this ship either suggested they enter the airlock or saw or heard them in there, and once they were in place that person seized the opportunity to get rid of them. That person wasn't me and it wasn't my brother. Twenty-two of you came aboard and three are now dead. If we discount the children, that leaves seventeen suspects.'

'I had nothing to do with their deaths,' said Sam from behind me. 'And I resent your insinuation. I've known everyone on board for many months and, in most cases, years. None of us are capable of committing such an act.'

'So you say,' said Vee, adding as she looked at me, 'But I don't know anything about any of you – except for what you choose to tell me.'

'Well, I'm telling you that every one of us has suffered over the last few weeks. We all lost friends or family back on Barros 5, not to mention watching our loved ones drop from disease, preventable accidents, exhaustion or ill-treatment on Callisto,' said Mum. 'Don't you think we've each had a bellyful of death?'

'If I hadn't just seen Jaxon, Mei and Saul sucked out of the airlock then I might've thought so, yes,' said Vee.

'This is outrageous. How do we know it wasn't you or your brother?' asked Sam.

'So Vee risked her life to rescue us, only to bump us off one by one?' I rounded on him. 'Sam, talk sense.'

He scowled at me but I wasn't about to back down. Vee had had about as much to do with my friends' deaths as I did.

'This is a serious business and it needs an older head and hand at the helm. Vee, you need to stand down and let the commander take over,' said Sam. 'You're too young to be the captain of this ship.'

'What the hell does her age have to do with anything?' I frowned.

'I'd rather take my orders from someone I respect and trust who knows what they're doing,' he argued.

'Which is a matter of competency, not years,' I replied. 'Don't be so damned ageist!'

The brief, unsmiling look Vee gave me was speculative. She wasn't sure about me. All the progress I'd made with her since I'd met her was slipping like water through my fingers. After what had just happened, she wasn't sure about any of us. The lift stopped. We'd arrived on the bridge.

29  VEE

I headed straight for my chair and lowered myself into it carefully when what I really wanted to do was go to my quarters and curl up into a ball. Death, the unwanted, unwelcome visitor, was stalking the corridors of my ship again. I closed my eyes, my head bent as I tried to marshal my thoughts.

Come on! Think, Vee.

What would Mum do?

She'd be logical and methodical and try to get to the bottom of what was going on. I needed to be like her. One thing Mum and I had in common: we hated real-life mysteries. They were usually unwelcome problems to be solved. I opened my eyes. There were now eight or more other people on the bridge apart from my brother, and all eyes were on me, waiting for answers I didn't have.

'Could all of you except the commander, Nathan and my brother please leave the bridge until further notice?' I said.

Glances were exchanged but I didn't need to say it twice. Sam, Hedda and all the others reluctantly trooped out.

'You two are only staying because I don't believe you

163

were responsible for what just happened,' I told them straight.

'Thanks,' Catherine said drily.

'Don't thank me yet. I may revise that opinion, but if you were going to kill someone, Commander, I think you'd have the guts to face them when you did it. And you, Nathan, I think you would only harm someone to protect yourself or someone you cared about.' And they could both take that any way they wanted. I turned to my brother. 'Aidan, talk to me. What do you know?' I said.

'I'm still trying to figure out how my security was bypassed.' Aidan shook his head, his expression grim. 'I locked everyone out of all but the most basic computer functions when Mrs Commandant over there tried to take over the ship.'

The commander cast Aidan a steely glare but he was oblivious.

'*Your* security?' asked Nathan.

Uh-oh . . .

'When it was just the two of us on board, my sister and I split the ship's tasks,' said Aidan. 'I was primarily responsible for the ship's security protocols and procedures – and I still am. Quite frankly, I don't give a damn if you have a problem with that and I resent it that one of you lot has infected my computer with nanites.'

'Aidan, what do we do to get rid of them?' I asked, trying to bring my brother back to the matter in hand.

'The only way to get rid of them completely is to shut down the ship's computer and do a full purge before a reboot, which is a twenty-four-hour job. If we attempt that here and now, we'll be dead in space with no navigation, weapons, environmental or gravitational controls. And if the Mazon come knocking at the door while we're out of commission . . .'

'OK, we get it,' I said.

Sometimes my brother liked to beat a point to death.

'That's why reboots are only supposed to take place at space docks, not when travelling in space,' said Aidan.

'So rebooting the ship's computer is out,' said the commander. 'What else can we do?'

'Not a thing until we get to a space dock,' my brother insisted. 'All we can do is react to what happens. We won't be able to stop it from happening in the first place. I have no way of knowing what the nanites might do next until they're doing it, by which time it'll probably be too late. This is not acceptable, someone messing with my computer like that . . .'

'Aidan, the more important point right now is that three people have died,' I said quietly. 'If we can't do anything from the computer side of things, then we need to find out who's responsible.'

'You monitor and record activity in every part of the ship except the sleeping quarters, I take it?' said Catherine.

'I'm way ahead of you,' I replied. 'Aidan, could you play

back the mess-hall recordings from ten minutes before the . . . incident.'

Aidan called up a series of recordings, each running in a three-by-three holographic grid that looked like one of those old-fashioned noughts and crosses boards. The commander sat down next to my brother at the navigation console as we all watched the images play out before us. The mess hall was heaving and practically every person who came and went used one of the utility dispensers in there. Some used them three and four times while others congregated around them.

'Utility dispensers weren't available to us on Callisto.' Nathan must've seen the puzzled look on my face because he squatted down next to me and spoke softly for my ears only. 'We had set rations which were dumped by automated planes at periodic intervals. Sometimes one or even two days could pass with no food drops, so when food did finally arrive there was always a vicious, desperate scramble for it. It's that scramble the Authority likes to broadcast whenever there's a news story featuring us drones. There's nothing like giving the people what they expect to see. Those back on Earth expect to see drones behaving like animals so that's what the Authority shows them. And no one bothers to ask why.'

I looked at Nathan then. His eyes as he watched the display matrix were narrowed, his lips a thin, angry line, and yet at the same time he looked so . . . hurt. The urge at that moment to put my arms around him and comfort him shook me. Quickly I turned back to the display. We all continued to watch in silence for a few moments.

'Aidan?' I said at last.

'I'm cross-referencing the time when the alarm started with all those within close proximity of a utility dispenser in the mess hall,' said Aidan. 'Discounting the children, there appear to be six possible suspects. Should I discount Khari and Simone, the children?'

'I think it's safe to do so,' I replied.

The heads and shoulders of Aidan's six suspects appeared on a new display grid. I recognized some of the faces instantly. Darren was one. Another was Erica. Hedda, who'd been working on the bridge almost constantly since she'd come aboard, was also displayed, as was Mike from hydroponics and the doctor and another person I'd seen around but hadn't spoken to yet – Alex.

'Can't you narrow it down any further than that?' the commander asked.

Aidan shook his head. 'Quite frankly, if the person who did this knew enough to hack into our computer system, they probably knew enough to delay the alarm going off until they were out of the mess hall or establishing a vacuum-sealed alibi.'

'Which means it could be anyone on board, not just those six on display,' I realized.

Aidan nodded, confirming my worst fears.

'That would only work if the whole thing had been set up.' Nathan frowned, straightening up. 'I mean, someone would've had to tell Mei, Jaxon and Saul to be in that air-lock at that particular time for a specific reason for that to work.'

'And that's probably precisely what happened,' I said. 'There's no other explanation for the three of them being in there at that time. Which means only one thing. The deaths of Mei, Saul and Jaxon were premeditated.'

'No. No way,' denied Commander Linedecker. 'I refuse to believe anyone I know could be capable of such a thing. And for what possible reason, for God's sake?' She glared at me, challenging me to come up with a motive.

I had none. For the time being, it might be better to keep my suspicions to myself, at least until I had proof positive. 'I'm just speculating,' I sighed. 'Maybe there's another explanation that just hasn't occurred to us yet.'

'Vee, that's nonsense,' Aidan dismissed. 'We definitely have nanites in our computer which weren't there before we picked up these people. Those nanites mean that some-one unknown can take control of the ship's computer at any time. The deaths of those three refugees had to be deliberate. No other explanation makes sense.'

'Yes. Thank you, Aidan.' Attempts at subtlety were entirely lost on my brother.

'But why would anyone want to do that?' asked Nathan.

I couldn't shake the feeling that I was missing some-thing, but random facts, fears and feelings were firing off in my head in all directions like a fireworks display. I needed to sleep to have any hope of making sense of them, but I knew from past experience that I was now too wired to do so. Just one fact kept playing in my head. Someone on board the *Aidan* was a murderer. I didn't want to believe it but the truth kept slapping me in the face.

'Vee, I'm going to talk to the crew to see what I can find out,' said the commander, standing up. 'And I want to set up a gathering tomorrow afternoon so we can pay our respects to all the ones we've lost. I hope that's OK with you?'

Whether or not the question was rhetorical, at least she asked.

'Yes, of course. The mess hall or the cargo hold are probably the best places. They have the most space,' I replied.

'A memorial service tomorrow at fifteen hundred hours in the mess hall it is then,' said the commander.

'Would you mind if I joined you?'

Catherine contemplated me for a few moments. 'You'd be more than welcome.'

I wondered how many of her friends would agree with her. Still, she knew the colonists far better than I did. I needed her help if I was going to get to the bottom of this. Then I had a thought.

'Commander, most of the sleeping quarters are on the mid deck. Aidan and I have sleeping quarters opposite each other on this upper deck, just outside the bridge. If you and Nathan would rather have quarters on the mid deck with everyone else that's fine, but there are two more unassigned sleeping cabins on this deck that are available if you want them.'

The commander nodded. 'Yes, I think that would be best. I'd like to remain close to the bridge.'

'Nate?' I asked.

Nathan nodded.

'OK.' I turned to my brother. 'Aidan, could you assign the commander cabin U-07 and Nathan cabin U-08?' I turned back to Catherine. 'Your rooms will be across the corridor from each other, close to the astrophysics lab.'

'It's done,' said Aidan.

Catherine gave me a nod before heading for the exit. As she left the bridge, Anjuli entered. It was obvious that she'd been crying. A lot. Last time I'd seen her was down in the cargo hold.

God, I'd just left her there. But she had the luxury of giving way to her feelings. I didn't.

'I need something to occupy my mind,' she announced to no one in particular. 'May I stay? Please.'

I pointed to the empty chair at the navigation panel that the commander had just vacated.

'I could show you some of the escape manoeuvres I've programmed if you like,' said Aidan.

Anjuli nodded gratefully. 'Yes, please.'

'In the meantime, Vee, you should go and get some rest,' Aidan told me.

'Not yet. I need to get to the bottom of all this,' I sighed.

'We'll work on that. Your shift is over. Go and get some rest,' said Aidan. 'You can't think straight when you're tired. The rest of us can manage.'

'Aidan's right,' said Nathan, standing up. 'It's been a long day – for all of us. You should get some sleep.'

Sleep? With everything that had just happened? But I was not just physically but mentally exhausted.

'I'm not sure I can,' I said, standing up. 'But OK, I'll give it a good try.'

Nathan and I headed for the exit. As we left, Sam and Hedda entered the bridge, with Sam giving me a look as if daring me to ask him to leave again. I said nothing. Neither Nathan nor I spoke until the bridge door hissed closed behind us.

'Vee?'

I stopped outside my cabin and turned to face him. Nathan was frowning at me. Why? I waited for him to tell me what was on his mind but he just kept frowning.

'Yes, Nathan?'

'I . . . er . . . I don't suppose . . . ?'

Pause.

'Never mind,' he said at last. 'It doesn't matter.'

'You sure?' I asked. 'You look like you want to get something off your chest.'

'Now's not the time. It can wait,' said Nathan. 'Sleep well.'

'Night.' I pressed my hand against the security palmlock of my door. My skin was prickling. The door slid open.

My heart was thumping against my ribs. I entered my room and turned to see Nathan still standing in the corridor watching me. 'See you in the morning.' My words tumbled out in a rush.

He nodded. My door slid shut, but not before I heard Nathan quietly curse to himself.

30

NATHAN

What the hell was I doing? Standing outside Vee's quarters staring at her opaque glass door like a lovesick jackass. I needed to get my shit together and go let off some steam but I needed to be somewhere where I could do so in private. There was a gym on the mid deck but I didn't believe for a second it'd be empty, even at this time of night.

The astrophysics lab . . .

Mei and Saul were the only ones assigned to that lab and now they were gone. Would I ever be able to forget the image of them and Jaxon being sucked out of the airlock? Somehow I doubted it. I needed somewhere quiet to be alone, to lose myself.

So the astro lab at the end of the corridor it was. I made my way towards it, forcing myself not to break into a run to get there. I entered the lab, relieved yet unhappy to find it empty. Workstations and equipment lined the perimeter of the room though the middle was strangely clear. Then I realized why. It was space left for the 3D mapping of star charts. Only how did I activate it?

'Er . . . Aidan, could you display a star chart?'

'*Which one?*' Hearing Aidan's voice coming at me from everywhere and nowhere made me start. It was just the computer but

I still wasn't used to it. Aidan, Vee's brother, was still on the bridge with Anjuli and the others.

'Show me Earth's star system,' I ordered.

The star chart appeared around me at once, swallowing me whole. It wasn't to scale of course. It just showed the relative positions of one planet to another orbiting around the Sun, but it was still chilling.

Earth . . .

It should've felt like home but it didn't. Far from it. And there was Jupiter with its many moons orbiting around it, including Callisto. The sight of it made me feel sick, actually physically sick. There was nothing in this universe and beyond that would ever make me go back there.

I reached out to push Callisto away. When I removed my hand, this particular moon moved back to its original position. Getting rid of it wasn't that easy. I stepped forward to hold the Earth in my hands, slowly pushing my palms together to crush it. The holographic image was immediately displaced but reappeared as my hands dropped to my side. I glared at the Earth, the sight of it fanning the hatred I felt towards it and everyone on it.

I had to move on, let it go, but I wasn't good at that.

'Aidan, display another star chart.'

'Which one?'

'Show me a star chart of the furthest galaxy from Earth that has been mapped,' I said.

Immediately the middle of the room was full of stars, planets, nebulae and asteroids which reached from floor to ceiling;

the whole thing was at least four metres wide as well as high. I stepped into it, the static energy around me slightly raising the hairs on my skin. Suns and planets moved aside and were displaced as I walked into them, only to reappear beside and behind me in their original space and place once my body was out of the way. I stood in the middle of it, drinking it all in. It truly was one of the most beautiful things I'd ever seen. I hadn't appreciated until this moment just how much I'd missed this: being on a ship, food and drink whenever I wanted it, relative safety and security. Comfort. Vee was going to give all of us what we wanted, she was going to take us to Mendela Prime. I should be ecstatic.

But I wasn't.

All I felt was . . . empty.

The deaths of my friends just reinforced that.

There was still something missing.

I'd felt like this on Callisto but I'd thought I was missing my old life. I'd felt like this on the transport ship even though it was supposedly taking us to freedom. I'd felt like this on Barros 5 and the feeling hadn't left me on board the *Aidan*.

Was this all there was or ever would be to my life?

Getting by? Surviving? Would I ever find a way to fill this void within me? Was this really how I was destined to spend the rest of my days, with this constant craving inside but with no idea for what?

Or maybe I did know and just didn't want to face up to the truth.

Vee.

When I was with her, it felt like . . . home. I'd only known her for a short while but it felt like so much longer. And when I was away from her I couldn't get her out of my head. I went to sleep thinking of her and woke up with her still on my mind, which was beyond pathetic. I was a drone. She wasn't, and that was the end of that. She may have decided to help us but that didn't mean she would want to hook up with the likes of me. I wore my drone status like a shirt of thorns, but it was *mine*. It was all I had and I couldn't shrug it off even if I wanted to. It was as much a part of me now as my bones. As a drone, I may not have been on the winning side but I was on the right side. I was convinced of that.

Slowly my fists clenched. I felt like I was going to explode out of my skin. I pulled off my jacket and threw it as far away from me as I could. My shirt followed. I unfastened my boots and threw them after my shirt and jacket. I wanted to *feel*, to connect with my body again. After all the death I'd seen today I needed somehow, in some way, to connect to *life*. Slowly I turned, my gaze intense as I focused on the positions of the astral bodies around me.

Close your eyes.

Focus.

Control.

I raised my left leg close to my body before extending it higher than my head to place the ball of my foot in the middle of the closest star system. I remained perfectly still for a few seconds, feeling the energy of it flow around me. That's how I knew I'd made contact. I drew my knee close to my body again, moving it in a different direction to make contact with a different star. My eyes still closed, I focused on my mixed martial arts kata training.

It was all about control.

Control I was fast losing.

31

A few minutes in my room were all I could bear. I felt like I was about to climb the walls. At times like these I usually headed down to the gym on the mid deck and ran for kilometres or went through my fitness programme in the holosuite at one end of the gym until I was much too tired to do anything but fall in a heap on the floor and sleep where I lay.

But a quick check with the computer informed me that there were six people in there already. I wasn't about to let off steam in front of spectators. Even the cargo hold had a couple of people in it. Mike was still in the hydroponics bay on the mid deck. What in the galaxy could he be doing in there at this time of night? Had he moved his bed in there? I wasn't going to head down to find out. After putting on my trousers and a T-shirt and pulling on my boots, I headed out of my quarters, only to stop abruptly in the corridor. Where could I go?

The astro lab.

That would be echoingly empty now. I still had some star mapping to do – a job which required total concentration – so maybe I could give myself over to that task for a couple of hours. The astro lab was the one place aboard the ship where I could truly lose myself among the stars and feel at peace. I headed along the corridor, but when I opened the door, I saw at once that I was not alone.

Nathan was in the middle of a 3D star chart of the Tau system, if I wasn't mistaken, and he was performing some kind of kata I'd never seen before – and I'd made an extensive study of the martial arts. He wore only his trousers, his chest and feet bare, and his whole body was wiry and ridged with muscle. I knew I should respect his privacy and just turn round and leave, but my feet were rooted to the floor. I'd never seen anyone move the way he did, with that degree of control and intensity. Each extended kick, each flick of his wrist, or sweep of his arm made contact with a star here, a planet there, or swept through an asteroid belt. I realized with a start that his eyes were closed, and yet he didn't miss. Not once. Had he memorized the positions of each stellar entity in the star chart? He must've done.

Damn!

Nathan's movements grew quicker but he never for one second lost focus. His arms flew out from his sides, his palms pushing against the star systems he came into contact with. He did a handstand onto one hand only, his left arm moving with precision to strike a moon close to a planet, and his feet simultaneously made contact with the binary stars that had been above his head only moments earlier. Nathan fell into a crouch, his breathing only slightly faster, his eyes open at last and looking straight at me. I hadn't moved during the whole performance, but I was the one having trouble catching my breath.

I opened and closed my mouth, struggling to find something apt to say. Nathan stood up slowly and held out his hand. I looked from it to him.

Turn round and leave.

My legs wouldn't cooperate. Instead I walked over to him and took his hand. What the hell was I doing? Nathan placed the fingers of his other hand under my chin to tilt up my face. I swallowed hard. The next moment his lips were on mine and we were kissing, in the perfect setting. We were at the heart of our very own universe. At first it was just our lips tentatively touching. His eyes were open, as were mine.

But not for long.

With a groan, Nathan took both my hands in his, our fingers intertwining, his eyes closing only a moment before mine.

Then the tone of our kiss changed. Nathan's mouth on mine became harder, more demanding. Heat began to spread throughout my body. My heartbeat quickened. Nathan's lips moved on mine, coaxing my mouth open. His hands began to drift slowly up and down my body, from my hips, over my waist, onto my breasts, along my shoulders, down my arms, all the while blazing a trail as they journeyed. My hands were doing some tentative exploring of their own. All this touching and contact after so many years alone was overtaking my ability to think straight. All I could do was feel, and this felt good, with the certain knowledge that Nathan could make me feel even better.

Moments turned into minutes of kissing and touching. Nathan peeled off my shirt before I even realized what he was doing. I didn't want it anyway. I wanted to feel his bare chest against my naked skin. Now I was burning up, hotter than when I'd been in the Mazon engine core. Nathan was still kissing me, his lips making their way down – from my earlobe to my throat before he nibbled at the crook of my neck. An involuntary moan escaped from my parted lips. Nathan's hands were still caressing wherever they landed and his touch against my bare skin almost hurt. He raised his head to kiss my lips again, his tongue darting into my open mouth. It was almost unbearably pleasurable. I wanted more. More of his kisses, his touch, his body.

Wait! What was I doing?

'Nathan, wait. Stop,' I gasped, pulling my mouth away from his.

Reluctantly Nathan stopped kissing me. We were both panting like we'd been submerged under water for too long.

'What's the matter?' he whispered.

'Nathan, I . . . this is too fast. I want to but we're moving at light speed.' Were my words as jumbled out loud as they were in my head?

Nathan nodded and smiled ruefully.

This was madness! What was I *thinking*? I wasn't

thinking, that was the trouble. I was just letting my emotions run away with me – something that had never, *ever* happened before. What was happening to me?

'You'll have to give me a moment to calm down, particularly one part of my anatomy,' said Nathan.

Huh? I glanced down his body and blushed.

'Aw, she's embarrassed!' Nathan teased.

'How could you tell?' I asked, surprised.

'You don't have much of a poker face, Vee,' he said.

No. I didn't. I looked at Nathan, scared to death by what I was feeling.

'I'm sorry I stopped us but—'

'Shush! You don't have to apologize,' said Nathan, before brushing his lips against mine once again. 'My regions may take some convincing of that, but it's OK. Really.'

'No, it's not. I want you, Nathan. I want to do this with you, I really do,' I said, eager for him to understand.

'Olivia, give me a break. You're killing me here,' groaned Nathan.

'Not helping?'

'Not even a little bit.'

All the kissing and touching we'd just done in the middle of this star chart had been mind-blowing. Good phrase that. Mind-blowing. I'd seen it used in a number of the films I'd watched but I'd never truly *felt* it until now. I still don't know why I'd stopped Nathan from making love to me, having sex with me – whatever. God, we'd got close enough and I'd wanted so much more of him. All of him, in fact. So what was I waiting for? The Mazon could catch up with us and blast us to smithereens at any moment. A stray meteor could hit the ship and knock out the life-support systems. Hell, I could eat some chilli and choke!

'Vee, stop looking at me like that,' he said.

'Like what?'

'Like you want to finish what we started.'

'I do.'

'I'm getting mixed signals here,' said Nathan.

I sighed. 'I'm sorry. It's just . . . you confuse me.'

'Back 'atcha!'

'Should we change the subject?'

'That would help – but after you've put your shirt back on!'

Mortified, I scrambled to grab my shirt from the floor.

'Hold on. What's that?' Nathan indicated the necklace I always wore. It was a platinum chain with the letter V set in an oval on the pendant at the end of it and a bolt of lightning running from the top to the bottom of the oval.

'Oh, that's my pendant. It used to be Dad's. He was wearing it when he died. Dad always said he'd give it to me for my eighteenth birthday.' I would gladly have waited for it if Dad had been around to give it to me personally. I sighed. 'It's all I have left of him now.' I looked at Nathan, surprised at his solemn expression. 'What's the matter?'

'What was your dad's name again?'

183

'Daniel Sindall. Why?'

'I don't know that name.'

'Why should you?'

Nathan pointed to my pendant. 'Because that's the secret symbol of the Callistan Resistance working against the Authority.'

I shook my head. One of us was confused. 'No, it's not. Dad designed it himself, he told me so.'

'Vee, that's the symbol of the Resistance. And only those in the Resistance know it.' Nathan stretched out his arm towards me, then turned his forearm so his hand was palm up. There, tattooed on his upper forearm, was the same symbol as formed my pendant. I reached out, my fingers stroking over his tattoo in bewilderment.

'I don't understand,' I whispered.

'Did your mum know about your necklace?'

'I don't know,' I replied. 'I always assumed she did. I thought the V stood for Vida, my mum's name, and for me – Vee. Was my dad a member of the Resistance then?'

'It seems likely if he gave you that.' Nathan pointed to my pendant.

'But Dad wasn't a drone.'

'Not everyone in the Resistance is. There are Elites who understand that what happens to drones is wrong and work in secret to do something about it,' said Nathan.

I took hold of my pendant to look at it again. I'd loved it because Dad had promised it to me and I thought it looked striking, but that was about the extent of it. Once again, my ignorance shamed me.

'Vee?'

'Hmm?' I asked, still studying my pendant.

'Could you put your shirt back on please?' Nathan said softly.

My head whipped up to look at him.

'I'm not made of stone . . .' he said drily.

Picking it up, I pulled it over my head. Cheeks flaming, I suddenly found the floor fascinating.

'She's embarrassed again,' teased Nathan.

'Shut up!'

Nathan sat on the floor, holding out his hand for me to do the same. I sat next to him, cross-legged, still holding his hand.

'Want me to hold you?' he asked softly.

Swallowing hard, I nodded.

Nathan lay down, holding out his arm to me. I lay with my head on his shoulder, and his arm immediately wrapped around me. We lay in silence for long comfortable moments, surrounded by stars. My heart rate was slowly returning to normal – as normal as it ever got around Nathan. This was seriously nuts! What was I doing kissing a stranger? But that was the trouble: he wasn't a stranger. Not even close. In such a short space of time, he had me thinking things I'd never contemplated before, acting in ways I didn't recognize. Quite honestly, it scared the hell out of me.

'Where is this galaxy?' Nathan pointed to the vast cluster of stars directly above our heads.

'All these are in the Tau Quadrant,' I said. 'If we travelled at max speed and made use of the seven charted wormhole jumps along the way, it would take around twenty years to get there.'

'I like the look of it,' said Nathan.

'From this angle, all the star systems in the Tau Quadrant look good,' I said. 'They probably don't look so compelling once you get up close and personal.'

'Well, at this moment we're at the centre of that quadrant and masters of all we survey.' Nathan smiled.

'Maybe that's what God does: sits in the middle of the universe and watches.'

'You believe in God?' Nathan asked.

'On good days – and bad days,' I replied.

I reached out a hand, displacing a spiral constellation when all I really wanted was to hold it closer. I was chasing the stars. Once the constellation had resumed its original position, I placed my hand beneath it. The illusion of holding a multitude of stars and myriad worlds in the palm of my hand seemed nothing less than miraculous. My hand dropped to my side.

'It's a shame it's not real,' I sighed.

'It's real enough. Every moment is real enough.'

True. This was so lovely, just being with Nathan like this. To have a little corner of the universe which was ours and ours alone. Nathan's hand stroked up and down my arm. He suddenly chortled.

'What's so funny?' I asked.

'I was just thinking that life is strange,' said Nathan. 'A while ago on Barros 5, I was sure I was going to die. Now I'm lying here, holding you and watching a galaxy full of stars.'

'A few days ago I wondered if I'd make it home to Earth or die of loneliness first,' I admitted out loud for the first time. 'Then there was that moment in the engine core of the Mazon ship when I nearly lost my balance. I really thought my last moments had come.'

Life was indeed strange.

Nathan kissed my forehead. 'We were obviously destined to meet and be together like this, as dictated by the universe.'

A moment's stunned silence, then I burst out laughing. 'Wow, but you talk some impressive nonsense!'

I expected Nathan to laugh too, but after a moment's silence he said, 'The first time I saw you . . . well, it was as if I'd been waiting for you my whole life. Damn, that sounds cheesy but it happens to be true. Didn't you feel it too?'

Attraction, yes, but it wasn't the kind of thing I was ready to admit. 'Nathan, I . . .'

He drew his arm out from beneath me and rolled on his side to face me directly. 'It's OK, Vee. I don't mind that I'm ahead of you in the way I feel. I'll just wait for you to catch up, that's all.'

'I love the way you're convinced I will,' I said with a smile.

'You wouldn't be lying here with me otherwise.'

He had a point. One thing I needed to clear up though. 'All that stuff you said about having dinner with my imaginary sister – you meant me?'

Nathan gave me a pitying look. 'Of course I meant you. Vee, I really like you. I mean, I *really* like you. My friends have been teasing me about it since we met, it was so blindingly obvious.'

Not to me. 'Next time just say, "Vee, I like you. Would you like to have dinner alone with me sometime?" Keep it simple!'

'I'll remember that,' said Nathan. 'So you and me, d'you like the idea?'

My teeth worried at one side of my bottom lip as I tried to find the right words.

'I'm moving too fast again, aren't I?' said Nathan, beginning to draw away from me.

I placed a hand on his bare chest. 'I was at the other end of all that kissing that just went on – remember?' I reminded him. 'Of course I like you; more than like you. And it's not that I don't want to be with you.' Uncertainty crept unbidden into my voice. 'It's just . . . I'm not sure. I've been away from other people for so long, I'm not sure if what I feel for you is genuine or just gratitude and propinquity.'

'What does that mean – propinquity?'

'Proximity. Nearness.'

'Oh.' Nathan nodded. 'I understand.'

I knew he would.

'Scared?' he asked softly.

'Terrified actually,' I confessed.

Then Nathan surprised me by saying, 'Me too.'

Maybe I shouldn't have admitted to being scared. Did Vee think less of me because of it? A glimpse at her expression calmed my anxieties. Her wide-eyed stare spoke of astonishment but nothing else. She was so cute when she looked at me like that, like she thought I had all the answers, when the truth was, I had none. And the moment I asked her what propinquity meant I regretted it. I'd spent the last few Sol years on Callisto with no access to books, films or music except that deemed 'appropriate' by the Authority. I didn't want Vee to think me ignorant but she'd told me what the word meant without being the least bit condescending.

'You're scared too?' asked Vee. 'Really?'

I nodded. Her sigh of relief made me smile.

She exhaled softly. 'It's just . . . my head is telling me one thing while my gut is telling me another.'

'What's your head telling you?'

'That what I'm feeling is just a rush of hormones to my brain, mixed with gratitude and three years of loneliness, shaken and then vigorously stirred. Bit of a lethal combination, that,' Vee admitted sheepishly.

'And what's your gut saying?'

'That this is real. That I should tell my brain to shut up and just trust my feelings,' said Vee. 'Though of course the feeling in my gut could just be from the chicken joluf I ate earlier.'

I smiled. 'Something tells me you're a pragmatist.'

'Not so as you'd notice at the moment,' Vee said, shaking her head slowly. 'I still can't believe I'm lying here like this. This is crazy. In fact—'

Another kiss halted anything else she was about to say. I didn't want her to have any doubts about us. Even out here in space, there was no room for doubts if we were going to make this work. She was an excellent kisser. Natural talent! When eventually we both came up for air, Vee was giving me a very strange look.

'What?' I asked.

'Nothing,' she said at last, laying her head back down on my shoulder.

'Not true. Tell me. Talk to me, Vee.'

'Just this,' she said, kissing my cheek. 'And some of this.' She kissed my eyebrow. 'And a lot of this.' She kissed my mouth, her lips soft against mine. Then she lay back down. We lay in silence for a while, but much as I might like to, I knew we couldn't stay here for ever. Sooner or later, the real world would come looking for us.

But not yet. Please, not yet.

'You're not ahead of me regarding how you feel,' Vee said softly. 'I'm right alongside you, or maybe slightly ahead. It's just . . . it's not where I expected to be.'

We gazed at each other, nothing hidden. I wanted her so much. But I needed her to want me too. I needed her to trust me, to feel she could open up to me about anything.

'Olivia,' I said, 'tell me something about you that no one else knows.'

33

I tilted my head to look at Nathan. He wasn't asking for much, he was asking for everything.

Something no one else knows . . .

'Sometimes I . . . I cry in my sleep. I wake up with tears streaming down my face,' I admitted.

Oh God! I lowered my gaze, unable to even look at him now. How pathetic must that sound?

Silence.

'Here's something others know but which I've never told anyone,' said Nathan. He spoke so quietly I could only just hear him. 'Sometimes I wake up screaming.'

My eyelids flew open as I stared at him. His expression immediately told me he was serious.

'Does that make you think less of me?' he asked softly.

Choking up and unable to trust myself to speak, I moved closer to him, wrapping my arm tighter around his waist. My heart ached for him. I swallowed hard, then took a deep breath.

'Nate, nothing you've been through or had to do in the past would ever make me think less of you,' I whispered. 'There's nothing you can say or do that would make me change my mind about you. D'you understand?'

A moment, then he nodded.

'Do you believe me?'

He nodded slowly.

Our faces were mere centimetres apart as I spoke. My gaze didn't once waver. I wanted Nathan to know that I meant every syllable.

'Vee, you say that—'

'I mean that,' I interrupted.

Nathan's green eyes were so dark as to be almost black as I looked at him. I willed him not just to see and hear the truth in what I'd said, but to feel it. A smile, slight and sad, twitched on his lips. Memories were eating away at him. I moved in closer to nibble on his bottom lip. Something else, hopefully more pleasurable, eating at him. It seemed like the natural thing to do. He looked so . . . lost. I just wanted him to know he wasn't alone. I was as lost as he was but we could be lost together. I drew back. Could he hear my heart pounding in my chest? It was deafening me. Nathan took my hand and placed it over his heart. My eyes widened. His heart was beating just as fast as mine.

We both moved forward at the same time to kiss again, our mouths open, our lips touching, our tongues dancing together. I closed my eyes as my hands stroked slowly up and down Nathan's chest and arm. I needed to touch him. Touching was good. I never thought I'd have this, certainly not before I made it home to Earth. Now here I was in the arms of someone who continued to occupy more and more of my thoughts and my time. Nathan pulled me closer until not even a breath of air could've got between us. He was holding me so tight, almost too tight, like he was trying to pull me right inside him to make us one and the same. Even I knew it didn't work like that. But I wasn't going to complain.

It was all good.

Better than good.

Delicious. Definitely edible.

I couldn't get over how glorious it felt, when only a year or two ago the thought of someone else's tongue inside my mouth would've made me gag. Hard. Now I was lying on my side, my hands moving over Nathan's back as we kissed. His skin was almost hot to the touch. I traced over his shoulder blades, his spine, his nape. I loved the feel of his skin and muscles beneath my fingertips, so soft yet solid. How had I survived for so long without this physical contact – a handshake, a hug, a kiss?

Was I abnormal to feel like this or did all people feel this way? Was this a basic human need, to be held, to experience basic human contact, or was there something wrong with me because I'd been alone with just my brother for far too long?

Nathan's hands moved under my T-shirt, one on my stomach, the other arm wrapped round my back, and they weren't still for a second. Slowly but surely they stroked and caressed, and each move made me catch my breath and scorched my skin. Nathan's hand moved up to caress my breasts. His thumb rubbed slowly back and forth across my right nipple through my bra and a bolt of lightning zinged through my body at his touch. Nathan raised me up slightly to pull my T-shirt over my head again. Then it was the turn of my bra. Once it was off, I wrapped my arms around his neck to pull him closer. We were skin against skin from the waist up. I wanted nothing to get in the way of my whole body touching his, no clothes, no more doubts, no inhibitions.

Nathan pulled away from me to unfasten my trousers. His fingers hooked into them at the hip and he slowly pulled them downwards. My breath hitched in my throat as I watched him, not sure at first what he was doing. I raised my hips slightly to make it easier for him. This was so strangely unfamiliar. To literally lay myself bare for this guy. All my senses were suffering an overload. Both of us were breathing so much faster. I was so glad I wasn't the only one having trouble catching my breath.

Once my trousers were off, it was Nathan's turn, only he didn't wait for me to reciprocate. He took them off himself – in about three seconds flat. I watched his eyes, too nervous to glance down, much as I wanted to.

We were naked. Alone. Together.

Nathan's gaze moved over my body, physical as a touch. Suddenly self-conscious, I drew up my legs and tried to cover my breasts with my hands. Nathan gently took hold of my hands and placed them at my side. Was there something wrong with the environmental controls in this room?

The temperature was way too high and the air had all but disappeared.

'You are so beautiful,' he whispered, his gaze moving slowly down my body. 'Flawless.'

Then his hands followed the path of his gaze, flitting lightly over my forehead, my eyelids, my lips, my neck, my breasts, my abdomen, and lower. Every time I raised my hands to do the same to him, he pushed them down at my sides. Frustrated, I finally left them there, especially when his lips followed the path of his hands. When his lips were kissing and licking around my navel, I thought that was as far as he would go.

But I was wrong.

His kisses were moving further down my body. I pushed myself up onto my elbows to watch. He wasn't seriously going to go where no one had gone before, was he?

Oh. My. God.

He was! I tried to raise a hand to push him away and stop him, but Nathan took a gentle but firm grip on both my wrists. With a groan, ripped from somewhere deep inside, I lay back down, completely supine. Nothing I'd watched or read had prepared me for anything like this. A series of shocks shot through me at every touch of his tongue.

It was so intense. Almost too much. My body writhed under his care until I was sure I was going to pass out from pleasure. When at last Nathan moved up my body, I was totally boneless and couldn't for the life of me remember how to breathe. And then Nathan was kissing my lips, my forehead, my eyelids, my chin, my cheeks. He raised his head to smile at me as the memory of how to breathe finally came back, making me pant in an effort to fill my starving lungs with air.

'Nate, let me . . .' I pushed at Nathan's chest. He immediately backed away from me, looking anxious. With a smile to reassure him, I pushed him onto his back, kissing and nibbling on his neck as I did so. I rained kisses over his chest. I wanted to taste him all over too. Reciprocity was a good thing.

'No,' whispered Nathan, rising up to cup my face with his hands. 'Next time.'

'Next time? There's going to be a next time?' I grinned.

He didn't want this to be just a one-time thing. I so liked the sound of that. I hadn't wanted to assume.

Nathan went very still, his green eyes suddenly cold, hard. 'Vee, I don't hit and run. If you're looking for a one-time one-off to scratch an itch, you're looking in the wrong place. I had enough of being used like that on Callisto.'

Already Nathan was pulling away from me. Appalled, I realized he'd misunderstood. I sat up, reaching out to cup his face.

'Nathan, that's the opposite of what I'm looking for,' I rushed to reassure him. '*You're* what I'm looking for.' Heat swept over my face at my inadvertent admission but I wouldn't have taken it back even if I could.

'You're all I'm looking for,' Nathan said at last, his gaze softening.

And then I was on my back with Nathan's body covering mine, his tongue darting in and out of my mouth as he slowly but surely pushed inside my body. He was so gentle, allowing my body time to awaken to this strange new feeling. Nathan lowered his head to lick and nibble at my throat. Already the discomfort I'd felt at his entry into my body was fading. I ran my hands up and down his back as we finally moved together. It was so slow, so sweet, so tender that with each second that passed I felt like I was melting into him and he was melting into me. Love was a word, an idea, a concept, something to be watched in films and read and sung about before this moment. Now it was something I could touch and feel, something tangible that held me up high till there was no air to breathe and dragged me down low until I was drowning – and I loved every second. Nathan had caught me, heart, body and soul, and the depth of what I felt for him frightened me. Actually frightened me. It would be too easy to completely lose myself in the way I was feeling.

Nathan raised himself up to look at me, his body still joined with mine, his gaze intense. 'You're mine,' he whispered.

I stroked one finger over his lips. 'Only if you're mine.'

'Always.'

As the pace quickened, all doubts, all fears were pushed aside. Here and now was all that existed. Nathan was all that mattered. And for now, for this moment, I wouldn't have had it any other way.

Nathan and I both got dressed in sated, smiling silence. As I pulled on my boots, I could only thank God no one had come into the astro lab while we'd been . . . busy. Or maybe they had and we'd just been too busy to notice. That thought was mortifying. I could feel my face burning at the prospect.

'No regrets, I hope?' asked Nathan.

'Not a single one,' I replied honestly.

'Good. Still scared?'

I considered. 'Yes, but for completely different reasons now.' I smiled.

Nathan's gaze was intense as he looked at me. I could so easily surrender to a look like that and never want to escape again. Listen to me! Like I hadn't already done so.

'Want to go all out and do something even more scary?' asked Nathan.

'Like what?'

He stood up and held out his hand. I took it and he pulled me to my feet. 'Promise me you won't think, you'll just go with your gut. OK?'

Intrigued, I nodded.

I kept telling myself I had to be cracked to put myself in the hands of someone I'd known for such a short space of time, but it felt so right, so . . . natural. It felt like I was on a gravity ride, being lifted up high and about to be dropped fast and hard. It was exciting and fear-inducing all at once. But while I was on this ride I was going to hang on for dear life and enjoy every moment.

NATHAN

There's nothing like seeing death, facing death, to put life in perspective. I swore when I was on Callisto that if I ever escaped from that hellhole, I would never hesitate to grab any and every opportunity that crossed my path. I promised myself I'd never be afraid of life or love and would celebrate both.

I have to admit though, I didn't see this one coming.

Vee kept casting me curious looks as I pulled on my jacket and led the way out of the astrophysics lab.

This was insane! She'd never agree to what I had planned but that wasn't going to stop me from trying. Even I couldn't believe what I had in mind. I was definitely losing it, but I didn't care.

All Vee had to say was yes and our lives would never be the same again.

'Vee, are you all right?' asked my brother.

'Yeah.' I yawned. 'Why?'

'That's the eighth time you've yawned in ten minutes,' said Aidan.

I frowned. 'Don't exaggerate.'

'You know I don't do that.'

'Why are you counting how many times I yawn in any given amount of time?' I said, irritated.

For heaven's sake! Couldn't a girl even yawn in peace? And though I knew I'd done nothing wrong, my face and neck were growing steadily warmer. Erica, who was perched at the edge of Aidan's console chatting to him, looked at me curiously.

What?

Luckily for me, the commander, Anjuli and everyone else on the bridge couldn't give a damn how often I yawned. I needed to pull myself together. We were still travelling through Mazon space and weren't out of danger yet. I needed to be on top of my game.

Focus, Vee. Focus!

Nathan chose just that moment to step through the

door – and, yep, he was yawning.

Crap!

'Morning, Nathan,' said Aidan.

Aidan's greeting almost made me feel sorry that I'd spoken in private to him about being more open and friendly with the crew.

'Someone else who didn't get much sleep last night,' said Erica pointedly.

What was that girl's problem? And thanks to her words and Nathan's untimely entrance, my face was now on fire.

'Nathan, are the oxygen levels on board too low?' asked Aidan. 'That might explain why both you and my sister are yawning. I shall check—'

'Aidan, where is everyone?' I asked, desperate to get my brother off the topic of the ship's lack of oxygen.

'Doctor Liana and Rafael are in the medical bay. Alex is in the science lab with Max. Dooli is with the two children in the cargo hold. Mike is in the hydroponics bay, Ian, Maria, Harrison and Corbyn are in the engine room—'

'I really don't need to know the exact whereabouts of every single person on board,' I interrupted.

'But that's what you asked me.' Aidan turned to me with a frown.

Sometimes he could be so irritatingly literal. 'I just meant . . . Never mind.'

I glanced at Nathan, who winked at me.

Bastard!

I smothered a laugh beneath my hand, which I placed over my mouth as if I were contemplating something deep and meaningful – which in a way I was.

Nathan walked over to me and squatted down. 'How're you feeling?' he asked softly.

'Tired. I didn't get much sleep last night,' I replied, equally quietly.

We grinned at each other, at that moment the only two on the bridge. But only for that moment. I looked up. Erica was watching us, a dawning light of realization in her eyes. She opened her mouth. I quickly shook my head at her. A satisfied gleam in her eyes, she closed her mouth again. With one gesture I'd been stupid enough to confirm her suspicions.

Damn!

I really was entirely out of practice at being with people. Erica resumed her conversation with Aidan, probably knowing I was watching her. She wasn't going to tell my brother, was she? But hell! So what if she did? What Nathan and I got up to in our own time was none of her business, or Aidan's business, or anyone else's for that matter.

'Thank you for my present,' Nathan said, bringing my attention back to him.

'Are you wearing it?'

'Are you kidding? I'm never going to take it off.' Nathan smiled. He unfastened the top of his work jacket, making it seem like a casual gesture. There, against his black T-shirt, was the V pendant my dad had promised to me and I in turn had passed on to Nathan last night.

'Be careful with it. The clasp is a bit fragile,' I warned.

Nathan nodded.

'Don't lose it,' I said softly. 'It's very precious to me, that's why I gave it to you. OK?'

'OK.'

'Vee, I've been going through all the logs recorded since we arrived on board the *Aidan*,' Catherine told me. 'Are you convinced by your assessment of yesterday's airlock . . . incident?'

I forced myself to look straight back at her rather than looking around to see who was monitoring our conversation. 'With the data I've analysed so far, yes I am.'

The commander nodded and turned back to what she was doing. She reminded me that I needed to get my head out of the clouds and back to work. Three people had died. I needed to find out why.

Beside me, Nathan straightened up. 'I wasn't given an assignment for today,' he said at his normal volume. 'Is there anything in particular you'd like me to do, Captain?'

I looked from Nathan to his mum and back again.

Oh, he was talking to me!

Nathan pressed his lips together to stop himself from laughing. Resisting the urge to kick him in the shins, I asked, 'What're you good at?'

With a devilish glint in his eyes, he replied softly, 'I'm good with my hands.'

God! My face was on fire. Again.

'Er . . . if you could help out on the landing craft down in the cargo hold, that'd be great. I haven't managed to get it running and I believe some of your colleagues are currently working on it. I'm sure they'd appreciate your input.'

Nathan bent down to whisper in my ear, 'I like it when my input is appreciated.'

Oh. My. God!

'Nathan, behave!' I muttered.

'That's not what you said last night,' he replied.

I glared at him. What was he like?

Before I could say another word, Nathan was heading for the door. And I knew that he knew I was watching him.

I had it really bad.

Focus, Vee.

In spite of everything else that was going on around me, there was a peaceful, easy feeling inside me that I'd never felt before. I intended to savour it, make the most of it, because I couldn't help wondering, *Just how long will it last?*

I was almost late for the memorial ceremony. The moment I entered the mess hall I immediately scanned the room for Vee. It was only as I looked around for her that I realized I did the same thing whatever room I entered. The first thing I did was look for Vee. It was as if I couldn't relax properly until I knew where she was and that she was OK. I moved to stand beside her as Mum cast me a disapproving look for my tardiness. I nodded my apology then turned to look at Vee. She wore her work uniform but beneath her jacket I could see her purple sleeveless shirt. The contrast between the purple of her shirt and her brown skin made me want to take her and hold her. Or better still, to hold her and take her. Highly inappropriate thoughts, given the reason for this gathering, but damn it, if a memorial service didn't make you appreciate love and life then nothing would.

I placed my hands behind my back and waited for Mum to speak. Vee stood with her head bowed. I looked around. Everyone on board was present – except Aidan. Someone had to stay on the bridge in case the Mazon put in an unexpected appearance. The mess hall wasn't completely silent. Some were trying – and failing – to suppress their sobs and tears.

Darren wasn't the only one who'd lost his entire family on Barros 5. Maria had lost her mother-in-law, who was the last member of her family, and Dooli and Rafael had also lost loved ones. To escape from Callisto only to lose the ones we loved now was especially cruel. Erica was fidgeting like she couldn't wait to leave, but then she'd lost all her family back on Callisto a long time before we escaped, so this ceremony was probably just hammering home that fact. And there was Max. He'd never had any family, but he had to be the most optimistic person I'd ever met. I'd never heard him say a mean word against anyone. As far as the rest of the crew were concerned, the deaths of Mei, Saul and Jaxon had been a tragic accident, nothing more. Mum reckoned, and Vee had agreed, that there was no point in revealing the truth. It would only spread fear and suspicion around the ship. I could understand their point of view. So here we all were with more lost lives to be remembered, more deaths to mourn.

It wasn't often that we had the time and space to collectively mourn our dead. As sombre as this occasion was, maybe it was the start of a new way of doing things for us. Maybe out of this commemoration of so much ending we'd find a new beginning.

And maybe I was just deluding myself.

'We are gathered here to pay our respects to all the loved ones we have known and lost – on Callisto, on the *Galileo*, on Barros 5 and aboard this ship,' Mum began. 'There's not one of us on board who hasn't suffered the grief of a loss. But we must continue to use that grief to unite us and to make us the stronger for it.'

Silence.

Vee was radiating sadness. Her hand moved to her chest, then dropped back to her side. Anyone watching probably thought she was about to cough or was placing her hand over her heart in a very over-dramatic way. But I knew that's where her dad's pendant used to lie against her skin. She was probably thinking of her parents and the rest of the crew of the *Aidan* who had died. I clasped my hands in front of me, forcing myself not to reach out and take Vee's hand in mine. I could only guess what everyone present would make of that.

'We may have lost loved ones,' Mum continued. 'But all is not lost. Everyone, look around. You are standing beside your old friends and we are, all of us, your new family. We will endure and we *will* make it to Mendela Prime where a better life awaits us. The best way to overcome a fear of death is to live and live well – and we will.'

But would we?

As I looked around, an unwelcome question sprang into my head.

Just how many of us currently standing here would make it to Mendela Prime? Something told me our troubles weren't behind us, but lay ahead.

Over the next few days, I'm sure more and more people were giving me funny looks, *knowing* looks. At first I tried to tell myself I was imagining things. But the smiles as I approached people in the corridors and the whispers as they passed me weren't all in my imagination. Nathan insisted Erica didn't know a thing but she must've shared her suspicions.

Nathan and I almost got caught – twice while kissing in the lift when we unexpectedly found ourselves in it together, and once in the malfunctioning landing craft when I went down to the cargo hold to enquire about progress. That really was all I went down there for – honest! Ian and Harrison were outside the two-man craft, recalibrating the engine, and Nathan was inside, relaying data back to those outside. When I entered the craft to tell Nathan that we had to be more careful about public displays of affection, he answered by kissing me breathless. When the data ceased to be forthcoming, Ian decided to come into the craft to find out what the problem was. The problem was, Nathan had his tongue in my mouth, not his eyes on the screen. That one had been close . . . but I think we got away with it.

And I was actually making friends. The commander and I now had a grudging respect for each other and I often asked her advice on matters regarding the ship and crew. To be honest, it was good to have someone willing to take on some of the responsibility of running the ship. The only thing I hadn't shared with any of the others was the executive command code which allowed me among other things to lock out or lock down any computer function at a moment's notice.

Anjuli and I in particular were already good friends. Her enthusiasm was endearing. If she could've, she would've slept on the bridge. She insisted that Aidan and I take her through every facet of the ship's controls, which I for one was more than happy to do. And she was no mental slouch either. In fact, I got on well with almost everyone – except Darren. And Erica. She got on my nerves, with her openly knowing looks cast in my direction, and her obvious plays for my brother. The atmosphere on board was slowly beginning to relax and warm up as we got used to each other. Don't get me wrong, I was happy about it – but it felt like the calm before a fast approaching storm.

I could only hope and pray that I was worrying about nothing.

And then there was Mei, Saul and Jaxon. I hadn't forgotten what had happened to them, even if our investigation seemed to have ground to a halt. Realizing that I hadn't had a proper chat with my brother in a number of days, I headed for his door about thirty minutes before the start of my next shift. Placing my hand against his palm-lock, I walked straight into his room. Aidan was seated at his desk. He swung round in his chair the moment I entered.

'Hi, Aidan, how're you?' I smiled.

He gave me a strange look, almost stony.

'Are you all right?' I asked, my smile fading.

'I haven't seen you in a while,' said Aidan.

'Yeah, I know. I've been . . . er . . . busy getting to know our new crew,' I mumbled.

'The whole crew or just one member of it?' he asked.

My face began to burn. 'What does that mean?'

'You and Nathan are together a lot,' said Aidan.

'Nathan has been telling me about the other members of the crew and teaching me things.'

'Like what?'

'Like what life was like on Callisto and how he survived,' I replied, my tone growing brusque. This wasn't what I'd come to talk to my brother about. Time to nip this subject in the bud. I took a deep breath. 'Aidan, I didn't come here to talk about Nathan. How is the investigation going into the deaths of Jaxon, Saul and Mei?'

At first I thought he wasn't going to answer, but at last he said, 'I've analysed all the available logs and cross-referenced the time of the nanite infection with the times of the deaths of the refugees.'

'And?'

Aidan shrugged. 'Any or all of the new crew could've done it.'

Distinctly unimpressed, I narrowed my eyes. 'All that brain power and that's the best you can do?'

'Let's hear your conclusions then,' Aidan challenged.

Silence.

'They're the same as yours,' I admitted. 'The person who infected our computer system was really smart to do it in a place which everyone uses and has access to. I don't believe it's a conspiracy though. This feels to me like one person acting alone.'

'Well, the only way to track down this person is to wait for them to strike again,' said my brother.

'And if they don't?'

'Then they'll probably get away with the murders of three people,' said Aidan.

'And if they do strike again?'

'Then more people on board this ship will die.'

The *Aidan* was in night-time mode and I was on the bridge instead of the cargo hold where I should have been. Guess I had it really bad. I just didn't like to be away from Vee for too long. Every couple of hours or so I always found an excuse to come up to the bridge, supposedly to see Mum. But from the way Vee tried to hide her amused smile every time I appeared, I wasn't fooling her for a moment. What I was doing was making a damn fool out of myself.

Sad, but true.

But I was addicted to her. More than addicted.

I loved the idea of the two of us spending more time getting to know each other. As far as I was concerned, a lifetime wouldn't be long enough.

So here I was again, asking my mum some inane question that could've waited until we were both off duty just so I could be close to Vee. Even if neither of us said a single word to each other, at least I got to see her for a few minutes. That would have to do me until the two of us could be alone together again.

Anjuli sat in Aidan's seat at the navigation controls next to Mum, with Darren at weapons and Sam and Hedda at the tactical panel. I was glad there'd been no more talk of Mum trying to take over Vee's ship. I still heard mutterings among some of the settlers about an eighteen-year-old running things and giving orders, but Mum always backed her up and Vee obviously knew what she was doing, so though the mutterings didn't disappear, they didn't get any louder – at least, not around me. Between Vee and Mum, they pretty much had the running of the ship covered.

The day after the memorial service Mum suggested to Vee that they run tactical simulations involving the whole crew. Vee took only a moment to consider before agreeing.

'Would you like to run them yourself or are you happy for me to handle that?' asked Mum.

'You go ahead. I'd like to be involved though,' said Vee.

So over the next few days they devised different scenarios and ran test alerts to see how the new crew of the *Aidan* would manage. The first couple were close to disastrous but we were getting better.

I was so proud of Vee. She wasn't afraid to get her hands dirty and she ate at the same tables as the rest of us in the mess hall. Unlike some of the commanders and captains I'd come across before Mum and I were exiled to Callisto, Vee wasn't standoffish and unsociable, thinking she was too good for anyone who wasn't of the same rank.

Aidan was a different story. After the first few days of sitting with us but not saying a word, he'd taken to chipping into our conversations with comments whenever he got the chance. The trouble was that most of his comments missed the mark or were inappropriate. He was trying too hard. And more than once I caught him watching me. No, not just watching me, *scrutinizing* me. Whenever I tried to smile at him to be friendly, he just continued to stare. Well, if that's the way he wanted it then that was his business. But the staring was unnerving, verging on creepy.

The ship was still on yellow alert and Vee said there it would stay until we were out of Mazon territory. No one was going to fully relax until we reached the wormhole that would take us out of their space.

So here we were, only a few days away from leaving Mazon territory for good, and I was actually daring to believe that luck might actually be on our side for a change.

'Nathan, when you've finished staring at Vee like she's suddenly sprouted an extra head, perhaps you'd like to tell me what you're doing on the bridge?' said Mum.

Damn! I needed to be more careful. I didn't realize I was staring.

'Mum, I was wondering if you wanted to have dinner with me in the mess hall some night soon?' I said to her as she looked at me expectantly.

Pathetic! That didn't even convince me!

'And you needed to ask me that at this precise moment?' said Mum drily. 'It couldn't have waited?'

Behind me, Vee cleared her throat, but when I looked at her she was avidly studying something on the panel which made up one arm of her chair. Everything on there could also be called up as an image before her by manipulating the two command bracelets she wore on either wrist. With the slightest subtle hand or wrist movement she could display information from any panel on the bridge. She had very clever wrists. And hands. And—

'Er . . . Nathan, I'm over here. I thought you came to see me. It's interesting just how many times a day you come up here to see me about this or that, none of which is really important,' Mum continued, looking from me to Vee and back again. 'I'm beginning to wonder—'

The ship's alarm began to scream. Any relief I felt at being saved by the siren was short-lived when I realized what the siren meant. The lights on the bridge kept flashing red.

'Aidan, get in here,' Vee called out. 'And shut off the siren.'

A metal harness came over the back of the captain's chair, pressing down on Vee's shoulders and clicking into place round her waist.

'What's going on?' Mum asked as she secured herself into her seat, as did everyone else around me.

Vee studied her monitor. 'We've got company,' she said grimly. *The Mazon*.

I ran to the environmental station and sat in the first available seat, securing myself in too. Aidan raced into the room. Anjuli got to her feet, looking shocked and ashen as Aidan sat in the chair she'd just vacated.

'I didn't . . . I didn't mean . . .' Anjuli wasn't making any sense.

'Aidan, report,' Vee ordered.

Aidan studied his console for a moment before his body stilled momentarily.

'A Mazon patrol ship has locked onto our signal and is heading our way at speed,' he said.

'How the hell did it manage to lock onto us?' said Vee. 'We're still scrambling our ship's energy signature – right?'

'We *were*,' Aidan said pointedly.

'I'm so sorry . . .' Anjuli's apology was a horrified whisper.

What had she done?

'Anjuli sent the Mazon ship a signal from my panel. She's alerted them to our presence,' said Aidan. 'Vee, we're in big trouble.'

I must've misheard. 'What?'

'Anjuli sent the Mazon a signal,' said Aidan.

Dahell? Much as I might want to leap across the bridge and kick Anjuli's butt, I had higher priorities at that moment. But what the hell was she thinking?

'Can we scramble our signal to lose them again?' I asked my brother.

'Not this time, sis. They'll know what to look out for now. And besides, the Mazon ship is closing in at maximum speed.'

'How long before it reaches us?'

'At its current speed, fifteen minutes.'

'The closest star system?'

'Over a day away,' Aidan replied.

'It's just the one Mazon ship?' I asked.

'So far.'

'One of the ones we encountered before?'

'I can't tell from this distance. I don't see what difference it makes. Whichever Mazon cruiser it is, when it fires at us, we'll be just as dead,' said Aidan. 'Anjuli, what were you doing? Why would you want to get us all killed?'

All eyes were on Anjuli. Tears rolled down her cheeks as she struggled to speak. 'I w-was just trying to monitor their communications,' she stammered. 'I wanted to find out if there were any other Mazon ships between us and the wormhole. I wanted to help. Tell them, Aidan.'

'Never mind that now,' I said.

Accusations and explanations would have to wait.

'Vee, long-range sensors indicate another three Mazon battlecruisers eighteen hours away and heading in our direction,' said Aidan.

'When the Mazon patrol vessel reaches us, I could try a phased-shift electron burst,' said Darren from the weapons station.

'That would only work if we hit their engine core straight on. With all the shielding the Mazon have around their engine, we wouldn't do enough damage to tickle them, never mind disable them,' I replied tersely.

'Nathan, get over here,' said Commander Linedecker. 'We need you at navigation.'

'We do?' said Aidan.

'My son can fly this ship or any other Earth vessel ever made. Plus he's studied the schematics of every alien ship Earth has ever had contact with,' she replied. 'He was not only the best flight pilot on board my last ship but he also knows every bolt and rivet of every ship he's ever studied.'

Nathan had told me that his mum had no idea of the full extent of his knowledge or interest in star craft. Looks like he got that one wrong. She sounded pretty savvy to me. I heard the sound of Nathan's safety harness being un-coupled. He went over to the navigation board and sat at the panel between his mum and Aidan. I wasn't about to argue. The monitor before Nathan immediately had his attention. Anjuli moved over to Nathan's vacated seat at environmental.

'Anjuli, don't touch anything,' I ordered. 'D'you hear me? Not a damned thing.'

Anjuli nodded. I turned back to Nathan. If the worst came to the worst, at least I'd get to look at him one last time before—

No! Don't think like that, Vee. You have too much to live for now. Figure something out.

Think, damn it. Think.

Nathan turned in his chair to look at me. I thought he might say something but he didn't. He just looked at me and then turned away. Did my expression mirror his – grim and resigned? So much for all the time Nathan said we'd have to get to know each other. So much for the life-time he'd promised me where we'd explore the universe together.

I turned back to my console, plotting distances and escape routes to the nearest star system where we might hide behind a moon or use the gravity of the local sun to slingshot us out of range of the Mazon weapons. Nothing doing. As Aidan had said, the nearest star system was over a day away.

The Mazon were only minutes away and closing fast.

'Vee, it's useless. We can't outrun them or outgun them,' said Hedda from tactical. 'To stand any chance at all, we need to surrender.'

'That's your plan? To surrender to them?' asked Vee coldly. 'D'you know what the Mazon do to their human prisoners? We'd be experimented on and tortured and they'd make sure to keep us alive for as long as possible for their own amusement. Is that what you want?'

'Hedda, we are not surrendering.' Mum frowned. 'That's not an option. If we go down, we go down fighting.'

'Aidan, what's our engine output capacity?' asked Vee.

'Making our way through Barros 5's atmosphere depleted some of our engine's power. We're running at seventy-two per cent capacity.'

'Vee, let me take command. I'll make sure we put up a good fight,' said Mum.

'How about we try something a little less suicidal first?' said Vee.

'Like what?' asked Mum.

Silence.

'Aidan, how far are we from the Zandari ion storm?' Vee asked.

As if it were rehearsed, every single person on the bridge turned in horror to stare at Vee – me included.

'You want to try and hide in an ion storm? You're not serious! D'you know what will happen to us if we get stuck in there?' said Mum.

I cringed. Mum was taking a bad situation and making it worse, even if she was right.

'Aidan, how far are we from the Zandari ion storm?' Vee repeated, ignoring my mum.

Aidan swung round in his chair, a deep frown cutting grooves at the sides of his mouth as he faced his sister. 'By the time we get there the Mazon ship will be close enough to target us.'

'We only need to outmanoeuvre them for long enough to enter the storm,' said Vee. 'You and Nathan will need to make sure they don't get a lock on us.'

Oh, is that all? I thought with what I admit was a touch of sarcasm.

An ion storm. Did Vee know what she was doing? If we entered an ion storm, the ship's engine power would drain away in less than a minute. The emergency reserves which ran the life-support and other essential systems would last maybe half a day at most. We'd be sitting ducks. I wouldn't have dreamed of challenging Vee's decision in public but it seemed to me all she was doing was prolonging our agony.

'Aidan, can you get us into the ion storm before the Mazon can attack?' asked Vee.

'I can try – but the probability of succeeding is zero point—' said Aidan.

'Never mind the maths. At this point I'll take any chance of success I can get.'

'Vee, what you're proposing is lunacy,' argued Darren. 'You obviously don't realize that the ion storm will drain the power from the ship's engine.'

'Not only do I realize it, but I'm counting on it,' Vee replied.

'You want us to be dead in the water?' he said, appalled.

'The Mazon have us in their sights now. Their primary objective is our destruction and they will follow us into hell itself to make that happen,' said Vee.

'All the more reason to turn and fight,' argued Darren. 'Hand over this ship to someone who knows what they're doing.'

'Look, I don't have time to argue with you. We're going to do this my way. If you don't like it, there's the exit,' said Vee, exasperated.

'You're condemning us all to a slow painful death within an ion storm,' Sam piped up. 'I wouldn't wish that upon my worst enemy.'

'We should surrender,' Hedda insisted.

They were all doing my head in so God knows what they were doing to Vee.

'For God's sake!' I snapped. 'Vee's the captain of this ship, not any of you—'

'Stay out of this, Nathan,' Mum ordered. 'Olivia, I've checked the ship's logs. You've never been toe to toe with a battle-cruiser and had to strategize your way out of a bad situation. I have. Let me take over.'

Vee studied my mum as she spoke, her unimpressed expression obvious. 'Have you all quite finished?'

'We need to do whatever is necessary to ensure our survival. If that means taking this ship from you by force, then so be it,' said Darren.

'No, Darren. We won't do anything of the kind,' said Mum. She turned to Vee. 'Olivia, you must see the logic in letting me take charge. I'm asking you to let me take over.'

'If you do, we're dead for sure,' said Vee. 'Commander, I'm a survivor. I'm asking you to trust me.'

Mum and Vee regarded each other. No one on the bridge spoke.

'I hope you know what you're doing,' said Mum at last.

'Cathy, you cannot be serious! You're going to place our fate in the hands of that . . . that child?' Darren leaped to his feet, beyond outraged.

'Being younger than you doesn't make me a child,' Vee snapped. 'And I'm sick to the back teeth of you and your attitude.'

'Like I give a shit,' Darren hissed.

'Sit down, Darren,' Mum ordered. 'I think I'm beginning to see what Vee has in mind.'

I'm glad Mum was because I sure as hell wasn't.

'Aidan, head for the Zandari ion storm. Maximum velocity.' Vee was busy at her monitor, her fingers moving at speed as she checked over her calculations.

'At maximum velocity we'll reach the ion storm in twelve minutes and eighteen seconds but by then the Mazon ship will be close enough to wave to,' said Aidan.

'As long as they don't get a clear shot at us and they follow us into the storm,' said Vee, her tone remarkably calm. 'That's all I care about.'

'I still don't see . . .' said Aidan. 'Oh!' A slow smile crept over his face. 'Oh, I get it.'

What?

'For us lesser mortals who haven't quite caught up yet, how about an explanation?' I said, exasperated.

'The Mazon will follow us into the ion storm and their engine power will drain just as quickly as ours,' said Mum. 'As Hedda said, they can outrun us and they outgun us. Vee's trying to level the playing field. This ship is much smaller and Vee's hoping to make that work in our favour.'

'Nathan, I need you to position us as soon as we enter the storm so that we turn through one hundred and eighty degrees to face the way we came,' Vee ordered. 'If my calculations are correct and you get us facing the right way, even with no power our momentum means we should drift out of the storm after about an hour.'

'Won't the Mazon do the same thing?' I said.

'Not necessarily, but if they do and both our ships manage to drift outside the ion storm, it will only take fifteen minutes for this ship to recharge with enough power to get us moving again,' said Aidan. 'It'll take the Mazon ship eighty-nine minutes before they can do the same and we'll be long gone by then.'

'And if we don't turn the ship round in time or Nathan gets the calculations wrong?' asked Darren, still not convinced.

He had to ask.

'We'll drift deeper and deeper into the ion storm with no

navigation system to help us get out. Eventually our emergency life-support system will fail and everyone will die.' Aidan's matter-of-fact tone was really unwelcome.

'The Zandari ion storm is this quadrant's ships' graveyard,' said Vee quietly. 'I don't intend for us to be another of its victims. Nathan, are you on top of this?'

'Yes, Captain. Don't worry. I'll get it right,' I said with a confidence I was far from feeling.

'That would be preferable,' said Vee.

'Aidan, drop a location buoy just before we enter the ion storm, and while Nathan is turning us I need you to drop us three kilometres, co-ordinates zero, minus three point two, zero. OK?' said Vee.

'Drop us?' Mum said sharply.

'Descend, then. Aidan knows what I mean,' Vee said impatiently. 'I know there's no up or down in space.'

'Why are we going to drop?' I asked.

'We don't want to be where the Mazon expect us to be,' Vee explained. 'Just in case they decide to try their luck at plotting our predicted course to blast us into nothingness before their power drains away completely. So we're going to move about three kilometres below them.'

Darren sat down again. He wasn't happy, but Mum was willing to go along with Vee's plan so he had no choice but to do the same. I turned to look at Vee but her head was bent over the panel in the arm of her chair. She had more important things to worry about than me at that moment, but I still needed to look at her, no matter how briefly.

'Attention!' Vee broadcast a ship-wide alert. 'We'll be entering an ion storm soon with a Mazon battlecruiser on our tail. Please don't use any electrical devices that might leave an electromagnetic footprint or the Mazon will use that to track us – that includes the food and utility dispensers. This will apply until the ship's engine recharges and restarts. That is all.'

No one on the bridge spoke as we raced for the Zandari ion storm. I kept a careful eye on my panel, checking and double-checking the timings of the manoeuvre I was about to attempt. I'd used a number of simulators and studied everything I could about Earth vessels before we were exiled. I'd even been allowed to sit as co-pilot at the flight panel of Mum's old ship, but none of that had been anything like what I was about to attempt. I knew all the controls better than the back of my hand, but if I messed up, there was no reset button. Much as I wanted to turn round and look at Vee again, much as I longed to mouth a message to her in case we didn't make it, I didn't dare. I needed to concentrate and get this right for any of us to stand a chance.

The silence on the bridge was a living, breathing thing. We hadn't even entered the storm yet, but no one spoke. Anjuli moved to sit next to Darren, who completely ignored her. Everyone was ignoring her. When . . . *if* we got out of this, I had a few questions of my own for her, starting with 'Why?' and closely followed by, 'Dafuq?'

The Zandari ion storm was now visible on the viewscreen of the bridge – and fast approaching. It was one of the most spectacular sights I'd ever seen. Spectacular and deadly. It was a vast green, purple and red gaseous entity which stretched on for many hundreds of thousands of kilometres, always shifting and changing. Some said there had to be a small star at the heart of it, creating its own gravity well, but no one had ever emerged from the ion storm to confirm that – at least as far as I knew.

Then I saw the alert on my panel.

Oh God! 'Incoming!' I shouted.

Our ship lurched to starboard to avoid an incoming Mazon blast. There was less than one hundred metres between the detonation of the blast and us. Much too close. But Aidan had made sure it wasn't a direct hit.

An alert sounded around the ship which Aidan immediately quashed.

'Get ready. Zandari ion storm coming up on my mark.' Pause. 'Three, two, one, *mark*,' Aidan announced.

I activated my program to get my own mark for optimal timing, then turned the ship through one hundred and eighty degrees as directed, while Aidan did his part. The instruments were already going nuts. The ion storm was bending and distorting signals. I was getting echoes and false and phantom readings, but luckily I had already compensated for that. I let the ship's momentum swing us round for the final thirty-three degrees, hoping fervently that my calculations were correct and I hadn't screwed up.

In about an hour's time we'd know one way or another.

41  VEE

An hour and seventeen minutes had passed and we were still within the ion storm. If Aidan and Nathan had done their jobs properly it shouldn't take too much longer to emerge from it. I looked up past the transparent dome of the bridge. All around us, forks of energy like white lightning flashed in all directions through the red-purple mist that currently engulfed us. A quick glance around the bridge revealed that no one was looking at anyone else, never mind speaking. The tension had wrapped around each of us like a shroud. Our engine capacity was at zero and we were drifting. It was impossible to tell if we were drifting out of the storm or further into it but I had confidence in Nathan. His knowledge of this ship and its capabilities was matched only by mine and Aidan's.

But just in case, I needed to formulate a plan B. Devising a plan C wouldn't hurt either. The only trouble was, no plan in the universe could get us out of this storm if we were drifting the wrong way, and without our instruments working properly it was impossible to tell.

'Cathy, you should never have left our fate in the

hands of that girl,' Darren argued. 'Your judgement since Barros 5 has been lacking to say the least.'

'Darren, enough,' the commander snapped.

But he wasn't listening. 'Sam, you agree with me, don't you? Those two women are going to get us killed, if they haven't already.'

Ignoring Darren's misogyny, I turned to Sam, curious to hear his response.

Sam looked from Darren to me and back again. 'Darren, why don't you sit down and shut the hell up if you can't find something more constructive to do?'

Casting an explosive look at Sam, Darren at last did as he was told. I had no time for Darren and his histrionics at that moment. I had other priorities.

'Aidan, if we were to fire just one plasma burst behind us to give us some momentum, how much would that deplete our energy reserves?' I asked quietly.

'Our energy reserves would drop by eighty-two per cent,' said Aidan. 'Plus we have no way of knowing if we're heading in the right direction. A plasma burst could send us even deeper into the ion storm. Also such a burst could allow the Mazon to locate our position. They may not be able to fire at us if their energy is depleted, but they could try to ram us, which would have the same effect.'

'OK. And how long before the location buoy activates?'

'Another forty-three minutes.'

'The location buoy . . .' Catherine turned to look at me. Was that new-found admiration in her eyes? 'That's your backup plan in case we're not out of the storm by then.'

'Yeah. It'll start pinging in forty-three minutes to give us something to move towards on what little power we may have left. The only trouble is, the Mazon will hear it too and it'll give them something to aim at as well. Still, I seriously doubt we'll need it.' I smiled reassuringly at Nathan, who was watching me. He turned away.

My smile faded. Was he mad at me for having a backup plan? Did he think that meant I didn't trust him to get it right? Nothing could be further from the truth. I wanted to tell him that, but this was neither the time nor the place.

There was nothing else to do now but play the waiting game.

42 NATHAN

We had now been in the storm for over ninety minutes. That, and the sick feeling in the pit of my stomach, told me that somehow I must've messed up. Big time. Since we'd entered it, I'd checked and re-checked my calculations at least ten times. I still couldn't see where I'd gone wrong, but what other explanation was there?

'Cathy, this is all your fault. This is what happens when you leave our fate in the hands of a still-wet-behind-the-ears kid.' Darren was off again. 'Thanks to Vee and her idiotic ideas, we're now stuck here to wonder which of us will die first when the air runs out.'

'Darren, that's not helping,' said Mum.

I turned in my chair to glare at him. 'Why take it out on Vee? I was the one who was supposed to execute the manoeuvre that would get us out of here. If you're going to blame anyone, blame me.'

'You were only following that girl's orders,' Darren dismissed. 'I can't understand why you all defer to her like she has a clue. If we ever get out of this, I won't be taking any more orders from her, that's for damned sure.'

'How long, Aidan?' asked Vee from behind me.

'On my mark,' Aidan replied.

What were the two of them up to? Tense, silent moments ticked by. What was going on?

'Five . . . four . . . three . . . two . . . one . . . *mark*!' said Aidan.

We emerged from the ion storm to find ourselves alone, with not a Mazon ship in sight.

'What happened?' Darren asked.

'The engine capacity increased by two per cent a second before we entered the ion storm, giving us a speed boost,' said Vee. 'Therefore we travelled further into it than originally anticipated, which meant it took longer to get out of it. Nathan's calculations were spot on though.' She smiled at me. 'Otherwise we'd still be drifting in there.'

'Why didn't you say so?' Darren raged.

Vee turned to him, the smile dropping off her face. 'You didn't ask me. And we're not out of trouble yet, so it'd be lovely if you could shut up until we restart the engine and are on our way.'

Darren scowled at her, but didn't say another word. I knew him and that expression on his face.

This wasn't over.

'Aidan, do we have enough power to deactivate the buoy?'

Aidan nodded. 'Already done. It's dead.'

Vee walked over to Aidan and Mum and they had a quiet conversation about how to lose the other Mazon ships that were still on our trail. Scrambling our engine signature at random intervals was no longer going to be enough but I didn't pick up much more than that.

I turned to look at Anjuli, wondering what on Callisto she'd been thinking to get us into this mess in the first place. If I knew Vee – and I did – Anjuli was about to get her arse handed to her.

43

The engine was back online and we'd been underway for a good fifteen minutes now with nothing following us. We weren't exactly safe, but safer would do. I finally allowed myself to relax, but only for a moment. I had a task to perform that I wasn't looking forward to, but as someone Scottish once said: 'If it were done when 'tis done, then 'twere well it were done quickly.'

'Anjuli, I'd like a word.' I stood up and turned to face her. The look of dread on her face told me she had a good idea what was coming.

'Anjuli, I like you, I really do,' I began, already hating myself. 'But I don't want you on the bridge any more. Commander Linedecker will see to it that you're assigned other duties elsewhere.'

Anjuli's mouth dropped open, her eyes wide with dismay. I felt so mean, but what choice did I have?

'Vee, please. I'm so sorry. I was just trying to help,' she pleaded.

'I understand that you were acting for the best of reasons, Anjuli, but the fact remains that your negligence put all our lives at risk.' It felt like I was trying to find a way to ever so gently knock her out. 'Whether this ship has a crew of two or two hundred, it only functions if everyone works as part of a team. And if we don't work as a team, then we don't work at all. That means that if you have a risky idea, you pass it by me or Commander Linedecker first so we can properly assess it before you run with it. You do not sit there doing your own thing just so you can flash your initiative hoping to make yourself look good. That doesn't fly, not on this bridge.'

'I get it. And I promise it won't happen again . . .' Anjuli's eyes pleaded with me for a second chance and in any other circumstance I would've given it to her – in a heartbeat. But I just couldn't take that risk.

'I'm sorry, Anjuli, but no. You need to leave this bridge.'

Anjuli's eyes glistened with unshed tears. Head lowered, her steps slow, she did as I ordered and left the bridge. I felt like a complete and utter bitch, but that didn't make me wrong. I took a deep breath and then turned to Darren. 'And that goes for you too, Darren. I welcome positive debate and opinions but you try to undermine me at every opportunity. The Mazon were breathing down our necks and I had to waste time arguing with you when I should've been concentrating on getting us out of danger. I'm not going through that again. So you will leave this bridge and not come back. I'm sure the commander will find you another assignment until we get to Mendela Prime.'

Darren stood up, his face slowly turning a vivid shade of puce. 'I don't have to take that from a snot-nosed little brat like you. Just who the hell d'you think you're talking to?'

Stay calm, Vee. Stay calm.

'Darren, I'm in command according to Article TOTV-1957, Section C-4 of the Earth Vessel Code which states that a crew member may assume command of a vessel in the event of incapacity, illness or death. We had all three on board this ship, and I was the last one left standing so that's what I did, and it's logged on the ship's computer and in the first sub-space report I sent back to Earth. So I'm telling you to get the hell off my damned bridge and don't return unless and until instructed.'

I didn't mean to quote regulations at the guy but I admit it, he'd stomped on my last nerve and I wanted him gone. But I'd barely got the last word out when, the next thing I knew, Darren was barrelling towards me. A blur moved between us and then two bodies were flailing around on the floor. What the—? It took a moment or two for me to realize that the person who had intercepted Darren was Nathan. The next moment they were on their feet and Nathan stood before me, his back to me. I sidestepped to get a better view, unwilling to lose sight of Darren even for a second. If he was coming in for the kill, I'd rather see it coming.

'Darren! Enough!' the commander ordered.

But Darren only had eyes for me.

'Get out of the way, Nathan!' he roared. 'This isn't your fight.'

'Fuck you, Darren. You lay one finger on my wife and I'll break it off,' Nathan told him furiously.

239

The air whooshed out of my lungs as if I'd just been gut-punched. Everyone on the bridge froze in stunned silence. You could've heard a feather drop.

'Your *wife*?' Darren echoed.

'Yeah, that's right – my wife. So back the hell up.'

'Your *wife*?' Darren repeated. His level of shock hadn't dwindled any.

'We went through the official joining ceremony and it was logged and legal. Doctor Liana and Mike were our witnesses. So I warn you now, harm Vee and I will end you.'

I'd never seen Nathan like that before. His anger burned not hot but ice-cold. The expression on his face was chilling. He didn't shout or yell, but then he didn't have to. His softly spoken words were full of quiet menace.

'Nathan, it's OK,' I said quietly. I placed a hand on his shoulder, which was so tense it might have been carved from stone.

As I watched, Darren's fists slowly unclenched.

'Nathan, you got married and you didn't tell me?' said the commander – only she wasn't his commander in that moment but his mum.

'You would've tried to stop us,' said Nathan, his eyes still on Darren.

'Of course I would've tried to stop you,' she said, scandalized. 'For God's sake, you two have known each other for five minutes. What the hell were you thinking?'

'I fell for Vee the moment I saw her, and luckily for me she felt the same,' said Nathan. 'I'm not going to apologize for that.'

I sighed softly. So much for keeping it a secret until we were at least out of Mazon territory. Nathan gave me a quick, apologetic look before turning back to Darren. He didn't trust Darren any more than I did. Here was a man neither of us was in a hurry to turn our backs on.

'I believe Vee gave you a direct order,' said Nathan.

'Cathy, are you going to let them talk to me like that?' Darren asked.

The commander looked from me and Nathan to Darren. 'Vee has the perfect right to call you on your bullshit, Darren,' she told him. 'It's her ship and she's the captain and I have no intention of asking her to put up with something I myself wouldn't stand for. I suggest you leave the bridge and go and make yourself useful in the engine room until further notice.'

With a look of pure venom that literally took my breath away, Darren turned and strode out of the room.

'Vee, you're not to go anywhere near that man unless I'm with you,' Nathan said quietly. 'D'you understand?'

I fought to keep the smile from my face but failed spectacularly. Bless! He was worried about me. How lovely to have someone actually worry about me while I concerned myself with everyone else on board.

'Olivia, it's not funny,' Nathan said when he saw the expression on my face.

My smile faded. 'No, you're right. It's not.'

A come-at-me-from-the-front attack I could defend myself against. But Darren was the kind of guy who'd sneak up on me from behind and garrotte me faster than I could blink.

I needed to be on my guard. When it came to Darren, one careless mistake could be my last.

44

NATHAN

I think Vee was finally beginning to realize just how dangerous Darren really was. He was a big guy with a short fuse and a long memory. And now that Mum had shown her support for Vee rather than him, he'd be even more hostile. It was only now that Darren had left the bridge that I allowed myself to relax. All I wanted was to grab hold of Vee and pull her into a tight hug, but if I did that in front of everyone on the bridge, she wouldn't thank me for it. In fact, she was already probably going to kick my arse. Our joining was meant to be a secret.

'Is it true? Did you go through the joining ceremony with Nathan?' Aidan's voice was strangely monotone, his eyes staring a hole straight through Vee.

'Yes, Aidan, it is,' she replied. Her gaze was equally intense and watchful.

'It's not on the ship's computer,' said Aidan.

'It was recorded as part of my personal log,' Vee replied. 'That's why you didn't know.'

Why would Aidan be following his sister's activities on the ship's computer? That was all kinds of weird, though Vee spoke not only like it wasn't a big deal but like it was normal. There was something going on here, some undercurrent between Vee and her brother from which the rest of us were excluded. From the way Mum was looking at them, I knew I wasn't the only one who thought so. If I didn't know any better, I'd have said that Aidan wasn't just peeved but actually incensed. His expression was carefully neutral, but there was something in his artificially even tone, and in the way he held himself, that had me on my guard.

'You didn't want me to know?' Aidan asked his sister.

'It wasn't that,' Vee denied. 'It was a spur-of-the-moment thing.'

'Why did you do it?'

Vee looked around the bridge, then at me, embarrassed. 'Because I wanted to, Aidan.'

Aidan tilted his head slightly as he continued to scrutinize his sister. He hadn't looked at me once. 'Do you regret it?'

What the hell?

Vee cast me a swift, intimate smile. 'Not even a little bit.'

'You will,' Aidan replied, before turning back to his control panel.

Two words, but they managed to annoy the crap out of me. 'Now wait just a damned minute . . .' I took a step forward, only to find Vee's hand on my arm holding me back.

She shook her head. 'It's OK,' she said softly. 'He just needs to get used to the idea.'

'He'd better get used to it fast then,' I replied tersely, before heading back to my workstation next to him. And still he wouldn't look at me.

Fine! If he wanted to be childish, that was his business. I glanced at Mum. She was looking at me. I smiled, but she immediately turned away. I sighed inwardly. Yes, I got that she was hurt. That was probably Aidan's problem too. I had promised Vee that I'd respect her wishes to wait a while before telling anyone on board about us, but Darren had provoked me!

He'd actually launched himself at my wife. Well, screw that!

My wife.

I never got tired of thinking that. How many times since our joining ceremony had I looked at Vee and thought, *My wife!* Sometimes I wanted to pinch myself to make sure I wasn't back on Callisto having one of the most intense, vivid, amazing dreams of my life. I still had trouble believing that Vee had gone with her gut instinct and agreed to join with me after such a very short time together. But sometimes you just knew – at least, that's the way it'd been for me. Within an hour of our meeting I knew I wanted to spend more time with her. Within a week I knew I wanted to share the rest of my life with her – whether that was an hour, a day or a century. My time on Callisto had taught me that life was short and I should never let fear hold me back. The thing was, even though I knew that Vee was perfectly capable of taking care of herself, I still felt responsible for her. And more than that, for the first time in my life I felt truly vulnerable. That bit I wasn't so keen on.

If something bad were to happen to her . . .

I understood now why the Authority not only allowed us to have families back on Callisto but actively encouraged it. The love of others made you easier to control and manipulate. If I'd met Vee back on Callisto, I wondered if I'd have been so quick to ask her to join with me? Back on that moon, I'd always sworn

I'd never hook up with anyone on a long-term basis for precisely that reason. It was too hard to care about someone knowing that at any moment they could be taken away from you, or to watch them being brutalized in front of you and to be helpless to do anything about it. I decided long ago that I couldn't and wouldn't live or love that way. Love made you weak. Yet here we were, light years away from Callisto, and Vee was all I cared about.

If anything were to happen to her . . .

Or, worse still, maybe she'd wake up one morning and realize she'd made a colossal mistake.

No! I couldn't think that way. I *wouldn't*.

She'd chosen me. *Me.* I wasn't going to spend our time together dreading the day the best living dream of my life came to an end. I had to take each day as it came and make the most of our every moment together. And I wasn't going to let my mum or Vee's brother, or anyone else for that matter, get in my way or make me regret my actions for even a second.

We were on our way to Mendela Prime and we'd survive.

We had to, we just had to.

Our long shift was finally over but Mum had insisted on having a word with Vee as we both made our way off the bridge. The look on Mum's face said that I needn't linger so I had no choice but to leave them to it. Thirty minutes later Vee joined me in her quarters which were now our quarters as we could at last openly share. No more sneaking along the corridor hoping I wouldn't get caught entering her room.

'What did Mum want?' I asked without preamble.

'To talk about running more tactical procedures, to discuss the ship's manoeuvrability,' said Vee, adding drily, 'And to question me about the two of us.'

'Oh, did she?' I'd suspected as much. Furious, I was practically out of the door, ready to have it out with Mum, but Vee pulled me back.

'Nate, calm down. It's fine,' she soothed. 'Your mum and I had a full and frank and cleared the air, that's all.'

'What did she say?'

'Nate, it's OK. Really.' Vee let go of my arm and headed for the bed, sinking onto it. Her shoulders were slumped, her head bowed. As she unfastened and pulled off her boots, I noticed for the first time how truly weary she was. It'd been a long day for all of us.

I headed over to the utility dispenser and ordered a cup of minestrone, one of Vee's favourites. Sitting beside her, I tried to hand her the soup. She waved it away.

'Nate, I'm not hungry.'

'Take it. I doubt you've eaten today, so go ahead,' I insisted.

'But, Nate—'

'Drink.'

Vee regarded me, a trace of a smile lighting her dark brown eyes. 'You're going to sit there and nag me until I do, aren't you?'

'You know it!'

Vee's smile broadened. She took the cup from me and started to drink, chewing on tiny pieces of pasta and vegetables in each mouthful.

To Vee's amusement, I sat beside her and watched until the cup was empty.

'Happy now?' She handed the empty cup back to me.

'Happier,' I corrected as I stood up to dispose of it.

What I was about to say next would probably go down like a cupful of vomit but, damn it, I was still going to say it.

'Vee, you don't have to handle the running of this ship on your own any more. You've got a crew now and we're not all like Darren. You need to learn to delegate or you'll burn out.'

Vee sighed. 'I know. I've been telling myself the same thing. It's just . . .'

'What?' I sat back down beside her on the bed. 'Talk to me.'

'It's just that I've spent so long rattling around this ship by myself. I used to examine every panel, every instrument, walk the decks for hours just so I'd have something to do, something to wear me out so I'd be too tired to remember just how alone I was. Old habits die hard, I guess.'

'You had Aidan.'

Vee lowered her gaze. 'Yeah, I had Aidan, but he handled the isolation far better than I ever did.'

'You could step back, you know,' I suggested. 'You could let my mum worry about the day-to-day running of this ship. Not only is she used to it but she's good at it.'

'Give her the executive command code, you mean?' asked Vee.

We watched each other. The stillness that came over her reminded me of her brother.

'I'm just saying it's an option,' I replied.

248

'You don't rate me as any kind of captain then?'

'That's not what I said. I'm not even thinking that,' I denied vehemently.

'But you wouldn't object to me handing over this ship to your mum?' said Vee.

'Let's get this straight,' I said, annoyed. 'I want to ease some of the burden of being captain of this ship off your shoulders. I want to see you smile more often and be less tired and stressed. I admit it, I'm selfish. I want to see more of you – and not just from across the bridge. I want to spend more time alone with my wife.'

Vee smiled. I loved her smile. It started somewhere down in her toes, and by the time it reached her face it shone out like light from a new-born star. I'd keep that to myself though.

'If you want me to give the ship's executive code to your mum, I will,' said Vee, her gaze falling away from mine.

I placed a hand under her chin and raised her head to give her a brief kiss. 'Don't do it for me, do it for you, and only if and when you're one-hundred-per-cent sure. OK?'

'OK.' Vee looked around her room. 'I guess there's nothing to stop you moving in with me permanently now – if you want to.'

'Of course I want to. I'll move the rest of my stuff in tomorrow.' I checked the bed was pushed and bolted against the bulkhead. Now that I was about to relinquish my old sleeping quarters I needed to sort out our permanent sleeping arrangements. I said casually, 'D'you mind sleeping nearest the wall?'

'No problem.' Vee shrugged, but then she took a proper look at my face. 'What's wrong, Nate?'

Damn it! My poker face was obviously asleep.

'Nate?'

'I just don't want to sleep next to the bulkhead,' I stated.

Vee looked at me with concern, which made it worse. 'Why? Nate, what's going on?'

I hadn't fooled her for a second. That troubled me.

'Nate . . . ?'

Silence.

'Nate?'

'For God's sake, I don't like to feel boxed in. All right? Happy now?' I shouted.

Vee flinched as if I'd struck her.

Double damn it. Vee started to get to her feet. I reached out, taking her hand in mine and gently pulling her back down to sit next to me again.

'I'm sorry, Vee. I didn't mean to take your head off. I . . . I just can't sleep next to the wall. I can't stand to feel . . . trapped.'

She was probably wondering what kind of man she'd joined with. A man who couldn't even sleep next to a damned wall without having a panic attack. Yeah, Vee had got herself a real bargain.

'We complement each other perfectly then,' she said gently. 'Because if I'm next to the wall and you're beside me, holding me, I'll feel truly safe for the first time in three years.'

She smiled at me, not a hint of scorn or disappointment in her eyes, and I fell further. I took Vee's hand in both of mine and raised it to my lips, kissing her palm. Her smile broadened.

'My dad once told me that the point of life is to get it right,' she began. 'When I asked him what that meant, he told me that it was different for each person, but that I would know instinctively when I experienced it. I think . . . I think the point of my life is to be with you.'

Simple words that would've had me running kilometres in the opposite direction just a short while ago. Now I welcomed them. They bound me closer and tighter to Vee and I wasn't fighting it. But I couldn't help feeling that the higher we climbed, the further we had to fall.

'And if for some reason we don't work out?' I asked at last, giving voice to my secret fear.

Vee cupped my cheek with her hand. 'Then I'll see you next lifetime.'

'I don't want to wait another lifetime. Let's get it right in this one,' I replied.

'Agreed.'

We shared a smile.

'Now, are we going to talk all night or are you going to make love to me?' said Vee.

'You're tired.'

'I'll be fine if we take it slow,' she said softly.

'Ah! A challenge. I'm up for that,' I agreed.

'I thought you might be!' Vee grinned, and we moved together to kiss.

45

VEE

The following morning I woke before Nathan. He was facing me, fast asleep, and he looked so peaceful. I smiled to myself, still not quite used to waking up beside him. I raised my head to check the time on the panel above our heads and saw I had a message from Doctor Liana. Carefully I tried to climb over Nathan ninja-style so I wouldn't wake him up but my ninja skills had deserted me. I was only halfway over him when his hands shot out to pull me down on top of him.

'Sorry, Nate,' I laughed. 'The plan was to get out of the bed without disturbing you.'

Nathan turned his head to check the time. 'Why're you getting up so early?' he asked sleepily. 'We have another hour before our shift starts.'

'Doctor Liana has sent me a message.'

'How about you read it later?' Nathan closed his eyes, weaving his fingers into my hair to pull me closer for a kiss.

I used the opportunity to roll off him completely and sprang to my feet. 'How about I read it now in case it's important?'

'Can't the doctor and everyone else on this damned ship give you a moment's peace every once in a while?' Nathan grumbled.

And he didn't stop there! While he cursed up a blue streak, I read the doc's message. She wanted to meet me in the mess hall before my shift started. Once I'd read it, I turned to Nathan who was still cursing.

'D'you kiss your wife with that sewer mouth?' I teased.

'Every chance I get. In fact, I was trying to when she hopped out of bed to read the doctor's damned message,' said Nathan.

'You're too old to sulk, Nate,' I told him.

'Come back to bed then.'

'No can do. I'm going to meet the doctor,' I replied.

'I want you,' said Nathan, indicating a certain part of his anatomy.

'I see that, but both of you will have to wait till later,' I told him. And I headed for the bathroom.

Once showered and dressed I headed off to meet Doctor Liana. In the mess hall, it took a few moments to find her. She was seated by herself at a table furthest away from the exit. She had a spoon loaded with food in one hand and was reading something off a tablet in her other hand, her focus totally absorbed by what she was reading. Her food fell off her spoon and she didn't even notice. I walked over to her.

'Nihao, Doc. You wanted to see me?' I sat down on the chair opposite.

'Ah, Captain. Yes, I did want to see you.'

'Doc, please call me Vee,' I pleaded.

'Why does my calling you "Captain" make you so uncomfortable?' asked Doctor Liana with interest.

My face began to burn. I glanced around but there was no one near us. 'I guess . . . I guess I still sometimes feel like a little kid wearing her mum's shoes which are far too big for her,' I confessed to the doctor – something I'd never admit to anyone else, not even Nathan. I wanted him to see me as sophisticated and capable, a woman oozing poise and self-confidence, not some tongue-tied, awkward noob filled to overflowing with self-doubts who sometimes felt like she was faking it.

'You want my advice? Stuff your mother's shoes with whatever you have to until they fit you,' said the doc. 'And from what I can see, your mum's shoes don't need any kind of padding. Why don't you give yourself a break, Vee?'

Doctor Liana and I considered each other. She was right.

'Thanks, Doc,' I said quietly.

'Ah, to be young again.' She smiled. 'But then again, maybe not!'

Which made me laugh. 'Anyway, you wanted to see me?' I said.

'I'd like your permission to go through the ship's medical logs from three years ago and earlier,' said Doctor Liana.

My smile vanished. Immediately my heart began to hammer. 'Why?'

'I'd like to try and learn more about the virus which

killed your original crew. I want to analyse everything about it, but I can't at the moment because I'm locked out of the historical medical logs,' said the doc.

My frown deepened. 'My dad and those who worked with him studied the virus. They didn't find any way to stop it spreading,' I said carefully.

'I'm not disparaging your dad's efforts,' she rushed to explain. 'I'd just like to take a look for myself. With your permission, of course.'

For the life of me, I couldn't think of a single reason to turn down her request, much as I wanted to. 'OK, but just the medical logs from the previous crew, nothing else,' I stipulated.

'That's all I need,' said the doctor. 'Thank you.'

'I'll set it up once I'm back on the bridge,' I said.

This would require careful handling. No way was I prepared to give her full access to each and every medical log from three years ago. Some editing would be required.

As I stood up to depart, the doctor asked, 'Am I right in thinking you've had no communication with Earth since your parents and the rest of the crew died?'

I sat back down again, shaking my head. 'There's no two-way communication with Earth this far out. When it was just me and Aidan, I used to send monthly sub-space reports, but I stopped that after about six months.'

'Why?'

'The content never changed, so what was the point? "The crew are still dead. My brother and I are still alone.

I'm still desperate to make it back home and be with my grandparents. The end." See? Always the same report so it was a waste of time. I'll start sending them again when I'm within six months of Earth's solar system.'

'You miss your grandparents very much, don't you?'

'God, yes. They're all I have left of my life as it was on Earth. They're my way of feeling connected to my past. I can't wait for them to meet Nathan. It'll be like the past, present and future all coming together for the first time in my life,' I gushed. Only then could I hear myself. I winced. 'That probably made very little to no sense.'

'It made a great deal of sense.' The doc smiled. 'Isn't that what we all crave? Somewhere to be? Someone with whom we can share our life and love? A green part of the universe to call our own?'

Some note in the doctor's voice made me pause. Here was a woman who didn't need a dictionary to know what lonely meant.

'Do you have someone back on Callisto or Earth, Doc?' I asked.

'I . . . I have a son back on Earth,' she said after a long pause.

'Really? How old?'

'Twenty-three. He's training to be a doctor.'

I smiled. 'Ooh. Like mother, like son.'

'Something like that,' the doctor said, her smile fading. 'I'll be accompanying you once we leave Mendela Prime. I want to go back home to Earth.'

'So your son is your reason for wanting to go back?'

'Something like that. Now tell me, how is married life?'

'Exhausting!' The word slipped out before I could properly think about my answer. At the wry rise of Doctor Liana's eyebrows, I burned hot, a curtain of fire covering my face. I rushed to explain. 'I mean, I've been alone for so long, too long, and all of a sudden I'm sharing my quarters, my shower, my bed, my time, my life. Nate and I try to spend at least an hour a day just talking to each other about anything – the past, the future, our hopes and dreams. We've even managed to watch a few of my favourite twenty-first century films together. And I love it, I truly do, but it's exhausting.'

'Have you told Nathan that?'

I shook my head. 'I don't want him to think I don't like being with him, 'cause nothing could be further from the truth. It's just . . . people are tiring.'

'I hear that,' said the doctor. 'Does Nathan talk about Callisto?'

I sighed. 'Not really any more. Not often. And he totally hates doing it, so I try not to push too hard on that subject. He told me a fair amount when we first met but now it's a bit here, a little there. I'm hoping the longer we're together, the more he'll open up to me. In the meantime we discuss his time spent on his mum's last ship and what he remembers of Earth – that kind of stuff.'

Doctor Liana nodded. 'You're right not to push,' she said carefully. 'Let him tell you in his own time, when he's ready. I like Nathan, and believe me, he's been through a lot. I had to patch him up more than once back on Callisto. I don't know if he told you this but I was the one who operated on him to attach his prosthetic lower leg when he lost his own.'

'No, I didn't know that,' I replied.

'It's a testament to just how much you mean to him that he told you anything at all about his time on that god-awful moon,' said the doctor.

'Doc, will you tell me more about Nate's life on Callisto?' I asked eagerly.

'No. No way,' Doctor Liana replied at once. 'Doctor–patient confidentiality.'

'I'm not asking for medical secrets, just more of an insight into his life there.'

'You'll need to get that from your husband, not me,' said the doc, repeating her previous mantra. 'Doctor–patient confidentiality.'

'Worth a try,' I sighed. 'Have you got any advice for me, then?'

The doc gave me a speculative look. 'I will say this. Sometimes Nathan can get a bit lost inside his own head and it takes a while for him to find a way through his thoughts. My advice? Just be patient with him.'

That I could do 'Don't worry, Doc. I'll be Nathan's safety net. I won't let him fall.'

The doctor smiled. 'Tell *him* that, not me.'

I decided to hit the gym before my shift started. I needed to work off my early morning frustrations. As I headed there, it didn't take long to realize that the news of my union with Vee had spread throughout the ship. Most people I passed offered me their sincere congratulations. One or two greeted me with a smirk or a knowing look. Well, let them stare if they had nothing better to do. I wasn't the first one of us settlers to get married and I very much doubted I'd be the last.

Going to the gym, however, turned out to be a mistake. I wasn't the only one who'd decided to work out before the start of the next shift. The moment I entered the gym, the ribald comments started.

'Way to advance your career on board, Linedecker,' Harrison called out.

Arsehat! I ignored him.

All eyes were on me as I made my way over to the first piece of apparatus I wanted to use – the programmable pummel bag.

'Thinks he's too good to associate with us common drones now that he's joined with the captain of the ship,' said Maria.

Laughter followed Maria's comment, then more remarks were made, a number of them snide. The others were using various pieces of equipment around the gym but that didn't stop the commentary.

'I wouldn't have thought you two had much – if anything – in common,' said Ian. 'I mean, she's an educated Elite and you're just a drone. What d'you two find to talk about when you're alone? Or have you not reached the talking stage yet?'

I glared at Ian, practically fusing my lips together so I wouldn't bite his inquisitive head off.

'What happens when she heads back to Earth?' Ian continued. 'You gonna stay behind on Mendela Prime and wait for her?'

'Are you kidding?' scoffed Maria. 'Bet the moment the captain sets foot on Earth and is among her Elite friends and family, Nathan will be instantly forgotten.'

Stay calm, Nathan. Don't let them get to you.

'Nathan, you'd better make the most of her while you've got her,' Harrison called out. 'I'm still trying to figure out how on Callisto you managed to persuade her to join with you in the first place.'

'He hypnotized her?' Maria suggested.

'Dicknotized her, more like!' Harrison laughed. 'Picked up a few tips and tricks from me over the years, Nathan? You were wise to learn from the sensei.' He took a bow.

I punched the pummel bag harder.

'What's she like in the sack? Bet she's learned a few tricks of her own from all those films she watches.' Corbyn winked.

'I wouldn't mind a go or two with her myself,' said Harrison. 'Have you seen that gravity-defying rack?'

'Nat, any chance of you sharing?' asked Corbyn.

I spun round. 'The next arsehole who opens their mouth in my direction is gonna end up in the medical bay.'

One glance at my stony expression and they all found something else to do, which was fine with me. Ian walked over to me and said quietly, 'Sorry, son.' Then he headed back to his apparatus. His apology did nothing to cool my mood. It was just as well I was in the gym and could take out my temper on the pummel bag. I beat the stuffing out of it – literally. My last kick brought it down from the ceiling. Sweat dripping off me, I turned to find four pairs of eyes watching me. They all turned and carried on with their various training programmes the moment I looked their way. Placing the destroyed pummel bag in one corner of the gym, I made my way out of there and back to my quarters.

It was my own fault. I was the one who'd let the cat out of the bag about me and Vee. I should've kept my mouth shut, but any more comments like those I'd just heard and someone would be in a world of pain.

47  VEE

When Nathan walked onto the bridge, I instantly knew that something was wrong. He had a face like stormy weather. He sat down at his workstation at the navigation panel without even a smile at me. For a brief moment I thought he was mad at me for not staying in bed with him earlier but I dismissed that notion straight away. Nathan wasn't that petulant. So what had happened to wind him up?

After a quick glance around the bridge to make sure no one was paying attention, I walked over to Nathan.

'May I have a private word with you?' I asked quietly.

Nathan glared up at me from his chair, then stood up. I led the way off the bridge and into the corridor.

'Are you OK?' I asked the moment the doors had closed behind us.

'Yes, of course,' said Nathan, his tone clipped. 'Now if you don't mind, I have work to do. *Captain*.'

Whoa!

'Why did you say it like that?'

'How else should I say it? *Captain?*'

I stared at Nathan, cringing inwardly from the venom

he managed to inject into that one word. Was I mistaken? Was he mad at me for not making love with him earlier?

'Talk to me, Nate,' I said. 'What's wrong?'

'There's not a damned thing wrong. I've just been reminded that you're an Elite and I'm not, that's all. *Captain*.'

Dahell!

'That's enough, Nathan,' I said, my temper flaring. 'I don't know which idiot you've been speaking to or what they said to put you in such a foul mood, but sort yourself out. And that's your captain talking.'

Bugger this for a game of soldiers! If he didn't know by now that I couldn't give a rat's behind about his drone status then he never would. I went to stalk past him and head back to the bridge but his hand shot out and caught me by my upper arm before I'd gone more than a couple of steps. I swung round to glare at him.

'I'm sorry, Vee,' Nathan said quietly. 'I was being a dick.'

'Yes, you bloody well were,' I said furiously.

'Forgive me?' Nate quirked an eyebrow, a self-deprecating half-smile on his lips.

It took a moment or two for me to calm down sufficiently to return his smile, albeit grudgingly. 'You're forgiven.'

Nathan gave me a quick kiss before stating, 'Then I shall go back to work and be a dick no more. Captain.'

He gave me a grin before heading back to the bridge, leaving me shaking my head behind him.

When I entered our quarters after my shift, the first thing that hit me was the mess. Vee's jacket, trousers and boots decorated the floor, as did a couple of her many colourful sleeveless shirts. I pulled off my clothes and hung them up, ready to wear the following day. Wearing just my shorts, I made for the bed and sat on top of the cover, picking up my tablet from the side table.

Vee emerged from the bathroom wearing an orange sleeveless shirt and shorts, nothing else. My breath hitched in my throat.

'Oh, nihao, Nate, I didn't hear you come in.' Vee's face lit up, her smile warm and immediate.

'Vee, I adore you but you are a slob!'

Surprised, she looked around our room. 'Oh dear! Sorry. I did plan to sort out this mess before you got here,' she admitted. 'I'll fix it.'

I watched her move around the room. My tablet was still in my hands so maybe she thought I was reading, but nothing could be further from the truth. She had all my attention. Vee was oblivious to the way I was watching her, which was probably just as well. She bent to pick up her jacket off the floor and my body sprang to life. She hung the jacket over the back of the chair by the desk then moved to pick up the rest of her clothes.

'Vee, I need you.'

'You need me to do what?' Vee wasn't looking at me as she placed her boots and trousers in a storage cupboard.

A trace of a smile hovered over my lips but it didn't last long. Unwelcome, unbidden memories of my time on Callisto had begun to whisper in my mind. Some days I could suppress the whispers. Some days I couldn't. 'Vee, I need you.'

Puzzled, she turned to me. I put down my tablet. The look in my eyes wasn't the only thing that clarified what I meant.

'Oh,' Vee breathed. 'I see.'

She smiled, tilting her head in a move that reminded me of her brother, not that I wanted to think of him at all in that moment.

She slunk towards me, still wearing that smile of hers that made my heart beat faster. When she reached me, she pushed me back against the bed and climbed on top of me. My heart started thumping, but not in a good way. As she bent to kiss me, I flipped her onto her back, my body immediately covering hers, my mouth pressed against hers. We kissed until we both had to break apart to gasp for breath.

'Wow! What brought that on?' asked Vee.

'That top you're wearing. It does it to me every time.'

'Then I'll never take it off,' she said.

'Wanna bet?' I replied.

Vee tried to sit up but I wouldn't let her. She placed her hands against my chest and pushed, trying to get me to lie back down, but I wouldn't.

'Can't I be on top for a change?' she laughed.

I froze. Inside I began to shut down. Slowly I shook my head.

Vee's smile disappeared. 'Oh, Nathan, I'm sorry. I wasn't thinking.' She looked up at me, stricken, as if she was the one who'd done something wrong.

'Vee, it's not you. It's just . . .'

She placed a finger over my lips. 'Nate, I understand. Really I do. And don't you dare apologize.'

I sat up, my head in my hands as I sat still, trying not to give in to the destructive storm swirling inside me. My head was messed up. I had to get out of here. I couldn't let Vee see me like this.

'I need to leave,' I muttered.

Where the hell did I put my trousers? I started to stand up but Vee curled her arms around me from behind. She kissed my shoulder, then the back of my neck, before resting her forehead against my head.

'Nathan, thank you,' she whispered.

Her words made me wince. I swung round to face her, stunned. 'What're you thanking me for?'

'For trusting me with your memories. For letting me share some of your past,' said Vee.

'For showing you how broken I am?' I said bitterly.

Vee moved round to cup my face with her hands, looking into my eyes. Her lips brushed against mine. 'When you're feeling broken, I will hold you in my arms, all the pieces of you, until you're whole again,' she said softly.

'You reckon you can fix me?'

'I can be there for you while you try to heal,' Vee amended. 'I'm here, Nate. And I'm not going anywhere.'

I buried my face in her neck and she held me tight until I stopped shaking.

Vee lay on her side, her head on my shoulder, her left leg over mine, her left hand gently stroking my chest. For my part, my arm beneath her shoulders pulled her closer, stroking slowly up and down her arm. Her skin was so smooth, so soft. Just one of the many reasons I couldn't stop touching her. These were usually the moments I loved the most, when Vee and I lay in an easy silence where not a word needed to be spoken. But I was troubled. We were close to leaving Mazon territory for good. And once we made it to our destination, what then? The comments made to me in the gym had been playing on my mind for a while now – one comment in particular.

'Vee, what happens when we get to Mendela Prime?'

Vee raised her head to look at me. 'What d'you mean?'

'Going back to Earth isn't an option for me. Escaping from Callisto made me a fugitive. I can't risk being recaptured by the Authority. I won't go back to Callisto. I'd rather die.'

Vee and I regarded each other as long moments passed. 'I understand,' she said at last. 'It's just that Doctor Liana wants to go back to Earth.'

That didn't surprise me. Doctor Liana had hated Callisto almost as much as I had. She'd kept herself apart from most of us drones on that moon, doing her job, no more, no less. If, unlike most of us, she had friends and family back on Earth who hadn't turned their backs on her, why wouldn't she want to return to her old life?

'Nate, I feel obligated to take her there,' Vee said unhappily. 'Her and anyone else who wants to go back. I said I would.'

'I know.'

She sighed. 'But it's taken my whole life to find you,' she said. 'I can't imagine being without you now – not even for a single day.'

'So what do we do?' I asked.

'Maybe we could travel back together until we reach the outer rim of Earth's star system,' Vee suggested. 'I could take Doctor Liana and any others who decide to go back to one of Earth's space stations before turning round to pick you up, after which we could head back to Mendela Prime.'

I sighed. 'Even the outer rim of Earth's solar system would be a dangerous place for me. Outer-rim spaceports are filled with bandits and bounty hunters who'd trade their own mothers to the Authority for a few extra credits. And besides, d'you really think you can just stroll into Earth's system and the Authority would allow you to stroll out again?

'No, they wouldn't,' Vee agreed at last. 'I guess I have trouble thinking straight where you're concerned.' She lowered her head to rest it against my shoulder again. 'So what do we do?'

Neither of us had the answer.

49  VEE

I sat on Aidan's bed waiting for him to speak. He was the one who'd asked me to come and see him, but he sat on his chair staring at me like I was something peculiar that had just started sprouting out of his floor.

'Today, Aidan!' I prompted. 'I do have other things to do besides sit here and watch you gawp at me.'

'Vee, how much do you trust Anjuli?'

'Huh? What d'you mean?'

Aidan shrugged. 'How much do you trust her? I mean, do you think what she says is . . . reliable?'

'I don't know. I was sorry to lose her from the bridge, I know that,' I replied. 'She was keen and a fast learner, just not very good at thinking things through.'

'I'm not talking about her competency,' said Aidan. 'I'm asking if you think she's trustworthy.'

'I suppose so. I don't really know her well though.'

'Not the way you know Nathan,' said Aidan coldly.

I sighed. Well, that didn't take long. 'If the sole point of this conversation is to wind me up, then you've failed. I'm outta here.' I stood up. If Aidan had asked me to come to his quarters merely to have a go at me in private, then good luck to him, I had better things to do.

'No, don't leave.' Aidan grabbed my arm. 'I'm sorry, OK. It's just that Erica's told me some things . . .'

'Erica? What kind of things?' I frowned.

Aidan gave me a studied look. 'You know what? Forget I said anything. And besides, I promised Erica I wouldn't tell anyone what she told me. It's just that you're my sister and it's my job to look out for you.'

I could see Aidan was conflicted but now I was intrigued. 'Did Erica say something negative about me?'

Aidan frowned. 'Of course not. D'you think I'd let her badmouth you to my face?'

'So she was badmouthing somebody then?'

'Vee, let it drop. I really shouldn't have said anything. Besides, what you and Nathan get up to is none of my business. It's just . . . I don't want to see you get hurt.'

'Why would I get hurt? And what's Nathan got to do with it? I thought we were talking about Erica – and Anjuli.'

My brother shook his head, his gaze falling away from mine.

'Aidan! What did Erica say?' I said, exasperated.

'Look, I'm sure it's all over now.'

'What's all over now?'

'Nathan and Anjuli.'

Stunned, I stared at Aidan. 'What?'

Aidan shrugged. 'Like I said, forget I said anything.'

'Something's going on between Nathan and Anjuli? That's bollocks. They're just friends.'

'If you say so,' said Aidan.

Once more with feeling. 'That's not worthy of you, Aidan, to take a piece of absurd gossip and treat it as fact,' I said, unimpressed.

'I know you've been too busy to notice but Erica and I have been together a lot,' said Aidan. 'She's been useful in helping me get to know the refugees. And after what she's told me about Nathan I don't trust him, that's all.'

'I'm not going to stay here and listen to you slam the guy I . . . I'm with,' I said icily. 'And if Nathan is so terrible, why didn't you say something before?'

'Did I know you were going to sneak off and join with him?' Aidan's sudden burst of anger caught me by surprise. 'I'm your brother and you didn't even tell me what you were planning. After everything we've been through over the last three years, you didn't even think to let me know, never mind include me in your plans.'

'I didn't sneak off. And I told you, it was a spur-of-the-moment thing.'

Damn! Aidan was actually hurt. I really didn't think he'd be that bothered.

'I'm your brother,' said Aidan.

We regarded each other.

'You're right. I'm sorry,' I said at last. 'If I ever go through another joining ceremony, I'll make sure you're there.'

My attempt at a joke fell totally flat. Aidan wore an expression I'd never seen before.

'I'm really sorry, Aidan,' I said again. 'Forgive me?'

Aidan nodded, though his gaze slid away from mine.

'Vee, be careful. OK?'

'Careful about what?'

'Just be careful.'

NATHAN

The following morning, after a quick shower in my quarters, I was ready to start my shift. After a quick stop at the science lab on the same floor I made my way along the corridor to the bridge. Footsteps came running up behind me.

'Nat! Nathan, wait.'

I turned to see Anjuli running towards me. My heart sank. I could guess what was coming. I raised a hand to ward her off.

'Listen, if you've come to bitch about Vee, I'm not interested. I know she bounced you off the bridge and I'm sorry about that, but my mum would've done the same if she'd been in charge and you know it.'

'Nat, I realize I messed up,' said Anjuli. 'But I need to get back on the bridge. That's where I belong, not in the poxy engine room.'

Anjuli just didn't get it. Her stunt had almost cost the lives of everyone on board but all she could see was her punishment, not the reason for it. I really didn't need this. Not now.

'What exactly d'you expect me to do about it?'

'Is it true that you and Vee are officially joined?' asked Anjuli hopefully.

'Yes, but—'

'Great!' Anjuli's eyes lit up. 'Make her take me back on the bridge.'

My eyebrows shot up. 'Anjuli, have you been drinking Prop? I can't *make* Vee do anything.'

'You're her husband, aren't you?'

'What has that got to do with the price of Garen meat on Callisto?' I frowned.

'She'll listen to you if you ask her to give me back my old job. If you managed to persuade her to join with you so soon after the two of you met, then you can get her to do anything. Tell her I know what I did was wrong and that it will never happen again. *Please.*'

'OK, Anjuli, let's get something straight right now,' I said, annoyed. 'I asked Vee to trust her instincts where she and I were concerned and luckily for me she did. That's completely different to interfering with her professional decisions and judgement. Vee runs this ship, not me. And I'm not going to start telling her what she should do and how she should do it. I'd like our joining to last.' Anjuli had to be seriously demented if she thought I'd jeopardize my relationship with Vee for her, or anyone else for that matter.

'Just get her to give me a second chance. Tell her I've learned my lesson. That's all I ask. Please, Nat, just try. You owe me . . .'

And there it was.

Silence stretched between us.

'I'm sorry to play that card, but you do owe me and I'm desperate,' pleaded Anjuli.

Yes, I did owe her. When I first arrived on Callisto, I'd had less than a clue. Anjuli had befriended me, shown me the ropes and taught me which guards and supervisors to avoid like primate flu and which ones were still relatively human. And she'd actually saved my life once. I would've sunk without trace if it hadn't been for her and we both knew it.

'OK,' I sighed. 'I'll have a word but I can't guarantee anything.'

'Thanks, Nat!' Anjuli leaped at me, her arms around my neck. I had to put my arms around her or she would've landed in a heap at my feet. She kissed me before placing her feet back on the floor. 'I knew you wouldn't let me down.'

'You did hear the part about my not being able to guarantee anything, right?' I asked.

'Yeah, yeah! This will make us even.' Anjuli beamed at me.

She spun round and headed back towards the lift and she was almost skipping. As far as Anjuli was concerned, it was a done deal. I shook my head. This really was one issue I wanted to stay the hell out of. I turned to make my way to the bridge.

Vee was standing outside the closed bridge doors, watching me intently.

'Hello, Nate,' she said as I approached her.

Vee was the only one who called me Nate. Most of my friends called me Nat. Mum called me Nathan. I liked the way my name sounded when Vee said it, but then I liked everything about her. A quick glance around to make sure we were alone, then I pulled her to me for a quick kiss. Vee turned her head and my lips landed on her cheek. She pulled out of my grasp.

What on Callisto . . . ?

'What's wrong?' I frowned.

Vee's fixed expression slowly relaxed into a smile. 'Nothing's wrong. I just don't want any of the crew to see us messing around when we should be working.'

'Well, I did check first and the coast is clear. Plus it's not messing around to kiss my wife, but fair enough.' I smiled.

'It's just that it's hard enough to get your colleagues to take me seriously as captain because of my age,' Vee said. 'I don't want them to think less of me than they already do.'

'Olivia, you've saved our lives twice now. If, after that, someone wants to think less of you because of a kiss, then you should tell them to kiss your—'

'Er . . . OK,' Vee interrupted. 'D'you wanna calm down now?'

'Or better yet, send them to me. I'll put them straight,' I said, still reluctant to climb down from my high horse.

Vee smiled and placed her hand on my cheek, stroking my face. 'My hero!' Her hand dropped to her side. 'Was that Anjuli I saw heading off down the corridor?'

'Yeah. She was telling me how upset she is that she let you down,' I replied.

'She didn't seem particularly upset to me,' Vee said.

'No, she really is. She was asking me how she could prove to you that it'll never happen again.'

'And what did you tell her?'

'That the running of this ship is down to you, not me,' I said.

'And that's what made her so happy as she walked away?'

Oh hell! Vee must've seen Anjuli flinging herself at me.

'Well, don't tell her I told you but she asked me to speak to you on her behalf. She wants me to try and get you to change your mind about having her on the bridge,' I admitted.

'And you said?'

'I told her I would try.' I shrugged. 'That's why she went away happy.'

'I see,' said Vee after a moment's pause. 'And are you going to?'

'Going to what?'

'Try and persuade me to change my mind?'

'It might be an interesting test of my persuasive powers, to have you know what I'm doing but still manage to do it anyway.' I smiled.

'You've already proven just how persuasive you can be,' said Vee, a strange note to her voice.

'Vee, are you OK?' I asked, concerned. 'You sound a little . . . off.'

'I've just got a headache,' she replied. 'I'm off to the medi bay to see if Doctor Liana can sort it for me.'

'Want some company?'

'No, I'll be all right. Besides, your shift is about to start and mine has just ended. See you later.'

Vee headed off down the corridor, leaving me frowning behind her. If I didn't know better, I would've thought she was in a hurry to get away from me.

51  VEE

Vee, don't be a moron, I told myself. *Nathan and Anjuli are good friends, nothing less and certainly nothing more.*

I mean, Nathan had known Anjuli far longer than he'd known me, and living on Callisto probably meant that you had to keep your friends close if you wanted to survive. I needed to get my act together. I couldn't get in a flap every time Nathan spoke to or hugged or kissed another girl. He was with me. When our shifts were over, he came home to me. What more did I want or need? I headed into the medi bay.

'Nihao, Doc.'

'Hello, Vee, or should I say "O Captain! My Captain!" and bow low?'

'You love teasing me about that word, don't you?' I groaned. 'And weren't those words from a poem used in the late-twentieth-century film *Dead Poets Society* starring Robin Williams?'

Doctor Liana stared at me. I'd done it again: quoted a film that no one else but me had a clue about.

'Never mind,' I dismissed, my face growing hot.

'Yes, they were used in that film.' The doctor grinned.

'And the original poem was written by Earth American poet Walt Whitman.'

'About the death of American president Abraham Lincoln,' I supplied.

The doctor and I exchanged a smile of genuine pleasure.

'It is so nice to finally meet someone who's into more than just a ship's nuts, bolts and weaponry,' she said.

'Well, I'm into that too,' I admitted. 'And to answer your original question, "Vee" will do just fine and we can discuss the depth of your bow some other time.'

I looked around the medical bay. The doc had moved the medi-pods around and reconfigured the data panels above each of the beds. It was now far more efficient and ergonomic.

'You've done a great job in here,' I said, impressed.

'Thank you. I take it you don't mind me making changes?'

Surprised at the question, I shook my head. 'Why on Earth would I mind? You're in charge of this medi bay, not me.'

'I wasn't sure if you'd see it that way,' said the doctor.

'How else would I see it?' I frowned.

Doctor Liana nodded, satisfied that I wasn't going to try and encroach on her domain. 'So what can I do for you?'

'I just came to get something for this pounding headache. I've had it all day and I can't seem to be able to shift it.'

'Take a seat on the bed while I scan you,' said Doctor Liana.

'Doc,' I sighed. 'I really don't need a full medical check-up for a headache.'

'Let me be the judge of that,' she said. 'Besides, all commanding officers are required to have a full medical check-up at least once every six months. Authority regulations.'

'Bugger the Authority,' I muttered.

'And so say all of us.' Doctor Liana smiled. 'Actually, I've issued a schedule for everyone on board to have a full medical check. For some of them, it'll be the first time they've had a proper medical assessment. Back on Callisto I was given just enough equipment and medicine to make sure the drones could work at maximum efficiency, but that was it.'

I sighed and sat down on the nearest bed. 'The more I hear from you and others about life on Callisto, the more I realize just how much the rest of us have been kept in the dark by the Authority. I know I've been away from Earth for a while but my ignorance of what's going on back in my own solar system embarrasses me.'

Doctor Liana laid a hand on my shoulder. 'I felt exactly the same way when I was exiled to Callisto. I had no clue about the lives of drones and I must admit I didn't really want one either.'

'You were exiled to Callisto? Why? I thought you were just one of the Authority's doctors assigned to that moon.'

The doctor's gaze fell away from mine as she picked up the MMS or mobile medical scanner. 'I was one of three doctors on the entire moon serving a drone population of over a million, but I was exiled there. No one in their right mind would volunteer to work in such a place.'

I noticed she hadn't answered my question about why she'd been exiled to Callisto but I decided not to pry further. It really wasn't any of my business, and if she didn't want to talk about it then I had to respect her wishes.

'Could I have something for my headache and come back some other time for the check-up?' I asked.

'Nope. Something tells me that if I let you leave now, I won't see you again unless I drag you in here,' said the doctor.

And she was right! I resigned myself to a full-body scan, blood tests, the works. I remembered how my dad had been the same. If I came into the medical bay with a cut or a graze, he'd perform a full battery of tests. It had to be a really annoying doctor thing. I looked at Liana. The sadness in her blue eyes that I'd noticed the first time I saw her hadn't gone away. If anything it was more pronounced.

As she passed her MMS slowly down then up my body, I asked, 'Doc, where were you born?'

'On Earth, the same as you,' she said.

'Is that where you met your husband?'

'How did you know I was married?'

I shrugged. 'When Nate and I came to ask you to be a witness at our joining ceremony, you kept telling us that being joined was a serious business and not a bed of roses and that we'd have to work at it and whatnot, and you spoke like you knew what you were talking about. I know you never mentioned a husband when you were talking about your son, but I just assumed.'

'Well, you're right. I was joined actually.'

'Where did you meet your husband?'

'He was the chief engineer of the first Earth vessel I worked on. I took one look at him and I knew I'd found my soulmate.' Doctor Liana was staring somewhere past my shoulder into her memories, a slight smile playing on her lips. 'He was an amazing man, fiercely loyal, loving and the best damned engineer the Authority ever had, mostly self-taught. That's how good he was.' She glanced at me and gave a rueful smile. 'But that was a long time ago.' She viewed my readings on her mobile scanner.

'So what's the verdict?' I asked. 'Will I live?'

'Would Nathan let you do otherwise?' said the doc drily. 'That guy dotes on you.'

'The feeling is mutual.' I smiled. 'In fact, sometimes I . . .'

'Yes?' the doctor prompted.

'I don't know what I'd do if he ever stopped loving me,' I admitted.

'He won't.'

I shrugged, feigning nonchalance. *Move on, Vee!* 'I know I've said it before, but thanks again for agreeing to be a witness at our joining ceremony. Nate and I really appreciated it.'

'You're welcome, and you don't have to keep thanking me,' Doctor Liana replied. 'Mind you, Catherine wasn't too thrilled with me. She verbally kicked my derrière all around this room.'

'Oh dear. I'm sorry.'

'Don't be. It does her good once in a while to realize she can't control everything in her life, including her son. In fact, especially her son,' said the doctor.

'So you're not one of those who thinks I should hand over this ship to her?'

Doctor Liana gave me a horrified look. 'Don't you know how to run this vessel?'

'Of course I do,' I replied with indignation.

'And you're the legitimate commander?'

'Yes I am.'

'Then I don't understand your question,' said the doctor.

She made it sound so simple. Maybe I was worrying about, if not nothing, then too much. So what if some of the colonists still viewed me with suspicion? I'd just have to show them with my actions that my age had nothing to do with my experience and competence. And if after all that they still couldn't accept me? Well, that was their problem. I refused to make it mine.

And then there was Nathan.

I could wish he hadn't blurted it out like that about the two of us but maybe it was for the best. Maybe it would convince some of the doubters that I really was on their side and wouldn't betray them to the Authority. Or maybe it wouldn't make any difference.

Or just maybe I shouldn't care so much about the opinions of others.

'So, Olivia, what d'you think of married life?'

'So far so good.' I shrugged.

The doc gave me a studied look. 'Is everything OK with you two?'

I nodded. 'Yeah. Nothing I can't handle.'

'Hmm. And how's your sex life?'

'Doc!'

'What? I'm your doctor as well as your friend, remember. Any problems in that area?'

Was I really having this conversation?

'None whatsoever, thank you.' I couldn't help my smile as I revisited a memory or two.

'Ooh, that smile on your face is verging on obscene,' said the doctor.

Face on fire, my smile vanished, making the doctor laugh.

'I'm just teasing, Vee. Not about your smile – that *was* obscene – but it's lovely to see a young couple who aren't afraid of life for a change. I know I questioned you both long and hard before agreeing to be a witness at your joining ceremony and insisted you sort out a method of contraception, but I hope you understand, I had to make sure that you and Nathan fully understood what you were letting yourselves in for.'

'It may have been spur of the moment, but it wasn't done on a whim or for frivolous reasons,' I said. 'I really do . . . care about him.'

'The way I care about all my patients?' teased Doctor Liana.

'Not quite,' I said drily.

'That's what I thought.'

My face was beginning to burn again. Why did I find that one word so hard to say? I didn't find it hard to feel, that was for sure. The way I had fallen for Nathan so hard and so fast still amazed me. I'd jump in the way of a Mazon blast for him without even thinking about it, and that was a fact.

'Nate and me, we just . . . fit. We understand each other,' I tried to explain.

'I gathered that from the moment I saw the two of you together,' said Doctor Liana. 'You two reminded me of me and my husband. That's why I finally agreed to act as a witness.'

'Did you tell the commander that?'

The doctor raised an eyebrow. 'Are you kidding? Besides, she did most of the talking, not me. I just let her get on with it. I find that's the best thing to do when Catherine goes off on one.'

I smothered a laugh. I did like Doctor Liana. She was a no-nonsense, straight-talking woman. I knew where I stood with her.

'Doctor, what . . . what d'you think of Anjuli?' I couldn't help asking.

'Anjuli? She has interesting clavicles.'

I wasn't really looking for information about her collar bones. 'Is she . . . ?'

The doctor looked at me expectantly, waiting for me to continue.

'Never mind,' I sighed.

She gave me a curious look but didn't press. 'OK. Your scan is complete. You're as fit as a flea.'

'I could've told you that,' I replied. 'Any chance of something for my headache now?'

Doctor Liana brought over a small plastic vial and snapped it in half beneath my nose. 'Inhale,' she instructed.

I leaned over it and did as she asked, inhaling deeply. A smell of something intensely minty hit my nostrils and caught in the back of my throat, making me cough. Moments later, my headache was considerably less painful.

'Great. Thanks,' I said, jumping off the bed. 'Why didn't the painkiller I took earlier work then?'

'You had a tension headache,' said the doctor. 'Are you feeling particularly stressed at the moment?'

'No more than usual,' I lied. 'And usually I can handle a headache with a standard painkiller patch. It didn't seem to work this time though. Thanks, Doc.'

'Any time. And, Vee?'

'Yes?'

'Take it easy. If something is worrying you, don't bottle it up. That's probably why the painkiller you took didn't work. OK?'

'Thanks for the chat, Doc.' I headed for the door.

'Vee, remember, you can tell me anything. I'm here for you.' The doctor smiled. 'Doctor–patient confidentiality is a sacred thing! I told Catherine that when she was ranting at me for not letting her know about you and Nathan, and I'm telling you the same thing.'

'Doc, can I ask you something?'

'I don't know. Can you?'

It took a moment to realize what she meant. She was questioning my grammar! My dad used to do the same thing. It was annoying then too.

'*May* I ask you something?' I amended ruefully.

Doctor Liana grinned at me. 'You're the only one I've ever met since leaving Earth who understood what I meant when I asked that. Bravo! What's your question?'

'You said you wanted to go back to Earth, but won't the Authority just send you back to Callisto?'

'No. I've served my time,' said Doctor Liana sombrely. 'All I want to do now is go home.'

It'd been a bastard of a day. My shift on the bridge with Mum in charge was exhausting. She had me checking this and analysing that all over the ship. My arse hadn't been stationary in any one place for longer than fifteen minutes at a time. And to top all that, Anjuli had cornered me at least five times to ask, 'Have you spoken to her? Am I reinstated yet?'

Until finally I snapped. 'Anjuli, for God's sake, give me a chance. Vee and I aren't even sharing the same shift.'

'When will you get to speak to her then?' Anjuli frowned.

Which was the final straw. 'Anjuli, stop pushing.' I spoke very quietly, at this point somewhere beyond severely pissed off. Anjuli became very still as she regarded me.

'Here I am, backing off very slowly,' she said. Never taking her eyes off me, she took slow, exaggeratedly careful backward steps away from me. OK, I admit it – that made me laugh. I'll say one thing for her, she could always tell when she'd pushed me too far and it was time to retreat. Literally.

And the worst thing of all about my day was I'd only seen Vee once during my entire shift. She was coming out of our quarters when I was walking along the corridor towards the bridge after completing another of Mum's assignments. Instead of waiting for me, she'd frowned and entered the bridge ahead of me. By the time I got there, Vee was having a quiet word with her brother. I went to my station next to him, smiling at Vee in the hope that she'd come and speak to me once she'd finished her chat with Aidan. Nothing doing. Once her conversation with her brother had finished, Vee headed straight for the exit without a backward glance.

I mean, what the actual hell?

By the time my shift was over I was mentally and physically wrecked. I paused outside our quarters, hesitating before entering. If I didn't know better, I'd've said Vee was giving me the cold shoulder. If that was the case, then I had no idea why. Surely not because I'd agreed to help Anjuli?

Placing my hand against the palmlock, I headed inside – only to stop abruptly at the sight before me. Our quarters glowed with the flickering light of at least thirty different artificial candles scattered around the room. The bed was strewn with white and red flower petals. There was a strange whiff in the air, not unpleasant but definitely noticeable. And in the centre of the room stood Vee, wearing a burgundy cloak which completely covered her body from neck to toe.

What was going on?

Vee smiled at the confused expression on my face.

'What's all this?' I asked suspiciously.

'I thought I'd do something special for you,' she replied.

'What's that smell?'

'Cinnamon spice. It makes all things nice. Do you like it?'

Not really, no.

289

'So what d'you think?' asked Vee.

I took another look around. 'It's very . . . colourful.' I frowned. 'You know I'm a guy, right?'

'Oh. You don't like it?' Vee's smile faded.

'No, I didn't say that.' I spoke hastily. 'It's great, really.'

Vee burst out laughing. 'I'm just pulling your leg, Nate. All this is for me, not you.'

Thank Christ for that!

'Your sense of humour will be the death of me,' I said ruefully.

'*This* is for you.' Vee winked. And she opened the cloak, letting it slowly slide down her arms and onto the floor. The breath left my lungs in an audible hiss.

God, but she was lovely – both inside and out. I couldn't imagine ever growing tired of her. The more I saw her, spoke to her, spent time with her, the harder it was to imagine my life without her in it.

Damn! I really, *really* had it bad.

Vee sat on the bed and held out her arms towards me. I didn't need a written invitation. Stripping off in about five seconds flat, I sat down beside her. After a prolonged kiss, we lay down. I didn't reach for her. She didn't reach for me. We just lay on our sides, watching each other.

'You OK?' I asked softly.

She nodded. 'You?'

'Yeah.' But I wasn't. Not entirely. 'Vee, did I do something to upset you?'

Vee cupped my cheek with her hand, which I immediately

kissed. 'No, you didn't. This is my way of making it up to you. Sorry if I made you worry. I was just feeling a bit . . . fragile today.'

'Why fragile? Aren't you feeling well?'

'No, it's not that . . . To be honest, my brother said something which upset me and I was stupid enough to let it get to me,' said Vee.

'What did he say?'

'It doesn't matter.'

'Tell me what he said.'

'Nate, trust me. It really doesn't matter.'

But it did.

'It was something about the two of us, wasn't it?' I realized. 'I'm gonna have a word with him.'

'Nate, no. It was my fault for listening to him and for letting his words crash around in my head causing havoc. I'll sort it, OK? Please?' Vee pleaded.

Inside I was seething. What had he said? Obviously something negative about me.

'This time I'll let it slide, but if he says anything else about us that upsets you, I want you to tell me,' I said. 'Promise?'

Vee smiled and kissed me. And then the idea of getting her to promise went right out of my head.

The following morning I awoke right where I wanted to be, in bed with my arm round Vee's waist as we spooned. The gentle bleep of the overhead alarm was already getting on my nerves.

'Alarm off,' I said softly, not wanting to startle my wife.

291

I *still* loved the way that sounded. *My wife.* The alarm immediately ceased. I kissed Vee's nape, then rose slightly to kiss her cheek.

'Time to get up. Our watch starts in thirty.'

Vee opened her eyes and smiled.

'I love you, Vee,' I couldn't help saying.

Her smile broadened. 'I know.'

I had yet to hear Vee say those words even though I knew she did love me. She showed it every time she looked at me or touched me. Yet there was something inside me that longed to hear the words. Maybe one day . . .

She yawned, then sat up. 'At least we're sharing the same watch today,' she said. 'Fancy dinner in an astro-lab star chart later?'

'Sounds good,' I agreed. 'And speaking of things we can do together, let's go and shower.'

'The shower is barely big enough for one.' Vee frowned.

'I know.' I winked.

Vee laughed. 'Our watch starts in thirty minutes, Romeo.'

'Romeo?'

'From *Romeo and Juliet*? The film with Leonardo DiCaprio?'

'Who?'

'Never mind. Anyway, I think it would be . . . faster to shower separately.'

'I suggested we shower together so neither of us is late to the bridge. I don't know what's going on in your dirty mind.'

'Yeah, right,' Vee scoffed.

I got out of bed and removed the platinum chain from round

my neck, placing it carefully on the table beside our bed. At Vee's quizzical look, I explained, 'I haven't had a chance to fix the clasp yet and I don't want to risk it disappearing down the shower's extraction hole.'

'It's not that fragile. Besides, you sleep in it.'

'That's different. If it comes undone in bed, at least I know where I'll find it. If it comes loose in the shower, it'll end up floating out in space. It's only the water that gets recycled.'

'Fix it then. Or were you exaggerating when you said you were good with your hands?' said Vee.

'Forgotten already? Let me remind you then.'

Sitting both of us back down, I ran my hands over Vee's waist, holding her to me. Mistake! What I'd intended as a teasing reminder morphed into something else. Burying my face in her neck and nibbling on her, I whispered, 'Want to feel my hands in action?'

Vee laughed. 'No need. I believe you.'

I drew back to look into her brown eyes. 'I want to provide you with more proof,' I repeated in all seriousness.

Vee's smile faded.

'Nathan . . .' she said huskily. 'What about our shift?'

I leaned in to kiss her and our shift was forgotten.

The moment we got our breath back Vee sprang out of bed. 'Damn! Our shift starts in six minutes. You, Nathan Linedecker, you're a bad influence.'

'That's not what you were saying about me a few moments ago,' I reminded her.

'That was then, this is now. I don't want to get on the wrong side of my mother-in-law!' said Vee.

'How about getting on the right side of me?' I suggested.

'I thought I just did that,' Vee replied, blowing me a kiss before heading into the bathroom for a shower. I followed her.

'Want some company?' I asked hopefully.

Vee gave me a kiss, then went into the shower cubicle firmly shutting the door behind her. Worth a try! I looked at the closed door and smiled before heading back into the main room. Whatever happened, whatever the universe might throw at us, Vee and I were going to be all right. I just knew it.

'Vee, we've got a problem.' The door to our quarters hissed open and Aidan strode into the room. 'Some of the—' He halted abruptly when he saw me.

'Dafuq, Aidan! Have you ever heard of knocking?' I fumed, grabbing for some trousers to cover my nakedness.

'Where's my sister?' Aidan looked around the room. 'What're you doing in here?'

'She's in the shower and I share these quarters – remember? So go and wait in the corridor and don't come into this room uninvited again,' I told him.

First chance I got, I was going to change the entry protocols to this room to exclude Aidan. I would've done it already if I'd known he had access. The guy thought he could just stroll in here whenever he liked? Hell, no!

Aidan didn't move but stood there glaring at me.

'Aidan, what d'you want?'

'To talk to my sister.'

'Well, you can't at the moment. D'you want me to give her a message?'

'No.' Aidan looked me up and down like I was an unwelcome specimen in the science lab. 'Why did you go through the joining ceremony with Vee?'

'Because I wanted to.'

'D'you always get what you want?' asked Aidan.

'No, not always. Like at this particular moment I really want you to be somewhere else,' I replied.

Aidan didn't take the unsubtle hint. 'Do you love Vee?'

'Of course I do.' This guy was really beginning to wind me up.

'Is it possible to fall in love so quickly?'

'Well, we're proof it is.'

'Will you fall out of love as quickly?'

'Don't hold your breath waiting for that to happen,' I told him. 'Vee and I were meant for each other. I'm not letting her go.'

Aidan looked me up and down again. Slowly my fists began to clench.

'Vee will come to realize her mistake, probably before we reach Mendela Prime. You and the others will depart and I'll get my sister back.'

'Don't count on that,' I replied.

'You can't return to Earth, Vee won't stay on Mendela Prime. Her home and everyone she loves are back on Earth. One way or another we'll both be rid of you. All of you.'

That did it. 'Are you going to leave or am I going to carry you out?' I asked.

'I'd really like to see you try,' Aidan said evenly.

I took a step towards him, more than ready to make good my threat.

Just then Vee emerged from the bathroom, wrapped in a towel. 'Nate, d'you think—? Oh, hi, Aidan. What're you doing here?'

'He just walked in,' I replied with a scowl. 'And I'm telling him to walk out again.'

Vee looked from me to her brother. 'Aidan, could you leave please? I'll see you on the bridge in a few minutes.'

Aidan gave me one of his creepy-arse smiles before he turned and left the room without saying another word. The moment the door was shut I rounded on Vee.

'What the hell, Vee? How come he can just saunter in here whenever he feels like it?'

'Calm down, Nate. When it was just me and him on board, we needed to have access to each other's quarters in case of emergency. If I were ill or if I fell and knocked myself out or something, he needed to be able to get to me in a hurry.'

'Why didn't you change the access protocol when I moved in here?'

Vee shrugged. 'I forgot. It's not a big deal.'

'Yes it is.'

'Why?'

'I don't like the idea of your brother being able to stroll in here any time he pleases,' I said.

'Well, there's the room's control panel.' Vee pointed to where it was set in the wall. 'Feel free to make sure he can't in the future.'

Too damned right I would. While I changed the access protocol, Vee got dressed in her work uniform and pulled on her boots. I watched as she quickly plaited her hair, tying it up into a ponytail before checking her appearance in the room's one mirror. She caught my reflection frowning at her.

'Nate, why're you so upset?'

'Why aren't you?' I asked. 'He could've walked in here when you were naked.'

'No way. I'd tear his head off if he did that.'

'Vee, he walked straight in. *I* was naked,' I said, still irate.

Vee frowned. 'You've changed the access protocol now. He won't be able to enter this room again unless it's an emergency and I'll make sure I have a word or fifty with him about our need for privacy. OK?'

'Why does your brother have a problem with me?' I asked.

'He doesn't. I mean, he's probably still getting used to the idea of you and me together. After all, it was just Aidan and me for years.' Vee's gaze slid away from mine.

Something was wrong. I'd told Vee before that she didn't have much of a poker face. She was hiding something.

'Vee, what are you not telling me?' I asked.

'I don't know what you mean. I'm going to be late.' Vee headed for the door, a plastic smile on her face. 'See you on the bridge.'

'Vee, wait.'

She stopped. A moment or two passed before she turned to face me. 'Yes?'

'I love you,' I said, walking towards her.

'I know.' She smiled.

I took hold of her upper arms, being careful not to hurt her, as I looked into her eyes waiting for her to confide in me. She stayed silent. Disappointed, my hands fell to my sides.

'As we probably won't get a chance for the next eight hours . . .' Vee wrapped her arms around my neck and kissed me like it was saving her life. At last I reluctantly pulled away. Much as I would've liked to lead Vee back to bed, Mum would give me hell if I was late for my shift on the bridge.

Thinking of the bridge . . .

'Vee, have you given any further thought to reinstating Anjuli? She really is sorry, and don't you think she's been punished enough?'

Vee's expression froze. 'Wait a minute. I'm kissing you and you're thinking of Anjuli? Really?' She glared at me.

Oh, man!

'No, of course not,' I said hastily. 'It's just that Anjuli and I are good friends and I promised her I'd have a word. That's all.'

'And that occurred to you while we were kissing?'

'Of course not.'

'Yeah, right.'

The next moment Vee marched out of the room, leaving me to stand there mentally kicking myself. Hard.

53

VEE

By the time the door to our quarters had closed behind me I'd cooled down. I was over-reacting. Nathan was just a good friend to Anjuli, that's all. Anjuli was lucky to have him fighting in her corner. And once we'd travelled through the wormhole and the Mazon threat was behind us I saw no reason why Anjuli couldn't come back to the bridge. She was wasted down in the engine room.

I turned round, ready to go back into our quarters to apologize to Nathan for biting his head off, only to hesitate. What if he asked more questions about what I was hiding regarding my brother? When Nate had questioned me, I should've looked him in the eye and told him the truth about Aidan and me. Sooner or later I was going to have to bite the bullet and do precisely that. With a sigh, I took the coward's way out and decided to wait.

I would tell Nathan the truth.

But not now. Not today.

Aidan's shift was over and I still had a couple of minutes left before mine began. I needed to have a few choice words with my brother. Crossing the corridor, I placed my hand on Aidan's palmlock. His door slid open and I walked in.

To my surprise, he wasn't alone. Erica sat on his bed while Aidan sat at his desk.

'Am I interrupting something?' I asked.

'No,' Aidan replied. 'Erica was asking me to have breakfast with her but I need to sleep.'

'Well, before you go to bed, I'd like a word with you,' I said. 'In private.'

Erica stood up. 'Never let it be said that I can't take a hint. Aidan, maybe we could have a late lunch then?'

Aidan looked from me to Erica before standing too. 'I'd like that.' He smiled as he walked over to her. He touched her cheek before giving her a swift but gentle kiss on the lips. 'I'd like that very much. See you later.'

I waited till Erica had left and the door had shut behind her. 'Aidan, what're you playing at?'

Aidan shrugged and sat back down at his desk. 'I don't know what you mean, sis.'

'Don't "sis" me. What's going on with you and Erica?'

'Is that what you came to ask me?'

'No. I came to tell you not to come into my room uninvited again unless I'm alone in there and dead or dying.'

Aidan regarded me, his eyes cold. 'Noted.'

'Now what's going on between you and Erica?'

'How is that any of your business? Do I ask you what you and Nathan get up to in private?'

'That's different.'

'Why?'

'Aidan, you know why,' I argued.

'No, I don't. That's why I'm asking.'

OK, so he was in one of those moods, was he?

'Aidan, don't muck about with Erica's feelings. She doesn't deserve that.'

'Whatever you say, sis.'

He was being deliberately aggravating. Time for a change of subject before we ended up arguing. 'So what did you come into my room to talk to me about?'

Aidan studied me for a few moments. 'It doesn't matter. I wanted your advice about something but I'll handle it myself.'

'Advice about what?'

'Like I said, I'll handle it.'

I didn't have time for this. 'Suit yourself. You know where I am if you change your mind.'

And with that, I left Aidan's room.

There was a time when Aidan wouldn't have hesitated to confide in me. How had things changed so much between us over the course of a few weeks? He was still my brother and I loved him but there was something going on in his head that had me worried.

54

I was three minutes late for my shift. Count them. Three minutes. But the moment I set foot on the bridge Mum started.

'Good of you to grace us with your presence, Nathan.'

Knowing when to keep my mouth shut, I headed for my station, which was Aidan's usual seat at the navigation panel.

'No, Nathan,' Mum said as I sat down. 'Your services will not be required on this bridge until you learn to turn up on time. You will report to Darren in the engine room and spend this shift down there. Dismissed.'

I leaped to my feet and scowled at her. 'Yes, Commander.'

Furious, I headed for the door. If Mum wanted to get pissy because I was three minutes late, then two could play at that game. From now on she was Commander Linedecker first and my mum second.

The first thing that hit me when I entered the engine room on the lower deck was the intense heat, followed swiftly by the raucous noise. I'd have to endure eight hours of this when I should be on the bridge. Thanks, Mum! Anjuli was the first to see me when I entered the room. She was just climbing out of a plasma conduit on the port side. And she was filthy.

She waved at me but I didn't acknowledge her as I needed to

report to Darren first. I couldn't afford to annoy any more people this morning. I saw him over by one of the flow panels, scrutinizing the screen before him. I sighed inwardly. I wasn't Darren's favourite person to begin with, and though there'd been no further hostilities since we'd escaped the ion storm, God only knew what task he would find for me to do. I walked over to him.

'Nathan Linedecker reporting for duty, sir.'

'Are you now?' said Darren, a slow smile of satisfaction creeping over his face.

Yeah, I was in trouble.

'Right, Nathan, you can take my place and join Corbyn over there in conduit S3. There's cabling in there that needs re-shielding. The plasma arcs have been switched off. You've got two hours.'

'Yes, sir.'

Well, I could've predicted that. He was giving me one of the filthiest, most back-breaking jobs on board to do. And too bloody right the plasma arcs had been switched off. If they hadn't been, the plasma energy in each conduit would fry anyone unlucky enough to be caught in there in less than a second. And to top it all off, I wouldn't even be working with Anjuli on the port side. I was on the starboard side with that arsehat Corbyn who got on my nerves and then jumped up and down on them some more. If he knew what was good for him, he'd keep any comments about Vee to himself. Darren started to input my assignment into the computer, effectively dismissing me.

'Harrison, you moron. Don't put that there,' he called out in a temper. He headed over to Harrison, who was looking sheepish.

I turned and gave Anjuli a discreet wave. She smiled at me sympathetically, retrieved a sonic calibrator from the floor and headed back into her tunnel.

'Hurry up, Anjuli.' That sounded like Ian in the conduit with her. He was never happy unless he had something to complain about, but then if I'd been born on Callisto and had seen half the stuff he had, I wouldn't find much to smile about either. He'd outlived his wife and his three children who'd all died back on that moon.

I headed over to conduit S-3 and peered inside. Corbyn was some ten or twelve metres up ahead, and to get to him I'd have to crawl through a conduit barely fifty centimetres high.

This sucked mightily.

'Well, look who'll be joining me in here. Is this your wife's way of asking for a divorce?' Corbyn called out.

Arsehat!

Not bothering to answer, I got down on my hands and knees, ready to crawl through what looked like years of dust and dirt with a trail cut through the grime where Corbyn had entered the conduit before me. Just then the engine's coolant alarm sounded.

'Damn and blast!' I heard Darren exclaim. 'Nathan, get your butt over here.'

With pleasure.

'Recalibrate the coolant ratios. That alarm has been sounding all morning.'

'Yes, sir.'

Fine with me! Darren reassigned himself to the conduits while I headed for the control boards. Once at the appropriate panel, I called up the data on the current levels of coolant in the appropriate parts of the ship's engine. I needed to come up with the optimum level of coolant for each fuel cell relay. I was barely five minutes into the task when another alarm sounded, far more serious this time. The open conduit portals were beginning to close. The trouble was that Anjuli and Ian were still in one and Corbyn was in another. The portals were never supposed to close when people were in there, but something had obviously gone very wrong. Once the portals shut, the conduits would be flooded with plasma energy and the people still inside them wouldn't stand a chance.

I ran to the conduit where Anjuli and Ian were working. Anjuli was frantically crawling towards me. In her panic she kept trying to rise to her feet and run but the tunnel was too low and she kept hitting her head and back against the roof.

'Abort the resetting of the plasma arcs!' Darren shouted.

'I can't, sir. The computer has locked me out,' Maria replied, panic in her voice.

'For God's sake.' Darren ran over to the control panel and shoved her out of the way to try and stop the plasma arcs from resetting. From his expression he was having either bad luck or no luck at all. I jammed my back against the closing portal door, pushing upwards to try and stop it from sliding down any further. The metal of the closing door cut through my jacket and shirt and into my skin.

'Nathan, move away from there,' Darren yelled at me. 'If those doors are open when the arcs reset, you'll flood the whole engine room with plasma energy. You'll kill us all.'

I reluctantly moved. 'Anjuli, move your arse,' I urged, reaching out for her. The moment her fingers touched mine, I hauled her out of there with the help of Harrison who'd run over to help. Darren was still trying to stop the arcs from resetting. Metres away I could see Maria urging Corbyn to hurry up and get out of his tunnel. With Anjuli out, I ducked down to help pull Ian to safety. Even though the portal door was moving slowly, it wasn't slow enough and Ian was a good three metres away.

'Ian, hurry,' I called out.

He carried on crawling for a moment, then shook his head and turned to sit with his back against the wall of the tunnel, his legs drawn up.

'Ian, what're you doing?' I yelled.

He turned to me and smiled. 'I'm going to see my wife and children.'

'Ian . . .' I tried to crawl into the conduit to get him but Harrison grabbed hold of me and pulled me back just as the conduit door closed completely. There was a whooshing sound as the plasma arcs ignited. I half sat, half collapsed against the wall next to the closed conduit door. Even through the shielded and tempered bulkhead I could feel the heat of the arcs in the conduit almost scorching my back.

For the second time since coming aboard this ship I'd had to watch people die. And once again there was nothing I could do about it. Across the floor, Maria was banging her fists against the conduit door. I stood up slowly.

'Corbyn?' I asked.

Harrison shook his head. 'He didn't make it.'

55

The atmosphere aboard the *Aidan* was poisonous after the second incident with Ian and Corbyn. I didn't know either of them very well but it didn't matter. It felt like I'd lost members of my own family. And where the colonists had begun to stop and chat to me in the corridors, now they kept walking; some actually turned round and went back the way they'd come when they saw me heading towards them.

The accident in the airlock was bad luck.

But two accidents? That had to be by design.

I began to realize that some of the crew seriously believed that I had something to do with the loss of their friends. After all, they had all lived together on Callisto, had escaped together and tried to settle together on Barros 5. I was the unknown entity, the outsider.

When my shift was over I made my bone-weary way back to my quarters. I expected Nathan to already be there but he wasn't. A shower, a sandwich and a change of clothing later and Nathan still hadn't come back to our quarters. I paced up and down wondering and worrying about where he was.

'Aidan, where is Nathan Linedecker?' I finally gave in and asked the computer.

'Nathan Linedecker is in his assigned quarters U-08,' Aidan's voice played back to me.

I half sat, half fell onto the bed. Did that mean what I suspected? Did Nathan, like the rest of the colonists, suspect that I had something to do with the deaths of his friends? Surely if he had doubts, he would come and at least talk to me first? Or maybe he had no doubts.

Should I go and see him? Try to reason with him? Or would it be better to leave him alone for a while?

God! My thoughts were driving me crazy.

Over the next hour my doubts wouldn't leave me alone. They writhed and grew, fed by fear. The door to my quarters hissed open. I jumped to my feet as Nathan entered, looking as tired as I felt. He stopped just inside the room and we both stood like living statues, watching each other.

'Have you come for the rest of your stuff?' I asked at last.

Nathan looked shocked, but only for a moment. Then the shutters came down and his expression set, mask-like and unreadable.

'Are you kicking me out?'

Now it was my turn to be shocked. 'No! Of course not,' I denied. 'But our shift finished hours ago and the computer said you were in your old quarters. I thought . . . does that mean you're moving out?'

Slowly Nathan shook his head. I still couldn't read his

expression. For the first time I wasn't sure what he was thinking.

'Nate, tell me honestly, d'you think I had something to do with the death of your friends?'

He walked over and wrapped his arms around me, hugging me to him, his embrace almost too tight, but I didn't care. The relief I felt then made tears spring to my eyes which I tried to blink away. I didn't want Nate to think I was weak.

'Nate, I need to hear you say the words,' I whispered.

'Vee, I know you had nothing to do with their deaths.' Nathan drew back slightly so I could see his face properly. The mask was gone. 'I've just spent the last few hours telling that to anyone who'd listen.'

'But you were in your old room,' I said, confused.

'Only for the last couple of hours. Anjuli and I were going through all the engine room and bridge logs and footage to try and find out what happened.'

'You and Anjuli?' I said sharply. 'You could've asked me, Nate. I would've helped.'

'I didn't want to risk anyone accusing either of us of a cover-up. That's why it was better if Anjuli and I investigated without you.'

Nathan had been alone in his old room with Anjuli for a couple of hours . . .

No! I wasn't going to travel down that path. As King Lear said, 'O, that way madness lies.' I had to decide whether or not I trusted Nathan, and what it boiled down to was that I did, and I would until it was proved beyond all doubt that I shouldn't.

'So what did you find?'

'Nothing. At least nothing out of the ordinary.' Nathan dragged a weary hand through his unruly hair. I could feel his frustration at his lack of progress. 'Everything points to it just being an accident.'

'But you don't think it was, do you?'

'Darren tried to shut down the arc reset from a panel in the engine room. He was locked out while there were people inside the conduits. After the accident happened the control panel worked just fine,' said Nathan.

'If it'd been a true malfunction, it still wouldn't have worked after the accident,' I realized.

'Exactly,' said Nathan grimly. 'Which means someone took control of the ship's computer, using the nanites to deliberately cause their deaths.'

'But why would anyone do that?' I asked, bewildered.

When Mum and Dad and the original crew had started dying, that had been because of a mystery virus which no one had been able to do anything about. That was a savage twist of fate. This was different. This was someone deliberately picking off crew members for no apparent motive.

'There's no other explanation, Vee,' said Nathan. 'And what's more, I think *I* was meant to be one of the victims.'

56

NATHAN

Vee's mouth dropped open, her face horrified. Her expression had to be the mirror image of mine when I first realized.

'Please tell me you're joking,' she whispered.

'It's not something I would joke about,' I replied.

Vee stumbled over to the bed and sat down. I sat down beside her, taking her hands in mine. Vee looked me in the eye and I could read every emotion as it crossed her face – disbelief, fury, fear.

'Tell me why you think you were the intended target,' she said at last.

'Darren assigned me the task of re-shielding the cabling alongside Corbyn in one of the starboard conduits. He entered the assignment into the computer but then the coolant alarm went off and he reassigned me to fix that instead. Only I don't think Darren got the chance to enter the new assignment into the computer.'

'So . . . the computer had you down as working in one of the conduits that got flooded with plasma energy.' Vee picked her way through the words.

I nodded.

'It has to be a coincidence. I mean, who in the galaxy would want to harm you?'

Aidan.

I decided to keep that thought to myself.

'Who on board has the technical knowledge to do something like that?' asked Vee.

Aidan.

I couldn't and wouldn't share my suspicions with Vee, not until I had titanium-clad proof.

'That's the same question Anjuli and I were discussing,' I sighed. 'The list is short. Eight people – my mum, me, Anjuli, Darren, Hedda, Sam, Doctor Liana and Mike.'

'Well, it's obviously not you,' Vee said. 'And I think we can cross your mum and the doctor off the list.'

'And Hedda, Sam and Anjuli,' I added. 'They're all on the bridge with us. And I doubt if it's Mike.'

'The list of suspects is going to be non-existent if we carry on like this,' said Vee.

'Yeah,' I sighed. 'Quite frankly, I can't believe it's any of them.'

'Darren?' Vee suggested.

'He's capable but this isn't really his style,' I replied. 'Besides, he's the one who reassigned me so I wouldn't have to work in the conduit – remember?'

Vee wrapped her arms around my waist, her head against my shoulder. We sat in silence for a few moments as it sank in that someone had tried to kill me. It wasn't a pleasant thing to contemplate. Surely I hadn't pissed off anyone enough for them to want to see me dead? The evidence unfortunately said otherwise.

'Tell me everything you know about those eight people,' Vee asked. 'Then tell me everything you know about all the ones who have died while aboard this ship.'

I could see where she was going with this but I doubted it would do much good. Still, Vee might see something that Anjuli and I had missed.

I could only hope.

The overhead lights were on their dimmest setting, casting subdued amber throughout the room. I lay in bed on my back staring up at the ceiling, unable to sleep. Nathan wasn't having the same problem. He lay on his side, his arm round my waist, and he was dead to the world.

Inappropriate phrase.

I'd seen enough of death to last me five lifetimes. I was so weary of it. And now someone was out to get Nathan. I glanced at him while he slept. He looked so peaceful, almost boyish. Why would anyone want to harm him? Was it because he'd gone through the joining ceremony with me? It was ironic that the refugees I'd picked up from Barros 5 considered me part of the Authority, an Elite, yet among this group I was the one on the outside. Because they saw me as part of the Authority, I knew that some of the crew still didn't trust me. I had hoped that over time, as they got to know me, they'd come to realize I was on their side. These so-called accidents had made the task that much harder. And if Nathan stuck with me, how soon before he lost his friends because of it?

Or, worse still, his life?

Quite frankly, I envied Nathan his ability to sleep. The wheels were spinning in my head. It rankled that some of Nathan's friends and colleagues thought that I might have had something to do with what happened in the engine room.

Like I would *ever* harm Nathan.

I had to admit, it'd hurt when I found out he'd been with Anjuli trying to figure out what had happened. Wasn't that the sort of thing the two of us should do together? I understood what he'd said about keeping me out of it so as not to be accused of manufacturing any data or evidence that might prove my innocence, but to be honest that didn't help.

I'd just have to find a way to accept that Nathan and Anjuli were good friends and probably always would be. I had to find a way to be cool with that. Besides, he'd joined with me, not her. That was the one fact I needed to cling onto whenever I got twitchy about Nathan and Anjuli's relationship. This was my problem to solve, not Nathan's. I could wish that my brother had kept his mouth shut about Erica's suspicions. Those words were like slow poison that had been dripped into my ears.

Slowly the hours ticked by and still I couldn't sleep. Sometime in the night Nathan had turned away and was now lying with his back to me. In the end I just stopped fighting it and decided to start my shift on the bridge an hour earlier than scheduled. Staring at the ceiling was serving no purpose at all.

I slipped out of bed, had a quick shower and was getting dressed in my work uniform when Nathan woke up.

'Wh-what're you doing?' he asked drowsily.

'Going to the bridge,' I replied.

Nathan checked the wall clock. 'Our shift doesn't start for another hour.'

'I can't sleep.' My tone was terse. I wasn't in a chatty mood.

'Wait for me to have a shower and get dressed and I'll come with you.' Nathan threw back the covers and swung his legs out of the bed. He started to take off his pendant.

'I'll see you in there then. I have a few things to take care of that can't wait,' I replied, already heading for the door.

'Vee . . .'

At that moment the door alarm sounded.

'Who the hell is that at this time of the morning?' Nathan grumbled.

I waited for him to slip on his shorts, before opening the door. It was Erica, and her expression was stiff to say the least.

'Nihao, Erica. Can I help you?'

'Hello, Vee. I was hoping to speak to Nathan,' she said formally. 'In private.'

Erica and I hadn't exactly been best friends since our first altercation but now the air between us was distinctly frosty. She definitely thought I had something to do with all the accidents on board the *Aidan*.

'What d'you want, Erica?' Nathan's tone wasn't much warmer than Erica's as he addressed her.

She moved past me, needing no further invitation. I turned to Nathan. 'I'll see you on the bridge,' I said, leaving them to it.

I crossed the corridor to Aidan's room, placing my hand against the palmlock. To my surprise, the door didn't immediately open. I pressed on his door alert. I had no right to feel aggrieved – after all, I'd told my brother that he couldn't just swan into my quarters whenever he liked. He'd obviously decided privacy should be a two-way street.

Aidan's door hissed open and he stood at the entrance, blocking my way.

'May I come in?' I asked when it became clear he wasn't going to move.

Almost reluctantly, he stepped to one side and allowed me to enter his quarters. I crossed the room to sit on his bed. He remained standing.

'Aidan, it feels like we haven't had a proper conversation in a while.'

'That's because we haven't,' he said.

My fault, I knew. I'd been a bit caught up in my new life with Nathan.

'How are you?' I asked.

'Fine,' Aidan replied curtly.

Well, my brother wasn't making this easy for me.

'Why are you here, Vee?'

'I wanted to talk to you about the . . . accident in the engine room yesterday.'

'Accident?' Aidan said pointedly.

'That's what the commander and I are officially calling it,' I said.

'I've got news for you, Vee. Everyone knows that what happened yesterday and what happened to Mei, Jaxon and Saul in the airlock weren't accidents,' said Aidan.

'How did they learn that?' I asked, dismayed.

'Vee, get real. We were never going to be able to hide that fact for long.' Aidan sat down beside me on the bed.

'But nothing has been officially confirmed by the commander or me,' I protested.

'Nothing has been denied either. The rumours are rife.'

I slumped back onto Aidan's bed, staring at the ceiling. I had hoped that by the time the majority of the crew found out the truth, we'd also have answers for them. I dreaded to think what this was going to do to crew morale.

I sat up again. 'Aidan, is there anything you can tell me about who's responsible for these deaths?'

He shook his head. 'The nanites were programmed to activate the plasma arcs and the order came from every control panel on board simultaneously.'

'That's impossible.'

'Nevertheless, that's how the computer recorded it – as coming from each command panel at once.'

'Maybe the command came from the original panel a millisecond before all the others?' I said hopefully. If so, then at least we could pin down the original command panel used and crosscheck it against who was using it at the time.

'Sorry, Vee, I already thought of that. When I say simultaneous, that's what I mean.'

I sighed. 'So what you're telling me is we've had two more deaths and we're no closer to catching the culprit?'

'In a word of one syllable – yes,' said Aidan. He regarded me. 'Still glad the refugees came aboard, sis?'

58

Today wasn't shaping up to be any better than yesterday. I'd arrived on the bridge thirty minutes before my watch was due to start and Mum had still sent me back down to the engine room. We'd barely said a word to each other that wasn't work-related in two days.

Thankfully Darren hadn't put me back on cabling duties. I had to finish sorting out the coolant ratios, and then work with Anjuli to find ways to increase the engine's efficiency by at least another three per cent. The modifications Vee had made to the engine already had it running at optimal capacity. I don't know where Darren thought Anjuli and I would find an extra three per cent, but I wasn't about to argue with him. Life was too short.

Hours later, the coolant ratios sorted, Anjuli and I were sitting at a panel trying various efficiency permutations. At least that's what I was doing. Anjuli, it turns out, was doing something entirely different.

'Nathan, I've been over these calculations five times,' she began, her voice barely above a whisper. 'D'you remember that story Vee told about how she sabotaged the engines of the Mazon ships before she rescued us from Barros 5?'

'Yeah?' Where was Anjuli going with this?

'Well, even wearing a protection suit, Vee would've lasted five, maybe six seconds maximum in the Mazon engine core, and that's with Aidan diverting most of the power from the ship's energy reserves to wrap her in a nano-field. Maybe seven seconds, if God was standing beside her at the time. But no more. She certainly couldn't have stayed in the engine cores for ten seconds or more like she said. So either she's lying about the time she spent in each Mazon engine core or—'

'Or?' I prompted.

'She's not telling the truth,' said Anjuli.

I frowned, unimpressed by Anjuli's attempts to be witty. So Vee was out by a couple of seconds. So what?

When she saw the look on my face, Anjuli sighed. 'Nathan, I'm not trying to stir up trouble between the two of you but, believe me, she's either lying or hiding something.'

'Like what?'

'If I knew that, I'd know as much as her,' Anjuli replied. 'I like Vee, I really do, but something is rotten in the state of Denmark. There's something Vee's not telling us.'

My frown deepened as I listened to her. I wanted to argue with her, but how could I when I was beginning to reach the same conclusion?

'And another thing,' said Anjuli, warming to her theme. 'Have you noticed how Aidan has changed since we got here?'

'Changed how?'

'His voice has got deeper.'

'Don't be ridiculous. Of course it hasn't.'

'I'm telling you, his voice has changed since we first arrived,' Anjuli insisted.

OK, Anjuli was definitely losing the plot.

'Don't look at me like that,' she protested. 'It's true.'

'No need to bite my head off. Look, if there is something going on, I'll find out what it is,' I said. 'But you're not to go round spreading gossip and rumours.'

'Of course not. But whatever it is, Nathan, be careful,' said Anjuli. 'I suspect it may have something to do with the reason people are dying.'

59

We'd been travelling through Mazon space for a while now and the tension on board was so thick I could almost taste it. Two days had passed since the accident in the engine room, and even in the mess hall the talk was subdued rather than the raucous chatter it had been a week ago. In a little over seventy-two hours we'd reach the wormhole which would take us out of Mazon space, but it felt like irrevocable damage had been done. Everyone was watching everyone else. Suspicion walked the corridors of the ship. And it had entered the sleeping quarters that Nathan and I shared. Conversation which had been unforced and easy before was now strained. More than once I caught him watching me, a strange, brooding look in his eyes.

'Nate, what's wrong?' I asked him more than once.

'I'm waiting for you to talk to me,' he replied.

I didn't know what that meant and I told him so. But that's as far as the conversation went. It hadn't taken long for our joining to hit its first hurdle. I was desperate to figure out what it would take to get us back to where we'd been. For the life of me, I couldn't think of a single thing.

I couldn't figure out what Nathan wanted from me and he wouldn't – or couldn't – tell me.

Eating in the mess hall had become an ordeal. As I sat down, others would get up and go to another table to eat. Conversations stopped when I drew near and started again once I departed. As a consequence, I took to eating alone in my room when Nathan was working or eating in Aidan's quarters when Nathan wasn't on shift. I learned it was possible to have people all around you and to still be alone. In fact, having people around just made it worse. Before, in my loneliness I'd had a whole ship to roam around in. Now, if I went anywhere except the bridge I felt I was looked on as an intruder. On my own ship.

The previous night, when Aidan and I were eating alone in his quarters, he'd said out of nowhere, 'Vee, I don't want to worry you but . . . you need to be on your guard. Now more than ever.'

'Why?'

'Too many people on board believe you had something to do with the deaths that have occurred,' Aidan replied. 'You're the topic of most conversations.'

'Why haven't you figured out who's really responsible for all those deaths yet?' I asked sharply.

'Why haven't you?' asked Aidan evenly.

'Believe me, I've tried,' I sighed. 'So what are people saying about me?'

'Maybe you should ask your husband that?'

'We haven't had a proper conversation in days,' I

admitted. 'We never seem to share the same shifts any more.'

'At his request,' Aidan said.

'What?'

'He requested different shifts to you.' Aidan frowned. 'I thought you knew that.'

Just for a moment my heart stopped beating. I swear it did. Just for a moment.

'That's news to me,' I replied quietly.

So Nathan was beginning to believe the gossip too? Why else would he request different shifts so we never had the chance to be together?

'Vee, you should have a conversation with Anjuli,' said my brother carefully.

I frowned. 'Why?'

'Speak to Anjuli, but not with Nathan present,' said Aidan. 'Or better yet, I'll speak to her and you can be hidden in the background listening to our conversation. That way you'll hear the truth.'

'About what?'

'Just trust me, sis. All right?'

'No. Not till you tell me what this is all about,' I said.

'Vee, you need to know what everyone else on this ship already knows and it's best you hear the truth from Anjuli,' said Aidan. 'I'm asking you to trust me. You know I've always got your back.'

'So you want to speak to Anjuli and you want me to be somewhere where I can eavesdrop without being seen?'

He nodded.

My gut was telling me this was a really bad idea but Aidan wouldn't have suggested such a thing if it hadn't been necessary, not to mention urgent.

'So when and where will your conversation take place?' I asked at last.

And Aidan told me exactly what he had in mind.

'Nathan, this is the second time in three days that you've been in here.' Doctor Liana frowned. 'What's going on with you?'

I shrugged, shuffling to move further along the bed. I just wanted her to patch me up, preferably without the inquisition. The medical bay really wasn't my favourite place. 'It's just gym aches and pains. I like to work out for a while after each shift.'

'Nathan, this is me,' said the doctor as she scanned my leg, also checking my prosthesis for damage. 'What's wrong?'

I sighed. 'The accident in the engine room is just preying on my mind, that's all.'

'Corbyn and Ian . . . Yes, that was tragic.' The doctor nodded.

'It was also deliberate,' I said.

Her head snapped up at that. 'What d'you mean? The rumours are *true*?'

'Hasn't Mum told you?'

Doctor Liana shook her head.

Why on Callisto wouldn't Mum tell the ship's doctor what was going on?

'Well, Mum and Vee haven't broadcast this so keep it to your-self, but someone hacked into the ship's computer and reset the plasma arcs knowing there were people still inside those conduits. I was one of the people who was supposed to be in there, so I think someone wants to see *me* dead.'

Deep creases ruled lines in Doctor Liana's forehead and around her mouth. 'No, that can't be right.'

'I've gone over it and over it. Someone tried to kill me along with Corbyn, Ian and Anjuli. Anjuli only just made it out, and if Darren hadn't reassigned me at the last moment, I would've been on the list of those who've died on this ship.'

'Why on earth would anyone want to kill you – or anyone else on board for that matter?'

I sighed again. 'No idea.'

Doctor Liana resumed her scan.

'The thing is, if someone does want me dead then I don't want Vee anywhere near me. I'd never forgive myself if she got hurt because of me,' I admitted.

The doctor frowned. 'Have you told Vee that?'

'Of course not,' I said. 'She's got enough on her plate without me adding to it. I'm just trying to stay out of her way to keep her safe.'

'But you two share quarters,' Doctor Liana said. 'You're sharing a life now. I would've said that was impossible.'

'Not impossible, but bloody difficult,' I replied. 'I've changed all my shifts so that we're working at different times and, like I said, I try to stay away from her as much as possible but it's so hard. I want to be with my wife. I didn't join with her to live like this.'

'Ah! Now I get the reason for the bruises and sprains all over your body,' the doctor said. 'You've been taking out your frustrations on the gym equipment?'

Damn it! I was blushing.

Her grin broadened. 'And using the training bots no doubt. Have you been running a few attack-and-defend scenarios? You against how many?'

'I'm up to eight,' I muttered.

'Eight! Are you serious?' The doc's eyebrows shot up. 'And you're still standing? Nathan, you're lucky you haven't broken something, or worse. As it is, you've sprained your right ankle and you have severe contusions all over your body and up and down your left leg in particular.'

'Well, if you fix me up and give me a painkiller I'll be on my way.'

'Back to the gym?'

'Well, yes. Vee's shift has just finished and mine doesn't start for another hour and she rarely goes to the gym.'

Doctor Liana's frown was back with a vengeance. 'For heaven's sake, Nathan. You need to have a conversation with your wife. Tell her why you've been avoiding her or she'll assume the worst.'

'What worst?'

'That you don't want to be with her, of course.' She sounded exasperated. 'That maybe you believe, as do too many others on this ship, that your wife had something to do with all these incidents that have been happening.'

'That's crap. Vee knows I don't believe any such thing.'

Doctor Liana shook her head at me. 'Your joining will fail if you and Vee don't find a way to communicate, and I'm not just talking sexually.'

'Doctor!'

'Oh, please. I'm a doctor and a married one at that. D'you want some advice – from one joined person to another?'

Something told me I was going to get her advice whether I wanted it or not. 'Go on then,' I said churlishly.

Doctor Liana glared at me, her lips pursed at my rudeness.

'Sorry,' I muttered. 'What I meant was, yes please, Doctor Liana, I'd love to hear your advice.'

She smiled reluctantly. 'Don't overdo it, Nathan. My advice to you is to talk to Olivia, share the good and the bad stuff, and more importantly, listen – that's if you want your union to last.'

'Of course it will last.' I frowned. 'I'll make sure of that. I'm not going to lose her.'

The doctor gave me a studied look.

'What?'

'You sound like you mean that.'

'Of course I mean it.'

'Just as long as you're not a fair-weather lover. Olivia deserves better than that,' said Doctor Liana.

'A fair what?'

'I mean someone who stays around when things are going well but then disappears when the going gets tough.'

'How can I disappear on a ship?' I asked.

'Don't pretend to be dense, Nathan. It doesn't suit you,' the doctor said impatiently.

'Doctor Liana, I'm really uncomfortable with this conversation. I'm not into all this emotional touchy-feely stuff,' I said. And certainly not with the ship's doctor, for goodness' sake.

'You're human, Nathan, therefore you're into it whether you want to admit it or not,' said Doctor Liana. 'Stop excluding Olivia from what you're doing and why you're doing it. Talk to her.'

'I'm not avoiding Vee because I like it, Doc. Far from it. I'm just trying to keep her safe. Besides, I'm not the only one keeping secrets.'

'What does that mean?'

'Nothing,' I sighed.

Doctor Liana looked thoughtful for a moment. 'On the day of the accident, why were you down in the engine room? I thought you were permanently assigned to the bridge.'

'I was, but Mum got the hump with me for being late and sent me down there to work with Darren,' I said. 'Nothing I do pleases her at the moment.'

'When you got to the engine room, had you already been assigned to the conduits?'

'No, of course not. Darren didn't even know I was coming. He just told me to take his place in the conduit and help Corbyn, but then he changed his mind and told me to sort out the engine coolant flows—' A light had finally switched on in my head. 'Oh my God!'

Doctor Liana raised an eyebrow, looking at me pointedly. 'The crew's assignments are usually entered into the ship's computer twenty-four hours before they're given out.'

'So I wasn't necessarily the target,' I realized.

'Exactly.'

'That means someone was after Darren, not me.' I beamed. 'Doc, I could kiss you.'

'I doubt if Darren will feel quite as joyful as you when he realizes he was the intended target,' the doctor said drily. My grin faded. Doctor Liana had a point. She placed a hypo against my ankle, and a moment later the pain there had lessened considerably.

I leaped off the bed and onto my feet. There was no pain at all now.

'Doc, you're a miracle worker,' I told her.

'If only I could bring the dead back to life, eh?' she said, her voice tinged with sadness. Sometimes I needed reminding that I wasn't the only one with inner demons to face and fight.

'Doctor, are you all right?' I asked.

She snapped out of her reverie to give me a smile. 'I'm fine. Now go be with your wife and stop beating up the gym equipment.'

This was ridiculous, not to mention undignified. What the hell was I doing skulking around in the hydroponics bay? Aidan had told me to enter the bay by the port-side door and to wait behind one of the hybrid fruit trees on the port side. So here I stood, *waiting*. Or should I say, hiding. And for what? Aidan insisted there was something I needed to hear. I looked around. Was I really going to do this? Was this really the level to which I had sunk?

Sod this! I needed to get back to my room; once there I'd try to figure out where I'd mislaid my self-respect. The moment I took a step away from the tree trunk behind which I'd been hiding, the starboard hydroponic bay doors slid open. In walked Aidan and Anjuli. I ducked back behind the trunk, hating myself.

'Why are we here, Aidan?' Anjuli asked.

'I needed to speak to you in private.'

'About what?'

'I want to help out with this situation between you and my sister,' said Aidan.

'Why?' asked Anjuli, eyes narrowed.

Aidan's eyes widened. He was thrown by the question, but he soon recovered. 'Trust me,' he said with an easy smile. 'I only want what's best for Vee, and that's for you and her to be friends again.'

'So you reckon you can get me back on the bridge?' asked Anjuli hopefully.

'I'm sure I can, with a little help. D'you mind me asking, how *are* things between you and Nathan?'

Anjuli looked puzzled at the question. 'The same as ever. Why?'

'I just want to make sure that we can count on Nathan's help.'

'Of course he'll help. Nathan would do anything for me.' Anjuli smiled. 'He owes me.'

What did she mean by that?

'Which brings us to why I asked you here tonight,' said Aidan.

'Oh yes?' Anjuli was immediately on her guard.

What was Aidan doing? I thought he wanted me to witness something that I should know. Aidan leaned in close to whisper something in Anjuli's ear. Something I couldn't hear even if I wanted to, which I wasn't sure I did.

'I just thought you should know that he's telling anyone who'll listen how revved he is that the two of you have started up again where you left off.' Aidan's voice was back to normal.

A moment's silence and then Anjuli burst out laughing. Aidan watched her, not joining in the joke. Anjuli's laughter ended abruptly, to be replaced by a look of outrage. 'Oh my God! You're serious?'

'He can't help bragging about the two of you together. Apparently you're the best he's ever had. He's going to try and come to your quarters tonight, as his are always occupied. You'll both need to be discreet for a while longer though. His words, not mine.'

'Discreet? Is he for real?' Anjuli spluttered, incensed.

'He said that once he's free again, he might even consider going through a joining ceremony with you. Once he's free,' said Aidan.

'Are you cracked? Is *he*? He must be! Once he's *free*? God, but he's such a lying whoremeister. Any man or woman stupid enough to join with him deserves everything they get. On Callisto he worked his way through every woman who looked at him twice and he's still at it on board this ship.'

'There are those on board who've crawled into his bed eagerly enough,' said Aidan. 'And I should know.'

'More fool them. Once he's had his fun, he'll move on. That's what he always does. He's a user.'

'So you won't be waiting for him in your quarters later?'

'Are you kidding me?' Anjuli dismissed. 'I have standards, even if some women don't.'

I couldn't bear to hear any more. I was turning round to leave when Aidan's next words halted me in my tracks.

'That's an interesting pendant,' he said. 'I haven't seen you wearing that before.'

Anjuli glanced down at the pendant hanging from a platinum chain and lying against the pristine white T-shirt beneath her open jacket. A jolt of recognition flashed through me. I knew that pendant. I'd know it anywhere.

'Isn't it beautiful?' Anjuli said with pride.

'May I see it?' Aidan asked. He didn't wait for an answer but pulled the pendant towards him for a closer look. 'You're right. It is beautiful.'

'Yeah, it was a present.' Anjuli beamed.

'From someone who obviously cares a great deal about you. Look, I hate to be rude' – Aidan ushered Anjuli towards the door – 'but I've just realized I'm late for another meeting.'

Within moments the two of them were out of the door and I was alone.

Minutes passed as I stood in the hydroponics lab, unable to move a muscle. I replayed the conversation I'd just heard over and over in my head. I must've misunderstood or mis-interpreted what I'd heard. I didn't even have to close my eyes to recall the image of the pendant hanging round Anjuli's neck. There had to be a reasonable explanation for why she had it now.

But I couldn't for the life of me come up with one.

It wasn't just the words I'd overheard – people said all sorts of things for all kinds of reason – it was what I'd seen with my own eyes. My joining gift to Nathan, the pendant I'd given to him with all my love, the pendant he swore he'd never take off, was now hanging round Anjuli's neck.

 # NATHAN

Where the hell was it? I'd turned the bed and the whole damned room upside down looking for the thing and it was nowhere to be found. The pendant Vee had given me had disappeared. I tried to think back to the last time I'd had it.

Was it at dinner tonight?

I'd definitely had it when I had my shower this morning. At least, I think I had. I distinctly remembered taking it off and putting it on the desk before stepping into the shower cubicle. Or was that yesterday? Damn it! I went over to the desk again, picking up books, data tablets and everything else. Then I examined the floor. It hadn't somehow been dropped and vacuumed up by the cleaning robot, had it? I picked up the cleaning robot from the side of the room and emptied its dust bales onto the floor, before dropping to my knees to search for the pendant with my bare hands.

Nothing doing. The only thing in the dust was dust. The moment I turned the cleaning robot the right way up, it set off across the floor having detected the dirt I'd just scattered everywhere.

Damn it! Where was it?

If Vee found out it was missing she'd never forgive me.

I'd meant to get round to fixing the clasp, I really had. I closed my eyes, resigning myself to the fact that I'd probably never see it again. That thing could be anywhere on the ship. I could've dropped it anywhere – in the engine room, the astro lab, the gym, the bridge, the corridors. Anywhere.

If I didn't find it before Vee noticed it was missing, there'd be hell to pay.

I don't know how long I stood still and alone in the hydro-ponics bay. My arms were wrapped around my waist as if to try and contain all the anguish I was feeling, but it did no good. If I moved my arms, my whole body would crum-ble to dust.

My brother. I needed to see my brother. I stumbled out of the hydroponics bay and made my way to his room. I pressed on his door alert. The moment the door opened and he saw me, he stepped aside to let me in.

'I take it you saw what Anjuli was wearing?' he said without preamble.

I couldn't speak, couldn't even nod, but Aidan already knew the answer. I collapsed onto his bed, my whole body shaking. Slowly, inexorably, I was dying inside.

My brother sighed. 'I'm sorry I couldn't tell you sooner, Vee. I wanted to but I didn't know how.'

'How did you find out?'

'Erica told me. Everyone knew about the two of them – except you,' said Aidan. 'They've all been having a good laugh at you behind your back.'

Everyone was laughing at me . . .

I closed my eyes against the battering misery inside. It did no good.

'Why didn't you tell me?' I asked. 'You should've told me.'

'Would you have believed me?'

My brother was right. I would never have believed anything he or anyone else said against Nathan. I was still having trouble believing the evidence of my own eyes.

I scowled at him. 'I hate you right now for what you've done to me.'

Aidan's mouth dropped open in astonishment.

'You never did like Nathan so you must be loving this,' I continued bitterly. 'Go on then. Say it. Gloat about how you tried to warn me but I wouldn't listen.'

Aidan glared, absolutely furious. 'Well, if this is what I get for being honest and for trying to protect you, then forget it. I wish I'd kept my mouth shut. In fact, from now on I think I'll do just that or, better yet, lie to your face like everyone else does on this ship.'

I closed my eyes and sighed. 'I'm sorry, Aidan. I'd rather you were honest. In fact, you're the only one I can trust to always be honest with me. I'm just so confused.'

'I should've been wiser and kept my opinions to myself,' fumed Aidan. 'Then at least you wouldn't have turned on me.'

'I'm sorry. It's just I close my eyes and I keep seeing Dad's pendant hanging round Anjuli's neck.'

That one image hacked through me, leaving destruction in its wake.

Nathan and Anjuli.

Lovers.

Anjuli was better than me. At least she was smart enough to see Nathan for what he really was.

'I still don't understand,' I murmured, replaying the conversation I'd overheard in my head. 'If Anjuli despises Nathan so much, why take his pendant as a gift?'

Aidan shrugged. 'The chatter on board says she's determined to make him earn his way back into her bed on a permanent basis. He knows that, so he gave her the pendant as a present. You're still captain of this ship and therefore an obstacle, so naturally they have to be discreet.'

Aidan's words were torturing me.

How was it possible to feel this much pain and still be conscious? I toyed with the idea of just giving them all the ship's command code and letting them do what they wanted to me. How much easier would it be to just let go?

'You could always share him,' Aidan suggested.

At my look of outrage, he raised his hands in apology. 'Tell me, would you be happy for Nathan to have sex with anyone he wanted as long as you didn't know about it?'

'No, I wouldn't,' I replied vehemently.

Though, to tell the truth, there was a part of me that wished to God I hadn't found out.

'Careful, Vee. Beware the green-eyed monster which mocks the meat it feeds on,' said Aidan.

'So I'm supposed to be happy that Nathan is screwing someone else, am I?'

Aidan shrugged infuriatingly.

'Why would he do it?' I whispered.

'You wouldn't hand over the ship to them,' he pointed out. 'Commander Linedecker probably felt she had no other course.'

'The commander is behind this?' I asked, aghast.

'Sounds reasonable to me.'

'So what was the plan? To have her son seduce the ship's command code out of me? He was so good I would've handed it over believing it was my idea, not his,' I said bitterly.

It had nearly worked. It was just a matter of time before I told Nate anything and everything.

'It's not your fault. Like Anjuli said, Nathan is a user, that's all, and he used you to get what he and the rest of the refugees want – which is this ship.'

'I told them I'd take them to Mendela Prime—'

'But playing devil's advocate, you could've changed your mind at any time,' said Aidan. 'You might've decided to alert the Authority to their whereabouts at any of the outposts we passed on the way. As far as they were concerned, the safer option was to have complete control.'

Gullible. Naive. Incredibly stupid. Reckless. The list of my better qualities went on and on. As if anyone could fall in love and want to spend the rest of their life with me, let alone after such a short acquaintance. I'd been dancing through a fairy tale and the music playing had drowned out all rational thought.

But now the music had stopped.

Nathan and the others must've hatched their plan soon after coming aboard. Maybe it was after I'd refused to hand over my ship to the commander that first time. Had it been so obvious that I was attracted to Nathan from the moment I saw him? It must've been, and they'd decided to use that against me. And, idiot that I was, I'd swallowed every kind word, every touch, every caress he had deigned to throw my way. That was the hardest thing of all to bear, just how easy I'd made it for Nathan to deceive me.

I realized something at that moment which squeezed my heart until I could hardly breathe. I'd been so desperate for love, had longed so much for someone to share my life with, that it hadn't taken very much persuading on Nathan's part for me to go through the joining ceremony with him. It wasn't desperately romantic as I'd originally thought; it was merely desperate.

But the truth of it was, I really had fallen for Nate.

Attraction at first sight. Love at second.

Before I met him I thought such a thing only happened in films and stories, but the first sight of Nathan had made my heart beat faster and my mouth go dry and my breathing erratic. Talking to him, being with him, making love with him after that had made those initial feelings deeper, more solid, much more real – or so I'd thought. Maybe the whole thing was just my delusion, a vision of love built on shifting sand.

Why had I joined with Nathan? It'd been such a rash thing to do. Why had he joined with me? I mean, why go along with it in the first place? A new sexual conquest? A brand-new adventure? A ship and his freedom at stake?

Nathan couldn't keep his hands off me. I'd been stupid enough to mistake desire for an extremely loving nature. I'd seen in him what I wanted to see and had believed that I'd be enough for him.

And yet . . .

And yet I could've sworn he only had eyes for me. I thought he was all mine, just as I was all his. I guess not all of him was mine alone. He felt free to satisfy his sexual appetite with anyone he wanted, he was just trying to be discreet about it. Discreet? Not if everyone knew what he was except me. What had Anjuli called him? A whore-meister. A master manipulator. Someone who wasn't above using sex and playing on the feelings of others to get what he wanted.

Stupid. I was so very stupid.

Reckless.

Foolish to join with him.

Now I couldn't get the image of him and Anjuli together out of my head. It was poisoning my mind, cell by cell. I closed my eyes and I saw them kissing. I opened my eyes and I saw them in bed together. In her bed or in the bed Nathan and I shared, the one that was supposed to be exclusively ours.

I sat up slowly, self-loathing scorching through me.

'So what do we do now?' I asked Aidan. 'There's fifteen of them, not including their children, and only the two of us.'

'Does Nathan know you're on to them?' asked Aidan.

'No, I don't think so.'

'As long as he and the others don't know for sure, then we do to them what they wanted to do to us, only we do it first – starting with Nathan.'

'Meaning?'

'Meaning we do whatever is necessary to survive,' said my brother.

'What about the ones who were killed? D'you know who was responsible for that?' I asked.

'I'm still working on that,' said Aidan. 'Though I suspect they were got rid of because they refused to go along with the plans to dupe us.'

Appalled, I stared at him. 'You really think that was the reason they were killed?'

'What other reason could there be? They lived on Callisto together, they travelled on the transport ship *Galileo* together, they lived on Barros 5 together. So why would someone suddenly decide to bump them off one by one now? The reason must have something to do with us and our ship. We have it, they want it.'

I hated the fact that Aidan's logic made sense.

'Vee, I hope you're not going to argue with me on this,' he went on. 'It's us or them. We need to neutralize Nathan, his mum, Darren and Sam. They are the refugees' leaders.

We get rid of them, then we strike at the others before they have a chance to regroup.'

No!

Think, Vee. Think.

This was all moving way too fast.

Nathan was my husband and that meant something to me. I wasn't going to rush to believe he could be such a treacherous rat. Our time together deserved more than that. Nathan smiling at me, hugging me, holding me, feeding me when I was almost too tired to hold my spoon – they were all images that played in my mind. I shook my head. I couldn't give up on us that quickly. I just couldn't.

'I'm not going to move against anyone without more proof,' I said at last.

'How much more proof do you need, Vee?' Aidan was exasperated.

'More than I've currently got.'

'Do we have to be floating out into space before you believe Nathan is no good?' he asked. 'Nathan is cheating on you, and not just him but everyone on board is having a good laugh about it at your expense. He's using you to get what he and the rest of the drones want. And once they have this ship they'll have no further use for either of us. It's us or them.'

Everything my brother said made sense, but I still wasn't prepared to believe it. Not yet. I had to think rationally about this.

'Let me speak to Nathan,' I said. 'Then we can decide what our next move will be.'

'If you insist on speaking to him first, then do me a favour. You'll know exactly where you stand if you ask Nathan one simple question,' said Aidan.

'What question?'

'Ask him where the pendant you gave him is.'

'I know where it is – round Anjuli's neck,' I said bitterly.

'Yes, but Nathan doesn't know that you know that. Ask him. See what he says. If he's honest, if he respects you, he'll come right out and tell you the truth. But if he lies or, knowing him, tries to change the subject . . .' Aidan left the rest unsaid.

I nodded reluctantly. Aidan smiled, satisfied.

I stood up, more tired than I'd ever been in my life. Every part of me was folding in on itself and I wasn't fighting it. I wanted to be as small as possible until I faded away from all the sorrow, the pain overwhelming me.

'Vee, you know I love you, right?' asked Aidan.

I turned to him and dragged a smile onto my face. 'Yeah, I know.'

I headed back to my room, sealing the door. I sat on the bed, my knees drawn up, my head resting on them. Every hope and dream I'd had which featured Nathan and me together was slowly but surely withering inside.

What the hell was going on? I placed my hand against the palm-lock for a third time. Once again the door failed to open.

'Computer, put me through to Vee in room U-02,' I ordered.

The image of Vee's face appeared on the control panel in front of me beside our door. 'Yes?'

'Vee, I can't get into our room.'

Damn! What was that look Vee giving me all about? Her eyes were narrowed and there was no spark of warmth or welcome in them. I must've been mistaken because, a moment later, she'd moved away from the screen and I heard our door unlock. I entered the room.

'Why're you here, Nathan?' Vee's voice dripped with enough venom to kill at twenty paces. So I hadn't been mistaken.

I frowned. 'Why did you lock me out? I live here now. Remember?'

'I remember. You obviously don't. Could you get whatever it is you came for and leave please?' Vee turned to walk away from me but I grabbed her arm, spinning her round.

'What's going on, Vee? Why're you mad at me?'

She looked me up and down in the same way her brother had when he barged into our room and found me naked. It'd irritated me when he did it and it was doing the same thing now. Vee was looking at me like I was somewhere beneath contempt.

'Where's my dad's pendant that I gave you as a joining gift, Nate?'

'What?'

'You heard me. Where is it?'

Shit! I'd lost that thing and still hadn't found it yet. Time for some fast talking.

'Never mind the pendant, why did you seal the door against me?' I asked, figuring to get Vee's mind on something else.

'Where's the pendant I gave you, Nate?' Vee repeated with slow deliberation.

'Don't try to change the subject,' I said. 'Why did you seal the door? If Darren or one of the others has threatened you then you need to tell me. We have friends on board, Vee, friends who won't let Darren or anyone else harm us. And talking of friends, when are you going to get round to recalling Anjuli to the bridge? Seriously. Don't you think she's suffered enough?'

If I thought Vee's look was cold before, it was at absolute zero now.

'Nathan. Where. Is. The. Pendant?'

'We're talking about Anjuli here,' I blustered. 'Not some stupid pendant—'

Vee's hand flew out as she went to slap my face. I grabbed her wrist, but only just before her palm made contact with my cheek.

'If you slap me, I warn you, I'll slap you back.' I was just as pissed off as she was now.

'Let go of me,' Vee ordered, her voice low.

I let go of her wrist as if it was red hot. Vee had actually tried to hit me. I swore when I left Callisto that no one would ever strike me again. *No one.*

'I'd appreciate it if you got your shit together and left,' Vee told me.

'Just like that?'

'Just like that.'

We scowled at each other, neither of us moving, neither of us saying a word. Something ugly was in the room with us and it was writhing, coiling ever tighter around us. Was that it then? Was our joining over when it had barely begun? It couldn't be because I'd lost the pendant she gave me. No one broke up over the loss of a piece of jewellery, for God's sake. Had Vee finally woken up to the fact that I was a drone, and realized just what she'd tied herself to?

An alarm blared. It sounded like it was coming from the upper deck. God forgive me but my first thought was, 'Thank God!' Closely followed by, 'Now what?'

I ran for the door, closely followed by Vee. Our issues would just have to wait. We both sprinted along the corridor to where the alarm was coming from – the mess hall.

65

We entered the mess hall to a scene of absolute chaos. Max, Dooli, Rafael and a number of others were doubled over, clutching their stomachs. Simone and Khari, the children, stood beside Dooli, crying at her evident distress. Simone tried to stroke Dooli's hair as the woman writhed in agony. Others were actually being sick where they sat. The smell was horrendous, bad enough to make me recoil the moment I entered the room.

'What's happened?' I asked.

'Vee, get over here,' Doctor Liana called to me. 'That utility dispenser over there has laced every meal that came out of it with some kind of poison. Everyone who was sitting at my table has fallen ill.'

What on earth . . . ?

'Everyone?' I frowned.

The doctor nodded.

'Did everyone eat the same thing?' I asked.

'No. We all had different meals.'

'Which table?'

The doctor pointed to the nearest one to the table.

'It must've been that particular utility dispenser,' she insisted.

But there was no way any utility dispenser on board could do that. There were too many checks and balances that had to happen before the food was produced in the first place. And if there was something wrong with the programming of the dispensers, then every dispenser throughout the ship would be affected, not just one. So either one particular utility dispenser had been sabotaged, or there was a much simpler solution.

I ran over to the nearest table and retrieved an empty cup. Hedda sat with her head on the table, lying next to a pool of foul-smelling sick. Her skin was pale, almost translucent. I used the cup to scrape up some of her vomit, which was mixed with blood. Hedda's eyes were beginning to roll back in her head.

'Doctor, you're needed over here,' I called out.

Doctor Liana spoke briefly to Mike before coming over to Hedda. Those who weren't ill were helping the sick in any way they could by wiping their faces and trying to make them comfortable. I took the cup containing Hedda's vomit and ran out of the mess hall to the science lab opposite. The lab was empty, everyone having hurried across the corridor to help out in the mess hall.

I needed to hurry, to confirm whether or not my suspicions were correct. Once at the nearest control panel, I placed some of the vomit on one of the specimen plates beneath the panel and pushed it into the elemental spectrograph inlet that was a feature of the panels in the science lab. It provided a fast way to analyse any substance, no matter how minute, which wasn't exactly the problem here.

'Aidan, analyse this sample and tell me if it contains any poisons or pathogens that are dangerous to humans,' I said to the ship's computer.

The answer came back almost at once. 'This sample contains Aetonella bacteria, species *A. pentadensis*,' said Aidan's voice.

'Are you sure?' I said, horrified.

'Positive. This sample contains five per cent Aetonella bacteria,' said the computer.

The lethal dose was less than one per cent.

'Aidan, what's the treatment for Aetonella bacteria poisoning?' I asked.

'It depends on the amount ingested and the time since ingestion. If the amount swallowed is small and recent, an emetic is suggested. Otherwise make the patient comfortable until they die.'

The computer knew nothing of euphemisms or breaking bad news gently.

I ran back to the mess hall. The cries of agony and the sounds of retching hadn't faded. A couple of bodies lay on the floor. Others at the tables or kneeling on the floor were not in a good way. Aetonella bacteria poisoning was a swift but brutal way to die. I looked around, trying to ascertain the possible source of the poisoning, 'cause it sure as hell wasn't the utility dispensers. There were jugs of water on each table but the water would've come from the same source, unless the bacteria had been introduced into one particular jug. But who would do such a thing – and, perhaps more importantly, why?

I ran over to the table where people had got sick. Half-eaten plates of food were at every place setting. And half-full cups of water as well as other drinks like Prop, that nasty purple stuff some of them drank once their shifts were over. There was a tablet next to one place setting and it was showing the film *Dead Poets Society*. I recognized it at once. That had to be where the doctor was sitting. Had she decided to watch the film again after our conversation about it? Her plate contained a half-eaten baked potato with cheese. The glass beside her plate was three-quarters full, with water round the rim. At the next place setting someone had been sick. There were patches of vomit scattered over this one particular table and some on the floor around it.

More people ran into the mess hall, assessing the scene of pandemonium at a glance. Among them was Darren, who took a swift look around before his gaze landed on me.

'This is your doing,' he shouted, pointing straight at me. 'You won't be satisfied until you kill every last one of us. Well, I'm not going to stand around waiting for you to decide when it's my turn to die.' He turned to those around him. 'It's too late for Max and Dooli – look, everyone, look at their bodies! And it's *her* fault. She needs to be put in one of the detention cells and to stay there until we get to Mendela Prime or none of us will get there alive.'

If Darren had come at me by himself, I could've kicked his arse. Three or four of them against me would've been a fair fight. But suddenly I was surrounded. Where was Nathan? My instinct was to search for him in this sea of hostile faces but I couldn't see him. Four of them came at me at once. A roundhouse kick sent Harrison spinning, as did an upward palm to Maria's chin. I punched and kicked as more piled in. If I was going down, then these bastards would know they'd been in a fight. I held them off for as long as I could but I was simply outnumbered. It didn't take them long to get the upper hand, but get it they did. My limbs were grabbed and I was being held by at least three of them.

'Let go of me!' I shouted. 'Have you lost your minds? Let me go at once!'

It was no use. Though I bucked and heaved and kicked out, I was carried like a rabid dog to one of the four detention cells down on the starboard side of the cargo hold. Darren held my arms, smirking viciously down at me, while Maria and Harrison held onto my legs. I was gratified to see that Maria's nose had been bleeding and Harrison already had a huge lump on his forehead and his eye was swelling shut. They must all have had glue on their hands though because I couldn't get out of their grip no matter how much I writhed.

When we reached the cargo hold, I was not placed but thrown onto the floor of the detention cell before those carrying me legged it. Darren activated the nano-field as I jumped to my feet, my blood racing. In a number of the old films I'd watched, steel bars, thick walls and reinforced doors were used to keep people locked up. Now my way was barred by an adapted nano-field which gave out a non-lethal but still significant plasma shock. I wiped the back of my hand across my bottom lip. Blood.

I was bleeding.

They'd pay for that!

'Let me out of here,' I demanded.

'You've been indulged for long enough,' said Darren. 'You can stay in here until you rot. At least this way we'll know where you are at all times. You won't be picking off any more of us.'

'You've been patiently waiting for this moment, haven't you, Darren? Any excuse to get rid of me,' I said with contempt. 'You know as well as I do that all these incidents around the ship have absolutely nothing to do with me.'

'There were no unexplained deaths until we came aboard this damned ship. Now we're dropping like zapped flies. You do the maths,' Darren replied icily.

The cargo bay doors hissed open and Nathan came running in. I hadn't seen him since we both entered the mess hall. He stopped abruptly when he saw where I was, only to then sprint across the hold to the cells. He made for the panel in the wall beside my cell, reaching out to tap on the command to drop the nano-field and release me.

Darren pushed him aside to stand in his way. 'What d'you think you're doing?'

'What does it look like?' Nathan tried to push past him again, but Darren shoved him back. 'Listen, Darren, no way am I going to let Vee spend another moment in there,' Nathan insisted. 'Move.'

'She's in there and that's where she'll stay until the commander says otherwise,' said Darren. 'We're all in danger with her on the loose. You did see what just happened in the mess hall, didn't you?'

'This was my mum's idea?' Nathan said, shocked. 'I don't believe it.'

'The commander knows how dangerous Vee is, and like the rest of us she's had just about enough of this one and her brother,' said Darren. 'That girl will stay in there until we decide what to do with her.'

More proof – if any were required – that Aidan had been right about them all along.

'This is all kinds of wrong,' Nathan insisted. 'You have no proof that Vee had anything to do with what just happened – or any of the accidents on this ship.'

'Accidents, my arse,' Darren scoffed. 'Someone is deliberately and systematically trying to wipe us out.'

'Someone. Not Vee,' Nathan insisted.

I tried to school my features as I watched the performance going on before me. Nathan really was a fine actor. I mean, he was right up there with some of my favourites.

Was I supposed to be taken in by this show of him suddenly being on my side? Was I supposed to be so moved that I'd give up the last of the *Aidan*'s secrets – like the command code to take over the ship?

'Nathan, you're skating on very thin ice,' Darren warned. 'It's time for you to pick a side. Either you're with us or you're against us. Which is it?'

'Why don't you just kill me and have done with it?' I hissed at Darren.

'Not until we have full control of this ship. And mark me, we will get it – no matter what it takes,' Darren shot back, confirming my suspicions. He returned to Nathan. 'Which is it? Do you choose to live with us – or die with that whore?'

'Screw you!' I replied.

Nathan gave me a long look before turning back to Darren. He shrugged and said, 'I choose to live.'

I gasped. I couldn't help it. Nathan had finally stopped pretending. I wrapped my arms tightly around my waist. So stupid to hurt like this.

I turned away before the sting in my eyes became apparent to all present, especially him. I wouldn't give any of them the satisfaction. It took a couple of deep breaths and immense force of will to control myself before I could turn round to face them. But as I turned, Nathan launched himself at Darren. Harrison rushed to help his leader while Maria grabbed a pulsar rifle off the wall and pointed it at Nathan. Nathan had Darren on the floor and was about to punch him for a third time when Maria fired a warning shot which only just missed Nathan's head. He froze. Darren kicked him away and leaped to his feet. Nathan stood up, glaring at Darren with loathing.

'This is your choice? To betray your own kind?' Darren spat blood out of his mouth.

'I choose to be with my wife. So if she's in the brig, then that's where I need to be too,' said Nathan quietly.

'You're a fool, Nathan.'

'You're not the first to tell me that.'

'You want to die with her?'

'I'd rather live, but whatever I do it'll be at Vee's side,' Nathan replied.

Tears streamed down my face and I didn't even attempt to hide them. Nathan sounded so sincere and I so desperately wanted to believe him, but how could I? With narrow-eyed contempt, Darren nodded to his cronies. Harrison pointed a newly acquired pulsar at me, Maria pointed hers at Nathan. Darren used the control panel to drop the nano-field. Maria dug her gun into Nathan's stomach, urging him to turn round. Giving his colleagues a look of dripping contempt, Nathan stepped into my cell. The nano-field sprang up again behind him. Now we were both being held captive. Nathan spun to glare at his so-called friends.

'When you finally decide where your loyalties lie, we'll let you out,' Darren told him.

'Darren, you, the rest of your mob and my mother can all go to hell,' Nathan said.

He and Darren scowled at each other, no love lost between them.

'You are making a huge mistake,' I told Darren. 'You need to let me out of here before Aidan wakes up.'

'The moment your brother emerges from his quarters he'll be joining both of you,' Darren replied.

I shook my head. 'Darren, you don't know what you're doing. If Aidan wakes up and discovers you've locked me in here—'

'Yeah, yeah,' Darren dismissed. 'The day I can't handle a teenage boy is the day I retire.'

I looked him in the eye. I had to make him believe what I was about to say next. 'Today is not the day you retire, Darren, it's the day you die. If you don't let me out of here by the time Aidan wakes up, you will be responsible for the deaths of everyone on this ship.'

66

Maria was left outside our cell to guard us. I knew from my time on Callisto that there'd be no reasoning with her. Darren had told her to guard us and that was exactly what she'd do until hell froze over or until she was officially relieved of duty – whichever came first. I raised a tentative finger to the nano-field.

'Ow!'

Well, that bloody hurt! I wouldn't be doing that twice. I drew back my finger and cradled it in my other hand. Vee gave me a pitying look as I sat down beside her on the bed.

'You're brave, but you're not very bright, are you?' she said.

'Excuse me?'

'If you really wanted to help, you could've pretended to go along with Darren, then waited for the first appropriate opportunity to get me out of here,' she said.

Oh, hell no! 'Well, to use your phrase, pardon me all over the place for displaying some loyalty,' I seethed.

Vee was actually giving me grief for defending her? Seriously?

'Loyalty?' she said with scorn.

Having lived on Callisto, I knew about cold, but the temperature on that godforsaken moon had nothing on the look Vee was currently giving me. I was sick and tired of her looking at me like that.

'Nathan, you can drop the act now. If all this is a set-up to get the executive command code to this ship, then you're wasting your time.'

I frowned. 'I didn't ask for it.'

Shaking her head, Vee moved to sit at the other end of the bed, as far away from me as she could get.

'I've had enough of this,' I said, holding onto my temper with difficulty. 'Why are you freezing me out? The least you could do is tell me what I've done to upset you.'

'U-upset me?' Vee sputtered. She closed her eyes briefly and took a deep breath. 'I know about you and Anjuli.'

'What about me and Anjuli?'

'I know that you two are together, having sex, making love, an item, lovers, screwing each other, having a great laugh behind my back. Any and all of the above,' said Vee. 'You must really think I'm stupid. No, I take that back. I *am* stupid for falling for you and your lies.'

My blood ran icy-cold at her words. If she'd taken a knife and stabbed me through the heart, I couldn't have been more shocked. Or hurt.

'What the hell are you talking about? Anjuli and I are friends. That's *it*. End of story.'

'Oh, please,' Vee dismissed. 'Nate, give it up. I know what's going on.'

'Then explain it to me because I haven't got a clue.'

She scowled at me. 'You won't be happy until you get your pound of flesh, will you?'

'I genuinely don't have a clue what you're talking about.' And

I seriously didn't. Anjuli and me? The idea would be laughable if it wasn't so ludicrous. Anjuli had eyes for one person and one person only – Mike. Mike, however, wasn't interested in anything that didn't grow out of soil and need regular pruning.

Vee stilled as she regarded me. I've been looked at before with contempt, with dislike, with disapproval. But I have never had anyone look at me the way Vee did at that moment, with such complete and utter hatred that my blood froze within me.

67

Ignoring Nathan, I walked as close to the nano-field as I dared to address my jailer.

'Maria, you need to let me out of here if you want to live,' I told her.

Maria gave me a filthy look and turned to face the cargo-hold entrance, effectively turning her back on me.

'I'm not joking,' I said urgently. 'When Aidan wakes up, he'll do whatever it takes to get me out of here, and he won't let anyone or anything stand in his way. People are going to die if you don't let me out.'

'Shut the hell up and sit down,' she hissed at me. 'I won't tell you again.'

'Listen, crap-for-brains, you have to let me out of here!' I insisted.

Maria turned and pointed her gun at my chest. 'Sit. Down.'

Reluctantly I did as she said.

Well, I'd tried.

Nathan was still glaring at me, annoyed that I'd rumbled his scam. Well, tough. He and his friends and colleagues had brought what was about to happen on themselves.

All I could do now was wait for my brother to get from his room on the upper deck to down here on the lower deck, and I didn't doubt that by the time he reached me he'd have blood on his hands.

Literally.

There was something else going on here, more than just Vee worrying about her brother being angry when he found out what had happened to her. Aidan would be one against many when he emerged from his quarters, and yet Vee seemed to be more scared *of* her brother than *for* him.

'Vee, what is it about Aidan that you're not telling us?'

Vee considered for a few moments. 'I'll tell you because then maybe you can persuade the bitch out there to let me out,' she said at last. 'My brother's first and most important mission is to keep me safe and make sure no harm comes to me. In the past, every time I've had to enter dangerous but necessary situations, I've had to order Aidan to allow me to do so.'

'Order him?'

'Otherwise he'd never let me do them – and that includes rescuing all of you from Barros 5,' said Vee. 'Aidan has constant on-going access to all non-private computer data. My imprisonment in here will be on the computer. The moment my brother wakes up he'll know that I've been thrown into this detention cell. He'll make it his mission to rescue me. The fact that I'm alive means you and your friends stand some chance. If you had killed me, you would've stood no chance at all.'

'There's only the two of you and several of us . . .' *You and us . . .* God, I hated saying that to Vee. When had it become 'you' and 'us'? It should've been all of us in this together. Why couldn't Vee see that I was on her side, that I'd always be on her side?

'It won't make any difference,' Vee sighed. 'Aidan will come to rescue me and God help anyone who gets in his way. Nathan, I'm not exaggerating. You've got to get me out of here before Aidan wakes up.'

'There's nothing I can do. I went to the bridge to find Mum when I saw what was going on in the mess hall but she wasn't there. I suspect this is all Darren's idea, but if Mum really is behind this then she's probably instructed Darren and some others to get into Aidan's quarters and detain him as we speak.'

'They won't get in there until Aidan is ready to come out. His quarters are the most secure on the ship,' Vee replied.

'Why do his quarters need to be any more secure than yours?' I frowned.

'In case we were ever boarded by an enemy,' Vee replied. 'It was crucial that Aidan survive.'

'What about *your* survival?'

'Mine depends on my brother's,' said Vee.

I scrutinized her. Her gaze fell away from mine. I knew what that meant.

'What aren't you telling me?'

Vee sighed, then gave me a long, hard look. 'Aidan is very special.'

That was one word for him. Not the word I'd use, but still. 'What d'you mean – special?'

'I mean, this ship and my brother are one and the same thing.'

69

Nathan frowned. 'Yeah, I know they both have the same name—'

'No, you don't understand. It's more than that.' Was I really going to tell him this? He should be aware of just what he and the rest of his friends were up against – not that it would do them any good – but I reckoned I owed him that much. 'Aidan is an extension of the ship's computer. He's an extension of the ship. He *is* the ship.'

Nathan's frown deepened and I could understand why. I wasn't explaining this very well at all. He remained silent, sensing that more was coming. His senses didn't deceive him. I'd never said the words I was about to say out loud before. It was a secret only my family knew, and Mum and Dad had taken it to the grave.

'D'you remember I told you that the original crew were infected with a virus that wiped them all out?'

Nathan nodded. I took a deep breath. God, this was so hard. Hearing the words spoken would make it impossible for me to push reality to one side the way I had been doing. That's how I'd kept calm and carried on until now. I had accepted what my brother had become without question. Now all that was about to change.

I swallowed hard, my gaze on my hands lying in my lap. 'When the virus invaded this ship, my brother was the first to die. You see, Aidan had set up the computer to transfer him in and out of a Mazon ship that was in range. My brother was a computer genius, so he knew how to bypass all the regular computer security protocols.'

A glance at Nathan told me I had his full stunned attention.

'He only transferred over for a few seconds, then he was back on our ship. But it was long enough to pick up a Mazon airborne virus. He brought it back to this ship and the rest of the crew got infected, but Aidan died first.'

Tell him the whole truth, Vee, not just the edited highlights . . .

But I couldn't.

If Nathan and I hadn't had so much hurt and misunderstanding between us then maybe it'd be different, but he wasn't ready to hear the whole truth and I wasn't ready to tell it.

I risked a glance at him, only to see Nathan frowning at me. 'If Aidan died, then who's the guy on board this ship calling himself your brother?'

'Before Aidan died, he was given a number of brain and body scans and his brain patterns were all mapped and stored. When it became obvious that he wasn't going to make it, Mum and Dad were frantic to find a way to ensure that even if Aidan died, what he was, *who* he was, wouldn't be lost. So all Aidan's brain patterns and engrams were implanted and amalgamated with the ship's computer, along with his memories, his speech patterns and all the data we had on him, including photographs, audio and visual recordings, DNA, the lot. Mum and Dad wanted to preserve as much of my brother as they could, but then something unexpected happened . . .'

'What?' Nathan prompted after a significant pause.

'What makes us who we are?' I asked. 'We're our memories, our experiences, our thoughts and dreams – and something else, something indefinable. Some call it a divine spark, some say being sentient and self-aware is the mark of true adaptive intelligence.'

'I don't get where you're going with this,' said Nathan. 'And how can your brother be dead? For God's sake, the Aidan I met wasn't a hologram.'

'No. Aidan *is* my brother.'

'You just said your brother died.'

'He did.'

'OK. I'm officially confused.' Nathan shook his head.

'Dad adapted the ship's automated robot to make it a physical manifestation and extension of the ship's computer. When he died, I turned the ship's robot into Aidan.'

'You said the ship's robot was destroyed during an exploration mission,' Nathan accused.

'I lied,' I admitted. 'I carried on Dad's work to make sure my brother didn't die. I've modified Aidan extensively over the years, so now he's much more than a mere robot. You asked me once what I did when my parents and the rest of the crew died. Well, most of my time was spent working on Aidan, making him as human as possible. I turned him into the brother I'd lost. He really is my brother, down to the way he looks and smells and talks and laughs – except when you all came aboard, I realized his voice wasn't quite deep enough for his age so I modified that.'

'Anjuli told me Aidan's voice had changed,' said Nathan, shaking his head. 'I told her she was imagining things.'

She'd spotted that? I'd altered Aidan's voice to change gradually over the course of several days. I hadn't expected anyone to notice. 'Your lover is really smart,' I conceded.

'How many times must I tell you, there is nothing between Anjuli and me except recycled air?' Nathan asked, exasperated.

'Yeah, right. You expect me to believe someone who can't keep his hands off others?' I said with scorn.

His green eyes spitting fury, Nathan opened his mouth, only to snap it shut without saying a word.

We glared at each other. It took Nathan several deep breaths before he managed to gain control of himself. Pfft! He was just pissed that I could finally see through him.

'I've seen plenty of robots before. None of them ever looked or behaved as realistically as your brother,' he said at last. 'They're deliberately built not to look too much like us humans.'

A change of subject? Fine with me. 'Well, I wanted to make Aidan as real as possible. I wanted my brother back.'

'And you did all that by yourself?'

'Aidan and I are twins. He wasn't the only one born with functioning brain cells.' I bristled. 'And, like I said, I had three years to dedicate to getting my brother back.'

'That's the reason why you gave the ship's computer the same name as your android brother and gave it his voice, isn't it? Because they're one and the same.'

My silence was his answer.

'Tell me more about this android who has been running the ship.' Nathan sounded dubious, not to mention belligerent.

'Listen, Nathan. Aidan is real, as real as you or me. His body is mostly cybernetics but he thinks and has emotions the same as us.'

'Hang on,' Nathan interrupted. 'When Darren hit him, Aidan's lip was bleeding. I saw it.'

'He has a rudimentary circulatory system containing some of my blood, which is packed full of anti-coagulants and plasma, and a small pump at the base of his spine to keep it all moving round his body.'

'But why? What's the point of that?'

I sighed. 'I didn't want Aidan to face any prejudice for not being fully human. A bit of blood leaking from any superficial wound would make sure no one got suspicious about him. And it worked, didn't it?'

'Your brother really is a robot? God, I'm still trying to

wrap my head around that one,' said Nathan. 'I'd never have guessed.'

'You're not listening to me. He's not just a robot. He's more than that. Don't you understand? He's Aidan the ship, Aidan the computer and Aidan my brother all at the same time. He's so much more than merely human and I couldn't love him any more than I already do.'

'How does he learn? How does he grow and adapt?'

Hadn't Nathan heard anything I'd just said? He was still trying to wrap his head around the concept of Aidan not being human.

'He's the same as us,' I replied. 'He's an AI unit, capable of learning from his mistakes as well as his successes, just like us. In fact, he learns faster and adapts quicker than we do. He's much stronger, faster and smarter – at most things. I can still beat him at chess though, but only because I initially programmed him not to learn from his chess game mistakes, but even with that handicap he's adapting and changing and growing. He's adapting his own programming. He's now almost as good as me at the game. He's his own person.' I was desperate for Nathan to see Aidan as I did, not as a machine but as a real, live person. Maybe not fully human, but a person nonetheless.

'If he's so much stronger and faster, why didn't he sabotage the Mazon ships instead of you?' Nathan asked.

'Because he's stronger than me but not invincible. The contamination from the Mazon engine core would've knocked out his neural network immediately. He wouldn't have stood a chance. Plus his reaction times are faster than mine. I needed him on the outside in case I got into trouble. With his help, everything on this ship has been adapted to work better and be more durable than standard Authority equipment.'

'Including the environmental protection suits?' Nathan asked.

I nodded, wondering why he asked about those in particular? Nathan was silent for a while. I could almost hear the wheels going round in his head.

'All those times Aidan was supposedly off-duty, he was recharging, wasn't he?'

'Yes.'

'So, he's not entirely infallible, then?' Nathan said with derision.

'He needs to recharge the same as us, only we call it sleep,' I replied.

'When Darren first hit Aidan, your brother got a strange look on his face and you had to tell him to stand down,' he mused. 'He was going to go for Darren, wasn't he?'

Oh God . . .

'Your brother isn't subject to the three robotic laws, is he?' asked Nathan, his voice low and filled with scathing contempt.

I stared at him. Did I look as guilty as I felt? I'd obviously underestimated just how sharp he was. One of the many things I'd got wrong about him.

'Did you alter him?' asked Nathan. 'Did you remove the robotic safeguards from his neural network?'

I said nothing, which gave him his answer. Appalled, he stared at me.

'When Mum and Dad and everyone died, I was terrified,' I rushed to explain. 'I was heartsick and grief-stricken and terrified out of my skull – all the time. There was only me left. Me and Aidan. I needed my brother to protect me, to look after me. To keep me safe as well as sane. D'you know it took me months after everyone died before I could even travel to any part of the ship on my own?' I bowed my head, the memory of my own weakness clawing at me. During my first year alone I had truly thought that I wouldn't make it. Each day was an immense, intense struggle just to get out of bed each morning.

'I was so far from home and all I wanted was to see Earth once again. Being back on Earth would mean I could stop living in fear, but I was so far away. So I decided early on that if a threat did find its way aboard this ship, I didn't want Aidan to hesitate in protecting me.'

'So you reprogrammed him so that the three robotic laws wouldn't apply?' Nathan's voice was gruff with disbelief.

'I didn't change them so they wouldn't apply at all. I just amended them.'

'Amended them how?' he asked frostily. 'The first law states that a robot may not injure a human being or, through inaction, allow a human being to come to harm.'

'I changed that one to—' My lips clamped together.

What I was about to say next would not show me in a good light.

'Yeah? I'm listening,' Nathan prompted.

'A robot may not injure Olivia Sindall or, through inaction, allow Olivia Sindall to come to harm unless she orders otherwise.'

'Christ on a bike!' Nathan exclaimed.

'I was only fifteen when I did it – remember?' I protested.

'And the second law?' asked Nathan. 'A robot must obey the orders given it by human beings except where such orders would conflict with the First Law.'

'A robot must obey the orders given to it by Olivia Sindall,' I admitted.

'That's it?'

'That's it.'

'And the third one? A robot must protect its own existence as long as such protection does not conflict with the First or Second Laws.'

'I left that one alone,' I replied.

'You really are a piece of work, aren't you?'

It wasn't a compliment.

I tried to defend myself. 'I was fifteen, OK. I was alone and terrified and fifteen. Give me a break.'

'The three laws were put in place for a reason. You bypassed the lot of them.'

Only the first two actually, but now wasn't the time to quibble.

'I was going to reinstate them when we got close to Earth again,' I said.

'So let me get this straight: Aidan is a robot with super strength and super speed, and there is nothing inside him to regulate his behaviour. I can't believe you'd be stupid enough to change his fundamental programming like that.'

'He thinks and feels just like any human. He has my brother's brain patterns and engrams so he knows right from wrong. Up until now that's been enough to make him consider his actions,' I replied. 'And I don't appreciate being called stupid.' Even if it did apply.

'So Aidan experiences emotions the same as us humans?'

I nodded. 'Yes.'

'All emotions?'

'I guess so, yes.' I frowned. 'There's no reason why he couldn't.'

'How old was your brother when he died?'

'Fifteen. Why?'

'Were you two close?'

'Very. We still are. We were and are best friends as well as twins. Why?'

Where was Nathan going with all these questions? What was he driving at?

'Did he have friends on the ship, apart from you?' he asked.

My frown deepened. 'Not many. He was probably the smartest person on board but he was a bit sickly and spent a lot of time in the medi bay or in his quarters with only me for company,' I said. 'Why?'

'Because I think your brother has set us both up,' said Nathan grimly.

'What d'you mean?'

'It was just you and your robot brother for years,' he said. 'And then you rescued us from Barros. Your brother has resented our presence ever since we came aboard, and he hates my guts.'

What? 'Of course he doesn't. That's ridiculous.'

'You said it yourself, he's capable of human emotions. *All* human emotions, even the negative ones,' said Nathan.

'Like what?'

'Like fear and jealousy.'

'Fear of what?' I scoffed. 'Jealous of whom?'

'Fear of losing you,' Nathan replied. 'Jealous of me, because suddenly *I* had all your attention, not him.'

'That's nonsense. He's my brother.'

'You're a fraud, Vee. You want the world to think of your brother as human when you yourself don't think of him that way. Not entirely.'

I glared at Nathan. 'What're you talking about?'

'Why is it so hard for you to believe your brother experiences emotions the same as the rest of us? Your brother loves you. He's devoted to you. So why won't you believe that he feels jealousy and hatred?'

'Hatred?'

'Of me, for taking you away from him. He's jealous of

me and would stop at nothing to drive us apart.'

'That's not Aidan,' I insisted. 'He doesn't feel those things. He's above all that.'

'Oh my God. Vee, open your damned eyes. Aidan hates my guts,' Nathan insisted. 'Emotionally he's a lonely fifteen-year-old boy who's always had you to himself. And then I came along. I bet he's the one who has been filling your head with all kinds of lies about me and Anjuli.'

'Aidan didn't need to lie to me,' I said bitterly. 'I gave you my dad's pendant to show you just how much I . . . I loved you, and you gave it to Anjuli.'

'D'you know, that's the first time you've actually said those words to me, even if it was in the past tense,' Nathan said quietly. 'And I did not give your pendant to Anjuli.'

I couldn't believe he still insisted on denying it.

'Nathan, I saw her wearing it with my own two eyes. I gave you a gift with love for you to keep. You gave it away like it was nothing, like it was garbage. And then you lied to my face when I asked you where it was.' I tried to swallow my anger but I was choking on it.

'You're saying Anjuli has my pendant?' Nathan shook his head. 'That's impossible. I know I should've told you I mislaid the thing somewhere in our quarters, but I sure as hell didn't give it to Anjuli. And she wouldn't just take it.'

For heaven's sake! Why was he still lying about it?

'Nathan, I saw it round her neck.'

'It can't be the same one,' he denied.

'Aidan examined it. He confirmed there's a tiny notch

on the back of it which I made by accident years ago. We'd both know it anywhere. It's my dad's pendant all right.'

'If it is, I never gave it to Anjuli,' Nathan insisted.

Eyes narrowed, I glared at him. Whoops! Was my scepticism showing? I could only hope so. 'Then how did she get it?'

'I don't know.' Nathan's tone was more vehement. 'But I intend to find out.'

I admit it, I was puzzled. Nathan seemed genuinely stunned that Anjuli should have my dad's pendant. No one's acting was that good, was it?

'And if you suspected me of something, why didn't you just come right out and ask me?' Nathan continued.

'Oh no you don't.' Was he for real? 'Don't try and turn this round onto me.'

'It's not all about you, Vee. It's about *us*. Why didn't you just ask me straight out?'

'I did. You lied to me.'

'I've never lied to you and I never will,' said Nathan coldly.

'Except when you do,' I dismissed. 'Even Anjuli called you a liar and a whoremeister.'

Nathan's mouth dropped open. He'd been caught in his colossal lie and was still trying to deny it. He thought that little of me.

'Yeah, checkmate,' I said with contempt. 'You know what? If you're just going to keep lying then I'm done talking to you.'

So much for Nathan being sincere. I can't believe the guy tried to make out that I was the one in the wrong. I turned away from him to underline the fact that our conversation, such as it was, was over.

'Olivia, why did you go through the joining ceremony with me?' Nathan asked.

'Why d'you think?'

'I thought I knew. I thought you felt the same way I did. Now I realize that wasn't the case.'

My head whipped round at that. 'I joined with you because I fell in love with you,' I told him. 'And what's more, you knew it. I would've flown into a star if you'd told me to, that's how much I loved you. You, on the other hand, had a completely different agenda – to seduce this ship out from under me. You've all been having a great laugh behind my back, haven't you? I've been the on-board entertainment. How did the conversation with your mum go? "Vee's been alone for so long and she's obviously attracted to me, so let me do whatever it takes to get the command code. *Whatever* it takes." Is that about right? You ripped my heart out, Nathan.'

Nathan stared at me. I glared right back. He actually opened his mouth to argue, but before he could utter a word the ship's alarm sounded.

I *really* hated that sound. My heart sank. Nathan looked at me, his expression grim. We both knew only too well what that noise meant.

'Aidan's awake.'

70

It didn't take long before I heard panicked shouts, screams and the firing of pulsar rifles. I leaped to my feet and headed for the nano-field barrier. Maria was on the other side of the cell, looking anxious, her head turning this way and that.

'Maria, you've got to let us out,' I pleaded. 'Vee is the only one who can stop her brother.'

'Move back,' she ordered.

'Listen, if you don't let us out, you will all die.' Vee had joined me at that the nano-field.

'I have my orders,' Maria said stubbornly.

'I hope that's a comfort to you when my brother rips your head off – literally,' said Vee.

'He's just a boy—' she began.

'Aidan is an android with super speed and super strength, and pulsar rifles and a few punches will not stop him,' Vee said, her voice low but urgent. 'The moment he discovered I was in here he went into protection mode. He will annihilate anyone who tries to stop him from getting me out.'

As if to reinforce her words, we heard the sound of pulsar rifle fire just outside the cargo hold.

'If you won't let us out, at least go and hide,' Vee said angrily.

'I don't want any more deaths on my conscience.'

The cargo door was blasted open, the noise deafening. Aidan strode into the room, turning his head slowly to scan the hold. I inhaled sharply before all the breath left my body and stayed away. His eyes – Aidan's eyes didn't look human any more. His eyes, including his irises and pupils, were now entirely white. He had blood on his clothes and I didn't doubt for a second that not all of it came from him. Two arms, two legs, one head as before, but he didn't look human. He strode across the cargo hold with relentless purpose.

'Maria, run,' Vee ordered.

A pulsar blast hit Aidan in the back but he didn't pause. He made his way towards our detention cell. Vee took a step back, her expression fearful. Instinctively I stepped in front of her. Maria raised her rifle, pointing it straight at Aidan's chest.

'Move b-back,' she stammered in fright. 'I'm w-warning you . . .'

Aidan walked towards us, his stride purposeful but unhurried. Maria opened fire. The rifle pulse ripped through his jacket and the shirt underneath but it didn't even slow him down, never mind stop him. The pulses bounced off his chest like she was firing air at him. Judging by the rips, tears and burns in Aidan's clothes, Maria wasn't the first to fire at him. His clothes were taking a beating even if he wasn't.

Aidan was only a few steps away now. And still Maria held her ground. He reached out for her, grabbed her by the shirt and tossed her across the cargo hold. She hit the opposite wall with a bone-cracking thud and fell without uttering another sound. If she wasn't dead, she was dying.

Aidan stared at me, then moved to the panel on the wall outside the cell to switch off the nano-field. The very thing that had kept me prisoner had also kept me safe, and I won't lie – I was sad to see it go. He stepped into the detention cell. Vee stepped forward but again I moved in front of her.

Aidan reached for me. I kicked out, my foot making contact with the side of his head. I managed to knock him off balance so that he had to sidestep to stay upright, but that's all I managed to do. Aidan's head turned and his expression altered. That slow, creepy twist of the lips that he called a smile was back. This wasn't Aidan the android in control, this was Vee's fifteen-year-old brother who loathed my guts for stealing his sister's attention and affection. I tried to jump backwards, away from him. His hands shot out and the next thing I knew he was holding me up in the air high above his head, ready to either bend me backwards to break my spine in two or pile-drive me into the ground. Either way, it was going to hurt.

I turned my head to look at Vee. That was about all I could do. If my last moment in this universe had come, that's all I wanted to do. Vee hadn't moved. She wasn't looking at Aidan but up at me, hurt and something else in her eyes. Something chilling, merciless. Then I recognized it for what it was.

Hatred.

She hated me.

Hated me enough to stand back and watch me die at her brother's hands.

Fuck.

71

Aidan raised his left knee. He was still holding Nathan above his head and obviously intended to drop him on his bent leg from a height to break his spine.

'NO! AIDAN, LET HIM GO!'

Aidan turned to look at me.

'Aidan, don't. Let him go. Please.'

He lowered his left leg to stand on both feet. Still holding Nathan high above his head, Aidan let him go and watched him drop. Nathan tried to break his fall, using his arms to impact the floor first. I heard a crack and he cried out in agony. He'd broken his arm or his wrist. Either way one of his arms was now useless. Eyes narrowed, Aidan hauled Nathan to his feet and put one hand round his neck, lifting him off the floor, kicking. Then he started to squeeze. It was impossible for Nathan to breathe. A few more seconds and it would all be over.

No!

'AIDAN, STOP! DROP HIM. NOW!' I ran over to my brother to pull his hands away from Nathan's throat. 'Aidan, you are not to harm him. That's an order. Stop.'

Aidan turned to face me, his head moving like his neck was stiff. He dropped Nathan, who fell to his knees, clutching at his neck with his good hand and coughing wildly.

'Aidan, stand down.' I placed my hands on his cheeks and looked into his eyes. 'Please, Aidan, stand down.'

He closed his eyes. When he opened them again, his irises were beginning to change back to normal. Across the hold, the lift doors opened. Darren and Alex raced over to us, their pulsar rifles blasting. Aidan pushed me to the floor and turned to face them, back in protection mode with a vengeance. Once again, his eyes were fully white, allowing him to see in a number of spectra at once.

'Darren, don't be a fool. Drop your weapon,' I called out. 'You need to show Aidan that you're not a threat.'

Darren charged at him, his pulsar rifle blazing while he cursed us both with words I'd never heard in that particular order before. I launched myself on top of Nathan, trying to cover him so that he wouldn't be hit by stray weapons fire. He groaned beneath me. I was hurting his arm but that couldn't be helped. I risked a glance up to see Aidan holding Darren off the floor by his neck.

Darren was kicking and struggling while Aidan regarded him, tilting his head as he slowly smiled.

'This is for my sister,' he said softly.

'Aidan, wait—' I began.

But too late. A quick upward jerk of Aidan's hand and Darren was still, his neck broken. I turned away, sickened.

Alex, Darren's colleague, immediately dropped his rifle and started to back away, his hands out before him to show that they were empty. Aidan didn't follow him. He stood like a sentinel between me and Nathan and the rest of the world. I rolled off Nathan and got to my feet, putting out my hand to help him up. He looked at me, his emerald-green eyes dark and ice-cold. Using his good hand, he pushed himself up. My empty hand fell to my side as Nathan and I watched each other.

He knew that I'd come within a hair's breadth of letting him die.

He knew.

 # NATHAN

Mum ran into the cargo hold flanked by Sam and Harrison, both of whom were armed. She made her way over to the detention cells, only to stop short when she saw Darren lying dead on the floor.

'Don't come any closer,' Vee pleaded. 'And for God's sake, put down your weapons. There's been enough bloodshed. If Aidan perceives you as a threat, he'll drop you where you stand.'

Mum turned to the men behind her and nodded. Harrison didn't need to be told twice. Sam wanted to hold onto his gun, but thank God common sense kicked in. Watching Aidan intently, he carefully lowered his rifle to the floor.

'Nathan, are you all right?' Mum asked me slowly, though she never took her eyes off Aidan.

No, I wasn't all right. My arm hurt like a son of a bitch and Vee wanted me dead.

I know which one hurt worse.

'I'm fine, Mum,' I replied quietly.

'Vee, I had nothing to do with this.' Mum was facing Vee now, speaking quietly but with real urgency. 'I had no idea what Darren and the others were planning. Darren only told me what he'd done after the event.'

I risked a glance in Vee's direction when she didn't reply. She wasn't looking at Mum but at me. I immediately turned away. I couldn't bear to look at her. It hurt too much.

'Nathan, you'd better leave,' said Vee. 'Go and get your arm sorted out.'

I walked out of the cell, quite frankly not caring if Aidan attacked me again. If he did then he'd be doing me a favour by putting me out of my misery.

Vee wanted me dead.

She'd got her wish.

Everything was so messed up. Two people were dead – Maria and Darren. Three more were injured, one of them seriously. The only small mercy was that Aidan hadn't hurt the children, Simone and Khari, who were distraught and grieving for Dooli. Rafael was currently looking after them.

Everything was so damned messed up.

Aidan was no longer in protection mode but it didn't matter. The bodies were removed from the cargo hold, but no one wanted help from me or my brother. The commander gave her quiet orders and everyone skirted round us, giving us a wide berth. When at last we made our way back to the bridge, no one came near us. And I do mean no one. And, as Aidan's sister, I was viewed as just as dangerous, if not more so because I controlled him.

We made one stop before we headed back to the bridge – the medical bay on the mid deck. Doctor Liana and Mike was busy tending to the injured, some of whom had their friends around them. The moment Aidan and I walked in all talk ceased. Every eye was on us. Fear was a living, breathing presence in the room. It was as if everyone had taken a step back from us even though no one had moved. I looked at Aidan. He was back to normal but he hadn't said a word since he came out of protection mode. I knew my brother could feel but, not for the first time, I wondered if he felt things in the same way I did. How did it feel to know he'd killed and injured so many people? Did he justify it in his cybernetic mind by telling himself that it was self-defence, that he was coming to my aid and that my safety was his priority? Did he tell himself it was just the way he was wired? Or did he not tell himself anything at all? He didn't say and I didn't ask.

'Back to work,' the doc ordered Mike. Her tone was terse but that could be put down to the pressure she was under.

'Doctor Liana, may I have a word with you?'

'Not now, Vee. Can't you see I'm busy?'

'It can't wait, Doctor,' I insisted.

Irritated, Doctor Liana came over to the now-closed medi-bay door where Aidan and I stood alone. She was the first person I'd seen since leaving the detention cell who hadn't viewed me and my brother with abject fear.

'What's so important that it can't wait?' she asked.

Pause.

'Doctor Liana, why did you do it?'

Her eyebrows raised, she looked at me with unconcerned patience, waiting for me to elaborate. 'You'll have to be a little less vague if you expect a meaningful answer,' she said.

'Why have you been killing your own?' I asked. 'You're

responsible for all the so-called accidents that have plagued this ship – the airlock, the engine conduits, the mess hall. One Elite to another, I'd like to know why.'

'I don't know what you're talking about,' said the doctor, giving me an indulgent smile. 'Are you ill, Vee? Stressed? Now that you've officially registered me as the ship's doctor, I'm the only one on board who can legitimately relieve you of your duties. You know that, right?'

'I know. And with your expertise and your nanites still in the ship's computer, I don't doubt that you could do it too. Like I said, I'd just like to know why. I give you my word as an Elite that I won't repeat a word of our conversation.'

The doctor swatted aside my question with a shrug and an imperious wave of her hand. 'What are you accusing me of? The only mindless killer on board is your brother.'

'Come on, Doc. No one else is around, it's just us. Let's face it, no one will believe a word I say now. Commander Linedecker will take over this ship and fly you all to Mendela Prime, and there you'll stay, which I suppose is what you really wanted all along.'

'NO!' The doctor raised her voice. She glanced around quickly, before lowering it to a more normal level. 'I want to go back home to Earth.'

'And I was going to take you there, so why set me up? Why make it look like I'm the one responsible for the incidents in the airlock and the engine room and the mess hall? What did I do to make you hate me that much?'

I'd confided in this woman. Trusted her. I'd sincerely thought we were friends. Apart from Nathan, she was the one with whom I felt I had most in common. She'd been like a second mum to me. God, but my judgement of people sucked.

'Of course I don't hate you, Olivia. You're one of the few people on this ship I can tolerate. I'm on your side; I always have been.'

'You have a strange way of showing it,' I scoffed. 'Setting me up to take the blame for your actions.'

'Olivia, the ones who died, they weren't your friends,' Doctor Liana insisted. 'Jaxon was plotting with Darren to take the ship from you from the first day they arrived. And Ian and Corbyn had agreed to join them.'

Stunned, I stared at her.

'Exactly. I couldn't let them do that,' said the doctor. 'I was genuinely sorry about Mei and Saul, especially Mei. She wasn't allergic to art and culture like most of them on Callisto. Her death was a real shame. It was just supposed to be Jaxon and Darren in that airlock, but Jaxon was alone when he met Mei and Saul to try and persuade them round to his cause. Jaxon reckoned the airlock was the only place on board where conversations weren't recorded.'

'They aren't recorded in the sleeping quarters either,' I pointed out.

'Yes, they are. They're just securely stored and never accessed unless someone dies in their room or something happens that needs investigating,' she said. 'Jaxon and

Darren held all their clandestine meetings in the airlocks until the . . . accident.'

'How d'you know all this?'

'They tried to recruit me too,' the doctor replied.

'And Mei and Saul?'

A pause, then she shrugged. 'Collateral damage. Accidents happen.'

I gasped. I couldn't help it.

'Like I said, I'm sorry about Mei and Saul, but they shouldn't have been in the airlock.'

Whoa!

Keep talking, Vee. Don't show your revulsion.

I had to appeal to the part of her that considered the drones beneath her. She thought she and I were alike. Elites. Kindred spirits. I needed her to go on thinking that.

'And those in the mess hall?'

'You mean the bores at my table?' said Doctor Liana with scorn. 'All they could talk about were the merits of utility dispenser Prop versus the stuff they used to swill back on Callisto. That and what their lives would be like on Mendela Prime. I could've told them their lives on Mendela would be exactly what they were on Callisto. That class of people take their ignorance with them wherever they go.'

'Max and Dooli *died*.'

'Then I did them a favour,' Doctor Liana said evenly.

Oh. My. God! I tried hard to keep my expression neutral but it was so hard. Now that the doctor was talking, she didn't seem to want to stop and I wasn't going to get in her way.

'What was wrong with talking about their dreams for their lives on Mendela Prime?' I asked. 'Was that a bad thing?'

'I want to go home, to Earth,' said the doctor. 'I don't want to go to Mendela Prime first. I don't want to go there at all. I'm sick of space: I'm sick of moons and miners and morons. I'm sick of transports and ships. I want to go home. And with what I know about everyone on board this ship and the Resistance movement and all the pirates and traders who help those on Callisto and the other moons to escape, I can easily buy my freedom.'

'So you were willing to trade their lives to get what you want?'

The doctor opened her mouth, only to snap it shut again. She seemed to realize that she was being a little too out-spoken. Her gaze grew speculative as she regarded me.

'If I were responsible for the incidents on board, which I'm not, but if I were, I'd be willing to do whatever it takes to get home with no detours along the way,' she said. 'Of course, I'm just guessing as to what the motive behind all these accidents might be.'

'Mei, Saul, Jaxon, Ian, Corbyn, Max and Dooli – you're responsible for all their deaths. Doesn't that mean anything to you.'

'Meh! Prove it.'

I shook my head. 'I don't need to prove it. Commander

Linedecker is no one's fool. She'll figure out what you've done.'

'Catherine? I don't think so. All she cares about are her precious drones. I suspect she's convinced you're responsible for all those deaths. She'd much rather believe you're responsible than her vulgar colleagues. There's a woman who's forgotten what it's like to be civilized.'

My jaw dropped. 'And murdering people? That's civilized behaviour, is it?'

'I was helping you,' said the doctor. 'Protecting you – just like your brother here.'

I was about to throw up.

'I could always tell the commander the truth,' I said through gritted teeth. 'Tell her about this conversation.'

'You gave me your word that you wouldn't, or have you been around drones for so long that you can't remember how to keep a promise? Besides, why would Catherine or anyone else on board believe a word you say?' asked the doctor. 'It's your word against mine and everyone knows that you and your brother are stone-cold killers.'

'I've restored the three robotic laws in my brother. He can't harm any more humans,' I said. 'What I did was wrong but I was all alone on this ship and acted out of fear. You? You're deranged. You're Norman Bates with a medi kit. That's the big difference.'

'Norman Bates from the film *Psycho*?' Doctor Liana smiled in amusement. 'I'm probably the only one on board this ship who would've got that reference, which shows the type of people I've had to associate with for the last several years. Well, no more. I want to go home. I want to be with my own kind, with people like you, not with ignorant drones.'

Oh hell, no!

'I'm nothing like you,' I said, outraged, my mask slipping somewhat.

'Of course you are.' The doctor smiled. 'You have a love of literature and films and music and art, all the things that separate us from beasts and drones.'

'Don't you think it's damned hard to care about music, literature and culture when you're close to starving, working in inhuman conditions in the mines and having to fight every day to survive?' I asked scathingly. 'Don't you have any empathy? D'you lack the imagination to realize that? If so, then perhaps you should read more books.' I clamped my lips together to stem my verbal tirade against this bitch.

Silence reigned between us.

'Tell me something – still speculating of course,' Doctor Liana said at last. 'What made you decide I had something to do with the deaths on this ship?'

'You had the technical know-how and everyone at your table in the mess hall got ill – except you,' I answered. 'I think you spiked the jug of water, probably after you poured out a glass for yourself, and then you poured a drink for everyone else and sat back to watch them all become violently ill.'

'Maybe I just hadn't got round to drinking my glass of water yet,' Doctor Liana suggested.

'Your glass was three-quarters full and there was water round the rim. You drank some but you didn't get ill. I didn't need to be Stephen Hawking to figure out the rest.'

The medical-bay doors slid open. A slight turn of my head confirmed that Commander Linedecker stood behind me, flanked by Harrison and Alex, who were both armed.

Doctor Liana frowned at the sight of them. 'What's going on, Catherine? Why are you here?' she asked.

Only when she'd finished speaking did she realize what had happened as her voice bounced back at her from the corridor outside the medical bay. With dawning realization she turned to stare at me.

'Aidan's been broadcasting our entire conversation everywhere throughout the ship, except for in this medical bay,' I told her. 'I gave you my word that I wouldn't repeat our conversation and I kept my promise. *You* told everyone what you did, not *me*.'

Doctor Liana shook her head. 'I'm disappointed in you, Olivia. Using such an old trick to catch me out.'

'I'm not ageist, Doc. I don't care how old a trick is as long as it works,' I told her.

'Doctor, you will be escorted to one of the detention cells and there you'll stay until we reach Mendela Prime,' Catherine told her.

'You can't lock me up. You need me,' she replied, her tone confident. 'These people in here will die without me.'

'I think more than enough people have already died with your help,' said the commander. 'You will come with me.'

'You can't do this. I may have made a breakthrough in finding a cure for the Mazon virus which wiped out the original crew of this ship. You need me.'

That made me start. Hope warred with disbelief inside me. Had she really made a breakthrough when it came to curing the Mazon virus, or was this a bluff? I glanced at Catherine, who slowly shook her head.

'You will not be given another chance to harm anyone else,' she insisted. 'You will have no further access to the ship's computer or any of the crew.'

Doctor Liana turned to me expectantly, like she was waiting for me to leap in and speak on her behalf. Part of me was stunned at her brazenness. I must admit, more of me was intensely sad that the woman I'd considered a good friend had turned out to be so morally warped. But what if she *had* found a cure? I dismissed the thought. The commander was right. She was too dangerous to be left to her own devices. Hopefully, if she was telling the truth, she had left all her notes in her computer logs so we'd still be able to access and study them.

'Liana, you'll be escorted down to a detention cell,' said Catherine, her expression hard as stone.

I thought the doctor might argue, but after shaking her head at me as if I were a disappointing specimen, she allowed herself to be led away by Harrison.

'Doc, feel free to run or try to get my gun away from me,' Harrison told her. 'I'd be only too ready, willing and able to shoot you where you stand.'

Doctor Liana didn't deign to reply. She just shook her head slowly and carried on walking.

The commander stayed put.

'Aidan, you can stop the ship-wide broadcast now,' I said.

Aidan nodded.

The commander beckoned me out into the corridor. Aidan and I followed her. She waited until the medi-bay doors had closed behind us and Alex had moved back a discreet distance.

'Vee, was it true what you said about reverting this robot's programming so that it can no longer hurt humans?' She pointed at Aidan.

I nodded, not appreciating the way she was calling my brother 'this robot'.

'Then I want this thing in a detention cell also,' she said. 'No one will feel safe with it on the loose.'

'It wasn't his fault,' I protested. 'I altered his programming. I never dreamed he'd end up hurting anyone.'

'But it did.'

'Please stop calling Aidan "it",' I snapped.

'Very well then. *He* is dangerous and I'm asking you, for the good of those left on board, to allow us to put him in a detention cell. I'm assuming the nano-field can hold him?'

'He can't pass through it without damaging himself,' I said unhappily. 'And he'll stay put until told to do otherwise.'

This was so unfair. Aidan shouldn't have to suffer because of my error in judgement.

'Commander, if you lock him up, then you should do the same to me. I'm just as responsible as he is,' I said.

'No,' said Commander Linedecker. 'We need your help to get to Mendela Prime. You're the captain of this ship.'

'Not any more. Go ahead and take over. You run this ship. I've had enough,' I said vehemently. 'I'll give you the executive code and my command bracelets. I'll tell you anything you want to know.'

Catherine stepped forward and lowered her voice for my ears only. 'Oh no you don't, Vee. You are the captain of this ship. That means you live with your failures as well as your successes. That means you do what needs to be done for the good of the majority, not yourself. That means you stand up and take responsibility for your actions. You don't get to go and hide in a corner. Not on this ship. Not in this lifetime. This crew needs you. So here's how it will work. Your brother will be escorted down to a detention cell, and there he'll stay until we work out what to do with him. And you will get your arse in gear and get back to the bridge.'

Stunned, I stared at her. 'Well . . . I consider myself bitch-slapped!'

The commander cracked a rare smile. 'Are we clear?'

'And the ones who died?'

'Let's concentrate on the ones who are still alive,' she said.

I nodded reluctantly. 'Aidan, I want you to go down to the cargo hold and place yourself in a detention cell. You will stay there until further notice. D'you understand?'

My brother nodded. 'Did I do something wrong, Vee?'

'Aidan, *you* didn't, but *I* did,' I replied. 'And now we both have to pay for it.'

He had followed his reprogramming in protecting me and the ship. But my human fifteen-year-old brother, who was a part of this Aidan standing before me, had enjoyed taking revenge on Darren and the others. He knew no better, because of me. Aidan hadn't matured emotionally because it had never occurred to me to look to that side of his development. He was a supercomputer with the mind of a genius and the emotions of a lonely, bullied fifteen-year-old boy whose sister was his only friend. Nathan was right. I'd made such a mess of things and others had suffered for my mistakes.

'I love you, Aidan,' I said.

'True?'

'True.'

Aidan looked at me sadly. 'OK.'

My heart breaking for both of us, I watched him walk away with Alex as his armed escort.

It was late at night and I was back in my original quarters next to the astro lab, trying not to think about the pain in my broken forearm. That was nothing, however, compared to the pain in my chest. I couldn't forget the look on Vee's face when her brother had held me high in the air, ready to break me in two. Aidan wanted to make me suffer before I died.

And Vee had wanted to see it.

She hated me that much.

Selfish, I know, but everything that had happened since then with Doctor Liana paled into insignificance when compared to that one fact. Vee hated me. I hadn't known until that moment in the detention cell, when death had had its hand on my shoulder, just how Vee truly felt about me. The worst moment of my life didn't even begin to cover it.

Funny, but I could've sworn—

I sighed again, wishing the pain in my chest would give me a break. And my damned eyes wouldn't stop leaking. No doubt a side effect of the painkiller Doctor Liana had given me earlier for my arm, before she'd been arrested. Yeah, it had to be a side effect of the pain medication. I mean, what else could be causing it?

For the life of me, I still didn't understand quite what had happened. How could what was supposed to be love turn into something so rancid and deadly that quickly?

Maybe because it hadn't been love in the first place.

It had suited me to think that what Vee and I had was special, instead of what it actually was – a heady mixture of lust, longing and wishful thinking. On Barros 5 I'd been convinced I was about to die. Vee had been alone for over three years. Was it any wonder that our mutual attraction mixed with desperation had made us gravitate towards each other? Now it felt like Vee and I had both clung to the idea of what our relationship could be instead of seeing it for what it was. I had genuinely thought what we had was . . . love.

Man, had I got that one wrong.

Just add that to the never-ending list of failures in my mucked-up life. Vee had clawed my heart out, and all because she was convinced that I'd been playing away with Anjuli. Well, if nothing else I was going to knock that one on the head. Swiping a hand across my eyes, I said, 'Aidan, where's Anjuli?'

Silence.

Damn it! I'd forgotten the way to access the ship's computer had now been changed by popular demand. 'Computer, where's Anjuli?'

'Anjuli is in her quarters.' Hearing Aidan's voice sent a shiver down my spine, but at least it was just the computer. The robot Aidan was in a detention cell and there he'd stay, where hope-fully he would rot.

'Computer, where's Vee?'

'Vee is in her quarters. U-02.'

Right. I swung my legs off the bed and, after putting on my boots, exited my old room. Heading along the corridor, I paused outside Vee's quarters. Would my handprint still allow me access via the palmlock? I wasn't about to try it and find out. Those days were over. Vee meant nothing to me now. I just wanted to clear my name. The fact that Vee thought I was the kind of scum-sucking lowlife who would go through a joining ceremony with her one minute and then crawl into bed with someone else the next hit hard to say the very least. I pressed her room alert. Almost immediately the door slid open.

Damn it!

Something in my chest leaped at the sight of her. More side effects of those painkillers. Vee looked so utterly miserable I almost stepped forward to wrap my arms around her.

Almost.

Repeat after me – those days were over.

'If you're not too busy, I'd like you to come with me.' God, my voice sounded gruff, like I was growling at her. I needed to stick to the point and keep it terse or God only knew what might spill out of my mouth.

Without a word Vee walked out into the corridor, waiting for me to lead the way. We took the lift to the mid deck in silence. I passed a couple of friends, but neither they nor I felt like smiling or speaking.

'Computer, where are Anjuli's quarters?'

'Anjuli resides in M-17 on the mid deck.'

Vee glanced at me, surprised. It took me a moment to figure

out why. She thought I'd already know the number of Anjuli's room. Even now, she still believed I'd been unfaithful.

Once outside Anjuli's door, I activated the room alert with my one good hand. She took her own sweet time getting to the door.

'Aidan, d'you know what time it is? It's three thirty in the morning,' Anjuli fumed, rubbing her eyes. 'Couldn't this have waited? Vee? What're you doing here? Is everything OK?'

'No, it isn't, and this isn't a social call,' I answered before Vee could. 'Where did you get that chain and pendant round your neck?'

Anjuli frowned and glanced down at her necklace. 'This?' she asked, holding the pendant between her fingers.

Which other one would I be talking about? She was only wearing one.

'Where did you get it?'

'Aidan gave it to me.'

'Aidan?' Vee's tone was sharp. 'Why would Aidan give that to you?'

'He said it was a gift from someone who wanted to get with me. Apparently this certain someone wanted me to have it but was too shy to give it to me himself.' Anjuli's smile was broad as she stroked the pendant lying against her chest.

'And who was that?' I asked.

'Well, Mike, of course.'

'Mike in hydroponics?' Vee asked.

'Who else?' Anjuli said. 'Took him long enough. I've been dropping hints for ages but he never seemed interested.'

'Where did Aidan get the pendant from?' I asked.

'Obviously Mike gave it to him to give to me. I've been waiting for Mike to say something about it ever since but he hasn't yet,' Anjuli replied. 'What's all this about?'

'Anjuli, you had a conversation with my brother in the hydroponics bay a while ago. D'you remember?' asked Vee.

'Yes, of course. Why?' said Anjuli.

'You called someone a whoremeister. Who was that?'

Anjuli's smile vanished, to be exchanged with an expression of total disgust. 'You mean Harrison?'

'Aidan whispered something in your ear at one point. What did he say to you?'

'How did you know that? I don't remember you being there.' Anjuli frowned.

'Anjuli, please. Just tell me what my brother whispered to you,' Vee pleaded.

'Aidan told me that Harrison had been boasting about how I couldn't resist him.' Anjuli made a face like there was a putrid smell under her nose. 'I mean, eww! As if!'

'Oh God . . .' Vee looked stricken.

I barely listened to what they were saying. I didn't care about some random conversation Aidan had had with Anjuli. I was still trying to figure out this pendant business. There's no way Aidan could've got the pendant. Once Vee had given it to me, I never took it off except each morning when I had a shower. And Aidan had only been in our quarters on one of those occasions and the pendant hadn't gone missing then. In fact, the only other person apart from Vee to enter our sleeping quarters was—

'Anjuli, could you come with me?' I asked.

'Come where? At this time of night?' said Anjuli.

'Please, Anjuli. It's important.' Too late, but important nonetheless. 'Computer, what's the number of Erica's room?'

'Erica is in M-53,' the computer replied.

We headed further along the corridor. I looked at Vee. She looked back at me. Was that an apology I saw in her eyes? Did she already know how this was going to end? Neither of us spoke. Once in front of Erica's door, I pressed the door alert. I had to press it twice more before the door opened.

'Nathan, what the hell?' Erica looked dazed. 'D'you know what time it is?'

Why was everyone asking me that?

'Why did you take my pendant?' I launched straight in, pointing at the chain round Anjuli's neck. I was not in the mood for pleasantries.

Erica's gaze slid over the necklace. 'Anjuli, what're you doing with that?'

'Aidan gave it to me as a gift from Mike,' Anjuli replied.

'Aidan gave it to you?' Erica said sharply.

'Yeah. Mike gave it to Aidan to give to me as a gift. He was too shy to give it to me himself. Isn't that adorable?' said Anjuli.

'Aidan gave it to you? You must be mistaken.' Erica shook her head.

'I'm not lying.' Anjuli bristled at having her word doubted.

'Erica, why did you take it?' I asked sombrely.

Erica looked at me, her lips pressed together, her expression mutinous.

'I'm not playing, Erica. Don't test me,' I told her stonily.

'Wait? What's going on?' Anjuli still hadn't caught up.

I turned to Anjuli. 'Erica's about to admit where that pendant really came from.'

Vee stood beside me, her head bent.

Looking resigned, Erica said, 'I took it from your bedside table when you went for a shower.'

'Huh? You stole it from Nathan?' Anjuli was completely bewildered.

Vee turned to me, remorse written all over her face. Far too little, much too late.

'I didn't steal it,' Erica denied vehemently. 'I took it.'

'Why?' Vee asked.

'Aidan told me to,' Erica admitted.

Back to Aidan again. The spider at the centre of this web of misunderstandings and lies.

'Why would he do that?' asked Vee.

'He said he just wanted to play a trick on Nathan for a day or two. He kept on and on at me to find a way to get the necklace,' said Erica. 'Nathan, I'm so sorry. I swear I thought Aidan would keep it for a day or two and then give it back. I thought he just wanted to get you into trouble with Vee for losing it – for a joke. You know, ha ha! I didn't know he was going to give it to Anjuli.'

I glanced at Vee, expecting her expression to hold fury or at least contempt as she watched Erica. Instead she just looked sad.

'Wait a minute. You mean, it's not from Mike?' Anjuli pouted.

'No, it's not from bloody Mike. Shut up about Mike, for God's sake!' I shouted at Anjuli. 'It was mine and Aidan gave it to you to stir up trouble between me and Vee. And he succeeded. You thought it was from Mike while Vee thought that you and I . . . that we . . .'

Anjuli looked from me to Vee, totally horrified. She'd finally caught up. 'Me and Nathan? We didn't . . . we've never . . . Vee, you can't believe that Nathan and I would do anything like that,' she protested. 'Nathan is nuts about you. He always swore on Callisto that he'd never go through the joining ceremony with anyone. He didn't want to be tied down or join with someone only to lose them, for whatever reason. But he took one look at you and all that went out the nearest airlock. I swear, we've never once—'

'It's OK, Anjuli. I believe you,' Vee said quietly. 'Excuse me.'

She turned and walked away from all of us. I don't know what I'd expected – an apology would've been nice – but anyway, I didn't get it. Vee carried on walking along the corridor, her head up, her shoulders back. However much she hated me, it was nothing compared to what I felt about her at that moment. Our union was well and truly dead.

A night spent crying in my room had done nothing but give me a pounding headache. The moment I'd had my shower and got dressed I headed down to the detention cells. Doctor Liana lay on the bed facing the bulkhead, her back to the outside world. I walked past her cell to my brother's. Aidan stood in the middle of the room, his eyes open, his stance relaxed yet alert. The instant he saw me his eyes tracked my movements. That was the only part of him that moved. We contemplated each other for silent moments.

'Why did you do it?' I asked at last.

My brother stood behind the nano-field of his detention cell looking out at me, his expression unreadable. Ever since I'd changed his self-preservation algorithm so that it would follow the three robotic laws, as adopted by the Authority, he'd changed. Now he only spoke when spoken to, and every time he looked at me I'd swear there was regret in his eyes. I'd failed him and he was punishing me for it.

'Aidan, why did you lie to me about Nathan?'

'I don't understand the question.'

'Why did you get Erica to take Nathan's pendant? Why did you want to convince me that Nathan was being unfaithful? Answer me, damn it.'

'I don't understand your questions.'

'Why did you try to kill Nathan? He didn't have a weapon aimed at you. He couldn't harm you.'

'He was a danger to you.'

'How, for God's sake? Nathan would never harm me.'

'He was a danger to you. He was making you unhappy,' said Aidan.

'He was making me unhappy because of you and your lies.'

Aidan didn't reply.

I shook my head, trying to put my scattershot thoughts into some semblance of order. 'Nathan says you were jealous of him. Is that true?'

His eyes briefly narrowed. At last, an emotional response.

'Is that it, Aidan? Were you jealous?'

Aidan made his unhurried way to the bed in his cell and sat down. He raised his head to look me in the eye and said, 'I don't understand the question.'

Who the hell was that at my door? I tapped my bedside table to check the time. If it was Anjuli trying to cheer me up again, then she was about to get the door closed in her face. I'd already told her that I didn't want company. I didn't know how to make my meaning any clearer. I'd had more than enough of Erica's apologies and Anjuli's attempts to 'take my mind off things' and Mum's sympathetic looks over the last twenty-four hours to last me a lifetime. I opened my door, ready to take someone's head off.

Vee.

Damn it! Another punch to the stomach. Every time I saw her it was like being hit. Hard. Every time I entered the bridge knowing she'd be there I had to steel myself not to react. But who was I trying to fool? If myself, then I was failing.

You may still affect me, Vee, but it's purely a reflex action now. I'll get over you, I swear I will, I thought as I glared at her. And I sure as hell wasn't going to speak first. These were my quarters. And, quite frankly, she was the last person I expected or wanted to see.

'May I come in?' she asked at last.

I stepped aside to let her enter. Vee moved into the middle of my room. I leaned against the door, my arms folded over my bare chest.

We stood there in silence, watching each other. I still wasn't going to speak first. It wasn't me being childish, I just didn't trust myself.

'I needed to see you,' said Vee softly. Her voice was honey laced with thorns. 'I know this can never be enough, but I wanted to tell you how sorry I am for doubting you.'

I didn't move. I didn't speak.

'I still don't know why Aidan set us up like that. He won't speak to me,' Vee continued.

I'd already given her my opinion as to why he'd done it. I wasn't about to go over old ground. What was the point? When you drilled right down to it, Vee had chosen to believe her brother over me.

'Can you ever forgive me?' asked Vee.

'For what?' I said. 'For not trusting me? For believing the lies your brother told you over the truth I gave you? For standing by when he tried to kill me?'

'I didn't,' Vee denied. 'I told him to let you go.'

'But there was a moment when you were going to let him do it. Admit it.'

Unshed tears filled Vee's eyes. She tried to blink them away, quickly wiping her fingers over her eyes as if I wouldn't notice.

I wanted her to cry.

I wanted her to be unable to sleep and to have to endure a fraction of the hurt I was feeling. At that moment her tears made me despise her even more.

'I know I have no right to ask, but please forgive me?' Vee asked.

I straightened up, my arms falling to my sides. I walked over to her, moving slowly, giving her a chance to flee. If she had any sense she'd leave, but she stayed put, though her expression spoke volumes.

I was scaring her.

Good.

I stood before her, looking down at her face. So many thoughts and feelings were swirling through me at that moment, none of them good.

'Nathan, please . . .'

'Please what?' I asked. Was that really my voice, so bitingly cold, so unrelentingly hard?

'Tell me what I need to do to make things right between us,' Vee whispered.

'What're you prepared to do?' I asked.

'Anything it takes. I promise,' said Vee. 'I'll do whatever it takes to get us back to the way we were.'

Her hand moved up to cup my face. I pulled away. Her hand fell to her side.

'Prove it,' I demanded.

'How?'

'Take off your clothes.'

A stillness swept over Vee as she looked at me. 'Why?'

'Because I asked you to,' I replied evenly. 'You did say you'd do anything it took to make things right.'

Vee and I regarded each other, something ugly in the room

with us. Vee raised her chin. 'I'm not about to let you hurt me, Nathan.'

'That isn't my intention.'

'What is your intention then?'

I shrugged. 'I'm horny. I thought we could spend some time in bed or against a wall or on the floor – I don't really care. And then you can leave.'

'You don't get to treat me like a whore, Nathan,' Vee said furiously.

'Why not? You were quick enough to believe that I was one,' I pointed out bitterly. 'Why was that, Vee? If I wasn't a drone, would you have been as eager to think the worst of me? I don't think so.'

'You being a drone had nothing to do with it. It wasn't you. Don't you see that? It was me. My doubts, my insecurities, my naivety. Me. I couldn't quite bring myself to believe that you felt the same way about me as I felt about you.' Vee's words cascaded like a waterfall. 'I couldn't bring myself to believe anyone outside my family could truly love me. Look at me. I've been nowhere. I've done nothing. I've been the only human inside this metal coffin for three years. Why would you want to be with me? That's what I kept asking myself. Whereas you and Anjuli, you'd been through so much together, shared so much. I could believe in you and her as a couple far more easily than I could believe in you and me. That was my mistake. I messed up.'

I hardly heard her. All I could see before me was someone who was supposed to love me the most, but who had been prepared to stand by and watch me die.

'D'you need help taking your clothes off?' I asked evenly.

Vee closed her eyes briefly. When she opened them again, they shone with unshed tears.

'I won't have sex with you, Nate, not like this.'

'So much for doing anything to make it right,' I said with contempt. 'Turns out that promise was as empty as all the others you made at our joining ceremony.'

'I do want your forgiveness, Nathan, but not at any price,' said Vee. Slow tears ran down her cheeks. 'I guess I was wrong about that.'

I turned my back on her. 'You need to leave. Now.' I closed my eyes, fighting to retain control of myself.

Moments later my door opened and then closed. I was alone.

77

I left my quarters, ready to start my shift on the bridge.
Anjuli was outside my room, obviously waiting for me.

'Yes, Anjuli?' I asked wearily.

After my conversation with Nathan I'd spent the rest of
the night staring up into the dark of my room. I had to face
the truth. Any love Nathan had felt for me was well and
truly dead. And I had no one to blame but myself. I hadn't
once shown that I had faith in him. I hadn't trusted him
because I hadn't trusted myself. I couldn't quite believe
that I'd fallen for anyone as quickly as I fell for him, and the
fact that he felt the same way seemed too good to be true.
So it was easy for Aidan to convince me that it wasn't.

Nathan said that Aidan had acted out of jealousy.

That made two of us.

A sibling trait obviously.

I should've held onto what Nathan and I had with all my
might. If I'd had more experience or sense or confidence, I
would never have let anyone get between us. But I'd let
self-doubts and suspicions drive us apart.

And I'd lost him.

'Vee, are you all right?' Anjuli frowned at me.

'What is it, Anjuli?'

'Well, I . . . I don't want to tell tales and I know you're going through a lot right now but I just wanted to clear something up,' said Anjuli reluctantly.

'I'm listening.'

'Aidan was the one who suggested that I should monitor the Mazon comms. He said my initiative would impress you.'

What?

'Aidan put you up to it?' I frowned. 'Why didn't you say something before?'

'Because it was my mistake,' Anjuli replied unhappily. 'I should've cleared it with you or Commander Linedecker first but I was desperate to make a good impression. And if I then turned round and said that Aidan suggested it, it would've looked like I was just trying to pin the blame on your brother.'

'I see,' I replied.

'And one other thing,' Anjuli began. 'Your brother was the one who suggested that I persuade Nathan to talk to you about letting me back on the bridge. Aidan said I should speak to Nathan about it every chance I got.'

I briefly closed my eyes. Just when I thought I couldn't feel any worse . . . Aidan had been ahead of me every step of the way.

'Thanks for letting me know,' I said.

Anjuli nodded before she turned round to head back to the engine room.

'Anjuli, you're needed on the bridge,' I called after her.

She spun round, her eyes hopeful. 'Really?'

'Yes, really. You're assigned to the bridge until further notice.'

'Oh thank you, Vee. I won't let you down again, I promise.'

Though I was also heading that way, Anjuli didn't bother waiting for me. She practically ran to get there. I followed her onto the bridge, too heartsick to dredge up a smile.

Nathan was already at the navigation panel, sitting in Aidan's usual place. The commander, Sam and Hedda were at the various stations around the bridge. Anjuli sat down next to Nathan, who was concentrating on the screen before him. I forced myself not to look at him. I had a job to do and I needed to get on with it. I'd do my grieving in private.

We were less than an hour away from the wormhole that would take us out of Mazon space. I needed to concentrate on getting us through that.

Anjuli and Nathan spoke quietly together. To my left, Commander Linedecker, Hedda and Sam did the same. I read the reports from the medical bay to get an update on the progress of those who'd been made ill in the mess-hall poisoning and those who had been injured by my brother. Then I had to steel myself to read the report on those who'd recently died – Max and Dooli, Maria and Darren. Their funerals had been scheduled to take place once we were through the wormhole, after which their bodies would be jettisoned. Closing my eyes, I rubbed my fingers slowly over my forehead.

So much destruction.

Space wasn't the place for those who didn't like adventure, but all of us on board had seen far too much of death. And there was more than one way to die. The death of hopes and dreams and desires was perhaps more cruel because you had to live every single day with the pain of their loss. In spite of myself, I glanced at Nathan. He was watching me. Embarrassed, I looked away.

Anjuli whispered something to him and he nodded. I turned my attention back to the ship's reports.

'Vee, we have trouble,' Nathan said.

My head snapped up. 'What?'

'There are two Mazon battlecruisers between us and the wormhole,' Nathan replied. 'They obviously couldn't pinpoint our exact position as we travelled but they must've guessed our destination and got there ahead of us.'

I sat back in my chair. The Mazon were ahead of us and there was no ion storm to hide in this time. We had come this far, only to fail.

78

NATHAN

This was so damned unfair: to get so close to escaping Mazon territory only to be ambushed at the last moment. What had been a lifetime to sort out my problems had turned into a mere matter of minutes. The promise of all the time in the world had been broken.

'How soon before we encounter them?' asked Vee with a calm I could only envy.

I checked my panel. 'Nineteen minutes.'

'How soon before they determine our exact location?'

'At our current speed, less than six minutes,' I replied.

'Orders, Captain?' said Anjuli.

'Put the ship on silent red alert,' said Vee.

'Captain?' Mum moved to stand beside her.

'I have a plan, Commander, but you're not going to like it,' said Vee.

'Does it beat dying?' asked Mum drily.

'Depends on your point of view,' Vee replied.

'Let's hear it.'

'There are a number of escape pods on board. I suggest we use them.'

'You want to abandon ship?' Mum frowned.

'No. I want to put your . . . our dead in the escape pods,' Vee replied. 'And we rig each one with false life-sign readings so the Mazon will think exactly as you did: that we're abandoning ship and individually making for the wormhole. They'll assume that's the plan because the escape pods are so small, they make for a much harder moving target.'

'A harder target but not impossible,' Mum pointed out. 'And the closer the escape pods get to the Mazon ships, the easier they'll be to destroy.'

'That's what I'm counting on,' said Vee. 'Because the escape pods won't only be rigged with false life-signs.'

Pause.

'You want to rig each pod with explosives,' Mum realized.

Vee nodded. 'If we're lucky, the pods will detonate close enough to the Mazon ships to do some serious damage and we can make a run for the wormhole while the Mazon are carrying out repairs.'

'Sounds like a plan,' said Mum. 'Why don't you look happier about it?'

Mum was right. Vee was looking troubled.

'For this to work, the escape pods can't be detonated until they are within striking distance of the Mazon ships,' she said. 'If even one of the pods is destroyed before then, the resultant force of the explosion will alert the Mazon to what we're up to and the plan will fail. It means that each escape pod will have to be controlled from our ship. They can't travel on a predictable trajectory. It has to look like each is under the control of its occupant.'

'I can use the computer to plot a course for each one,' said Anjuli.

'Plotting a course won't do it. We need to remotely fly all four simultaneously and make all the micro adjustments necessary when the Mazon open fire on them,' Vee said.

'Can you do that, Anjuli?' asked Mum.

Anjuli shook her head. 'I can't fly four escape pods all at once. That's not humanly possible.'

'Nathan?' she queried.

I shook my head.

'It can't be done.' Mum echoed what I was thinking.

'Aidan can do it,' Vee said quietly.

My blood ran cold. Was she seriously suggesting we allow that killing machine back on the bridge?

'Your call, Commander,' Vee said to Mum.

Mum looked around the bridge. 'Sam, get him up here,' she said.

'Mum, you can't be serious,' I protested.

She scowled at me. 'Are you questioning my orders, Nathan?'

Slowly I shook my head. 'No, Commander.'

Sam issued the command to the guards outside Aidan's detention cell to bring him up to the bridge. Then he put a work detail on filling the escape pods with those who had been killed and packing plasma explosives around each body. Time was of the essence. Less than a minute later Aidan was standing beside me at the navigation panel, flanked by Erica carrying a pulsar rifle even though she had to know that they were useless against him.

Aidan looked at me pointedly. For two credits I would've gladly kicked his arse. What was I talking about? I'd gladly kick his arse for free. Instead I reluctantly relinquished my seat. Vee walked over to him as he sat down and squatted down beside him, looking into his eyes.

'Aidan, the Mazon are between us and the wormhole. It's vital that we make it past the Mazon ships. We're going to launch four escape pods which are packed with bodies and explosives,' she said.

'Why do they contain bodies?' asked Aidan.

'In case the Mazon scan the pods. Their instruments need to detect people in those pods. I want you to manoeuvre the pods towards the two Mazon battlecruisers – two towards one, the other two towards the second ship. When they're close enough, the Mazon will destroy the pods and the resulting explosions should disable their ships for long enough for us to make a break for the wormhole. D'you understand?'

'Of course . . . sis,' said Aidan evenly.

I didn't miss the way Vee flinched.

'Sam, are the escape pods ready?' she asked.

'Yes, Captain,' Sam replied. 'They'll be launched on your mark.'

'Nathan, how soon before the Mazon know our position?'

'Ninety seconds,' I replied.

'Nathan, if this doesn't work, I need you to plot our own escape route. We'll need to head away from the wormhole at maximum speed,' said Vee.

'My assessment is that the Mazon won't move too far away

from their current position. They know we need to travel through the wormhole so they'll play a waiting game,' said Mum.

'I agree, Commander,' Vee told her.

'Nathan, launch the escape pods eight seconds after the Mazon start coming towards us,' she ordered. 'Aidan, the moment the pods are launched I want you to take over their flight, OK? Make it seem like they're heading for the wormhole but are inadvertently travelling too close to the Mazon ships. They must not under any circumstances be destroyed before they reach the Mazon ships.'

'Understood,' said Aidan, his hands poised on the controls.

Our lives resting in his hands? Well, that didn't sit well with me at all. I was going to make sure I kept both eyes on every-thing he did when those escape pods launched. I didn't trust that android as far as I could throw him.

Thanks to him, I'd lost Vee.

As if reading my thoughts, Aidan turned to me – and smiled.

If our survival hadn't depended on him, I would've gladly taken a pulsar to the base of his metallic skull where it would do the most good.

I knew from my time on Callisto that hatred didn't do any good. It ate away at you like acid until very little that was still human was left.

But when it came to Aidan – and his sister – I'd happily make an exception.

79

Well, it was a good try.

The escape pods travelled at speed towards the Mazon ships. I watched their progress on the bridge's viewscreen. The Mazon were fast advancing, just as I knew they would. One of the Mazon ships was approximately two kilometres ahead of the other one, and it was that one which targeted the nearest escape pods. Only the ship did its job a little too well. Three, instead of two, of the escape pods closest to it exploded. The Mazon ship immediately listed to starboard, dead in space. However, one escape pod wasn't enough to put the other ship out of action. And it was forewarned. Two directed energy blasts later, and the remaining escape pod had been destroyed before it got anywhere near close enough to do damage to the second ship.

We couldn't fully retreat and go back the way we'd come because there were more Mazon ships behind us. We couldn't go forward as the second battlecruiser was now between us and the wormhole, waiting for us to make our move. The first Mazon ship wasn't the only one that was dead in space. We were between a rock and a hard place and I could see only one way out – and only then if I moved fast.

I pulled off my command bracelets and handed them to Catherine.

'Commander, you're in charge. Make sure you get your people safely to Mendela Prime. Once I'm aboard the landing craft I'll hand over command of this ship to you.'

'What d'you mean? What're you going to do?' she asked sharply.

'I'm going to disable that other Mazon ship by using the landing craft to ram it. If I time this right, with enough speed and momentum I should be able to get right through their hull and reach their engine core. The moment you see an opening, just head for the wormhole and don't look back.' I was already heading for the door.

'WAIT!' Nathan's voice behind me stopped me in my tracks.

I turned. He was on his feet, staring at me.

'Vee, hang on.' The commander walked over to me. 'D'you know what you're doing?'

I nodded. 'Of course. I'm going to manoeuvre the landing craft until I get close enough to the Mazon ship ahead of us and then I'm going to aim straight for their engine core. I'm a good pilot, Commander. Actually, I'm a great pilot! I can do this.'

'It's suicide,' she said.

I smiled, feeling strangely at peace. 'It's my life and my

choice. Like I said, the moment I cripple them, head for the wormhole.'

I turned towards the door.

'Vee . . . ?' Nathan called after me.

I took one last look at him, no doubt an expression of regret and remorse and love and longing sweeping over my face. I took one last look at him to create a memory for myself, a memory to last me a lifetime. Maybe one day he'd be able to think of me without loathing.

Time to go.

'Vee, I have another idea,' said the commander. 'And I want you to agree to it.'

Puzzled, I said, 'There is no plan B. This is your only shot at escaping.'

'I'm not proposing that we change the play,' she said. 'Just the player.'

And she turned to give my brother a significant look.

80

NATHAN

I am so full of shit.

Vee was ready to sacrifice her life for the rest of us, and with each step she took to leave the bridge, fearful panic shredded my insides. She was going to give her life so the rest of us would have a chance, and all I could think was that I was going to lose her. For good. I couldn't let that happened and yet I was frozen on the spot and the words I wanted to say were lodged somewhere in my throat and wouldn't budge.

Mum saved my life.

If Vee didn't agree to Mum's idea, I knew what would happen. Vee would give her life to save ours – and I would die inside without her.

'You expect me to send my brother to his death?' Vee argued, horrified.

'Vee, listen to me. No one doubts your bravery, but your brother's reflexes are far sharper and faster than yours so he'll be better able to make all the micro adjustments required to evade the Mazon weapons fire before ramming their engine core. He stands a better chance of completing this mission suc-cessfully and we both know it.'

'I can do this,' Vee insisted. 'I've flown in and out of tighter spots before.'

'I don't doubt it, but this is a one-shot deal. If you fail, this ship doesn't stand a chance. For your plan to have the best chance of succeeding, it needs Aidan. You're only human.'

Vee wasn't the only one to start at that last comment.

Only human . . .

'You're asking me to send my brother to his death,' said Vee after a pause. 'I won't do it. I can't.'

Mum took hold of Vee's hands and looked her in the eye. 'Vee, as a captain sometimes you have to ask others to make sacrifices. Sometimes the ultimate sacrifice. Your primary concern has to be the welfare of this ship and the needs of the many.'

'That's why *I'm* prepared to do this,' said Vee. 'I won't be responsible for any more deaths.'

'An effective leader needs to be able to make the hard decisions,' said Mum.

'And I am. I'm not suicidal, Commander, but my brother is of more use to you than I could ever be,' Vee argued. 'You need him.'

'No, we need *you*. You haven't let us down so far and I won't let you start now.'

'Let you down? Are you serious? I altered Aidan's programming, and look what happened because of it. How can you say I haven't let you down?' Vee's derision was entirely directed at herself.

'If it wasn't for you, we'd all be dead,' said Mum. 'You need to remember that. Now we don't have time to argue about this. You need to order your brother to fly the landing craft into the Mazon ship's core. He's our only hope. We're all dead otherwise.'

Seconds ticked by. Vee closed her eyes, looking defeated. She pulled her hands out of Mum's and headed over to her brother.

'Aidan, I have a job for you.'

'I heard,' said Aidan. 'Is this because I failed to disable both Mazon ships just now?'

'No one's blaming you, but we do need to destroy that other Mazon ship or we don't stand a chance.'

'You want me to do it?'

'No, I don't want you to do it,' said Vee. 'But I do need you to do it.'

'Is this because I protected you against Darren and the others who wished you harm?'

'No. I'm not punishing you, Aidan. I promise.'

'Don't you love me any more, Vee?'

The question made me start. A tear spilled over onto Vee's cheek. She cupped her brother's face in her hands. 'Oh, Aidan, of course I love you. You're my brother. You've looked after me and kept me safe for three long years and you're the only one left who shares my memories of the past. You have no idea what that means to me, what you mean to me. But I need you to help save the lives of everyone else on board,' said Vee.

'You love me?'

'I love you.'

'True?'

'True.'

'Who will protect you if I die?' asked Aidan. 'Who will look after you? That's my primary function.'

That should've been my job after Vee and I had joined together. I wanted to leap in and interrupt their conversation to tell Aidan it was still my job, but how could I? Vee had only ever told me that she loved me once, and even then that had been in the past tense, but she could say it easily enough to her brother. My head was spinning. Thanks to her my pride was not just bruised but thoroughly battered. After everything that had happened between Vee and me, I had no idea where I stood any more. I had no idea where I wanted to stand either. Except . . . except I didn't want to lose her.

'I'll be OK, Aidan.' Vee smiled sadly. 'If you succeed, then so will I.'

'Vee, we need to hurry,' Mum urged.

'So will you do this, Aidan? For me?'

Aidan leaned forward to whisper something to Vee. She was suddenly very still as he spoke for her ears only. He kissed her cheek before standing up and heading off the bridge without a backward glance. Vee straightened up slowly, looking stunned and upset.

What had Aidan said? I didn't have the right to ask any more. It took a moment or two for Vee to pull herself together.

'Status update on the Mazon ship please,' she turned to me to ask.

I checked my neglected panel. 'They've placed themselves directly between us and the wormhole.'

434

'The other Mazon ship is still disabled?'

'Yes, Captain,' I replied.

Vee headed back to her chair. 'Let me know when the landing craft leaves our ship.'

I got up and resumed my original position in Aidan's chair, monitoring our landing craft and the remaining functioning Mazon ship closely. The atmosphere on the bridge was tense to say the least. This was our last chance to put some distance between ourselves and the Mazon.

If Aidan failed . . .

Well, as Vee said, there was no plan B.

I turned to take a quick look at Vee, maybe for the last time. She was watching me.

'Nathan, could you move us to a safe distance so that we're not hit by any of the debris from the destruction of the Mazon engine core. Anjuli, the moment Aidan rams the Mazon ship, you need to get us through that wormhole quick, fast, and in an almighty hurry. OK?'

'Understood, Captain.' Anjuli was already plotting out the most efficient route to and through the wormhole. Me? I couldn't take my eyes off Vee. She looked so sad, so alone. I got up and went to stand before her.

'Nate? Is . . . is something wrong?' Vee asked as she stood up to face me.

I pulled her to me and wrapped my arms around her. After only a brief moment's hesitation, she wrapped her arms around my waist, her head on my shoulder. God, I'd missed this, the warmth of her, the feel of her in my arms.

435

'What the hell, Nathan?' Mum exploded from behind us. 'Get back to your post.'

I put my hand under Vee's chin to tilt her head so she could look directly at me. I smiled at her. She smiled back. It was tentative and hard to do, but it was there. I headed back to the navigation panel, ignoring my mum, who was glaring at me.

'Captain, the landing craft has left the ship,' I announced half a minute later.

We sat in silence watching the landing craft head for the Mazon ship. The moment it was within range the Mazon opened fire. Aidan made that craft dance like a leaf on the wind. Some of the Mazon blasts came close, but none managed to catch him. He drew closer and closer to the Mazon ship, which was firing at him in earnest now. Mum was right. No way could anyone but Aidan have reacted fast enough to dodge their weapons fire. The landing craft was now within kissing distance of our enemy.

'Bye, Aidan,' Vee said softly from behind me.

The landing craft disappeared, swallowed up by the Mazon ship. There was a huge explosion and then nothing. No Mazon ship, no landing craft.

Nothing. Just debris firing out in all directions into space. I thought the landing craft might disable the Mazon ship. It had destroyed it.

'Captain, there was an anomalous reading just before the landing craft hit the Mazon ship,' Anjuli said with a frown, her head bent over the instrument panel.

'What kind of reading?' asked Vee.

'I don't know. It was there for a split second and then it was gone.'

'Could it have been an energy flux from the landing craft?' asked Vee.

'Yes. That was probably it,' said Anjuli. 'I'm sorry, Captain, I just thought I should mention it.'

'Anjuli, don't ever apologize for doing your job properly,' said Vee.

Anjuli nodded and continued to check the panel before her. The bridge was silent for a moment as we all contemplated what had just happened.

The Mazon ship and Aidan were gone.

And all I could think was, *That might've been Vee.* She and I weren't right, maybe we never would be again, but I wished her no harm.

That's all it is, I told myself.

And maybe if I told myself that often enough, I'd start to believe it.

'Get us the hell out of here,' Vee ordered.

Vee, like the rest of us, had had enough of Mazon space to last a lifetime.

81

I'd only ever travelled through a wormhole once before. The last time had been a rare and beautiful experience that I'd shared with my brother. We had both sat at the navigation panel watching in awe as we travelled. It was like moving through a fluid light show and nothing I'd seen before or since could compare, not even the deadly beauty of the Zandari ion storm. But now I closed my eyes against the sight of it.

Aidan . . .

My brother was dead. His engrams and brain patterns were still stored on the computer, but that was all my brother was now, data stored as bits and bytes. He should've been here to experience this with me, the sights, the sounds, the sense of acceleration and exhilaration.

But he wasn't.

There was no reason I couldn't try to recreate him, to acquire another robot and see if I could turn it into a sentient replica of my brother. But even as the thought entered my head, I dismissed it. He'd never have free will if he had to follow the three robotic laws, and I'd never, ever tamper with those again. Without free will any android replica would always just be a robot, no matter how intelligent it might appear.

It was finally time to let my brother go.

I needed to grieve for him, mourn his loss – and move on.

The commander had been right, of course. Aidan had been our best chance of disabling the remaining Mazon ship to allow us to travel through the wormhole, but if this was the nature of the captain's job, then I didn't want it. I was captain by proxy only. I didn't have what it took to ask anyone to sacrifice themselves.

But that was exactly what I had just done.

Aidan was gone.

Nathan wasn't mine any more.

I had no one.

Minutes later we emerged out of the wormhole and into the Gamma Quadrant. There was still a long way to go before we reached Mendela Prime but at least now we were less likely to encounter any Mazon ships. There would be pirates, and scavenger and Authority ships to avoid though, so it wasn't going to be all plain sailing from here on in by any means.

And I'd have to navigate through it all without my brother.

'Vee?'

I blinked out of my sombre reverie. I hadn't even realized that Catherine had moved to stand beside me.

'I'm sorry. Yes?'

She bent to address me so that no one else would hear. 'Would you like to have some time alone? I can take over for a while.'

I nodded gratefully, then stood up. 'Computer, Commander Linedecker is now in charge of the *Aidan*. Executive Command Code Authorization MIRA dash five four.'

Catherine looked at me with surprise. Not only was she taking over from me but I'd just handed over full command of the *Aidan*. She and her colleagues could now do what they wanted with it – and me. I was no longer necessary to their survival.

'My chair is yours, Commander,' I told her, then headed off the bridge before she could say another word.

As far as I was concerned, she could have the ship and everything on board.

I'd had enough.

Vee disappeared into her room for over twenty-four hours. None of us saw or heard a peep out of her during all that time. More than once I asked the computer where she was. More than once I stopped outside her door, my hand hesitating over her door alert. Only I never pressed it and I didn't disturb her. I wasn't sure if I had that right any more. Besides, before I could help her, I had to straighten myself out first. I couldn't for the life of me figure out which way my head was facing.

Did I care about Vee or not?

Did I care that she was hurting or not?

Did I still love her or not?

I'd spent the night in my own quarters, lying in bed, staring up into the darkness of my room and trying to find some answers. Come the morning, I was still no wiser. I was doing my own head in.

The following day, during a break in my shift, I headed down to the engine room with a long list of items Mum had asked me to check. Once down on the lower deck, I decided to have a word with Doctor Liana so I headed to the cargo hold first. To my surprise there was no security guard outside her detention cell. As I got closer I saw why. The cell was empty.

'Computer, where is Doctor Liana Sheen?' I asked.

'Doctor Sheen is no longer on board,' came the reply.

'Computer, where is she?' I asked.

'Doctor Sheen is no longer on board.'

It had already told me that. Impatient, I said, 'Computer, what happened to the doctor?'

'Doctor Sheen is no longer on board.'

Only then did it click. A chill ran down my spine. I raced back to the bridge and buttonholed Mum.

'What's the matter, son?' she asked when I dragged her to one side of the bridge for a private word.

'Where's the doctor, Mum?'

A wary, watchful look swept over Mum's face, going some way to confirming my worst fears.

'Mum!' I said, appalled.

'She was tried, found guilty and justice was meted out accordingly,' she said.

'Justice?' I was surprised the word didn't burn her tongue.

'Grow up, Nathan,' Mum snapped, though she was careful to keep her voice low so no one else could hear us. 'What did you think would happen to her? She was a murderer who saw us all as expendable in her bid to get what she wanted. We certainly weren't going to take her back to Earth, and if she came to Mendela Prime with us, then what? She would've made it her life's work to betray us to the Authority the very first chance she got.'

'So is that how it works now? Anyone you deem unfit or expendable is ejected off the ship?' I asked. 'You're in charge now and what you say goes?'

Mum shook her head. 'One day you will learn that life isn't just black or white with nothing in between. People aren't either good or bad and that's it. There are infinite shades, variations and possibilities between those two extremes.'

'Then why kill the doctor? If that's true, we could've talked her round to our side,' I said.

'And how many should she be allowed to kill before the decision is made that enough is enough? Some people and situations are beyond redemption.'

'You keep telling yourself that, Mum,' I said with disgust.

'Get off your self-righteous high horse, Nathan. You of all people should know that we don't live in a perfect universe with perfect people who achieve perfection in everything they do. You carry on thinking like that and people will always disappoint you.'

It was as if I was seeing this side of Mum for the very first time. Maybe this ruthlessness had always been there but I had chosen not to see it. And then a horrifying thought struck me.

'Computer, where's Vee?'

'Vee is in the astrophysics lab,' the computer replied.

I breathed a huge sigh of relief.

'Oh my God! You thought . . .' Mum frowned. 'Nathan, what the hell—?'

'I didn't think you'd do what you did to the doctor,' I told her. 'I'm just beginning to understand what you're capable of.'

'I'm capable of the same things as your wife,' she said coldly. 'I'm capable of making mistakes. I'm capable of sacrificing everything I want for the good of others. I'm capable of putting others first. I'm capable of doing the wrong thing for the right reason. I'm capable of regret and remorse. And I'm capable of taking responsibility for my actions even if it means I end up vilified and alone. I don't know everything that went on between you and Vee, but I do know that you failed her.'

'I . . . *what*? Are you kidding me? You obviously don't know that Vee was prepared to stand by and let her brother kill me,' I said, outraged.

'But she didn't, did she? She thought you were unfaithful and had been using her to get this ship as well as making a fool of her, and she still stepped up and saved your life,' said Mum.

'You're taking her side?' I couldn't believe what I was hearing.

'Nathan, my hand is itching to give you an attitude-adjustment slap.' Mum scowled. 'Didn't I just tell you to grow up? I'm not taking anyone's side. I'm saying, try seeing things from Vee's point of view – just once will do. Now I have work to do, and I could've sworn I gave you an assignment in the engine room. You can stop glaring at me now.'

I'd moved past glare and into full-blown glower, so Mum had got that wrong too.

'I swore I wouldn't do this but I'm going to anyway,' she sighed. 'Nathan, let me give you a piece of advice and then I'm going to butt out of your business.'

'What?' I said belligerently. 'I don't need any advice from you.'

'First of all, remove the bass from your voice. I am still your mother,' said Mum, annoyed. 'Now if you decide that your join-ing with Vee is over, make sure it's what you really and truly want and that it's not just your pride doing your thinking for you. Vee is very like me, that's why I like her. You keep pushing her away and one day she won't be there to push any more. If that's what you want, all power to you. But if it's not, you and she need to find a way to move past this. I've said my piece, so I suggest we both get back to work.'

I marched off the bridge. Mum didn't have a single clue what she was talking about. And how on Callisto did we end up talking about Vee and me when I'd wanted to confront her about what had happened to Doctor Liana?

Oh, Mum was good!

That was quite a skill she had there.

I headed along the corridor to get to the lift that would take me back to the engine room on the lower deck.

There ahead of me was the astrophysics lab—

No! I needed to get back to work.

But Vee was in there.

What was she doing?

Was she alone?

Even though I kept telling myself to go to the engine room before Mum got on my case, I found myself opening the door to the astro lab and stepping inside. I told myself it was just for a moment. I'd make sure Vee was doing OK and then I'd leave.

Vee was alone in the room and standing in the middle of the Tau star system. Her head was tilted up and her arms were raised as she tried to touch the stars, to clasp her hands round them, but no matter how slowly and carefully she moved, they all eluded her grasp.

I didn't mean to but I must've made a noise because she spun in my direction, her arms now at her side. Neither of us said a word. Neither of us moved. Tentatively Vee stretched out her hand towards me. All I had to do was move forward a few paces and take her hand in mine.

I turned and left the room. I needed to get back to work.

It took me forty-eight hours to return to the bridge. Staring at the walls and crying for my brother and all I'd lost wasn't making me feel any better. I needed to be up and doing. Though when I finally made the decision to get back to work, I was surprised at the trepidation I felt at the prospect. I didn't know what to expect. Maybe Catherine had decided that she wasn't going to give command of the *Aidan* back to me. It wouldn't surprise me to find I was persona non grata anywhere on the ship. Dressed and ready for work, I actually stood in the corridor outside the bridge doors, trying to muster up the courage to enter.

How ridiculous was that?

A deep breath later I entered the bridge.

'Captain on the bridge,' the commander declared and immediately vacated the captain's chair.

She smiled at me and handed back my command bracelets, then moved to the tactical station next to Sam and Hedda. I mean, did those two sleep at their stations? I took my seat, slightly stunned that walking onto the bridge was all it had taken.

'Captain, may I suggest that we head for the Edwardes

base?' said the commander. 'It's five Sol days away and we need to dock to effect repairs and to try and pick up a replacement landing craft. Plus some of our fuel cells were contaminated when the accident happened in the engine room conduits and they need realigning.'

'Fair enough,' I replied. 'Nathan, could you set a course for the Edwardes base?'

'Yes, Captain.'

Nathan didn't look at me, I didn't look at him. We just got on with it. Our personal relationship was dead. Long live the professional one.

Hope deferred maketh the heart sick.

Funny how I couldn't get that saying out of my head. I had no clue who had originally said it or where it came from but I knew exactly what it meant.

I had held out hope that somehow—

But anyway, that was then and this is now.

Hope was no longer deferred. And my heart? My heart was just a pump, circulating blood around my weary body. I had no other use for it.

I'd got what I wanted, hadn't I? Vee had finally got the message that I wanted nothing more to do with her. We spoke to each other only when necessary. Yesterday she had tried to join us at our lunch table in the mess hall and I had taken my tray, got up and moved elsewhere to finish my food. At dinner yesterday and at breakfast this morning Vee had sat down at an empty table to eat alone.

I'd got what I wanted.

So someone tell me why I felt so damned miserable.

During my break I couldn't face the mess hall again. Vee shouldn't have to sit by herself just because I was in there. So I made for the hydroponics bay. With Mike in the medical bay, it was the one place on board apart from my quarters where I was almost certain to be alone.

I was in luck. The hydroponics bay was empty. I ordered a bowl of Vee's 'special recipe' chilli from the dispenser and sat down on the bench to eat it. The first time I'd found it so hot I'd thought my head was going to catch fire. Now I couldn't eat any other kind. All the others tasted bland and insipid.

My chilli finished, I made my way over to the waste disposal beside the dispenser to get rid of my spoon and bowl.

'Hi, Nathan.'

Mike's voice made me jump. He stepped out from behind some tomtato plants, a satisfied grin on his face. He knew full well that he'd startled me. That was probably the effect he was going for.

'Hell, Mike! Are you trying to give me a heart attack to give you something to do in the medi lab?'

'Nihao to you too.' Mike smiled.

'Sorry,' I mumbled. 'I didn't mean to take your head off. But don't creep up on people like that.'

'You were lost in a world of your own,' said Mike. 'Got anything you want to get off your chest?'

'What's on or off my chest is no concern of yours,' I replied.

'Tell me something. What's going on with you and Vee? Are you officially over?' he asked.

'I don't want to talk about it.'

'Nathan, d'you want some advice?'

Oh, for God's sake.

'Not you as well. Why does everyone want to give me advice all of a sudden?' I fumed. 'What happened between me and Vee is our business, no one else's – so butt out.'

'Then answer my question and I'll never comment on your business again,' said Mike calmly.

'What question?'

'Are you and Vee over?'

'Why? Are you interested?'

'I might've been if I didn't have Anjuli.'

'So you two are together at last? Congratulations,' I said tightly.

'Said grudgingly and with more than a hint of venom, but I'll take it,' said Mike. 'And don't think I haven't noticed that you still haven't answered my question. Are you and Vee over?'

'For God's sake, Mike. What d'you want me to say? As far as I'm concerned, she's just somebody I used to know. That's all. OK?'

Furious, I spun round, only to freeze when I saw who was standing in the doorway. Vee. And she'd heard every word. Stricken, I stared at her. In that moment I couldn't have moved or said another word if my life depended on it.

Vee turned and left the hydroponics bay.

I spun round to glare at Mike, who shrugged apologetically.

'Man, she came in when I asked the question and put her finger over her lips before I could warn you that we had company. What was I supposed to do?' said Mike.

'Thanks a lot.'

He shrugged again. 'If you meant it, what's the problem?'

The problem was, I now felt like shit. This had to stop. Vee and I couldn't carry on this way.

I couldn't carry on this way.

I'd been putting it off for too long. It was time for Vee and me to sort out this mess we called a joining once and for all.

85

This watercress and potato soup had to be one of the nastiest things I'd ever put in my mouth. It was truly vile.

'So what d'you think?' Mike asked eagerly.

'It . . . er . . . maybe it needs a bit more salt and pepper,' I suggested. And the last rites read over it.

'You hate it, don't you?' Mike said, disappointed. 'Everyone on this ship is a philistine. I'm making food from real, honest-to-goodness, properly grown ingredients, and you all prefer that stem-cell-based muck that comes out of the utility dispensers. You do know those dispensers are descended from 3D printers, don't you?'

'I don't really care about their ancestry, Mike, as long as they dispense edible food,' I admitted. Which was more than could be said for this foul-tasting concoction before me.

'I'm casting pearls before swine!' Mike said, leaping to his feet and heading off in a huff.

'As long as the pearls are edible, Mike,' I called after him.

I couldn't help the smile that crept over my lips. Ever since the overheard conversation in the hydroponics bay

Mike had gone out of his way to be kind to me. He sat with me for meals in the mess hall if we shared the same shift and he insisted on letting me try his latest culinary experiments. I could've done without the last effort though.

'Can I join you, Vee?' I started in surprise at Nathan's voice from beside me.

'Actually, I need to get back to the bridge.' I grabbed my tray and stood up so vigorously that the plate and glass rattled in protest.

'Please,' said Nathan. 'It'll just take a minute.'

I looked around the mess hall. We were the focus of most people's attention. Reluctantly I sat back down again. I was all kinds of a fool for sitting with this guy. He'd humiliated me enough times in public by running a kilometre in the opposite direction every time I approached. I didn't need to be dropped on my head to finally get the message.

For want of something to do with my hands, I took another sip of Mike's soup. Big mistake. It hadn't improved. In fact, I came close to gagging.

'You're braver than me,' said Nathan. 'I put a spoonful of that stuff in my mouth and spat it straight out again.'

'In front of Mike?'

'Of course. He was sitting next to me waiting for my reaction,' said Nathan. 'Don't tell me you actually swallowed that stuff.'

'I didn't want to hurt his feelings,' I admitted. 'Anyway, what was it you wanted to say to me?'

453

Just get it over with, Nathan, please. It hurts to sit here so close to you like this.

'I want to call a truce,' he said quietly. 'I was thinking that maybe we could . . .'

Pause.

'We could – what?' I prompted.

'I don't know.' Nathan shrugged. 'Be civil to each other?'

'We are being civil,' I pointed out. 'Here we are having a conversation and there's no battling with drawn spoons, no plates flying across the room, no drama.'

'I was thinking we could maybe be a bit more than that . . .'

What? Why the sudden desire for détente? Confused, I studied Nathan. Did he want us to be friends, lovers, roommates, lunch partners? What?

'Nathan, what're you trying to say?'

He ran a hand through his raven-black hair. 'Aren't you prepared to at least meet me halfway?'

'Halfway to where? I don't understand what you want from me?'

Nathan frowned, irritation deepening the creases around his mouth. 'Give me a break. I'm trying to figure this out as I go along.'

I stood up, tray in hand. 'Well, when you do figure it out, let me know.'

Nathan's hot-and-cold, on-again, off-again attitude was confusing the hell out of me. He needed to make up his mind what he wanted regarding the two of us. I couldn't figure it out for him.

Time to head back to the bridge.

'Vee, I have the name of a contact at the Edwardes space dock, but we need to be cautious as this outpost services both the Resistance and the Authority. D'you mind if I present myself as in command of this ship?' asked Catherine.

I shook my head. 'Not at all.'

I headed for the vacant seat next to Anjuli at the navigation panel, just as we were hailed by the space dock.

'This is Lieutenant Moore of the Edwardes base. May we have your designation please?' The face filling the viewscreen looked vexed to say the least. What was her problem – because it couldn't have been us?

'This is Commander Catherine Linedecker of the Earth Vessel *Aidan*. We would like to request docking clearance. We need repairs and we'd like to requisition a new landing craft.'

Lieutenant Moore at the space dock was shoved out of the way and a handsome black guy with an intricately patterned beard and twinkling dark eyes appeared, his face filling the viewscreen as he got closer to the transmission camera.

'Cathy! You old she-goat! You took your own sweet time getting here!'

'Leon? LEON BRIKES! Oh my God!' The commander's

face lit up in a way I hadn't seen since I met her. 'It's so good to see you.'

'Back 'atcha! We have some catching up to do and I have a bottle of Hive wine in my quarters with your name on it.'

'I see you haven't changed,' the commander said with amusement.

'You can't improve on perfection, sweetie. You of all people should know that.' Leon winked theatrically.

To my surprise, Catherine burst out laughing. 'Oh, but it's good to see you. You always did know how to make me smile.'

'Excuse me!' Lieutenant Moore was trying to push Leon out of the way so she could get back to her job. 'I have to assign them a docking port. Could you move please?'

'Hold your horses, sweetheart.'

'I am not your sweetheart,' Lieutenant Moore replied.

'You could be if you worked on your attitude!' Leon told her.

As the lieutenant glared at him in high dudgeon, Leon turned back to the screen, his smile fading somewhat. 'Cathy, I'm so sorry about what the Authority did to you and your family. It wasn't right and I said so at the time to whoever would listen.'

'You were and are a good friend, Leon,' said the commander. 'But you should've kept your mouth shut. If you hadn't spoken up for me, you'd still be commanding your own ship.'

'I would do the same thing again tomorrow,' Leon

replied. 'It's a cold universe, Cathy. We know that better than most. If we don't look out for each other, it gets a lot colder. Besides, I have my own vessel again now.'

'The Authority reinstated you?' the commander asked, surprised.

'Are you joking?' Leon scoffed, adding with glee, 'I'm a wanted man. We're like Harriet Tubman's underground railroad, except in space.'

'Huh?'

'If fugitive vessels make it this far, we escort them to Mendela Prime. We're trying to set up a chain of vessels with sympathetic captains to help drones escape from the Authority. Admittedly there are a few gaps in the chain, but we're getting there.'

'You could give us safe passage to Mendela?' the commander asked, her voice sharp.

'For you, sweetheart, anything. You and your husband Josh were always good friends to me and Chi. I don't forget my friends, Cathy.'

She smiled. 'So how is Chi? Where is she? On the space dock with you?'

Leon shook his head, his expression sombre. 'She was executed by the Authority for refusing to reveal my location. And they made sure they broadcast it on every sub-space channel so that sooner or later I'd get to see it. Plus it would act as a deterrent to anyone else who even thought about denouncing the Authority.'

'Oh, Leon, I'm sorry,' said Catherine, stricken.

'I console myself with the knowledge that one day I will help to bring the whole corrupt, rotten Authority edifice crumbling down,' said Leon.

His expression at that moment was forbidding. There was no doubting the depth of his hatred. The Authority had made a dangerous enemy. But then he dredged up a smile, and just like that his face was back to normal.

'And in the meantime I enjoy ferrying drones to Mendela, where we are slowly building a rebel army,' said Leon. 'This war with the Mazon is unfortunate. They would've made useful allies. Their xenophobia mostly keeps them to their own territory in space but it also makes it harder for us to travel back and forth to Earth's star system in a timely fashion.'

'I'd very much like to help with that rebel army, if I can,' said the commander, fire in her eyes.

'We'd love to have you,' said Leon, a genuine smile back on his face now. 'How many of you are there?'

'Is it safe to talk?'

'Oh yes. Don't let the lieutenant's surly expression fool you, she loves me really,' said Leon.

Lieutenant Moore's eyes were shooting daggers through Leon as she glared at him.

'There are ten of us plus two children. Thirteen including the captain of this vessel.'

'That isn't you?'

'No, I'm second in command.'

'Hang on . . . only twelve of you made it?' Leon said,

aghast. 'The scuttlebutt said that over a hundred of you escaped from Callisto.'

'Eighty-five of us were dumped on Barros 5 by Stefan Jersecky of the transport ship *Galileo*. He decided it was too risky to travel any further into Mazon territory.'

'Jersecky was paid a great number of credits to bring you as far as this space dock at the very least,' said Leon. His dark eyes were once again ice-cold.

'He was already paid?' Catherine said sharply. 'That bastard took every credit we had to transport us to Mendela Prime and then, like I said, he dumped us. When the Mazon learned we were on Barros, they attacked and then detonated a proton bomb on the planet.'

Leon was horrified.

'Then thank God at least some of you made it this far.'

'We survived thanks to the captain of this ship,' said Catherine. 'If it wasn't for her, none of us would be here now.'

A hot flush crept up from my neck and over my face. I wasn't used to hearing good things about myself.

'So who is the captain? Let me see her,' said Leon.

I stood up. 'I'm Acting Captain Olivia Sindall. My mum Vida Sindall used to be the captain of this vessel but she died—'

'Vida Sindall? You mean you're Vida and Daniel's little girl? Look at you. You're all grown up.' Leon beamed at me.

I smiled faintly, not quite sure what to say to that. Leon was behaving like an uncle!

'You don't remember me, do you?' said Leon, his smile fading.

'I'm afraid not, sir.'

'Ah, pity. But you were, what? Six or seven when I saw you last? Well, if your ship is on its last legs, I'm prepared to give you all safe passage to Mendela Prime aboard my cruiser, the *Ashley*. She's seen better days but she flies true.'

'Captain Brikes, d'you think you could save your conversation for when they actually dock?' said Lieutenant Moore, exasperated. 'It would be great if I could get my workstation back.'

'Righto, sweetcheeks. You only had to ask,' said Leon. 'Cathy, I'll see you when you dock.'

'Looking forward to it, Leon. Looking forward to it.'

86

NATHAN

Our time aboard the *Aidan* had come to an end. In another eighteen hours the ship would be ready to depart with a refitted engine and a rebooted ship's computer, and a state-of-the-art landing craft which could be remotely controlled was now in the cargo hold. In less than twenty-four hours the rest of us would be on the battlecruiser *Ashley* and travelling to Mendela Prime. Vee would be alone on the *Aidan*, going God only knew where.

Earlier this evening Mum had tried hard to persuade her to come with us to Mendela Prime. Mum, Leon, Vee and me had all had a meeting in a booth in the space-dock bar – away from prying eyes and ears. We'd got to the bar about thirty minutes ahead of Vee. Leon and Mum sat on one side of the booth, leaving me to sit opposite them with a narrow table between us. The width of the table was obviously designed to encourage private drinking, not eating. When Vee arrived she had no choice but to slide in next to me. Her thigh was lightly touching mine, but there was something wrong with me. I had to be coming down with some type of fever or something because just the touch of her leg against mine had me burning up. So much so that I had to keep surreptitiously wiping my forehead.

Once our drinks order had arrived Mum didn't waste any time.

'Why won't you come to Mendela with us? Think of all the good you could do,' she said to Vee.

'The Resistance needs you,' said Leon.

Vee took a sip from her bottle of beer before answering. 'I have my own plans.'

'You'll return to Earth?' asked Mum.

Vee shook her head. 'No. I've decided to do what I can to rescue as many drones as possible from the mining moons in Earth's solar system. And I intend to be a deep thorn in the side of the Authority.'

'Then work with us,' urged Mum. 'We need your skills, your expertise.'

'Cathy has filled me in regarding everything that happened on board the *Aidan*,' said Leon.

Vee bent her head. He put a hand over her free one, which was resting on the table. 'What happened with your brother was . . . unfortunate.'

'That's one word for it,' said Vee with a bitterness that surprised me.

'You weren't responsible for the two deaths he caused,' said Mum.

'Two deaths? Hmm.' Vee closed her eyes and inhaled slowly but audibly before exhaling in a rush. Her eyes opened. 'I thank you for your offer, and under other circumstances I'd probably jump at the chance, but I think it would be best for all concerned if it was a clean break.' Though her eyes were on Mum and

Leon, her words targeted my gut. 'So you all go on to Mendela Prime and I'll head back to Earth's star system. That way, if I get caught, I can't compromise any of you because what I don't know I can't tell.'

A clean break? Had that been said for my benefit? Is that what Vee wanted? Is that what *I* wanted? God, this was so hard. Vee had told me to figure out what it was I wanted from her, but my thoughts and feelings were still a jumbled mess.

'If you work against the Authority and they catch you, you'll be executed. You know that, right?' said Leon.

'That would happen whether I ran with you guys or not,' Vee pointed out.

'We have plenty who are prepared to fight against the Authority. We have very few with your proven skills,' said Leon. 'Isn't there anything we can say or do to make you change your mind? The Resistance needs leaders.'

Vee gave me a swift look before turning back to Leon. 'I'm afraid not.'

She and the others argued back and forth for another fifteen or twenty minutes but her mind was made up. She was going to stay on the *Aidan* and travel back alone. I sipped occasionally on my bottle of beer, saying nothing. Once Vee had gone, Leon frowned at me then turned to Mum.

'I'm not being funny, Cathy, but I thought you said your son could help persuade Vee to throw in her lot with us. The man didn't say a word,' he said, unimpressed.

'Vee has her own mind,' I said. 'I don't tell her what to do.'

'Nathan, what the hell is wrong with you?' Mum said. 'What is going on between you two? Are you together or not?'

'It's complicated.'

'No, it's not,' she shot back.

'You don't understand everything that happened—' I said.

'Nathan, never make the mistake of thinking that because I stay out of your business I don't know your business,' said Mum. 'I know *exactly* what went on. In fact, I probably know more about Vee and her brother than you do.'

'What does that mean?' I frowned.

'It means you need to talk to your wife,' said Mum, exasperated.

'It's complicated,' I insisted again before taking another mouthful of my beer.

'Well, I don't know about you, Cathy, but I'm ready to kick his arse,' said Leon, glaring at me.

'Nathan, I'm going to ask you one question which should sort out all your confusion,' said Mum quietly.

There wasn't a question in the world that could do that.

'Go on then,' I challenged, putting down my beer.

Leon sat back in his chair, his arms crossed as he continued to glare in my direction.

Mum leaned forward to look me in the eye and asked, 'Nathan, do you still love Vee?'

87

'Computer, what time is it?'

'According to which time reference?' asked the computer.

I winced. I couldn't get used to the computer's new voice. The repair crew who'd been assigned to overhaul this ship had changed its audio output on my instructions, but this anonymous woman's voice jarred with me every time I heard it. I thought it would be easier on my heart not to hear Aidan's voice every time the computer spoke. Now I wasn't so sure.

'Use the Sol time and calendar,' I directed.

'It is twelve-fifty a.m.,' the computer replied.

I had chosen to sleep on board the *Aidan* while the ship was being repaired. The rest of the colonists had been assigned temporary quarters on the space dock. It seemed the right decision at the time, but with less than twelve hours to go before my scheduled departure I wondered if I had made the right choice. I would miss the settlers – the commander and her support, Mike and his hideous watercress soup, Erica and her forthright, pain-in-the-backside opinions, Anjuli and her enthusiasm, Sam and Hedda with their dedication to their jobs and their 'secret' romance which they thought no one but them knew about.

And Nathan.

'Captain, Nathan Linedecker is requesting permission to come aboard.'

Huh? 'Er . . . permission granted.'

I pulled on my boots and walked out into the corridor. I headed towards the lift to meet him when he reached the upper deck, then decided against it. That would seem too eager. I couldn't go back to my quarters either as I didn't want him to get the wrong idea. The bridge. I headed for the bridge and sat in my chair, first reclining to the left, then lounging to the right, wondering from which angle I'd look best.

'Vee, get a grip!' I told myself and sat up properly.

Moments later the bridge doors hissed open and Nathan entered. He stopped for a moment when he saw me, but only for a moment. He took a couple more steps. I stood up.

'Hi,' I said.

'Hi.'

Silence.

'Er . . . shall we sit at the navigation board?' I suggested.

Nathan nodded. He sat in Aidan's seat. (I really had to stop thinking of it as that.) I sat down next to him in the seat Anjuli had made her own.

'What brings you aboard?' I asked.

'It's time for us to talk,' said Nathan.

'OK,' I said cautiously.

Why here? Why now?

'So no more secrets between us, Vee. D'you promise?'

Pause.

'I promise.' I owed him that much.

Nathan took a deep breath. 'How many people has Aidan killed?'

Shocked, I stared at him. Of all the questions I'd expected, this one hadn't made the list. 'What?'

'Earlier in the bar, Mum said you weren't responsible for the two deaths Aidan had caused. I saw the look on your face when she said that. There've been more than two, haven't there? I want to know how many people Aidan has killed,' said Nathan.

I tried to school my expression, to paint my face with inscrutability. Too little, too late, to judge from the way he was looking at me.

'What possible purpose would it serve for you to know the truth?' I asked. 'If this is just curiosity on your part, then I beg you, leave it alone.'

'It's not just curiosity,' Nathan denied.

'Then what else is it?'

Damn it! Tears were pricking at my eyes. This guy before me and my brother were the only ones who'd ever made me cry. 'Please, Nathan, don't do this.'

He took one of my hands in both of his. 'Vee, no more secrets between us. You promised.'

Please, Vee. Just trust me.

We stood very little chance as it was. With secrets between us, we stood no chance at all. Vee closed her eyes. Her whole body slumped but she didn't pull her hand away from mine.

'Did you know that this ship was one of the first to encounter the Mazon?' she asked at last.

How would I know that? But then I realized the question had been rhetorical.

'It was just over three years ago,' Vee continued. 'My mum on this ship and Captain Walker of Earth Vessel *Wrigman* were tasked with negotiating with the Mazon to try and establish a trade route through their territory. Mum said that even though the Mazon were xenophobic, they could see the benefits such trade would have for both sides. We were a day or two from agreeing not just a peace treaty but a trade route through Mazon space.'

'What happened?' I asked.

'The hostilities between Earth and the Mazon started. No doubt the Authority believes the Mazon were the aggressor, start-ing the war to gain more territory or because of their irrational fear of other species. But that's not entirely true.'

'What does the situation between Earth and the Mazon have to do with your brother?' I asked.

'I wish you could've known Aidan three years ago.' Vee smiled, but it wasn't directed at me. It was directed at her memories of long ago but not so far away. 'He was so amazing. He was fun and funny and so kind. He'd do anything for anyone. And he was so smart, an absolute genius. I mean, his IQ was off the charts, but he wasn't physically strong, not like some of the other boys on board ship. A couple of them started bullying him and they wouldn't let up. I was his sister. They knew better than to mess with me, but when Aidan was alone they made his life hell. I threatened, I pleaded, I gave them all the credits I had to try and get them to stop. I didn't realize at the time, but showing I cared so much just made it that much worse for my brother. When it got too much for Aidan he decided to prove to them and everyone else on board that he wasn't the wimp and the coward they said he was.'

'Did he do something to the Mazon ship?' I asked.

Vee nodded. 'You could say that. He hacked into this ship's computer and changed the necessary protocols to allow him to carry out his plan. There was no direct visual contact between us and the Mazon but we were negotiating over the audio comms system and using the universal translator. The only contact made was voice contact, but as I said, it was working. The negotiations were going well and apparently we were only a day or two away from formalizing the agreement.'

'So what happened?'

'The Mazon ship had a breathable atmosphere so Aidan put

on a protection suit and attached a recorder to his arm. Then he had the computer transfer him to the Mazon ship, just for a few seconds so he could record the fact that he was the first human to board one. He was there and back before any of us were the wiser.'

'Did the Mazon catch him?'

'No. It was worse than that.' Vee lowered her gaze, her voice soft, sorrowful.

'Go on,' I prompted.

She took a deep breath. 'I'm the only one who knows this,' she admitted. 'It's not easy sharing it.'

I didn't speak. This had to be Vee's decision.

'Computer, play Aidan Sindall's last personal log – date three zero seven. When people die on board an Earth vessel, the captain has access to all their personal logs,' Vee explained. 'This is my brother's last personal log entry. He can explain it better than I can.'

A solitary tear rolled down her cheek. I knew I was hurting her by making her do this, but it was necessary. Aidan's fifteen-year-old voice from three years ago began to play, filling the bridge.

It's all my fault. None of this would be happening if I hadn't done it.

I'm so sorry.

I just wanted to prove that I wasn't a coward. Prove it to everyone aboard this stupid ship. Prove it to Mum and Dad so they'll be proud of me. Prove it to Matt and the others who won't stop hounding me. But most of all, prove it to Vee. Every time she looks at me, all I see is her disappointment that I'm not more like her. She'd never let anyone bully her. She's strong and smart. She never backs down from a fight.

I just wanted to show her that I could be brave like her.

So I waited until I was alone in my quarters, then put on a protection suit and strapped a recorder to my arm, making sure that the lens was facing forward. I didn't want to make the transfer only to have no one believe me because the recorder was facing my chest or up under my armpit.

Vee had left her helmet in my room so, when I couldn't find my own, I just borrowed hers. I didn't want to take any chances even though the computer said that the atmosphere on the Mazon ship wouldn't be harmful to me as long as I didn't linger. Their air was made up over thirty per cent oxygen and sixty-seven per cent nitrogen with carbon dioxide and other gases making up the rest, but better safe than sorry.

I was ready.

'Computer, transfer me on my mark.'

Even though I was alone, I spoke softly, terrified that Vee would come into my room and catch me. I'm not stupid. I knew that what I was about to do was wrong, not to mention dangerous. My heart trying to punch its way out of my chest and the sick feeling in the pit of my stomach told me that much. But I had no choice. If I wimped out now, I'd never be able to look at myself in the mirror again.

But if I went through with it—

If I actually went on board the Mazon ship and came back with proof—

Matt and the others would be so jealous when they knew what I'd done! I could already see the awe on their stupid faces. And maybe then they'd leave me alone.

I looked around my room, feeling guilty, even though I hadn't done anything yet. I was still alone, but for how much longer? I had to do this.

'Computer, transfer me to a part of Mazon ship where there are no Mazon present and bring me back after ten seconds. OK? On my mark. Three. Two. One. Mark!'

An intense, uncomfortable feeling of being squeezed hard and pulled at speed hit my body. A moment later I was in a vast room full of capsules filled with swirling, translucent, viscous liquid. Each capsule was suspended a metre or more off the floor. And there was some kind of curled-up creature floating in each one but I couldn't properly make out what they looked like. What hit me next was the heat. The room was almost unbearably hot. I fell to my knees. My stomach heaved. Without warning, I threw up inside my helmet, against the visor. It was gross. Unlocking my helmet, I pulled it off. Vomit dripped all over my protection suit and onto the floor.

God! Everyone was right about me. I was pathetic. I couldn't even perform my first transfer without puking.

Subdued sickly yellow lighting and a smell like rotting meat struck me next. Still feeling sick but knowing I didn't have much time, I forced myself to turn through three hundred and sixty degrees, wanting to record as much as possible. That smell really was disgusting. It was catching in the back of my throat and something in the air was tickling my nose. I sneezed, then coughed. I couldn't help it.

That's when I heard it.

A clicking, chirping sound that was approaching at speed. I ducked down behind one of the suspended capsules, but too late. I heard a scrambling noise, then a face was looking at me from the top of the capsule I was hiding behind. A face like nothing I'd ever seen before. I cried out as a limb from the creature stretched out towards me. Flailing in terror, I knocked the creature's arm away. The squeezing, pulling sensation was back. A second later I was in my room again.

But I'd been seen.

I'm so sorry.

I didn't mean for any of this to happen. I deserve what's happening to me, but it's so unfair that others are beginning to suffer for my mistake. And if anything happens to Olivia, I'll never forgive myself. She's my sister. It's my job to protect her. She's the only one who has always been on my side and at my side, no matter what. I wouldn't tell her this but she really is the best sister in the world.

She's sitting with me now, fast asleep in the chair beside my bed. She's exhausted but she won't leave the medi bay until I do.

When I get well, I swear I'll never let her down again. I will look after her and protect her and never let anyone harm her. I'll be a proper brother.

I'm tired.

Time to sleep.

The recording ended. Silence reigned. Vee was looking at me expectantly, waiting for me to speak.

I was missing something.

'Are you seriously telling me that the hostilities between the Mazon and humans started because your brother transferred onto their ship for a few seconds?' I asked, unconvinced. 'Even the Mazon can't be that petty.'

'When Aidan returned to our ship, he brought back a Mazon virus. He infected the entire crew,' said Vee. 'There were

474

seventy of us before Aidan went onto the Mazon ship. Less than a month later there was just me.'

'That's what killed the crew – including your parents?' I asked, aghast.

Vee nodded, her expression grim.

'Oh my God! But I still don't see what that has to do with the war between Earth and the Mazon.' I frowned.

'Nathan, viral infection didn't just travel in one direction,' Vee said unhappily. 'Aidan infected the Mazon with some virus or pathogen. Something completely harmless to humans.'

And only then did the whole truth begin to dawn on me. 'Shit!'

'Yeah.' Vee confirmed my worse suspicions. 'Sixty-nine people died on board this ship. Three *billion* Mazon died on their home planet because of a virus Aidan introduced onto one of their ships. Three billion. That's why they hate us so much. I've tried since then to explain to them that it was a tragic mistake but they won't believe it. They believe such devastation must've been the result of a deliberate human plot, instead of what it really was – a tragic accident.'

'This is what you've been hiding from me all this time,' I realized.

'It was my burden to bear, not yours,' said Vee.

'When we were joined, it became mine too,' I pointed out. 'You should've trusted me, Vee.'

'You're right. I should've,' she said softly. 'It should've been more than just a word between us. But what I've finally figured out is that love is an act of courage. After living in constant fear

475

for the past three years, I had none. I spent my time alone using my wits to avoid confrontation, to survive. That didn't change when I rescued all of you from Barros. I guess . . . I guess that's why you and I failed. I wasn't brave enough to believe in just the two of us because we were too new to hold onto.'

I hadn't expected that response. I guess we'd both grown up a lot over the last few weeks. Too little. Too late?

'This Mazon war, this whole damn mess was the result of one catastrophic mistake,' sighed Vee. 'My brother paid for that mistake with his life. Hundreds of thousands of drones and Mazon have been paying for it ever since. That's part of the reason why I wanted to help you and the other colonists reach Mendela Prime. And that's the reason why I can't travel with you now.'

'Vee, none of this was your fault,' I said. 'You can't spend the rest of your life trying to make up for this.'

'That's not what my head tells me,' she replied.

I placed a hand under her chin to tilt her head. I had to try and make her believe me. 'It wasn't your fault.'

Vee licked her lips. She tried to smile and failed miserably. 'Thank you for making me share this. It's good that someone knows the truth and I'd rather it was you than anyone else.' She exhaled softly and I could feel her warm breath against my skin.

Vee looked at me with complete trust in her eyes. And her lips were so close to mine. What had happened to all the air in the room? Should I kiss her? One last kiss for old times' sake? Reluctantly I dropped my hand back down to my side and drew back. It wouldn't be fair to take advantage when she was vulnerable.

Mum's question in the bar replayed in my mind.

Nathan, do you still love Vee?

I still didn't know the answer.

89  VEE

There was a time when I loved the stars. Once I could stare at them for hours – watching them, wishing on them, dreaming about them. They represented potential. Possibilities.

Not any more.

Now I was sick of the sight of them. You didn't need water to drown. Emptiness was just as effective. More so. You didn't need to touch it, feel it, breathe it, to be engulfed by it. It swallowed you whole and spat you out, only to swallow you down again.

I'd been swallowed whole and spat out so many times over the last few years, but there had always been a light on the horizon called Earth, a goal called home. It might've been far away but it'd been there. Now I was alone again, just me and my ship called the EV *Aidan* which would serve as a constant reminder of my brother. I belonged nowhere. I had nothing. And for all my talk, I knew the chances of making it back to Earth's solar system in one piece without my brother's help were practically non-existent.

It was time to depart.

I had thought about leaving the Edwardes dock without saying goodbye to anyone but, after everything we'd all been through together, the commander and the other settlers deserved better from me than that.

So here I was on landing dock EB-09 with my ship ready to go behind me and, to my stunned amazement, all the colonists had turned up to say goodbye. I thought after everything that had happened that maybe Anjuli and Commander Linedecker would turn up and that would be it. They all stood in a line waiting for me to speak, but I had no clue what to say.

'I . . . er . . . I want to tell each and every one of you that it has been an honour to meet you and work alongside you. Er . . . we've had one or two differences . . .' A few guffaws at that. 'But I want you to know that if I had the chance to do it all again, I wouldn't!' More guffaws. 'What I mean is, there's a lot I would change, but I'm sincerely grateful to have met each and every one of you. I wish you all . . . peace and a place to call home.' The words dried up after that, so I walked down the line of people, shaking their hands and wishing them well.

When I reached Catherine, to my surprise she didn't just take my hand, she hugged me tight. I hugged her back. I was going to miss her so much. She was what I hoped to be one day – if I lived long enough. She was the personification of grace under pressure.

Last in the line was Nathan. When I reached him, the others beat a discreet but hasty retreat. Within seconds we were the only ones left in this section of the landing dock. I tried to smile but it kept falling off my face so I gave up.

Our story might have had a very different ending if I hadn't been overwhelmed by doubts and taken in by Aidan's lies. I'd thrown away everything we had and, worse still, everything we could be.

I knew now that Nathan would never forgive me, nor would I ever ask him to again. What I'd done was inexcusable. The fact that he was prepared to be alone with me and courteous on top of that was more than I deserved. In his shoes, I'm not sure I could've been so generous.

'When do you set off for Mendela?' I asked.

Nathan shrugged. 'Within the next couple of hours. Mum is anxious for us to be on our way.'

I nodded. 'And what will you do when you get there?'

'No idea. It was never about the destination with me. I just wanted to be with someone who'd make the journey worthwhile,' said Nathan quietly.

That could've been me.

'What about you? Will you be OK?' he asked.

I smiled. 'Of course. I intend to make trouble for the Authority wherever I go. I'm going to disrupt their trade routes and give them hell. I should be good at that.'

'I don't doubt it,' Nathan said drily.

Pause.

'I've dissolved our union,' I said. 'All you have to do is sign the declaration form in your personal log.'

Nathan said nothing; his expression was unreadable.

'Your mum thought it would be for the best. She said you should be free to move on, unencumbered. Her word, not mine. I had to look it up,' I admitted.

'And what did you think?'

'I think . . . no, I *know* you'll meet someone to love and care for one day. You have a lot of love to give, and if you ever decide you want to be joined again, you shouldn't have to track me down or wait five years to dissolve our union first. I'm saving you a trip across the galaxy.'

'Am I supposed to thank you?'

'No. God, no.' Why did Nathan sound so . . . bitter? I was giving him what he wanted, wasn't I? Why was this so hard? All I had were words and they were so inadequate. If I could've ripped my heart out of my chest and placed it still beating in his hands, then I would've done so. Maybe then he would feel for himself how truly sorry I was for everything that had happened.

'Nathan, we had something really special, didn't we – at least for a while?' I said.

Even now I still couldn't quite let go of the faint hope that Nathan would want to cling onto and fight for what we once had.

Moments passed before he finally nodded. 'Yeah, we did. For a while.'

Past tense. I tried to read his expression but he was far better at masking his feelings than I was.

'Thank you for making me feel so loved – for a while.'

Nathan slowly shook his head. 'Well, even that turned round to bite me, didn't it?'

'What do you mean?'

'I needed you, Vee. Just holding you close made me feel . . . at peace. But because I couldn't keep my hands off you, you took that to mean I couldn't keep my hands off anyone,' said Nathan.

'Well, you were kinda insatiable,' I pointed out.

'Only for you, Olivia. Only for you,' he said. 'I thought you understood that, but you didn't.'

I bowed my head. Just one more thing to add to the list of all the things I'd screwed up since I'd met Nathan.

'It wasn't just about sex, Nathan. You made me feel special in so many ways.' I looked into his eyes, making a final memory. 'You stood beside me and in front of me and you had my back and you cared for me like no one else. That's what I'm thanking you for.'

Nathan looked at me but he didn't speak. Moments passed as we watched each other. Our ending was rushing towards us and there was nothing I could do about it.

'I'm sorry we didn't work out, Nathan,' I whispered.

'So am I. D'you remember all the promises we made to each other during our first night together?' he asked.

'Of course. But we live in a universe of broken promises. You promised to love me for ever, and it was implied, though never stated, that I wouldn't try to kill you.' I smiled.

Nathan's mouth fell open. Then he smiled reluctantly. 'Your sense of humour will be the death of me.'

'So I didn't need Aidan after all,' I mused. '*Now* he tells me.'

We both started to smile and it was shared and genuine though it didn't last long. The need to wrap my arms around Nathan and hold him close was almost overwhelming. So much so that I had to press my hands into my thighs before I embarrassed myself. But what the hell? Embarrassment was the least of my worries at that moment.

'Nathan, can I make one last request?' I asked.

'Anything,' he replied softly.

I moved as close to him as I could. 'Kiss me,' I whispered.

A moment's silence and then Nathan's mouth was on mine. I closed my eyes, allowing myself to get lost in that one last special moment. He wrapped his arms around me, his mouth slanting on mine. I buried my hands in his hair, pulling him closer. But all too soon it was over. Almost reluctantly, Nathan stepped away from me. I looked at him, drinking him in. I had to say it. Just once, I had to say the words.

'I love you, Nathan.'

Nathan regarded me for a moment. 'I know.' Pause. 'Perhaps one day I'll send you a message telling you how I feel about that.'

And perhaps one day would never come, but it didn't matter. All I wanted was for him to know the truth.

One more question, though it made me wince inwardly to ask. 'Nate, will you ever be able to forgive me?'

A moment's stunned silence. 'You don't want much, do you?'

No, not much. Just to roll back time, yet to be older and wiser. I would've gladly exchanged my soul for a second chance.

'You take care of yourself, OK?' he said at last.

'Only if you do the same,' I replied.

God, I couldn't do this any more. For all my bold talk, seeing him like this, knowing it was the last time we'd ever be together was killing me.

'I wish you only good things, Nathan.'

'Goodbye, Vee.'

One last silent moment between us, then I turned away and walked back up the ramp onto my ship.

In the cargo hold, a single workman with Pearson-Singh printed on his overalls was left doing something or other to the outside of my newly requisitioned landing craft. I nodded to him out of courtesy.

'Captain Sindall, your ship will be ready to depart within thirty-five minutes,' said the man.

'Thank you. I appreciate all your efforts,' I said.

He nodded and I carried on towards the lift, desperate to get to my quarters. Once there, I sat down on my bed, my head in my hands. Moments turned into minutes before I found the strength to even move. The *Aidan* had been fixed and groomed and looked like new and I hated the sight of it. It would be my prison for the rest of my life.

But at least now I had a purpose. If, by some miracle, I

did manage to make it back to Earth's star system, then the Authority was going to learn my name and the name of this ship – with a vengeance.

I had lost the love of my life, but I would survive.

Yes, I could do that, if nothing else.

'Captain Sindall, we are cleared to leave,' stated the computer.

Forty minutes had passed since I'd first come aboard the *Aidan* and I was still in my quarters. I had yet to get used to the computer's new voice. The first chance I got I was going to change it back to my brother's.

But then again, maybe not.

Perhaps it was better to accept some losses, because with acceptance came a chance to move on.

But then again, maybe not.

I headed for the bridge, sitting down in the captain's chair. After the influx of Callistan settlers there were a number of times when I'd wished to see the bridge exactly as it was now, devoid of people. Just me and silence. But the bridge looked so empty. A ship without people was nothing but metal and circuits with no heart or soul.

'Set a course for Earth's star system and take us out,' I ordered wearily.

'Yes, Captain,' the computer replied.

The ship moved slowly away from Edwardes base and everything I loved.

Without warning, the bridge door hissed open.

'Captain, permission to enter?'

I stood up slowly and stared. What on earth . . . ? What was Sam doing here? I thought I was alone. When did he come aboard? And why?

'Permission granted,' I said slowly.

'I would like to offer my services as your first officer,' said Sam. 'I have taken the liberty of uploading my credentials onto the computer. If you'd care to check you'll see that—'

I shook my head. Sam frowned at me, misunderstanding the reason.

'No, I mean . . . I'd be more than happy to have you as my first officer, Sam. In fact, I'd be honoured, but I still don't understand what you're doing here,' I said in a rush. 'I thought you'd never serve under a captain you didn't respect and trust.'

'And that still applies – Captain,' said Sam, the merest trace of a smile dancing over his lips.

A lump came out of nowhere to lodge in my throat as we looked at each other. I had to cough twice and swallow once to get rid of it.

'Er . . . welcome aboard.' I said gratefully.

'Something about taking the fight to the Authority really appealed to me,' said Sam.

'You know they'll stick a price on our heads and every bounty hunter in the galaxy will come after us, right?'

'If they don't, then we aren't doing our job properly,' said Sam.

That was indeed a point of view.

'Why didn't you just ask to join me back on Edwardes base?' I asked, trying not to look a gift horse in the mouth and all over.

'You might've decided you could take on the Authority by yourself, and that would never do. Why should you have all the fun?'

'Fair enough,' I said. 'As long as you know what you're letting yourself in for.'

'Always. Now may I register the rest of the crew and assign them their duties?' asked Sam.

'What rest of the crew?' I frowned.

Sam walked over to the door of the bridge and opened it. The queue of people in the corridor took my breath away.

'Anjuli, you'll be the flight officer,' said Sam.

'Yes, sir.' Anjuli beamed at him before she headed over to the flight panel and, after a wink at me, immediately made herself at home in Aidan's old position.

'Erica, you will be on weapons,' said Sam.

'Yes, Sam,' said Erica. At his immediate scowl, her response quickly changed. 'I mean, yes, sir.'

She gave me a brief nod as she took up her post to the left of the bridge. And so it went on. Those who had been on the ship before were assigned to their roles immediately. Hedda was sent to defence and tactical, Mike to the medical bay – I hadn't realized he was actually a qualified doctor, albeit a junior one, and Harrison to engineering.

Four newbies I didn't recognize – Becca, Andy, Zach and Valianta were registered and scanned by Sam. Andy and Valianta were assigned the engine room alongside Harrison. Becca was assigned to the medical bay when required to work with Mike, otherwise the astrophysics lab. Zach, who had to be no older than fifteen or sixteen, was assigned to the mess hall but was warned to make himself available to anyone who needed him. After their assignments I introduced myself to each of them and shook their hands. I needed to get to know them all, to learn their strengths and their weaknesses if we were going to make an effective team. But I had time. We all did.

Valianta was the last in the queue. I peered surreptitiously after her but there was no one else waiting to come onto the bridge.

'Is that everyone, Anjuli?' I asked, with what I hoped was just the right combination of professionalism and detachment.

'Yes, Captain.'

Anjuli and I exchanged a look. I hadn't fooled her for a second. She almost imperceptibly shook her head. The hope that had flared within when I saw Sam and the queue of people in the corridor guttered and died.

Nathan hadn't come.

I leaned back in my chair, briefly closing my eyes. Hope was such a dangerous thing. Its loss had scooped my heart out anew but I would survive.

I didn't need my heart for that, just my head and my wits.

Anjuli smiled briefly but sympathetically before turning round to face her instrument panel.

'Lay in a course for Earth's star system,' I directed. 'I'm going to make sure the Authority gets to know the name of this ship.'

'Course laid in, Captain,' said Anjuli.

We were on our way.

An alert flashed up on the panel that was part of my captain's chair. A personal message was coming through for my eyes only. I checked the sender.

Nathan.

A quick glance around the bridge, but no one was paying me any attention. My heart thumping hard in my chest, I opened the message and read. Then read it again and a third time.

Vee, I forgive you.
Nathan

A tear may have escaped and slipped down my cheek, but that was OK. I closed my eyes. Maybe one day, by some miracle, Nathan and I would be together again.

But if not . . .

Goodbye, Nathan. See you next lifetime.

Have you read Malorie Blackman's award-winning, ground-breaking Noughts & Crosses series? Soon to be a BBC TV series!

'Unforgettable'
Independent

'Flawlessly paced'
The Times